Each Little Universe
CHRIS DURSTON

Copyright © 2020 Chris Durston

All rights reserved.

ISBN: 9781656968227

For Hannah, without whom this could never have happened.

(It's actually had to happen three or four times now, but this one's for real. None of them would have been possible if not for her.)

And for you, of course, friendly reader. I worry that this story might be so idiosyncratic to *me* that it won't make any sense whatsoever to anyone else, but I'm gonna be optimistic and hope that you enjoy it nonetheless.

CONTENTS

1	The Octobike	1
2	Hot Bread	10
3	OMG, TV	24
4	Suplex Complex	31
5	The Rest of the Party	37
6	A Hero's Adventure	43
7	In Medias Noctis	56
8	Roll Up, Roll Up	60
9	Cheese That Isn't Your Cheese	79
10	Rainmaker I (The Spiders From Mars)	90
11	The Rent	100
12	No, You Rock	107
13	Two Steps to Success	117
14	Antiquity	130
15	The Dry Run	139
16	Boss Battle	155
17	Tenseless and Inadequate	168
18	The Others We Carry On	178
19	Plot Twist	183
20	Wrestler Intelligentsia	196
21	Extreme Hardcore Parkour	203
22	Rainmaker II (Fame)	209
23	But Siriusly Though	217
24	A Slightly More Blank Sheet	221
25	We Got A Real Job, Kinda	224
26	Hunky Dory	227
27	Oddity	234
28	Re-Entry	237

29	An Inauspicious Communication	243
30	Wait, We're Actually Getting To Do It This Time?	250
31	Precipitation	262
32	Station to Station	267
33	Because 'Gary's Mackerel' Would Have Been Too Obvious	273
34	Ultimate Showdown of Ultimate Destiny	280
35	Meow, Bitches	293
36	See, It All Came In Handy	300
37	Rainmaker III (Ch-Ch-Ch-Ch-)	306
38	Lady Stardust	312

PART ONE
Before

1. The Octobike

'Octobike,' said TM firmly. Veggie digested this for a moment.

'Octo... bike.'

'Octobike.'

Veggie withdrew the spoon he had been absently swirling around his mug of tea and tapped it against his jaw, leaving watery brown droplets collecting on his chin. 'I don't follow.'

TM groaned. 'Alright, hear me out -'

'I thought I *was* hearing you out. And very proficiently, too.'

'Okay, okay, fine, so get this.' TM spread his hands wide, fingers splayed, and bobbed his palms with each syllable for emphasis. 'Octo.' Veggie nodded. 'Bike.'

Veggie considered the prospect. His head turned to one side, then the other, considering the suggestion with all the weight and magnitude it deserved. He looked all around the little café, taking in the gaudy plastic tables and the offensively neutral walls. He looked at TM, then up at the heavens.

'... Octobike?' he said eventually.

'Octobike! Come on, Veg.' TM plonked his elbow down on the table between them, then rested his chin with what he hoped was compelling exasperation in his palm. 'Bike. Trike. Skip a few steps. Octobike. Ta-da. Next big thing, one hundred percent guaranteed.'

'Not sure I'm seeing it.'

'For heck's - fine - just - okay, imagine a quad bike. Quad - right? Four wheels - four flipping - quad bike.'

'Quad bike.'

'Then... *shananaaaa*... double it.'

'Two quad bikes.'

'Kwaaaaaa,' TM burbled, head flopping forwards.

'I'm trying,' protested Veggie, watching his friend suffer. 'It's not, like, the super most easiest thing to envisualise.'

'Not a word,' said TM, resurfacing and stretching out in his too-small chair. 'Anyway, all that shows is your lack of imagination, which is in no way indicative of the definitely amazing future in which the Octobike takes the world by storm.'

'Hm,' said Veggie. The two looked at each other in mutual expectation for a moment, each curious as to what the other might say next, followed by the realisation that neither actually had anything more to say on the topic.

'Eh,' said TM eventually, just so they wouldn't be staring silently at each other any more. 'You got cash?'

Veggie plucked a twenty pence piece out of his pocket and placed it on the table with pride, like a checkers player making what he thought was a genius move. 'Yup.'

'Amazing.'

'You get this one,' Veggie said, grinning.

TM dug out a couple of pound coins from his back pocket - they were the old kind, the ones that had been out of circulation for a couple of years, but beggars couldn't be choosers of the relative fanciness of their coinage. He slapped them down next to Veggie's tiny heptagonal fortune, did a quick count, and nodded. 'That'll do.'

The two stood, feet of their chairs scraping against the floor with a noise like a climber sliding painfully down a chalk cliff by their fingernails.

'Look, TM,' said Veggie quietly, when the last echoes of the cacophony had faded. He pronounced it long: Teeeeyum, like a Texan saying 'Tim'.

Veggie was one of those people who neither looked nor sounded hugely memorable: average height, neither skinny nor big, mid-length brown hair, easily absorbed vocal tones that were neither unpleasant nor melodic with an inoffensive accent that could have been from anywhere on the British Isles. TM, on the other hand, was taller, leaner, with short hair and wide eyes surrounded by neat lashes; still not exactly striking, but more distinctive on paper. Yet, somehow, the real-life experience that was Veggie constituted one of the most magnetic phenomena TM had ever come across. Veggie himself claimed alternately that it was down either to pheromones or hypnosis, both of which TM personally thought were probably BS. Whatever it was, his easy charisma regularly got them a long way.

'It's not a bad idea. I think.' Veggie tucked his chair neatly under the table, careful to lift the feet off the floor rather than scrape it along the ground. 'Still not clear what it actually is. But hey, it *sounds* kinda cool, and that's, like, ninety percent of all product design these days. We just need... y'know, an actual *thing*. Something easy to market, patentable. Quick sell and we're done, right? Prototyping ain't exactly within budget right now.'

TM sighed. 'I know,' he admitted. 'It's barely even a prototype of an idea for a prototype anyway.'

'Listen, bud,' said Veggie, in the sort of egregiously calming voice employed primarily by burglars begging house-proud dogs not to bite them, please, 'there might well be a gap in the market for, uh... some sort of... Octobike. Type... thing. Probably. But we gotta build us and our brand, like, waaaay up before we start thinking about doing something that big. And niche.'

'Hnnnnnnng,' TM moaned. 'I know.' He sighed and half-heartedly picked up one of the pound coins on the table, then plonked it down again; the noise of the coin hitting the hard plastic surface made him feel as if he actually had money to spend. 'Let's go?'

Veggie nodded, and they wandered out and under the dreary mid-January sky. There might have been no clouds in the grey heavens, or the whole thing might have been one big one. TM crossed his arms in his thick-knit jumper; Veggie, in a loud-patterned shirt with the sleeves rolled up over a loud-patterned T-shirt with the sleeves cut off, flapped his hands around to ward off the cold.

'Anyway,' said TM, as they headed for home, 'I reckon we might need to ditch the Dogapult.'

'Yeeaaaaaaah, possibly,' Veggie conceded, flexing his fingers a few times before stuffing his hands into his pockets. 'Maybe we didn't really think through what that... actually involved.'

'Maybe we need to stop trying to sell inventions based purely on the strength of the punny name,' TM mused. 'I mean, cat-apult, dog-apult, it doesn't even really make sense if you think about it.'

'Maybe we need to *keep* trying to sell inventions based purely on the strength of the punny name,' Veggie countered, 'if what you're saying is that the pun wasn't good enough.'

It was hard to argue that *something* wasn't good enough, TM reflected: their career, such as it was, depending on their ability to come up with useless inventions that people would nevertheless *really* want to buy, and then market those on the Internet. They made their money - or, more accurately, their business model specified that they made their money - through a system of investments made by faceless Internet moneyspinners who would give them a bit of a cash injection in order to let them develop products in return for some of the profits when they got around to producing the things and selling them on their own online stores.

It worked on paper.

Not the paper on which was printed their financial accounts - oh, no, definitely not *that* paper. An idiomatic sort of paper representing a beautiful and fantastical land in which ideas that worked 'in theory' did, in fact, work.

The café was a sort of it's-not-going-well-is-it tradition, a tacit acknowledgement that things really needed rethinking, and fast.

'Not my best idea, anyway,' TM admitted. 'I mean, even if it were humane and that, there's not that many breeds of dog small enough for what we were going for.'

Veggie gazed skyward as they wandered; TM thought he was probably ticking them off in his head. 'Hm,' he agreed, after a moment.

They turned a corner, heading for home. The walk took them through the retail-oriented streets of the city, down past the arcade that had once housed independent shops but had now been remodelled into an urban hub for fine dining - much to the scepticism of the locals, which had proved well-founded when three of the six new restaurants had folded within the year - and into the quieter residential areas that were generally quite pretty, but often smelled a bit funky.

'You ever hear of Giordano Bruno?' TM asked, trundling along beside his business partner and longtime best friend. Their footsteps beat a loose syncopated rhythm against the pavement.

'Should I have?'

'Prolly not,' TM said. 'He dead.'

'Ah.'

'He had this thing about what it means for the universe to be infinite, right?' TM watched Veggie's face; his friend raised his eyebrows by way of saying something to the effect of *it may not seem like it but I am paying attention, honest, albeit more because you're a mate than because I care.* 'So it's, like, if you stand at the edge and fire an arrow, then... it's not the edge.'

'You're *terrible* at explaining,' Veggie declared. 'No wonder the Dogapult didn't get over - I'm relinquishing your title as Head of Marketing at *Veggie TM Limited.*'

'I did not know I was that.'

'Well, now you know you're not any more.'

'Hang on, anyway,' TM spluttered, waving his hands around in the hopes that Veggie would somehow derive something meaningful from the flapping of appendages. 'If you stand at what looks like the edge of the universe, right, and shoot an arrow outwards - away from the middle -'

'I know what outwards means,' Veggie said. 'I looked at a geometry book once.'

'- then either it keeps going, in which case you weren't really at the edge, or it hits a wall. And - and if it hits a wall,' TM burbled, trying to remember, 'then you can stand on the wall and shoot another one, and so on.'

'Waste of arrows,' Veggie opined, shaking his head.

'It's supposed to show that the universe doesn't really have an edge,' TM said, put out.

'Neither does a round... thing.' Veggie cupped his hands around an imaginary ball.

'Does too, just not corners.'

'Well, that's a loss for corners.' Veggie scratched his nose. 'Is there a point to this?'

'Not really,' TM said. 'I just thought it was cool. Unknowable cosmos made even more unknowable by mundane but mildly badass image, y'know?'

'Sounds like someone else talking,' Veggie said, 'if you know what I mean.'

TM opened his mouth, then closed it again. 'It's the sort of thing she *might* have said, I guess,' he conceded.

'Are you kidding?' Veggie demanded, giving TM a full-force stare in the face. Veggie's stares were like being hit by a shovel made of charisma. 'It's, like, the only sort of thing she *ever* would have said.'

TM blinked.

'You gotta be less...' Veggie rolled his head around on his shoulders a few times. 'Less then, more now. You'll only get bummed out.'

'This *is* me now,' TM said.

Veggie sighed and patted his friend on the head. 'I know,' he said. 'I was a right wotsit after the whole Swede thing. Thing that sucked the most about it was that even after getting rid of him, there were still bits of him floating around in my head. Stuff he'd have said, thoughts he'd have had.'

'You got better,' TM said.

'Heck yes,' Veggie proclaimed, nodding regally. 'It all embetters once you've stuffed yourself full of pick and mix a few times. Anyway, we need to be not focusing on people that happened and focus on making money, like, now, and stuff.'

TM sighed in agreement.

'What we need,' said Veggie thoughtfully, 'is something simple. Reeaaaaaally simple. Like, cable tie simple.'

'Cable tie?'

'You know, those little do-whats: bind cables together, attach guff to other guff, string up your uncounted helpless victims by the wrists.'

'Oh, those.'

'Point is,' Veggie elaborated, slowing and punching the pedestrian crossing as they approached a crossroads (on the pavement of which was a single wooden bench trying its best to pretend that the dirty intersection was somehow *a view*), 'it's like the most basic-est thing - must cost, like, a billionth of a penny each to manufacture, I reckon - and I bet you anything that the guy who came up with them is *totally* loaded.'

'He was, but then he died,' said the girl sitting on the bench.

'Oh,' said Veggie. 'Right. Thanks.'

The crossing light flashed the green man at them, and they went a few steps out into the road before Veggie realised what had happened.

'Wait,' he said, walking backwards until he was face-to-face with the girl; TM elected to simply turn around and walk back. The drivers who had been so rudely forced to stop at the lights made a few gestures at the ignominy of having stopped for someone who hadn't even been grateful enough to actually cross the road. 'What?'

'Cable Tie Guy,' said the girl. She had bright red hair, aggressively quiffed; thick, obtrusive neon eyeshadow; a slim-fitting powder-blue suit; a red lightning bolt painted from her hairline across one eye and onto her cheek. 'Maurus Logan, died in twenty-zero-seven aged eighty-six. He *was* pretty well-off, though - well, up to that point, obviously, and I guess it probably didn't make too much of a difference to him after that.'

Veggie glanced sidelong at TM. 'Of all the things I thought might happen today,' he said, deadpan, 'being told the life story of Cable Tie Man by Ziggy Flipping Stardust was... like, seventh, eighth at best.'

'You wouldn't happen to have any bright ideas for an invention that would make us equally loaded and slightly less dead, by any chance?' TM said to the girl, who stretched languidly on her bench and thought about it for a moment.

'Nah,' she said eventually. She spoke, TM thought, as if she could have been from just down the road or from thousands of miles away. 'I'm kinda new around here.'

'So you thought you'd cosplay as the hecking Starman, fit in a bit better?' demanded Veggie.

'I did a bit of research,' she said, smiling faintly. 'Asked people what someone who came from the stars might look like, this is what I got. Not good?'

'Why d'you need to look like someone from the stars?' TM asked.

'Honesty is the best policy, right?' She ran a hand through her towering quiff. 'I thought it would be best to be upfront about it.'

'Natch,' said Veggie. 'Give us a sec, wudya?'

He marched TM a few steps away, holding his partner by the upper arm. 'What's going on, TM?' he asked with an air of helplessness.

'We're... having a conversation with a nice lady?' TM hazarded.

'This *nice lady* hijacked our conversation, gave us the low-down on Mister Cable Tie, and then said she was from outer space,' Veggie amended. 'That the understanding you got of the situation too?'

'Oh, yeah,' said TM. 'Something like that.'

Veggie bit the inside of his cheek, an unusually thoughtful expression which generally signified that he was considering doing something really dumb. 'She's smart, though,' he said after a moment. 'I assume. Possibly.'

'What are you -'

'I dunno, maybe we could use her brain. For money.'

'That sounds weird and very sketchy,' said TM. Veggie had a keen glint in his eye, which TM knew all too well. 'This is one of your ideas that makes no sense but if it didn't happen you'd lock yourself in your room and listen to Merzbow for days, isn't it?'

'Not sure yet,' said Veggie. 'Also, she's kind of doing something for me.'

'Early seventies Bowie is doing something for you,' TM corrected, accurately, 'and you've never met a person you didn't instantly both trust with your life and want to try to sleep with.'

'Fair point,' said Veggie, but he turned back to the girl without further consideration.

'Hello again,' she said, beaming.

'If you're from space,' said Veggie curiously, 'where d'you live?'

'Oh, heck,' said the girl. 'Hadn't thought about it.' She folded her arms, slouching; then she sat sharply upright and looked eagerly from TM to Veggie and back again. 'Can I come live with you?'

'Um,' said TM.

'Absolutely,' said Veggie at the same time.

'You can come hang out,' TM hastened to correct him. 'Like... I dunno, if you need somewhere to be... for a bit.'

'Sweet,' said the girl, bouncing to her feet. 'Thanks! I like you guys.' Then she turned - it was almost a hop and a spin, rather than a step in a direction - and marched merrily in the direction of TM and Veggie's flat.

'She knows where we live!' TM whispered.

Veggie ruffled TM's hair. 'It's fine,' he said reassuringly. 'I'm sure this one encounter isn't gonna define the rest of our lives.'

2. Hot Bread

Thus TM found himself bringing a strange girl back to the flat, which was unusual for him. Their tiny, extremely rubbish abode was leased under their business name of *Veggie TM, Inventors Incorporated*.

'Nice place,' the girl commented, as Veggie waded through the pile of bills, takeaway menus, and other assorted junk mail in the direction of the toaster.

'Thankee,' Veggie acknowledged. 'I got bread, if you want hot bread?' He reached the toaster, whereupon he leaned down and removed a few slices of bread from a cupboard filled mostly with instant noodles and sachets of ketchup stolen from fast food restaurants.

'Isn't it just called toast?' the girl asked. Veggie shook his head firmly.

'Oh no, Ziggy, my friend,' he reprimanded her. 'Living off *toast* is for people who haven't got their stuff together - but hot bread, that's a meal of *kings*.' He busied himself at the toaster - *bread heater*, TM reminded himself.

'I like this,' she declared, plonking down on the floor. 'I think I might stay forever. If that's OK.'

TM picked up a couple of the bills lying on the carpet and tossed them half-heartedly in the direction of the bin, which was mostly hidden underneath a pile of faded envelopes. 'Um,' he said. The girl sat there, cross-legged in her blue suit. 'You don't have anywhere else to be? Nothing, nobody to go home to?'

'Nah,' she said, gazing around the flat in all its cramped glory. The room contained all the essential components of a kitchen, a lounge, an office, and a dining room, and all in fewer square metres than would usually be afforded to a single one of them. 'Like I said, I'm sort of new.'

TM considered this.

'I like the layout, by the way,' she said, gesturing around. Her hand waved past the part of the flat that Veggie had termed the *studyining* room: a wooden table, half of which was invisible under piles of papers, stress balls, and other assorted stationery, and the other half of which bore a Christmas-themed tablecloth and placemats which had been purchased in a January sale and not changed since. 'Pretty high item-per-square-metre ratio.'

'That's a very nice way of saying we have more detritus than we can fit in our tiny-ass flat,' said TM. Then he sniffed. 'Veg?'

'Mm.'

'Am I having a stroke?'

'Nope,' said Veggie, perfectly calmly, 'the bread heater's just caught fire.'

'Heck,' said TM.

'Aww, who's this?' the girl said as TM flapped about. He looked down, following the direction of her pointing finger, and saw a black-and-white cat slinking over her crossed legs.

'Um -'

'I got it,' Veggie announced lazily, sauntering over to the table and snatching the seasonal tablecloth out from under the assorted debris like a magic trick.

'Er, this is Michel Furcoat, the cat,' said TM, choosing to tentatively accept that Veggie did in fact got it. 'We've got Maurice Meow-Ponty around somewhere, too, but he's not as big a fan of people.'

'I'm not sure I'm people,' she said.

'Anyway, er, they're not actually ours. Not originally, like. We were testing this idea we had for catnip-scented microwave meals - we used to have a microwave before it blew up - and they showed up and they've just sort of stuck around since.'

'Never did get around to actually selling that one,' Veggie piped up, throwing the tablecloth over the toaster. It immediately caught fire; he gave a sigh of mild exasperation and wandered back over to the table, where lay revealed a second, plain white and slightly shiny tablecloth that had been hidden under the red and gold fabric. He yanked it out with less precision, sending paper fluttering across the room, and tossed it atop the conflagration. With an underwhelming *pffft*, the blaze died down.

'Good names,' the girl said, watching Michel Furcoat the cat weave his lazy way across her lap, around TM's ankles, and into the warm nest of the many envelopes by the bin, where he buried himself and disappeared.

'What about yours?' TM asked. She looked blank. 'Name, I mean.'

She bit her bottom lip for a moment, then clicked her tongue. 'Ziggy is fine,' she said, unhelpfully. 'Although, you know this is Aladdin Sane, the one *after* Ziggy Stardust and all that?' TM shrugged. 'Most people don't,' she conceded.

'You must have an *actual* name,' TM reasoned. 'Like, one what's yours, and that.'

'It's kinda long,' she said. 'I was sort of hoping to leave it behind, to be honest. Fresh start and whatnot.'

TM nodded thoughtfully. 'Ziggy it is.'

Veggie lifted up the white sheet smothering the embers of the heated bread, releasing a cloud of thick black smoke. 'Balls!' TM heard him splutter from behind the sheet, and the smell of merrily afire stale carbs filled the flat.

'Oh, not good,' said Ziggy, watching wide-eyed.

'We should probably go outside, or something,' TM suggested half-heartedly.

'I think it's alright,' Veggie said tentatively, peering at the covered conflagration. The glossy sheet seemed to have done its work, no more unsolicited flames springing up. Veggie hummed for a moment, then glanced up at TM with a curious look. 'Bedsheet-Tablecloth-Whiteboard-Fire-Blanket?' he wondered. TM shrugged.

'Eh?' said Ziggy, looking between the two of them with interest.

'Oh,' TM said, 'yeah. So... we invent stuff.'

'Oooooooh,' murmured Ziggy. 'Stuff.'

'Like,' Veggie explained, 'like... er... TM?'

'Mm.'

'Examples of stuff?'

TM cast about for something suitable. The flat was full of their useless creations, but none seemed sufficiently brilliant as an exemplar of their creative ability. There was the coaster set with wheels ('for maximum coastage'), but that usually resulted in spills. Or the revolving lampshade, to ensure that the entire room got the same amount of light, but it turned out that light didn't work in quite the way they'd been thinking. Eventually, TM pointed at the white sheet covering the toaster; Ziggy gazed at it obligingly. 'Well,' he began. 'We invent stuff, like that.'

Ziggy blinked at him.

'It's the *Veggie TM* Bedsheet-Tablecloth-Whiteboard,' TM continued, wandering over to give the sheet a fond pat. 'Multi-function fabric in the shape and shade of your choice; serves as table cover, snuggly bedding, or reusable drawing surface - whichever you need at the time, for ultimate convenience.'

Veggie pulled a crayon out of a pocket and doodled it over the cloth, helpfully illustrating the 'whiteboard' part. 'Also, maybe, fire blanket,' he said, 'except that that sounds like a potential insurance thing and we can't be doing with that.'

'In essence,' TM said, 'we come up with ideas for broadly useless stuff that people might hopefully want to pay us lots of money for, and then we submit them to a board of faceless merciless bureaucrats -'

Veggie tapped his chest with a fist and raised a finger to the sky.

'- and hope that they might invest some money so we can make the things at bigger scale, sell them as, like, actual products or whatever. Then we wait, then hopefully profit. That's the theory.'

'Not that we're all about the dollar,' Veggie told Ziggy with a wise nod. 'Annoyingly, turns out money is quite an important thing to have in today's society, and since we can't beat the wealthy we'd really rather like to join them, if only so we can eat something other than bread every now and then.'

'Our ideas have to be mass-producible and cheap to make, too,' TM continued. 'The B-T-W is literally just some fabric that we ran through a laminate-y thingy and then branded with as many uses as we could come up with.'

Ziggy nodded thoughtfully; she hopped to her feet, trotted over to the counter upon which the toaster sat, and brushed a few crumbs around with a finger as if positioning toy soldiers in formation. 'What's your best one?'

'Our best -?' TM trailed off.

'Idea,' she clarified.

'Well,' he said, leaning in, 'I've been working on this thing I like to call the Octobike -'

Veggie gave TM a look. It was a look that, to most, would have looked like a fairly normal look, perhaps a little unusual in the degree of contortion Veggie could achieve with his eyebrows, but which to TM very clearly meant 'don't you dare tell her about the hecking Octobike'.

'- but it's a bit shit really,' TM finished.

'Huh,' said Ziggy, and turned to Veggie. 'What about'chu?'

Veggie swivelled in his chair and pointed proudly at Michel Furcoat the cat, who was lazily pawing at the door. 'Hear him scratching?' Veggie asked.

Ziggy shook her head.

'No, you do not. That is because Michel Furcoat, the cat, over there is wearing Veggie TM Feline Claw Silencers. Tiny little plastic sheath-type things, like them tips what go on scissors so kiddies don't cut themselves – and all this practical value available inexpensively and in a range of colours including Smooth Purple.'

'You put plastic tips on his claws?' Ziggy repeated, sounding somewhere between fascinated and appalled. 'Isn't that... a bit cruel?'

'Um,' said Veggie. 'I mean, I hope not. It's definitely cruel to whatever poor git has to actually put them on a cat what don't wanna wear none, though.' He gestured to TM, who held up a scratched forearm. 'Michel Furcoat, the cat, he's okay with them, sorta. We think.'

'And Maurice Meow-Ponty?' Ziggy asked.

'The cat,' TM finished for her. 'We've never actually managed to get them on him. I think they offend his phenomenological worldview somehow.'

'Makes sense,' Ziggy agreed knowingly.

'So,' said Veggie. 'Here's the deal. Ideas.'

'Ideas,' Ziggy concurred. She thought about it for a moment, then tilted her head. 'Ideas?'

'We need 'em,' Veggie said, tapping his crayon on the tabletop. 'If we don't come up with no ideas, we don't got nothin' to sell. TM's usually the one who comes up with actual decent stuff, and then we just sort of... I dunno, make it happen through sheer force of will.'

'Really?' Ziggy asked, eyes twinkling. 'I like the sound of that.'

Veggie lifted up the Bedsheet-Tablecloth-Whiteboard again, then - when no smoke billowed from underneath - whisked it up and slung it back over the dining table (and most of the detritus that still sat thereon, giving the impression of an extremely lumpy table under the sheet). 'Let's brainstorm,' he said, and then the toaster made a noise like a panda sneezing and a huge cloud of black, yeasty vapour mushroomed out and filled the room. 'Balls.'

'We should, er, probably go outside for a bit,' TM suggested.

'Smoke is bad,' Ziggy agreed. Michel Furcoat popped out from underneath his cosy pile of paper and buggered off out of the open window, as if by way of agreement.

Veggie huffed in frustration, threw his crayon down (causing it to break in two) and strode out of the door with an attention-demanding whine. Ziggy gave TM a quizzical glance; he shrugged, and they followed Veggie outside with significantly less melodrama.

***

Outside turned out to be airier than inside, and smelled a bit better (even before accounting for the noxious bread fumes currently circulating around the flat).

'What's so bad about being outside?' Ziggy asked, rhythmically prodding Veggie in the face as they wandered down the street. His stoic expression didn't shift once.

'He just prefers not to, if he can avoid it,' TM told her.

'You were outside earlier,' she pointed out.

'He'll go out when he needs something from the world, and then that's his outside time done for the day,' TM explained. 'It's a bit like having a pet, in that he needs a walk every now and again but then the rest of the time he just licks his balls and does basically naff all.' He sighed. 'He is toilet-trained, though.'

'Ah,' said Ziggy. 'So you *do* have a bathroom. I was looking for one, and I was thinking if you didn't have one I might have a problem with that. What with staying forever and all.' She fixed TM with an earnest stare, bright eyes boring into him; with the stark lightning bolt painted on her face, hands on her hips in her powder-blue suit, it was still somehow very difficult *not* to take her seriously.

'It's behind the filing cabinet on the other side of the table,' TM said, carefully ignoring the last bit. 'We couldn't be bothered to get another door after...' He paused, remembering the testing phase of a device he'd been provisionally calling the Ultimate Hinge Motion Ensmoothener. 'Anyway, we put some wheels on the filing cabinet, and now it's a sliding thing that you can kind of think of as a door. Most things in our place do more than one thing.'

'Nothing interesting in the universe only does one thing,' said Ziggy absently. 'Hold on a sec, would ya? This look isn't really working out as well as I hoped.'

'Um,' said TM. Their trundling down the street came to a halt - Veggie, too, ceased his steady, insistently harrumphing stride, and glanced around with interest.

'I'm just gonna - two secs,' Ziggy said, and then she'd pulled a hairpin from her crimson quiff, causing it to sink down limply across her face in a bright red wave, hopped down an alley perpendicular to the road, and disappeared.

'Where'd she go?' Veggie cheeped, peering after her.

'Somewhere, presumably,' TM murmured. 'Swear hair doesn't work like that.'

A moment later, a young woman with dark purple hair, light caramel skin, and soft eyes with corners accented like a swallow's wingtips emerged.

'...' said TM, somehow.

'I feel like this is more me,' said the young woman in Ziggy's voice. She was wearing dark jeans and a gaudy, tie-dyed T-shirt topped off with a leather jacket.

'Are you -' TM leaned around, looking behind her.

'Am I...?' She looked at him, questioning. The face was different, but the expression was her. TM looked down at her feet, upon which were dark grey high-top sneakers, and then back up at her face. He was almost sure Ziggy hadn't been carrying a change of clothes on her; he was *definitely* sure she hadn't taken them from the flat, because they definitely hadn't had any clothes like that just hanging out, and definitely definitely not in her size. He wondered why he was fixating on the clothes rather than the fact that her face was completely different.

'Are you Ziggy? Like... still the same Ziggy?' he asked eventually.

'Yeah, course,' she said, tucking a few loose strands of hair behind one ear; it stuck out like a dolphin's fin clearing the surface of the ocean. 'Well, I guess I'm technically not, in some sense, but you can keep calling me that. I'm still the same *me* as I was before, I think, depending on how you define *me* and whatnot. Just... trying out a different look.'

'You're still hot,' Veggie piped up.

'You think *everyone*'s hot,' TM said over his shoulder. Veggie made a dismissive, nonchalant noise like a wood pigeon settling down on a comfortable branch.

'So it wasn't just the Bowie after all,' Ziggy mused, to which both TM and Veggie felt they probably ought to respond. Neither did, so they just traipsed along after Ziggy as she merrily resumed strolling in the direction they'd been going.

'What actually *are* you?' TM asked after a while, more because he felt someone ought to than because he particularly needed to know the answer.

'I'm me,' said Ziggy. Her eyes - her new eyes - twinkled. 'I'm a *staaaahhr*, bay-bay.'

'Yeah, you said something like that,' TM mumbled. 'But, like, you're not making it up?'

Ziggy flicked her tongue off the roof of her mouth thoughtfully. 'It's complicated,' she said. 'Well, it's not really, but it's probably not super easy to explain. Or believe.'

'Is this some hippy thing?' TM asked. 'Like how we're all from the stars, eventually?' He put on his best Carl Sagan voice: '*Made of star stuff*, and all that.'

Ziggy considered the point. 'It's not some hippy thing. Although you're not wrong - you're all from the stars if you go back far enough, but I'm... a closer descendant, so to speak.'

TM considered this for a moment; Ziggy scratched her nose.

'Look,' she said, 'all people have star stuff in them. Like how all KFC chicken has a bit of secret spicy special sauce recipe, or all fictions have something of the people who came up with them. I'm just... a packet of one-hundred-percent special sauce.' She paused. 'Well, like, ninety-six percent, after you factor in all the packaging and manufacturing shit.'

TM blinked. 'That's a really weird analogy.'

'Sorry,' said Ziggy. 'Still getting used to... well, everything.'

TM couldn't argue with that. 'So you... are literally an actual star who's just dropped down to Earth? No BS? I mean, this –' he gestured at her appearance, which none could deny was significantly changed from what it had been only minutes before '- is weird, I'll give you that. It's convincing. I'm just not sure *what* it's convincing me of. Can *all* stars change their face, is that a thing that's always been a thing? 'Cos I didn't know that.' He stopped talking and hiccupped.

Ziggy came to a stop and exhaled loudly through her nose, one hand on her hip and the other tapping a finger against her cheek. 'What's an electron?' she asked abruptly.

'Um,' said TM.

'It's a tiny sub-atomic particle. Right? A probability density function, a negatively-charged electrical field generator, a fermion.'

'Um,' said TM, again.

'But if I tried to talk to you about electrons a couple of centuries ago – well, not *you* specifically, obviously, I didn't know you back then – what an electron was, even if I tried to explain it, you would think I was making it all up.'

'...'

'Nowadays, it's a theoretical term – which makes it, in some sense at least, a real entity. Right?'

TM felt that he ought to respond, but even ellipses began to evade him.

'Language is meaningless unless it refers; even if the referent doesn't actually exist, a thing of sorts is brought into reality when you talk about it, if only in your head. Point is –'

'There's a point?'

'The point is,' Ziggy repeated firmly, 'what's the actual difference between *terminology* and *made-up*? And besides, I could call anything an electron. Or I could claim that electrons *do* exist, but every theory about them so far has been completely wrong. Like, they're necessarily something, not necessarily anything in particular, but necessarily not anything that anyone's previously said they might be.'

'I have absolutely no idea what you're on about,' said TM.

Veggie yawned.

'Good,' said Ziggy. 'Forgotten what your question was yet?'

TM nodded.

'Sweet,' she said, and carried on. Her head turned in every direction as she walked, deep breaths taking in as much of the air as she could. Her fingers moved gently as if touching the atmosphere around her, feeling it.

TM watched her curiously, staying a few steps behind. He could hear Veggie keeping up with them, scuffing his shoes across the pavement with every step. A squirrel jumped out from a bush and went careening across the road, weaving around the wheels of a trundling car; Ziggy looked enthralled by it. Veggie spotted it too; TM heard him mumble the word 'Frogger'.

'So let's say you're a star,' TM said.

'I very much am,' Ziggy confirmed.

'What are you *doing*, like, being a person and that?'

Ziggy turned so that she was walking backwards, continuing to move smoothly along the road without ever stumbling or coming near to walking into anything, and turned her gaze on him. He wasn't entirely sure how he felt about it, but it was a gaze that remained indistinguishable from the one she'd had back when she was still Bowie Cosplay Ziggy. At least there was some continuity to the whole thing. 'You said it,' she said: '*being a person*.'

Veggie bumbled up alongside TM, scrunching his face up in what seemed to be an attempt to make himself look as confused as he possibly could. 'Right,' he said, 'I think I'm gathering something here about you being literally a star, and all that -'

'We just went over it five seconds ago in your earshot,' TM said.

'- but I can't say I totally follow,' Veggie finished, undeterred.

Ziggy sighed. 'You don't really need to,' she said. 'Just think of me as new to everything, and... eager to try it all.'

'So you were up there,' TM said, flicking his eyes towards the heavens, 'and you were being a star and all that, and now you're down here and you're being a person.'

'That's basically it.'

'And this works... how...?'

Ziggy harrumphed. 'Stop trying to reduce stuff down to parts, or how it works. Just take it as what it is as a whole thing, you'll feel better for it.'

TM thought about that, but didn't manage to formulate a response before Veggie interrupted.

'So let's just take it as read that you have in fact beamed down to Earth, or whatever you did, and this is the first day of Human Ziggy doing people stuff,' Veggie proposed, kicking his stone off into the bushes.

'Much obliged,' Ziggy said.

'And you picked us to be your guides on how to be a people and live a people life?' Veggie spluttered, as if it were the most ridiculous thing in the world. 'I mean... *us*?'

'Why not?' Ziggy shrugged, a laugh-like melody slipping into her voice. 'You're as qualified as any other person, so... just show me the world, and I'll owe you pretty much everything.'

'You'll owe us,' Veggie repeated, turning the phrase over in his mouth like a fresh piece of super-minty gum, or a coin he was testing for gold. 'Alright, then, make us rich and we're even.'

'Fair play,' said Ziggy. 'Quid pro quo and whatnot.' She scanned around for a moment, then her gaze settled on a man strolling casually by on the other side of the road with a plastic bag full of groceries. 'Right, got it.'

She sauntered over to the happy shopper, beckoning TM and Veggie to follow. They did so, scurrying through the light traffic.

'What's she doing?' TM whispered.

'I dunno,' Veggie replied, eyebrows furrowed. 'Maybe she's gonna invite this guy to join *Veggie TM Limited*.'

'I thought we were *TM Veggie Limited*.'

Veggie shrugged. 'Maybe she's gonna invite him to be a junior partner.'

'That's not even a real position - and she doesn't have that kind of authority!'

'Do you think she knows that?'

'Heck.'

'Hiiiiii,' said Ziggy.

'Um,' her mark said, holding his bag a little tighter, 'I'm not… buying, donating, whatever this is.'

'Nothing like that, no worries,' she reassured him, beaming. He relaxed, and she struck: her finger punctured the flimsy plastic of the bag, tearing it in two. Fruit, instant noodles, and other sundries cascaded forth, spilling onto the pavement like the jackpot from a slot machine in which all the prizes were overpriced groceries.

'What the hell,' said Shopping Guy, with which TM secretly agreed.

'This upstanding young man here,' Ziggy declared, 'was on his way home after a hard day in a very respectable job, having used his hard-earned money to procure necessary goods for his lovely wife and beautiful children!'

She picked up an item from the selection of fallen purchases by way of demonstration, and found herself brandishing a copy of *Tits* magazine aloft. 'Imagine that's baby food,' she said chirpily.

'There's a magazine literally just called *Tits*?' Veggie demanded of the hapless shopper, who nodded reluctantly. 'We could have come up with better than that!' A look of realisation spread across his face, and he turned to TM with a dawning excitement. '*We* could come up with better than that!'

'No,' said TM. Veggie deflated.

'Anyway,' Ziggy pressed on, 'this charming and professional young fellow was on his merry way back to his abode, when – oh no! – tragedy struck! He finds his goods scattered about!' She flailed her arms about with theatrical gumption, demonstrating the sheer horror of the situation. 'So what does he need? Why, a *Veggie Ziggy TM* Bag Puncture Repair Kit, of course!'

'A what now,' said TM. She wagged a finger in his direction.

'Why, a *Veggie Ziggy TM* Bag Puncture Repair Kit, of course!'

'Oh, of course,' said TM, who was rapidly forming the impression that it might be best just to go along with this sort of thing. It wouldn't take much effort, since Veggie's whole lifestyle was broadly *this sort of thing*.

'One simply takes the damaged bag,' Ziggy declared, demonstrating – Shopping Guy didn't try to resist as she tugged the thin plastic from his confused grip, 'repairs it like so – I mean, we obviously haven't got a prototype yet, but you get the idea. Don't worry, though,' she confided in Shopping Guy, 'the product is gonna be totally –' she winked and held her hand up in an OK sign with a click of the tongue.

'Oh, good,' said Shopping Guy. TM gave him a reassuring nod.

'And then, with a little *Veggie Ziggy TM* magic, the bag is repaaaaired!' Ziggy almost sang, holding the limp piece of non-biodegradable plastic in the air as if sacrificing it to the gods.

'Huh,' said Veggie.

'Here ya go,' Ziggy said, stuffing the bag back into Shopping Guy's hands with a friendly pat on the shoulder. 'Sorry about your stuff, but we're making money here.'

He nodded dejectedly, making no effort to pick up his scattered groceries. The trio left him there; Ziggy led the way with a cheery bounce, heading for Veggie and TM's flat.

'So… just to be clear,' Veggie said, 'your idea is that we design a thing for repairing holes in shopping bags.'

'Yup.'

'Single-use, disposable shopping bags.'

'Well, *yuh*. Just cos they're single-use doesn't mean that that one use shouldn't be as enjoyable and stress-free as possible.'

Veggie stopped in his tracks. 'TM,' he declared, 'I think she might be a genius.'

'You're serious.'

'Heck yeah,' said Veggie, the corners of his mouth moving further from each other as his grin widened. 'This product is *absolutely useless*. People'll buy it in their thousands!'

TM thought about it for a moment. 'You… might actually be onto something,' he admitted, and Ziggy burst into a wide smile.

'*Awesome*,' she said. 'Now, look, let's go make *mon-ay*, yeah?'

'Um,' said TM, as she strolled back down the road with her arms swinging enthusiastically. 'You know we can't just, like, conceive of something and make money, right?' he piped up. He felt almost reluctant to puncture the atmosphere that had both Ziggy and Veggie grinning so happily that between them they had more exposed teeth than he'd ever seen outside of a shark documentary, but *somebody* had to point these things out.

'Nah,' said Ziggy, waving a hand dismissively. 'Tim Berners-Lee will just give us a ring and be like *oh hey, is that Ziggy? I made the Internet but I just realised your idea's better, so here's a bunch of cash.*'

'That doesn't make sense,' TM started to say. Then he shook his head. 'You know what? Yeah, he will.'

Ziggy patted him on the back, smiling almost gratefully, then carried on her merry way. 'Eff yeah,' she said.

3. OMG, TV

They didn't make it all the way back to the flat before Ziggy delivered on her promise. (Tim Berners-Lee never called, but Veggie and TM weren't going to complain about that.)

She turned sharply off, a few roads before the turning for the flat, and strode straight into the city's public library. TM didn't hear what she said to the young man at the desk (with whom Veggie had had a brief fling, a few summers back), but somehow she was able to wander to an unoccupied computer, plonk herself on a chair, and set straight to logging into *Veggie TM, Inventors Incorporated*'s business accounts.

'Did we leave the login details lying around?' TM asked under his breath as he and Veggie stood watching over Ziggy's shoulders.

'I wouldn't trust me not to,' Veggie muttered back.

She hummed quietly as her fingers flew across the keys, entering information with blistering competence. Within moments she'd submitted the Bag Puncture Repair Kit to an online portal, where - in TM's experience - it would sit for months without ever being viewed and then have about a five percent chance of attracting funding for development and eventual retail.

TM and Veggie went to leave, but Ziggy just sat gazing benignly at the screen.

After less than a minute, TM's phone buzzed; he pulled it out of his pocket and peered at the screen. Ziggy leaned her head back, smirking upside-down at him.

'That's absolutely flipping ridiculous,' TM said after a moment.

'Eh? Whazzat?' Veggie leaned over and saw the screen. He blinked. 'That's never happened before,' he said after a few moments.

'Is good?' Ziggy asked, grinning wickedly.

'Is ridiculous,' TM said again.

'Absolutely,' Veggie agreed, 'ridiculous.'

Ziggy flipped around in the plastic library chair, crossing her legs and draping an elbow over its back. 'So can I be a junior partner and also live with you?'

'Are you serious?' Veggie asked, giving her a hard stare straight in the eyes.

'Uh, yuh-huh.'

Veggie held her gaze for a moment, then picked her up off the chair and embraced her; she gave a gurgling gasp, like a surprised chicken, as he lifted her up. 'You're a blooming senior flipping... executive... CEO, that's what the heck you are!'

'Woo,' said Ziggy breathlessly as Veggie's arms squeezed the air from her lungs.

'You're in,' TM agreed, high-fiving one of her flopping hands, 'for good.'

'Thanks,' Ziggy spluttered, then wiggled herself up and out of Veggie's bear-like grip and alighted softly on her chair. She promptly hopped down and resumed her languid seated position. 'I think I did pretty good, can't lie about that.'

Veggie trumpeted a blustering hoot, waving his hands about in wild excitement - drawing disapproving glances from several of the library's patrons - and tried to hug her again. She whipped up to her feet and stepped deftly behind TM, who patted Veggie on the head to calm his rampaging hug-mood.

'That's the most awesome thing that's ever happened to us in our whole life,' Veggie said, directing his words over TM's shoulder to Ziggy with total seriousness. 'It's usually, like, nothing nothing nothing PROVISIONAL PAPERWORK and then if you're lucky you get a little bit and then you see if it sells MORE PAPERWORK and then if you're *really* lucky you get a bit more - but I've never even *heard* of that much upfront. Upfront? *Upfront?!* It's ludicrous!' He finished his rant and took a few deep breaths, looking as if he might fall over with the sheer excitement of it all.

'It's almost unbelievably convenient,' TM summarised. Ziggy grinned.

'Well, it's *awesome*,' Veggie spluttered. 'I mean, this is the first actual *money* paid to *Veggie TM* - sorry, *Ziggy Veggie Ziggy TM*,' he corrected, when TM's eyes rolled pointedly in Ziggy's direction, 'because I'm so hecking chuffed that I'm gonna put your name in there twice - in... like, *ages*.'

Ziggy beamed, leaning over (balancing her chair deftly on two legs) to give Veggie a friendly punch in the arm. 'Happy to be of assistance,' she said, and Veggie made an affronted squawk.

'Of assistance? *Of assistance?!*'

'Veg,' said TM.

'Mmyeah.'

'I think she knows she did good.'

'Oh, right,' said Veggie, instantly deadpan. He shook Ziggy's hand politely, giving a clumsy curtsy. 'Not sure I ever properly introduced myself, so... pleased to meet you! I'm Veggie, two-time regional *Guitar Hero* champion and founding partner of this most lucrative and innovative business enterprise, and I look forward to many profitable years together.'

'Ziggy,' said Ziggy. 'Star, person, friend to cats.'

'*Awesome.*'

She hummed happily for a moment, then shivered. 'It's, um. Does anyone else...?'

Veggie and TM looked at each other, made the same bemused face, then looked back at her.

'You OK there?' TM asked; her gaze wandered around the large open space of the library, skittering across the walls until it settled on a widescreen TV set high up in a corner.

'Whoaaaaa,' she said, looking and sounding as if she were spacing out somewhat. 'That's TV, right?'

'That's TV,' agreed TM, correctly but not without concern. He glanced back at her. 'Are you, like -' his eyes flicked back to the screen: '- oh, hey, Veg, it's that show you like.'

Veggie bounded over towards the TV, bouncing on his toes. '*Awesome Survival*'s on? Sweet!' he called back towards them, attracting several more disapproving looks.

'You know it's not really called that,' TM said, attention focused on Ziggy as she slowly pushed herself to her feet and wandered after Veggie.

He logged her off the computer, just in case someone stole their identities right as they were actually achieving something.

'It *should* be,' Veggie sulked. Ziggy and TM joined him, looking up at the screen.

A copper-haired woman in a long, slim-fitting khaki shirt with a thick leather belt, practical but fitted trousers, and sturdy-looking boots was busy hacking away at an enormous tree branch with a sharp-looking machete.

'This tree,' she said (which none of them could hear, as the TV was muted, but luckily there were subtitles), 'is a redwood.' She gave the camera a knowing look, as if checking her audience were following along. 'It's incredibly old, and incredibly beautiful. And now it's going to help me in my quest for survival.'

'Ahhh,' Veggie declared eagerly, pointing at the TV and tugging on Ziggy's sleeve, 'I know what happens next!'

In a short sequence crammed with zooms and fancy transitioning shots, the woman fashioned wood from the tree into a long, elegant bow and strung it with what was apparently real animal gut. 'There's, like, a super-awesome montage song playing right now,' Veggie whispered to Ziggy. Sure enough, the subtitles read '*[CATCHY MONTAGE MUSIC]*'.

The presenter pulled a set of sharp arrowheads from a pouch on her belt, which seemed to have pouches and straps for just about everything; in a series of shots which alternated between sped-up and slow-motion, she fastened them to shafts cut from more of the tree's wood and hand-fletched with crisp feathers. In a few seconds, a small pile of homemade arrows lay before her.

'The direction's, like, kinda pretentious,' Veggie admitted. 'Slow-mo and hi-speed in the same sequence? C'mon. But nothing against you, we forgive you,' he told the woman on the screen quickly as she drew and loosed an arrow in a wide shot, hair blowing in what was probably artificial wind.

The TV changed channel.

'Aaaaawwww,' Veggie moaned, pulling a face at the person whose image now filled the screen: a weatherman, pointing at some area of either high or low pressure - TM never was sure which symbols meant what, but it was apparently significant. The new channel must have had a lower budget, for its image was washed-out and old-looking. 'I was enjoying that.'

TM glanced at Ziggy, who was utterly transfixed. He didn't think she'd breathed for a while.

'Who are these people?' she murmured.

'Erm,' said Veggie, as if it were the dumbest question he'd ever heard. 'That was Riegel O'Ryan, only the best wilderness survival presenter in the entire cosmos. And *that* is Al Tyer, local weather man and extremely minor celebrity. Not that anyone cares about him.'

Ziggy was trembling, TM realised, as if with great exertion. It was as if she were tensing all her muscles as hard as she could, turning herself into a rock-like, dense, solid object - as if she thought that something might pull her away if she didn't resist. 'I am,' she said after a moment, 'incredibly attracted to these people. I think.'

'Um,' said TM.

'Fair enough,' said Veggie with a nod of understanding. 'Well - on one count at least.'

TM looked back up at the TV. The weatherman - Al Tyer - was staring into the camera, saying something about the atmosphere. Maybe it was too intense, having someone appear to be staring right at her spouting reminders of the cosmos, the stratosphere, the world beyond the world.

'Not all is as it should be, meteorologically,' Tyer said via the subtitles, gazing blurrily at TM. 'But we'll put that right.'

TM frowned at him.

'You alright, though, for real?' Veggie was saying, a hand on Ziggy's shoulder.

'Er,' said Ziggy. Then she blinked and shook her head, and then she gave the two of them a small smile. 'Yeah, sorry. I just... it's hard to explain.'

'No worries,' said Veggie knowingly. 'You just witnessed your first ever celebrities of the televisual netwaves. That's a pretty big dealio.'

TM narrowed his eyes at his business partner, just to let him know he wasn't convinced. 'You sure you're OK?' he asked Ziggy.

'I think so,' she said. 'Let's just... go home, yeah?'

She walked slowly away, her partners following after a moment of confused hesitation.

'You think she's okay?' TM muttered to Veggie, not wanting Ziggy to hear.

Veggie shrugged. 'She made us more money today than we've made in... probably literally years. If she needs a minute to get over that, I'm more than happy to give her one.'

TM rolled his eyes and punched Veggie's upper arm. 'I doubt that's it, somehow,' he said. 'She's probably just a bit overwhelmed.'

'Yeah,' said Veggie, as if it were obvious, 'overwhelmed with how amazing our triple partnership is.'

TM sighed, watching Ziggy as she led them out of the library and down the road towards the flat. Her arms hung by her sides, but her fingers were outstretched as if trying to make some sort of contact with something solid. 'We'll see,' he said quietly, and he trotted up to catch her.

'So, look,' he said. 'I think Veggie and I are decided that you can... like, *stay* stay. Forever, or whatever.'

'Thanks,' she said, watching her feet on the pavement.

'So you don't have to worry about that.'

'That's good.' She paused. 'Really good. I mean... thank you.'

TM leaned in, trying to get her to look at him without overdoing it. In the end he just sort of wobbled in her direction. 'Are you... hiding?'

She looked sharply up at him, then back at her feet. 'Sorta,' she admitted quietly.

'If you're really a star,' he said, then mentally kicked himself - not the time for that, 'I mean. You're a star, but you're here. So... isn't someone going to want you back?'

She bit her lip, then sighed. 'It's a possibility.'

They passed a shop window crammed with TV screens, on every one of which was repeated the same image of Al Tyer. Either the picture had frozen or he was sitting very still, looking down the camera as if trying to see the audience on the other side. TM gave the window the finger, ushering Ziggy past. She shook her head a few times as if trying to dislodge something.

'Let's just get home for now, OK?' he muttered.

'Ahoy, abode,' called Veggie, strolling past TM and Ziggy; TM glanced up and realised that they were, in fact, home. He and Ziggy followed Veggie through the door, up the stairs, and into the flat.

4. Suplex Complex

The flat was quiet when they returned. That was a good thing, TM reflected: the expected way of things. The smoke had dispersed, leaving the air pleasantly clear, if mildly pungent. Ziggy took a few hesitant steps over to the sofa and sank down into it, elbows on knees. It was a decent sort of sofa, actually: a moving-in present from TM's parents, and thus one of the only things in the place that wasn't second-hand, third-hand, or rubbish-dump-hand. (They did have a real, proper set of wooden chairs - all matching and everything - most of which had all their legs and all of which had been liberated from a recently evicted neighbour's unoccupied apartment.)

She was still sitting in the same position by the time Veggie had scraped the atomised remains of the previous round of hot bread from the toaster, slipped a few fresh slices in, and slapped piping hot crispy bread down on three plates. He'd also somehow found time to nip to the bedroom and change into pyjama bottoms. Veggie could somehow make literally any look work; he'd worn triple-denim and a purple scarf once, and absolutely rocked it.

'Veg,' TM said, nudging his partner, 'I don't think she's OK.'

Veggie glanced over at Ziggy slumped on the sofa, and stuck his bottom lip out in what TM assumed was supposed to be a thoughtful expression. 'Sometimes people aren't,' he pointed out. 'We can't all be alright all the time. Remember how I was after the Swede - remember how *you* were, for heck's sake, after -?'

'That doesn't mean people *want* to be not okay,' TM interrupted. 'Shouldn't we try to… cheer her up?'

Veggie considered the proposition. 'I would go buy her pick and mix, but the shops are probably closing by now. Also, I don't want to go out, so you get this one.'

'Pick and mix does always help,' TM murmured, half-listening.

Veggie's eyes widened, a gasp of disbelief escaping his lips. 'Dude,' he said, as if it were the most important thing of all time, 'I just realised she's probably never had pick and mix before.'

'That's a pretty horrific state of existence,' TM concurred.

Veggie looked down at the plates on the counter before him. 'This'll have to do,' he resolved, and he picked up two of the three plates and went to plonk himself down next to Ziggy.

'Bread,' he said loudly, thrusting it in her face. She wriggled away; TM picked up his own plate and sat on the floor in front of her. 'Bread,' declared Veggie again; the look TM gave him told him in no uncertain terms to stop.

'It's OK, honestly,' he said to Ziggy, rather more calmly than Veggie had been going for. TM took a bite of his own toast, sighing happily as it crunched; Ziggy snatched her slice off the plate in Veggie's outstretched hand and nibbled at it tentatively.

There followed a silence, of sorts, albeit one punctuated by the sounds of crunching bread. Ziggy's eyes had widened slightly at the first bite, and she was tucking in ferociously.

'Right,' said Veggie around a mouthful of toast. TM imagined his words struggling to get out of his mouth, clambering around the crunchy chunks of toast crumb like tiny spelunkers in a delicious cavern. 'So you're obviously a goldmine. Which is tip-top, 'cos we *really* needed to hit the jackpot, like, several years ago.' He swallowed. 'To use a technical term, we're a little bit fucked. Financially speaking.'

'Never would have guessed,' Ziggy said quietly.

'And,' Veggie pressed on, sensing a path to up-cheering, 'since you have no other attachments...'

'None whatsoever.'

'I'm prepared to offer you the opportunity of a lifetime.'

Ziggy chewed for a few seconds, then gulped. 'Is it being in the company and living with you and all that? 'Cos we already covered that.'

'Oh,' said Veggie. 'Yeah.' He folded his slice of toast, rolling it up into a weird little stick of crispy bread, and took a hefty bite. 'I was gonna suggest you could be an unpaid intern - valuable work experience, you could totally have put it on your CV - and then, because we're probably too trusting of people, you could live here with us, call it a perk, but... as I now remember from incredibly recently, you're already a full partner and a significant part of our home life to boot. So... all good!' He downed the rest of his toast, chomping with glee.

'I think we have a deal,' said Ziggy.

'Cool,' said Veggie. 'I'll get you the paperwork. Where are you from again?'

'The stars.'

'Oh, yeah, you did mention.'

'There's no paperwork,' TM chimed in.

'I figured,' said Ziggy, polishing off the rest of her toast.

'So look,' said Veggie, 'since you're our new star employee - hehe, get it? - first order of business is to drain your brain of all your lucrative ideas. Mmkay?'

Ziggy tilted her head at him. 'How do?'

'How do ideas?'

'Mm.'

'Well, what we usually do is... ideas!' Veggie popped up to his feet and swanned over to where the Bedsheet-Tablecloth-Whiteboard still lay on a counter by the frazzled toaster. 'And then... I write 'em. On...' he gestured widely.

'There's no structure to this, is there?'

'Absolutely not.' Veggie retrieved the longer half of the crayon he'd broken earlier and raised it over the Bedsheet-Tablecloth-Whiteboard.

There was another silence, this one more silent than the last on account of TM having finished his hot bread.

'So how do you usually... do the thing?' Ziggy asked as the silence came to an end.

'We just sort of think and see what happens, really,' explained TM, staring fixedly at the blank expanse of the Bedsheet-Tablecloth-Whiteboard. 'It's not often particularly successful.'

'Oh,' said Ziggy. 'But this is what you *do*?' She said the word *do* in the sort of way that it might be used by a grandparent discovering that their grandchild had taken up professional blogging.

'Pretty much, yup.'

'It's lucrative, when it works,' said Veggie, by which TM assumed he meant 'mostly for people who aren't us'. 'I'm more of the business guy;

TM comes up with most of the real hotspot moneymaker concepts. He's one of them creative types. Although... maybe that's you now. So I don't know what we need TM for at this point.'

'Got one,' TM piped up quickly. Veggie raised his crayon with a ceremonious flourish. 'A thing that helps you reach Mexican food on high shelves.' At that, Veggie lowered his crayon. 'And we call it the *Enchi-Ladder*.'

'It's been done,' said Veggie, grinding the broken tip of his crayon into the Bedsheet-Tablecloth-Whiteboard with forlorn aplomb.

'Serious?'

'Must have been. No way a pun that good hasn't been taken already.'

TM tapped a finger against his pouting lips. 'How about... *Veggie Ziggy TM Super Grease*? Like grease, but more greasy.'

Veggie practically wailed in despair. Ziggy blew air through her lips like a camel inflating a balloon, filling the air with the sound – and, TM was almost sure, the smell – of a raspberry.

'I'll come up with something for you at some point,' she promised, then turned back around on the sofa to face towards the TV. Glancing at it, she shrank down and huddled up again, making herself small. Michel Furcoat, the cat, appeared from somewhere within the sofa and plonked himself on her lap.

TM took her plate - and his own, and the one Veggie had unhelpfully left on the sofa - over to the sink, which was behind where Veggie still stood with his crayon drifting through lazy loops in the air above the Bedsheet-Tablecloth-Whiteboard.

'How do you cheer up a star?' TM muttered. It was hard enough cheering a person up, let alone an astronomical entity who might potentially be a little more emotionally complex.

Veggie sighed. 'She's kinda bumming me out,' he said. Then he looked up at the ceiling and narrowed his eyes, evidently thinking hard.

'I know that face,' said TM with concern.

Then Veggie punched him in the stomach.

'Oof,' said TM. Ziggy's head poked out over the top of the sofa; Michel Furcoat's black-and-white cat head popped up next to her. TM just had time to wonder whether Maurice Meow-Ponty, the cat, had also come home before Veggie swung his fist again.

TM grabbed Veggie's arm, zipped around behind him and yanked hard, wrenching Veggie's shoulder into a painful, contorted hold. Ziggy cocked her head and, TM thought he heard, giggled quietly. Michel Furcoat coughed up a hairball, which was what he usually did when he was amused.

'Aha!' declared Veggie, wriggling like a krumping ferret in TM's grip. 'We got a smile!'

TM released his friend. 'Did you really just make me fight you for Ziggy's entertainment?'

'Natch.'

Ziggy rested her chin on the sofa back, peering at the two of them like a very comfortable owl eyeing up a juggling vole. 'Again,' she demanded.

'Really?' TM muttered - though he couldn't help a slight grin – but Veggie was already taking another shot. TM ducked under his arm, grabbed him around the waist from behind and heaved, letting himself fall backwards. Veggie landed with a thud on his shoulders, TM still holding him tightly in a reverse bear hug.

'You German suplexed me?' Veggie wheezed, sounding impressed.

'Not on purpose,' TM apologised. 'You try to hit me, it's all instinct. I can't be responsible if my uncontrollable badassery gets you hurt, man.'

'How come you can fight and whatnot?' Ziggy asked with interest.

'TM watches a lot of wrestling, plays a lot of fighting games, that sort of thing,' Veggie explained, hopping to his feet.

'That doesn't actually explain it,' Ziggy observed.

'I guess if you pretend to train at something long enough, eventually you actually get good at it,' reasoned Veggie. Ziggy looked unconvinced.

'This is good, though,' she said thoughtfully. Michel Furcoat (the cat) gave a sage nod. 'I might need protection.'

'Right,' said TM, 'yeah, so… I don't wanna make a big deal out of this, but, erm. Um. You know how you said someone might *possibly* be after you? What sort of someone are we talking, and how possibly?'

Ziggy thought about it for a brief moment. 'It's almost impossibly implausible not to be the case that it's unlikely it isn't already happening,' she intoned sincerely. 'As for the someone... *like me* someones.'

'More stars,' Veggie mumbled. 'Whatever. What's a star anyway? Just old light.'

'I'm sat right here,' Ziggy said.

'Why does TV freak you out?' TM asked, trying to bring the conversation back to questions that might (if he were feeling very optimistic) have more concrete answers.

She pondered this. 'It's... too much,' she answered eventually. 'Those people, they can reach me no matter where I am. That's a lot.'

'We'll watch movies later,' said Veggie. 'You can pause those.'

'That... actually sounds helpful,' Ziggy said.

'Anyway, look,' Veggie continued, 'whatever happens, we got you now. So that's what's happening there. We got you.'

'And,' said TM, trying to be helpful and encouraging, 'even if there *is* someone after you, how are they gonna know where you are? We're not gonna have to worry about that for *ages* -'

There was a knock at the door.

5. The Rest of the Party

Ziggy yelped and retreated to the furthest corner of the sofa; Michel Furcoat, knocked to the floor by her movement, did the closest thing to a harrumph that a cat could do and went to sit under the TV.

'Oh, heck. I forgot about - don't worry,' Veggie said to Ziggy, bounding over to the door. 'It's a friend.'

He pulled the door open.

'Oh, yeah: *friends*,' he corrected. 'Forgot you were all coming together.'

'When do we ever do *anything* as individuals?' said the well-dressed individual standing on the other side: sharp-eyed, willowy, a neat, straight wave of blonde hair framing one side of a lean face.

They entered the flat, giving Veggie a quick, affectionate hug on the way past; a young woman in a Columbo-style raincoat ambled in after, winking in TM's direction with pale green eyes set in a face partly hidden behind a curtain of dark, straight hair. She was followed by a mane of wild blue hair on top of a skinny, barely-out-of-his-teens man with dark eyes and a long-sleeved punk rock T-shirt who walked as if he were plucking at the strings of a bass guitar with every step.

'Hey, TM,' said Punk Shirt, clapping him on the shoulder. 'We got a new player?'

Ziggy looked at TM uncertainly, like a shy child dragged along to a Christmas party at an aunt's with whom she had absolutely no interest in spending time.

'Everyone,' said TM, 'this is Ziggy. She's... joining the business.'

'Awesome,' said the well-dressed person with an appreciative nod. TM watched Ziggy's reaction: she sat a little less stiffly, still keeping her weight planted at the far end but leaning towards the group.

'Ziggy, this is everyone,' Veggie said, spreading his arms wide. 'Well - not *everyone*, obviously, this is three people. That's Derrida -' he indicated Well-Dressed, who gave a thumbs-up and instantly looked horrified at having done such an obviously lame thing, '- this over here is Dominika -' the dark-haired girl, '- and that over there is Marty.' Punk Shirt gave a cheery wave. 'They're all nice, honest.'

Ziggy nodded and exhaled, her body relaxing. She climbed up on top of the sofa and sat there, waving shyly.

'Jack Derrida,' Derrida announced, striding over and holding out a smooth, well-looked-after hand for Ziggy to shake. She looked at it for a second, then took it between finger and thumb and wiggled it about a bit.

'Not *the* Jacques Derrida, obviously,' Veggie confided to Ziggy, 'although - you ever hear of nominative determinism?'

'Pff,' said Derrida, flapping their hands. 'Not boy Jack, but not girl Jack either, just to get that out of the way.'

'Person Jack,' Ziggy said, nodding. Derrida smiled at her.

'Most people have more trouble with it than that,' they said.

'Why?' she asked, sounding genuinely curious.

'Never mind,' Derrida said, though they looked more pleased than TM had seen them in a while. That was usually ominous, but seemed OK this time.

Dominika slinked over next, perching on the sofa-top next to Ziggy. She pushed her straight hair out of her face with an index finger and stared straight into Ziggy's eyes for slightly longer than was comfortable before nodding happily and wandering over to the table, where she sank into a chair and sighed.

'She doesn't talk much,' said Veggie. 'I'm not sure she speaks English, come to think of it.'

'How does that work?' Ziggy asked.

'You'll see,' he explained, or didn't.

'And I'm Marty Rook,' Marty said from across the room, making a fist with index and little fingers extended in greeting. 'You might have heard of me.'

'Hm,' said Ziggy noncommittally.

'Or my band?' Marty prodded. 'The Inciting Incident? We're, uh... kinda big around here.'

'We'll bring her to see you play some time,' TM promised, and ushered Marty to a chair. He sat, though not without a deflated whine.

'What's going on?' Ziggy asked. She peered over her seat atop the sofa, arms folded around herself and one hand holding on to the other elbow protectively; she watched curiously as everyone took their seats around the table.

Veggie whipped the Bedsheet-Tablecloth-Whiteboard up and threw it aside in a crumpled ball; then he shunted the assorted seasonal and stationery-ish debris off the table and onto the floor. Mess redistributed to his satisfaction, he reached under the table - on top of which could now be seen a mat bearing a fantasy-esque map covered in gridlines - and pulled out a stack of paper and cards, which he plonked in the centre of the tabletop.

'It's *Hero's Adventure* night,' TM explained. 'We all get together, once a week... or sometimes once a month, or sometimes nine times in one week, and we play -'

'The greatest tabletop role-playing game that ever there was,' Veggie finished with gusto.

'Did you guys invent it?' Ziggy asked. Veggie burst into peals of laughter.

'*Heck*, no,' he said eventually, wiping a tear away. 'We're not *that* good. Well, TM might be, but I'm not that good at long-term development and whatnot.'

'Want to join the game?' TM invited, pulling out a chair. It was astonishing, really, how many chairs and how many people could fit around the tiny table in the tiny kitchenette of their tiny flat. TM - looking proudly around at their living-dining-office-kitchen area and the many, many items littering it - put it down to good space management.

'Er,' said Ziggy.

'We'll help ya,' Marty offered. 'We're playing together, not against each other.' He glanced over at Dominika, who smirked. 'Unless we decide to,' he added.

'We're a band of brave adventurers, out doing our thing. Y'know: adventuring, and that,' TM explained. 'It's hella fun, once you get into it.'

'I'll help her make a character,' Derrida suggested, in response to which Veggie threw part of a broken crayon at them.

'No, you don't,' he said warningly. 'TM, if you wouldn't mind.'

'Yup.' TM took a sheet of paper covered in complicated-looking tables and charts and placed it in front of the chair he'd pulled out for Ziggy, then rummaged around under the table from whence Veggie had pulled his papers and cards. After a moment, he pulled out a thick book titled *The Definitive Player's Guide to Hero's Adventure (sixteenth edition)*.

'So first thing is you gotta make a character to join the adventure,' TM explained. He slammed the book down on the table; Michel Furcoat, who had remained lazily under the TV, jumped in surprise, yowled when his head made contact with the underside of the TV stand, and promptly absquatulated. 'Each of us has a character that we play as - well, except Veggie. He's the Adventure Master.'

'Whoaaa,' breathed Ziggy, sliding down into the offered chair.

'It's both way cooler and way less cool than it sounds, depending who you ask,' said Veggie.

'Soooo,' Marty said to Veggie as TM began helping Ziggy fill out her character sheet (a laborious process, since character generation version six-point-three - colloquially, '*The One That Nerfed Paladins and Made Non-Heterosexual Marriage Mathematically Advantageous*' - demanded an awful lot of statistics to be calculated before so much as coming up with a name), 'what sort of quests are we planning to embark upon today, O wise and frequently vindictive Adventure Master?'

'Who knows?' Veggie said, leaning back in his chair. 'We'll just have to see what awaits in this strange and magical world, won't we?'

Derrida snorted. 'You know exactly what awaits,' they said. 'You wrote the campaign.'

'You're absolutely no fun sometimes,' Veggie declared. 'Just accept the magic of the adventure. Besides, just because I *came up with* the story doesn't mean I know where it's gonna end up. Wouldn't be any point doing it if I did. I'd just write it down.' His eyes glinted. 'And then... sell it.'

'Thought for a later time,' said Derrida hurriedly. 'All I'm saying is that I like it when there's a neat plot, a worthwhile conclusion, and some sort of meaningful point to the whole thing.'

'Well, that's just not how things work around here,' Veggie said.

'Why does it need one anyway?' Marty asked Derrida across the table.

'There isn't always a point - that's just how the universe is sometimes. Not everything ends up being didactic.'

'I'll find a point somewhere,' Derrida said firmly.

'I believe you,' said Marty with a grin, 'just don't go writing your magnum opus... *Of Grammatology* equivalent of... I dunno, some weird post-structuralist deconstruction of one of our pointless role-playing games, 'kay?'

Derrida harrumphed.

'So how do you all know each other, anyway?' Ziggy asked, looking up at them all as TM jotted down a series of numbers on her character sheet.

The trio looked at each other, then at Veggie.

'Derrida and Dominika are Veg's exes,' TM told her without looking up. 'Marty isn't. Yet. But we like him, so we'll see where it goes.'

Marty gave him the finger.

Ziggy's head bobbed from side to side, gazing from Derrida to Dominika to Veggie and back again. 'You were... together?' she said, sounding enthralled.

'Not all at the same time,' TM pointed out.

'What was it like?' she asked, leaning forwards curiously.

Derrida scratched their nose. 'It was good,' they said with a shrug. Dominika nodded sagely.

'And... you're all still friends?'

'Hell yes,' Veggie boomed.

'There isn't a man or woman Veggie's loved that he hasn't somehow stayed in touch with,' TM told her, with an air of grudging impressment.

'Except the Swede,' Derrida said gravely.

'If I loved 'em,' Veggie said, waving a pencil around and ignoring Derrida entirely, 'why the heck would I not want to stay friends with 'em?'

'It didn't end badly?' asked Ziggy, her wide-eyed gaze travelling over them all.

'Nah,' said Veggie.

TM laughed, the movement shaking his arm so that he accidentally wrote a seven instead of a two in one of Ziggy's stat boxes. He moved to erase it, but decided to just leave it.

'Veggie here is what's known as *a real people person*,' he said to Ziggy. All present nodded as one. 'He just gets along with people. Loves them, leaves them, loves them again but in a mate way, and it's never really been a problem for anyone.'

'Except the Swede,' Derrida said. Veggie threw his pencil at their head, then turned to Ziggy.

'I don't want you to think I'm some sort of cheap lover,' he said seriously. 'I care very deeply about a lot of people, and that's just the way I am.'

'He actually means that,' TM clarified. 'It's kind of weird, given how easily he seems to be able to make people extremely annoyed with him, but general consensus is Veggie's just a genuinely pretty decent guy.'

'Huh,' said Ziggy. Then she looked at TM. 'What about you?' she said. 'Exes, I mean.'

TM made one final entry on her sheet, then put his pencil down. He thought about answering the question, then decided to pretend he hadn't heard it.

'She's good to go,' he said, and the ensemble picked up their own sheets as one. Veggie placed a few miniature figures on the map on the table, then straightened a stack of paper in front of him bearing the heading *'Hero's Adventure Campaign of Excellentness, by Veggie'*.

'Righto,' said Veggie. 'Where were we?'

He reached down into the heap of miscellaneous stationery that had until recently adorned the 'office' half of the table, but which was now just a miserable pile on the floor, and pulled out a pair of wire-framed glasses, pushing them up his nose. Then he leaned over his campaign paperwork, and began to speak.

6. A Hero's Adventure

In a voice that flitted between mellifluous and wrathful, gentle and harsh as the situation demanded, Veggie described the goings-on of the group's adventure. He'd done some voice acting once, hired for impressing the director with his ability to immediately adopt the necessary tone and immediately fired for refusing to do so unless he could get an introduction to Jason Momoa (who was not remotely involved in the production in any capacity).

A dark, cold wind is in the air tonight. The four heroes, who made camp last week –

'Oh, yeah, I remember now,' said Marty. Veggie shushed him theatrically.

The four heroes are awoken by the rustling of leaves and the sound of footsteps. The sound, perhaps, of somebody sneaking around in the woods not twenty feet from their soundly sleeping tushies.

'Perception check,' Derrida said quickly, rolling a six-sided and an eight-sided die. Ziggy watched them skitter across the table as if they were the most amazing things she had ever laid eyes upon.

Atgard, the Serpent-Man monk whose stats are all... like, so much higher than they ought to be because Jack 'The Exploit' Derrida decided to minmax the heck out of things –

'Entirely within the rules,' Derrida interjected.

'True,' conceded Veggie, 'but you have this habit of doing shit that's technically legal but is actually really douchey and makes you way overpowered.'

Derrida sank back into their chair, folding their arms and sticking their bottom lip out.

'Don't sulk at me, bitch, it'll get you nowhere,' Veggie said, and continued.

Anyway, Atgard scans his surroundings with his really abnormally good vision, but – Veggie made a dice roll of his own, and gave a wide grin at the result – *he simply can't see anything through the trees and the heavy darkness.*

'Balls,' said Derrida.

Dominika riffled through her hand of picture cards, each emblazoned with details – names, icons, the occasional graphic drawing of an enemy being disembowelled – and pushed one in Veggie's direction, tapping it with a pastel-nailed finger.

Iveline, the blind and mute half-elven ranger, uses her enhanced sense of hearing to pass the detection check and instantly knows exactly what's up: four orcs are making their way towards the heroes, trying to surround them.

Dominika folded another card down on top of the first; Veggie glanced down at it and adjusted his glasses.

Iveline nocks an arrow to her bow.

Dominika turned her character sheet so that he could see it, indicating the 'equipment' section.

The really high-stat-bonus bow that she won a couple of weeks ago from that travelling carny mage who turned out to be the king of… somewhere.

She nodded judiciously.

She looses the arrow into the trees, but hears it strike wood.

'Cock,' said Derrida.

'Okay,' said Marty thoughtfully. 'It's still the middle of the night, yeah?'

Veggie blinked and shuffled through his campaign papers. 'Uh, yeah. Didn't I mention?'

'You said it was dark or something.'

'Okay,' Veggie said with a sigh. 'Not that I didn't already set the scene in a masterful way, but for Marty's benefit –' everyone groaned, and Marty blushed '– let me reiterate.'

You four heroes are still in the deep darkness of the night, in the middle of the woods. Hence the trees. Also, you're still really sleepy 'cos you just got woken up, and who the heck can deal with that? So everyone take a penalty to all perception bonuses. Clear enough? Good. Okay, so the shuffling around you starts to intensify, and a ripping sound reaches your ears as one of the orcs pulls Iveline's arrow from the tree with malicious... maliciousness.

'Pff,' said Derrida.

'Shut it, you,' said Veggie. 'I ran out of words.'

'Wouldn't it be "malice", anyway?'

'I cast Shining Beacon,' Marty interrupted them, slapping a card down on the table.

Malachi, the sorcerer of the half-demon Rithling race, raises his hand. A bright ball of light springs forth and shoots into the air, where it hovers and illuminates the surroundings. The orcs flinch away from the sudden bright light, but now they know that there's no more hiding, they quickly draw their weapons with no more fear of detection.

'Nicely done, Rook,' said Derrida, poring over their character sheet. 'I think my passive reaction bonus of... nine should allow me to get a priority attack on one of these scumbags, since they're flinching?'

'Why not,' said Veggie. 'You'll find some weird way of engineering a sneak attack anyway. Deconstructive bugger.'

Derrida rolled the dice, watching intently. 'Natural max roll,' they announced as the polyhedrons came to a halt, clapping their hands together with excitement. 'Critical one-hit KO, I should think?'

A noise somewhere between a sigh, a groan, and whale song escaped Veggie, who looked fully ready to slam his head on the table in exasperation. Ziggy put a hand gently on his forehead.

Atgard, being who he is, leaps towards the nearest distracted orc and rips his head from his body, pulling the whole spine out in one intact piece from skull to ass.

'And eats the brain, don't forget,' said Derrida smugly.

'So subtle,' Marty groaned.

And, of course, he eats the brain.

Veggie made a quick roll.

Or, at least, he would, if it weren't for the fact that one of the other orcs has instantly jumped him.

Veggie dropped a few counters on the table to illustrate the placement of each character, and slid a red one violently in Derrida's general direction.

'I'll save it for later,' Derrida conceded.

'TM, you've been relatively inactive,' said Marty. 'You wanna get that, I'll sort out these two?'

'Yeah, go on,' TM said, leafing through ability cards. 'I'll... um.'

Marty and Derrida exchanged glances.

'What?' said Ziggy, sensing something.

'TM's famous for having a hard time with the first decision,' Marty explained. 'He gets into the swing of it, but deciding how to start things off always takes a minute. Especially since - I mean.'

'I'll slip through here,' TM said suddenly and decisively, sliding counters and miniatures around the table, 'behind this one, and then backstab.'

'Hm,' said Marty, sounding half-impressed.

'Roll for it,' Veggie instructed.

TM rolled. Ziggy patted his arm encouragingly at the result.

Barry the Shadowguard –

'I still can't believe you actually named your character Barry,' said Marty.

– former prince of the Ascended Humans, bearer of the Blessing of the Summoner Queen... um.

'Keeper of the Peace of the Sister Nations of Water, Mist and Low Cloud,' TM reminded him.

'Wow,' said Ziggy with a note of admiration. 'You've done a lot.'

'He hasn't actually *done* a lot,' Derrida said. 'He just wrote a really long and detailed backstory, and he was so proud of it all that we just decided to let him have it.'

Anyway, that guy *descends into the shadow of Iveline, his elfishly tall comrade. He travels through her shadow in the form of a black mist, then arises from the earth right behind the orc as it approaches Atgard.*

Veggie cross-referenced a couple of bits of paper, mumbling to himself. 'Sinks his dagger into its neck, aaaand... it's got one hit point left,' he announced, making a note on one of his many sheets of paper.

'Finish it with an attack roll,' Derrida completed, throwing their dice down.

Atgard's long Serpentine arms plunge into the orc's belly and rip out its intestines, shredding them into confetti before his enormous teeth bury themselves in its throat and tear its trachea apart as if it were rice paper. Then he crushes its brain and tramples on its eyes. It is now quite dead.

'Subtle,' Marty said again.

'You keep using that word,' Derrida told him. 'I do not think it means what you think it means.'

'It's sarcasm, you dolt.'

Dominika shot one of the remaining two orcs in the eye, though it stayed on its feet; Marty attempted to summon a lightning storm, but failed the roll and achieved precisely nothing. The two orcs smacked him in the face a couple of times, and then Veggie paused.

'Righty-ho,' he said, folding a couple of sheets over. 'I gotta instruct Ziggy, y'all.'

TM gave him a questioning look.

'Well, she hasn't joined up with the rest of you losers yet,' Veggie pointed out. 'She needs a storyline, some sort of intersection par excellence, you dig. I gotta make sure she acts independently, anyway. Them's the rules.'

Ziggy leaned over, putting her head close to Veggie's, and the two of them exchanged a series of brief whispers. After a moment they nodded and broke the huddle; Veggie scribbled a few lines on a piece of paper.

Okay, so. The two orcs approach Malachi, who's helpless to resist on account of it not being his turn. But wait! Lo, what light shineth forth from yonder mysticism?

Derrida spent a few moments gurning as if trying to work out how best to rudely tell Veggie just how terrible they considered that sentence, but shook their head and gave up.

The light from Malachi's floating light ball shines on, and he looks up to see a figure nimbly making its way through the branches of the surrounding trees.

'Shouldn't he have to roll some sort of check for that?' Derrida interjected.

His eyes are just drawn to the movement so he doesn't need to roll a check, okay? Christ. Anyway, he sees a figure skittering about in the trees, leaping between thin branches with all the grace of a ballet-dancing flying squirrel. Which is to say, really really gracefully.

'Agility check!' Ziggy declared, rolling the dice around in her hands before letting them fly across the table.

Veggie looked down his nose at them, then nodded. She looked quickly from the dice to Veggie, from Veggie to the dice, and back again.

'That's not good,' she said.

'No such thing as not good,' Veggie proclaimed. 'It'd be super uninteresting if nothing ever went wrong. Roll strength and reaction, would ya?'

Ziggy complied sadly.

The figure crashes down wildly out of the trees, smashing to the ground with the force of a descending meteor. Leaves fly in every direction; the new arrival forgoes acrobatiness entirely and charges the rest of the distance like a raging hippo.

TM raised an eyebrow.

'Hippos are terrifying, and fast,' Veggie said.

'I'm good with this,' Ziggy said, narrowing her eyes with dangerous intent.

The charging person mows down the fresher of the two orcs, stampeding over it and ramming its face into the ground with a knife to the base of the skull. Then she instantly whirls about and sinks a hidden blade into the remaining good eye of the other orc, the one Iveline shot in the face. It falls dead with a thump.

'That's awesome,' said Marty appreciatively.

'Overpowered, more like,' Derrida said. 'How come you get mad if *I* do that?'

'You know as well as I do that it's in the rules that new characters get inflated stats for when they first come swooping in for some heroically establishing moment,' Veggie told them.

'I gaze majestically around,' Ziggy declared in a theatrical vibrato, 'and then I lower my hood in a super-dramatic way and do, like, this really badass stare at them all.'

'I munch on brains,' Derrida added.

Atgard feasts upon the grey matter of his kills, imbibing their strength and gaining a temporary boost to his signature skill of Berserk Attack thanks to the Serpentine racial skill of Parasitic Consumption. The others...?

Veggie glanced around at each of them with a placid smile of anticipation.

'I could have taken them,' Marty grumped.

Malachi stares warily at the stranger. She lowers her hood and the half-mask covering her face from the nose down.

'What's your charisma score?' Veggie asked Ziggy. She held up her character sheet, rather than bother to look through it. 'And Marty, judgement modifier?'

Marty rolled. 'Critical fail,' he said.

Malachi, who considers himself a pretty good judge of character, divines that the stranger is an obese man holding a trombone in each hand, who is clearly very evil.

'Well, if that's a critical fail she's obviously decent,' TM pointed out.

'Yadda yadda,' said Veggie dismissively. 'There's stuff the characters know, there's stuff the players know. Use your knowledge wisely, metagaming dork.'

'I introduce myself,' said TM, after giving him a scathing look.

'I am Barry,' says Barry, 'with a whole ton of suffixes.'

Ziggy gave something like a giggle and put on a mysterious voice of her own.

'I am known as L,' says the stranger. Now that her face is visible, it is clear that she is a young human. A high-born one, judging by her cheekbones and immaculate hairstyle.

The rest of the team introduced themselves - Iveline spent a moment patting L's face, which Ziggy seemed to find immensely interesting - and L bound Malachi's wounds with medicinal plants from the forest, making sure he regained health the next time he slept.

In the real world, Dominika wandered over to the fridge and came back munching on a slice of leftover pizza which TM had forgotten was still in there. He was confident that there were no more stray slices left, though, which - now that he remembered he could have had one - felt tremendously disappointing.

'What do now?' Ziggy asked, bouncing in her chair.

'Well,' said TM. 'We were...' He turned to Veggie. 'What were we doing again?'

'You'd just finished a bunch of questlines in the west of the world so you were looking to find new fortunes in new lands.'

'Ah,' said Derrida knowingly; 'we ought to head to the nearest big city, then. A hub of adventure.'

'Malachi's no good with directions,' Marty said. Dominika, still munching on pizza, spared a greasy finger to point meaningfully at her own eyes. 'Oh, yeah: Iveline's also understandably not brilliant at that.'

'We weren't expecting to get jumped, though,' Derrida said. 'Either those orcs patrol through this forest, or... someone's hunting us. Like, on purpose.'

'I hope not,' said Ziggy quietly.

TM cleared his throat. 'Barry tells L that we're on our way to a city but have pretty much no idea how to get there, so if she knows what direction we should be going then that would be convenient.'

Ziggy shook her head, recovering, then slammed one palm down on the table and pointed sharply at TM with the index finger of the other hand. She opened her mouth to make some great proclamation, then shut it again. 'Um,' she said, looking at Veggie. 'Do I?'

'Yeaaaaaah,' Veggie conceded. 'Don't need to roll for this one, L knows it.'

'*I know these forests well,*' L says.

'Atgard gives his companions a questioning glance,' said Derrida thoughtfully. 'Do we trust her?'

'Well, yeah,' said TM. 'It's Ziggy.'

'Our heroes don't know that, though,' Derrida pointed out. 'For all they know, she's an evil... NPC... no-do-gooder.'

Marty snorted. 'You,' he said, shaking his head, 'are the absolute last person I would expect to be a stickler for role-playing verisimilitude.'

Derrida shrugged. 'I'm surrendering myself to the experience.'

Dominika tapped the end of her crust on her character sheet, staining it with crumbs and grease but effectively indicating something she wanted to say.

'Good idea,' Veggie said, 'everybody roll. Z, what's your deception stat?'

'Er,' said Ziggy. 'Twelve?'

'That's pretty high,' said Derrida. 'Must be good at... hiding things.'

Everyone shook their dice and threw them onto the table; Veggie totted up the numbers and nodded. 'She good,' he said.

'Lead the way,' says Barry.

L starts to examine the earth, checking for... whatever sort of signs and stuff people who know thingies about forests check for, and then turns her gaze to the heavens and scans the stars. She stares up for a moment, then nods decisively and leads the heroes into the forest. They fetch their belongings as she starts to ascend the branches, silently making her way through the trees above and in front of them. A small light dangling from her hip shows them the way to follow.

Dominika cocked her head and pointed.

'How'd you know?' Veggie asked.

She shrugged.

'Roll perception, at least,' he said. 'And... nature, and your Ranger's Blessing ability.'

She complied.

Iveline hears a scuffle of movement from just behind the trees. She makes her way over quietly, and there on the ground lies a young falcon, injured and abandoned.

Dominika nodded. Veggie handed her a token bearing a badly-drawn falcon.

Iveline takes the bird into her arms, her ranger's instincts and elfish affinity for all nature's creatures kicking in.

'You gain the power of pet!' Veggie declared. Dominika did a surreptitious fist-pump. At the sound of the word 'pet', a muted scratching sound reached their ears from somewhere across the flat; TM dashed over to let Michel Furcoat – the cat – out.

And then you all keep going through the forest again and -

Veggie stopped suddenly and flipped through a few pages. 'Z, perception check.'

'That's never a good sign,' Derrida lamented.

Ziggy rolled the dice.

L continues on her way through the trees.

'Wait,' said Marty. 'What was she checking for?'

'Well, she failed it,' explained Veggie, entirely unhelpfully. 'Anyway, you'll find out next time.'

'Oh, yeah,' said Derrida, standing and stretching, 'I better get going.'

'Whaaaaa,' Ziggy pined. 'We've only just started!'

'We've been playing for six and a half hours,' TM told her.

'Whaaaaaaaaaaaaaaaaaa,' Ziggy said again.

'Yeah, tabletop RPGs tend to take… like, waaaaay longer than you plan for,' Marty said with a wide yawn.

'To be continued, then,' said Veggie, sliding his glasses off his nose and throwing them down on top of his pile of papers.

'Oh, hey, TM,' Derrida said as Marty and Dominika slipped out from their seats and made for the door, hugging Veggie affectionately on the way out. Derrida, with their spot nearest the wall, was always last to get out. 'How come you weren't at the park today?'

'The park?' TM asked, confused.

'Day one of the fair, man.'

'Wait. We still go to that?'

The fair was a yearly event held in a large field not too far from their flat. It was generally something of a letdown, with poorly-made attractions, rickety rides, and extremely expensive sweets. Plus mid-January was a *really* bad time to hold a yearly fair, what with it being cold and overcast and the ground being either frozen solid or boggy, muddy mush. (This had been pointed out to the organisers, whose principal counter was that this made the field significantly cheaper for them to hire.)

There was at least Derrida's unusual ability to win at seemingly stacked-odds games, which was one of its only redeeming features and had regularly provided *Veggie TM Limited* with several cheap toys to sell on the Internet.

'Your parents do,' Derrida said. 'They seemed surprised you weren't there.'

'Oh, heck,' said TM. 'Look, I was makin' dollars, playa.'

Ziggy turned to TM. 'You blew off your parents?'

TM scratched the back of his neck. 'We'd just met you, we were trying to introduce you to the world, then you came up with the invention and the pitch, and...' He sighed, avoiding eye contact, and rubbed his scalp. 'I was kind of excited just to be hanging out with you.'

Ziggy blinked at him. 'So you skipped hanging out with your friends and your family so you could... hang out with *me*?'

TM nodded.

'I am... kind of flattered,' she said uncertainly. 'But that's not cool.'

'We're all gonna be at day two tomorrow, and your parents said they're coming again,' Derrida said, sliding out from behind the table and towards the door. 'You better show, okay?'

'Uggggggghhh,' replied TM.

'Do you not get on with your dad, or something?' Ziggy asked curiously.

'Nah, we get on fine,' TM told her. 'My family just get a bit weird if I introduce them to girls.'

A sly smile spread across Ziggy's face. 'Sounds like fun.'

'See ya, Veg,' Derrida said, kissing Veggie on the cheek. Veggie carried on gathering up his campaign papers obliviously. 'TM, quick word?'

'We just had words,' TM said.

Derrida gave him a look.

TM patted Ziggy on the shoulder, leaving her to sit curiously watching Veggie pack up, and followed Derrida out into the hall.

'What?'

Derrida nodded back through the open door of the flat, through which TM could see Ziggy still sitting at the table. 'What's the deal with her?' Derrida asked quietly.

'I don't -'

'I mean, she seems cool, but far as I can tell you'd never met her until yesterday and suddenly she's living with you and in on *Veggie TM, Inventors Extraordinaire* or whatever it's called these days?'

TM looked at the ceiling.

'That's your *baby*,' Derrida said. 'You've never let anyone else in.'

'She's... special,' TM said, which he knew was unsatisfactory.

'Oh, good,' said Derrida. 'You know, I have a theory.'

'Of course you do.'

'She seems like a bit of an outsider to me, you know? A misfit.' Derrida gave TM a pointed look. 'And you have a bit of a thing for misfits.'

'I do?'

'Of course you do!' Derrida exclaimed. 'You both do! You both just want to feel part of something with other people. Veggie's always taken people in way too quickly, and heaven knows that's had mixed results, and since Aster you -'

'Fuck off, Derrida,' said TM lightly, 'you're meant to be a deconstructionist, not a psychoanalyst. Go home and rethink your worldview.'

Derrida laughed. 'You know I'm not wrong,' they said.

'I appreciate it,' TM told them. 'I do. But either I don't think this is a mistake or I just don't want it to be, and either way it's mine to make. And Veg's,' he added, slightly too late.

'Extremely true,' Derrida said, nodding. 'See ya in the morning.' They patted TM on the shoulder and strolled away.

'Night,' TM said, and headed back inside.

Veggie was still there, of course, picking up the remaining sheets and stacking them away neatly. TM picked up the Bedsheet-Tablecloth-Whiteboard and dragged it over to the sofa, intending to make full use of its rarely-seen but often-advertised 'bedsheet' feature. He wasn't going to make Ziggy sleep on the sofa, not when he'd been looking for an excuse to do it himself for *ages*. He'd always secretly thought it'd be a rather cool and bohemian thing to do, plus Veggie snored.

Ziggy hopped up out of her chair and over to the door of the bedroom usually shared by Veggie and TM, opening it and peering inside.

'Do you actually sleep?' Veggie asked, wandering up behind her.

'Yeah, why not,' said Ziggy. 'Seems like a thing I might enjoy.'

'Night, then,' TM said with a wave, making up his bed on the couch.

'See ya in the morning,' Veggie said, saluting.

'We're going to this fair thingy,' Ziggy told TM firmly; TM nodded. She stepped out of Veggie's way as he meandered into the bedroom, and gave TM a look. 'Hey, look at it all optimistic-like,' she instructed. 'It sounds like fun. And besides, if I'm gonna be living with you, I should probably meet your family, no?'

'Possibly,' TM admitted.

Ziggy beamed and dashed back into the bedroom, leaping up into the top bunk. 'Night,' she called. Veggie made as if to tell her off, but gave up and took the bottom bunk.

'Night, all,' TM said, and tucked himself in.

7. In Medias Noctis

'I think it's sweet how you don't think you understand something until you understand every tiny component,' Aster told him, as they lay in bed. Aster's bed, in Aster's flat, of course, since TM's happened to be in the same room as Veggie's, and that was rarely conducive to anything. 'I mean, how small do you want to get?'

'I don't know,' TM said thoughtfully. 'I guess once you get as small as you can name –'

'Like, get down to the subatomic level, because that's the smallest level that science has given names to?'

'I think so.'

'That's pretty arbitrary, don't you think? Just deciding that you're satisfied that you understand something once you've broken it down as far as anyone's got terminology for?'

'Well, I don't actually manage to get that far most of the time.'

Aster laughed quietly. TM felt the vibrations of it travel through his chest where his skin touched hers. 'So most of the time, you just have to be satisfied that you do actually understand what something is, despite the fact that you haven't broken it down into every individual particle?'

'I guess if I didn't, it'd be pretty hard to get anything done.'

'I'm just imagining you trying to open a door, but you can't do it until you know exactly what the chemical makeup of the handle is. You'd be super late for everything if you had to go off and research every door you had to open on the way.'

'You've got to break it down somewhere, though,' TM suggested. 'If I don't break the whole thing that is the universe down into some sort of component parts, saying that a door has a handle is meaningless in the first place 'cos everything's just… universe.'

'I guess it's about figuring out where it's appropriate to make those divisions, then. Whether for utility or… something else. Heck, maybe the universe itself is just a component part of some divided thing. Like, for all we know, this universe is just one hemisphere of a brain made up of *everything that we know exists, and there's some cosmic corpus callosum in the fabric of reality joining us to the other hemisphere. And then maybe that brain's part of a head, which is part of a body, and that body's part of another species on another planet in another universe –'*

'Ad infinitum.'

'Exactly that.'

'It probably goes both ways, then,' TM mused. 'We're probably just an indeterminate number of layers into an infinite sequence of universes inside universes.'

'So you'll never be able to break it down completely, 'cos you'd have to keep breaking down entire universes.'

'Hm.'

'I can tell you're already trying to break down the logic of this whole thing.'

'Actually, I'm trying pretty hard not to.'

***

TM awoke suddenly to see Ziggy's face peering down at him.

'Er,' he said, blinking.

'Hi,' said Ziggy. Then she closed her eyes – TM imagined that he could feel the ever-so-light brush of her eyelashes displacing air, a tiny breeze winding its way to his face – and leaned in.

'Whoa, whoa whoa,' TM spluttered, putting his hands firmly on her shoulders. 'What are you... er...?'

Ziggy looked down at him, wide-eyed. 'I thought...'

TM sat up. She shuffled back, sitting on her feet at the end of the sofa. 'It's okay,' he told her. 'Just... why were you going to...?'

Ziggy rubbed her forearms as if trying to keep all of her limbs as close to her as possible. 'I'm sorry,' she said. TM couldn't see well enough through the darkness to be sure, but it sounded as if she were biting her lip.

'Hey,' TM said. He rolled out from underneath the Bedsheet-Tablecloth-Whiteboard and draped it around her with one arm, sidling up beside her. 'It's okay.'

'I just thought this was what people did,' Ziggy said quietly. 'To say thank you, or to show some sort of feeling, to let you know how much I appreciate how good you're being to me…'

TM sighed, rubbing his face with his free hand. 'It's more complicated than that,' he said slowly. 'People… do this together… when they really love each other. They really want it to mean something.'

'I want to have that,' Ziggy said, staring off. 'To be a person, with another person.'

'I get that,' TM said, and pulled her closer. 'I think wanting that might be one of the most human things you could feel. But it's got to be the right person, and the right time, and I don't think *me* and *right now* constitute that, you know?'

She nodded.

'I don't want you to think it's because I don't like you or something,' TM said quickly. She rested her head on his shoulder and looked up at him; strands of her hair fell down the neck of his T-shirt, tickling his skin.

'Oh, I know that,' she told him. 'I think you and Veggie might like me more than anyone else in the world ever has.'

TM grinned. 'I reckon we might do.'

'Thanks for not letting me do something that's meant to be meaningful without really thinking about it,' Ziggy said. 'And thanks for everything. You two are my first friends, I think.'

'So you've got no other experience of friends to compare it to, meaning we could be the worst friends ever.'

'I doubt that. Anyway, I think I might have made three more today.'

'Oh, well, you can compare us to Derrida, then.'

Ziggy made no sound, but TM felt her shoulders bob gently. He thought that meant she was laughing, which was probably a good thing. 'Oh, hang on,' he said. 'You didn't… try to do this with Veggie, did you?'

'I did, actually,' Ziggy said. 'He said no, too. Think he was considering it a bit more than you did, though.'

'He's alright, really,' TM said.

'He is,' she agreed.

When TM looked down at her again a minute later, she was asleep on his shoulder.

8. Roll Up, Roll Up

'Moooooorning,' Veggie trilled, flicking the light on. TM blinked himself awake, lifting his arm; it was protectively draped around Ziggy, who lay curled on her side on the sofa next to him.

'This isn't what it looks like,' TM started to protest, but Veggie held up his hands.

'I know,' he said. 'No worries. Looks like you two make good nap buddies, though.'

TM grinned; Ziggy yawned and stretched her arms out, somehow rocking herself upright. 'I have never slept so well in my whole entire life,' she declared.

'TM's pretty comfy,' Veggie said, taking a mostly-empty box of cereal from a cupboard. 'We snuggle up sometimes, don't we?'

'When there's nobody else in there with you,' TM said.

'Soooooo… are we going to the fair?' Ziggy asked eagerly, as Veggie handed her a bowl of cornflakes. She turned it around in her hands for a few moments, inspecting it with interest from all angles, then put a flake in her mouth and smiled excitedly as it crunched.

'Er, yup,' said Veggie, tipping his entire bowl into his mouth at once.

'I've never been to a fair,' Ziggy said wistfully.

'Well, today's your lucky day,' TM told her between spoons of milky cereal. He reached down between the cushions of the sofa and yanked out a brightly coloured flyer, handing it over.

'Celebrity appearances?!' she read with astonishment.

'Oh, yeah,' Veggie said with a merry crunch. 'It's always just some minor local who-the-heck-ever peeps, though. Marty got asked to do it one year.'

'Awesome,' said Ziggy dreamily.

They took turns showering; TM was relieved to see that Ziggy, when she slid across the filing cabinet that served as a bathroom door and emerged, looked much the same as she had when she went in. Slightly wetter hair, admittedly, but TM could deal with that.

'Think I'm sticking with this look, for a bit,' she said, noticing TM's glance. 'Wouldn't want to confuse everyone.'

'It works for you,' TM told her honestly.

'Aw, thanks,' she said, beaming.

'Get a room,' Veggie called half-heartedly, tying his shoelaces with gusto.

'I bagsy *this* room,' said Ziggy obliviously.

***

When the three of them were ready, they headed out into the world of Outside the Flat. TM wore a thick burgundy shirt, the sleeves of which he usually kept rolled up but had today deigned to roll down against the cold, while Veggie - who as per usual had simply refused to acknowledge the weather when deciding what to wear - proudly sported a T-shirt emblazoned with the logo of Marty's band. Ziggy had somehow found a pair of thick leggings, a long, slim-fitting checked shirt, and a baggy cardigan made of heavy orange wool – none of which belonged to her flatmates, TM was certain, but somehow he was both entirely unsurprised and entirely fine with it.

'Can we get candyfloss?' Ziggy asked.

'Yeah, why not,' TM said, patting her on the shoulder. 'We owe you that much, at least.'

Veggie hooted with laughter. 'We owe you… like, your entire weight in candyfloss,' he declared. 'Which, since candyfloss weighs pretty much nothing, would be an absolute heckton of candyfloss. Not that I'm saying you weigh a lot. I mean, stars weigh a lot, but… you don't look like… but it'd obviously be fine whatever… you're looking good,' he concluded sheepishly.

'Aww,' said Ziggy. 'That's nice.'

They wandered down the streets towards the fair; the usual feeling of low-expectation anticipation was offset somewhat by Ziggy's enthusiastic presence, which lent a certain novelty to the ordeal. As they turned a corner, TM thought he heard an unaccounted-for set of footsteps coming up behind them; he turned to look, but saw nobody.

'Whassup?' Ziggy asked, poking him in the shoulder. TM shook his head.

'Nothing, I think.'

Her head started swivelling, at first with excitement and then with panic.

'Is someone after me? Us? Following us?' Her eyes were wide, flicking back and forth in search of unfriendly movement.

'I don't think so,' TM said, in what he hoped was a reassuring voice. 'There might be someone behind, but they're probably just going to the same place, not... us.'

Ziggy shook her head and walked a little faster. 'I don't like not knowing,' she said. 'I knew more when I was up there. Like the stuff about Cable Tie Guy. Now I don't even know if someone's walking along the same road unless I can see them with these weird gooey thingies.' She indicated her own eyes.

'I don't think anyone's -' TM started to say, and then a man clapped him on the shoulder as he jogged past. TM very nearly punched him in the face in surprise, but realised just quickly enough that it was a familiar face. 'Why are you jogging, Gary Mackerel?!' he called after the man; a local entrepreneur of sorts not unlike themselves, Gary Mackerel had often shared a cheap cuppa with Veggie and TM over shared stories about not having much luck with anything. His latest venture was Gary's Fish, a chippy just around the corner.

'He's probably doing a food stall at the fair,' Veggie mused, beaming. 'I love that guy. Have I told him that lately? I should tell him that. I love Gary Mackerel. Great guy.'

He continued on his merry way, wittering about the virtues of Gary Mackerel, Esq.; between him and TM, Ziggy looked down at her feet and shuffled along.

'We're alright,' TM said to her under the sounds of Veggie's rambling. 'It's all good.'

She nodded, looking unconvinced.

'Ooh, lookee,' said Veggie, breaking off his stream of Gary Mackerel-themed odes. 'They got one of those wheely thingies this year.'

TM looked: a bright pink Ferris wheel loomed large above the rows of houses in the direction of the field where the fair was held. 'I'm not going on that.'

'I wanna,' said Ziggy, piping up.

TM glanced at her; she was looking up now instead of her feet, which seemed like an improvement. 'We'll see,' he said.

In a few brief moments they drew closer to the venue, bright banners and more attractions of dubious-looking construction coming into view. Ziggy started to smile as they approached, revealing gradually more teeth as they came near to the entrance; Veggie eventually asked her to put her canines away.

'This seems pretty nice,' she said, complying. TM exchanged a glance with Veggie, who shrugged and winked.

'Yes,' said TM. 'Nice.'

They entered the field, Ziggy leading the way. She twirled around to take in everything, from the food stalls that looked as if they might collapse at any moment to the lurid carnival games emblazoned with slightly creepy pictures of clowns and celebrity caricatures. The space around her seemed more open for her being in it.

TM remembered another girl, one who was always trying to connect herself to the world. One who wasn't around any longer, but who would always be in his brain, whether he liked it or not.

Ziggy hopped over, snapping her fingers in TM's face.

'Hey. Earth to TM.'

'Hello,' TM said, then wondered why he had said that.

'You looked a bit spaced out,' Ziggy told him, examining his eyes with concern. 'Back in the room?'

TM blinked. 'I think I was just appreciating the world, and you being a part of it.'

'That's cool,' Ziggy said. 'Hey, a Zen Buddhist goes up to a burger stand and says "make me one with everything". Can I have a burger?'

'Absolutely,' Veggie said, taking her by the arm. He marched her towards the nearest food stand; her head whipped side-to-side as they went, taking in all the sights. 'Except - TM,' he called back, 'I'm saving up for... something really important, so you get this one!'

TM shook his head and moved to follow them, but stopped in his tracks when an enormous, muscular frame put itself in his way.

'Hi,' TM started to say, then let out a yelp as the man wrapped his arms around him and hoisted him into the air,

'Juuunioooor!' he declared, raising TM almost above his head.

'Hi, Dad,' TM said.

Thomas Major, Sr. was an unusually large man, dark-skinned and boisterous. 'And is that Jonathan over there?' he asked, shifting TM's entire body weight to one arm so that he could gesture towards Veggie, who was trying in vain to remember Ziggy's order as she rattled through almost the entire food menu.

'That's him,' TM said, wheezing slightly through constricted ribs.

'Ah!' exclaimed Senior, throwing his son up into the air and catching him under the armpits to look him straight in the face. 'You weren't here yesterday! Or if you were, you didn't say hello. So you'd better not have been here!'

'We were in a business meeting,' TM explained, half-truthfully. 'Can I go back to being on the ground now?'

Senior glanced down at TM's dangling feet, as if he'd forgotten that he was lifting his son bodily from the ground. He plonked him down. 'There you go,' he said apologetically, and gave TM an affectionate pat on the head. TM felt his feet sink a few inches into the ground, as if he were an unusually-shaped nail bashed down by his father's hammer of a hand. 'Who's that girl with Jonathan, then?'

'You know nobody calls him that,' TM told his father.

'Does anybody else call you Junior?' Senior asked pointedly.

'Er…' said TM. 'Oh, there she is.'

'Hi, Junior,' said TM's mother.

'Hi, Mum.'

'Junior here was just telling me about Jonathan's new girlfriend,' Senior confided; TM scratched his ear awkwardly.

'Another one?' TM's mother asked, looking half-impressed. Lily Major was, in all outwards appearances, the opposite of her husband: petite, blonde – now greying, though gracefully – and wallflowerish, but they were as close a couple as TM had ever come across.

'She's actually not,' TM told her, kissing her on the cheek. 'She's our new business partner.'

Lily gave him an intrigued look. 'Really? How's that working out?'

'Well, we've made more money since yesterday than we did for the entire lifespan of our business up to that point, so I'd say pretty well.'

'Hm,' she said, a twinkle in her eye. 'She's pretty, isn't she?'

TM rolled his eyes. 'No grandchildren on the immediate horizon,' he said. 'But yes, she is.'

Senior marched over to Veggie and Ziggy, who had eaten her mountain of delicious greasy fast food and bounced along to hook a duck. 'Jonathan!' Senior bellowed; Veggie jumped, causing Ziggy to whack him in the face with her plastic fishing rod.

'Good morning, Mr Major,' said Veggie, standing straight upright. Ziggy looked him over in confusion, then gave Senior a casual nod.

'Sup,' she said.

'How are you doing?' Senior boomed, shaking Veggie's hand. It looked like a cocktail sausage in his enormous grip.

'I'm well, thank you, sir,' Veggie said timidly.

'No need for all the politeness, you know,' Senior said, leaning in slightly too close. TM thought that it was supposed to be a reassuring gesture. 'You're my boy's life partner, after all!'

Veggie coughed.

'And you are...?' Senior took Ziggy's hand - TM had the sudden image of a bull elephant holding an egg in its trunk without cracking it - and kissed the back of it.

'Hm,' Ziggy said.

'He's a real charmer,' TM told her, patting his father's forearm.

'I'm Ziggy,' she said, with a small bow.

'You kids and your weird names,' Senior guffawed. 'I just can't keep up,' he said to Lily, who embraced Ziggy.

'Nice to meet you,' she said; Ziggy returned the hug, smiling widely.

'You too,' she said.

TM spotted Dominika a couple of stalls away, collecting an enormous bear as a prize from a can-shooting game. Derrida and Marty stood by her, leaning on the stall; Derrida was applauding reluctantly. TM waved them over.

'She's a really worryingly good shot,' Marty said, making the bear wave at them. 'Hi, TM's mum and dad.'

'Hello, Benjamin,' said Lily, kissing him on the cheek.

'Your name is Benjamin?' Ziggy gasped.

Marty shrugged. 'Can't be a frontman without a stage name. *Benjamin Miles Parekh* isn't particularly rock-and-roll, but *Marty Gosh Dang Rook*...' He shrugged. 'It sells better.'

'Looks like your merchandise is doing well,' Lily said, gesturing to Veggie's T-shirt. Veggie pulled the hem proudly, stretching the front out so as to better display the logo.

'We're not doing too bad,' Marty agreed with a grin. 'Not as well as these three, though.'

'Yes,' said Lily, with an affectionate look at her son, 'it's nice to see them finally having some success.'

'Oh, thanks,' TM huffed.

Senior shook Marty's hand, kissed Derrida on the forehead, and gave Dominika a tight one-armed hug, then picked up one of the tiny plastic fishing rods between two fingers and smoothly swung the hook through the air, lifting a yellow duck from the water. Ziggy applauded politely.

'I win!' Senior exclaimed, examining the number on the duck's underside. The teenager manning the stand handed him a bear even larger than Dominika's, which still looked much smaller by comparison in his massive arms. He held it out to his wife, who took it and beamed.

'You two are *adorable*,' Ziggy said with admiration. TM thought he heard a hint of sadness in her words.

'Aww,' Lily cooed, turning her infectious smile on Ziggy. 'This one's a keeper, you know,' she told TM pointedly.

'You wanted candyfloss, right?' TM said loudly to Ziggy, taking her by the arm. 'We'll be around, okay?'

Senior nodded his approval and smacked his son on the back with what felt like more than enough force to win the strongman contest. TM stumbled, but smiled.

'I like your family,' said Ziggy, as TM led her away.

'They're not bad,' TM admitted.

'Do you think they like me too?' she asked, biting her lip and wringing her hands as if it were the most important thing in the world to be liked by the parents of a bloke she'd only met yesterday.

'Course they do,' TM assured her. 'They like most people, to be honest. They've got this theory that if... let's use me and Veg as an example, right? If I hate Veg, for whatever reason, that's still fundamentally my problem and not his.'

'What if he's a really bad dude?'

'There's kind of justified disapproval and then there's outright dislike,' TM mused. 'Point is, if you're just being yourself and not hurting anybody, then the only people who won't like you are people whose opinion you shouldn't really care about.' He paused. 'Although Veggie really, *really* does hate the Swede.'

'Makes sense,' Ziggy said. 'Can't help really wanting everyone to like me, though.'

'Oh, yeah, that's called being part of human society, you'll get used to it. Most of it sucks.'

'Your family's better than mine, anyway.'

'You have a family?'

'Yeah, sort of. I think I have a twin, somewhere, but... I don't know if she came down, too. I don't even know if she's a she. And then I've got some sort of... undefined relatives going on somewhere.'

TM gave her a searching look. 'I don't understand.'

She returned his gaze without flinching. 'I don't really expect you to,' she said kindly. 'Now buy me candyfloss.'

TM shook his head, having accepted by now that there was generally very little point in trying to get more out of Ziggy than she wanted to give. 'You're on,' he said, trotting over to the appropriate stand.

'Heyyyy,' trilled Veggie, joining them in the queue. 'Celebrity host reveal in a few minutes, apparently.'

'Ooooh,' said Ziggy, eyes widening.

'Don't get your hopes up,' TM advised her, handing over a bouquet of pink candyfloss. She took a bite, then stuffed the entire thing into her mouth aggressively.

'Hm,' said Veggie. 'Enjoying that?'

She nodded, cheeks bulging.

'May as well check out the stage, at least,' TM said; Ziggy gave an enthusiastic thumbs-up. 'Seriously, though, it's not likely to be anyone decent,' he warned her, in reply to which she flicked a dismissive hand in his direction.

'Everyone is decent,' she said, the words leaving her mouth in a cloud of pink sugar.

'Except the Swede,' said Veggie darkly.

***

They made their way to the stage, which was really just a small platform under a large banner bearing the legend 'THE STAGE'. A small, vaguely-defined crowd was in the process of gathering itself; the trio made their way through to the landmark that was TM's father.

'Are... you... ready?' intoned an unenthusiastic voice. A young man holding a large microphone climbed onto the stage, making wide gestures into the crowd in a way that suggested he really didn't want to be there. There was a general mumble of half-interest from the assembly. 'Then, without further ado, I present to you this year's special guest hosts and selectors of the raffle winners –'

'Get on with it,' Senior said in what was intended to be an undertone. His unusually projective voice carried his words to every ear in the vicinity.

'Anyway,' said the young man tiredly. 'Give it up for local hero and reputable weatherman, Al Tyer!'

'Pff,' said TM, though Ziggy applauded with mild excitement.

'He was on the TV!' she told TM. Then, memory apparently moving from having seen him on the telly to the strange feelings the viewing had instilled in her, she frowned and put her hands down.

Tyer took to the stage carefully, every hair and fold of his suit precisely in place, and gave a practised wave.

The interim host flicked through his note cards for a moment until he found the right one. 'And, joining us straight from wrapping up the filming on her latest adventure, it's the Huntress herself –'

'No way,' Veggie breathed.

'Riegel O'Ryan!'

'Holy *shit*.'

O'Ryan came into view behind Tyer, ascending up the stage with a graceful leap. An enormous dog padded after her; more than waist-high, with a shimmering golden coat, it looked more like a happy blonde wolf than anything TM would have referred to as a dog. It was the sort of dog that people would be drawn to, that would demand every ounce of attention as soon as it passed; nobody was going to give a second glance to the person holding the lead, not when an animal like that came along. Unless, of course, the person on the other end of the lead happened to be Riegel O'Ryan.

'Hiya,' she called with a broad wave. 'We're very happy you could have us!'

She was striking on the TV, but that was no comparison to the Huntress in person: long hair like red stone dust blowing down a cliff towards a tumultuous sea, and an accent to match.

'She's, like, Irish-Greek, or something ridiculous like that,' Veggie explained to Ziggy, who was staring unblinkingly at O'Ryan.

'We'll be around, enjoying the attractions,' O'Ryan continued. Tyer nodded, hands clasped behind his back and the smile of a professional presenter firmly assembled upon his lips. Unlike his fellow celebrity guest, nothing was lost in translation when transmitting Tyer's image by television. Even in the flesh, it was as if the colour saturation had been turned down. 'Raffle winners to be drawn later! So, er... have fun!'

'OH MY GAH,' said Veggie, as the two – plus dog – disappeared from sight and the crowd dispersed, having slaked their thirst for celebrity-spotting. 'Riegel O'Fucking Ryan!'

'Jonathan,' said Lily sternly.

'RIEGEL O'EFFING RYAN,' Veggie trumpeted.

'He's got a bit of a thing for her,' TM said; Senior roared a boisterous laugh and slapped Veggie around the shoulders with a resounding smack.

'You dog, Jonathan,' he said, somewhere between reproachful and amused.

'She's an excellent presenter,' Veggie huffed.

'She's... here,' Ziggy breathed, still staring at the space O'Ryan had occupied on the stage.

'Ziggy also apparently has a bit of a thing for her, maybe,' TM said, watching her with concern.

'Don't we all,' Veggie agreed.

Senior took all three under one arm with a happy chuckle, and bought them each a raffle ticket from a bored-looking girl. 'Good luck,' he wished them, reaching for his wife's hand. She took it, the enormous bear still tucked under her other arm. Between the oversized bear and her oversized husband, it looked as if she had been shrunk. 'I'm taking your mother for lunch, so we'll be off.'

'Nice seeing you,' TM said honestly. Senior hugged his son again, gently this time.

'Take care,' he told his son. Lily planted a kiss on TM's cheek.

'I will,' said TM.

Ziggy watched TM's parents go, hand in hand. 'I wish I had that,' she said.

'You do,' TM assured her. 'You've got me, and Veg, and that lot –' he waved in the direction of Marty, Dominika and Derrida, who appeared to be hustling a card-tricking stall attendant, '– and now them too.' He nodded towards his parents' retreating backs.

'Thanks,' Ziggy said. Her gaze was wandering all over the place, fixing only for brief moments: on the stage where O'Ryan had been, in the direction in which TM's parents had headed, on the laughing Marty, on nothing in particular.

'Not to interrupt this moment, or anything,' Veggie interjected, 'but *I* am going to go and stalk Riegel O'Ryan, so if you two don't mind I will see you for the raff-*elle*.' He sauntered off, waving his raffle ticket around like a fancy paper fan or a very flat, very wobbly conductor's baton.

'That boy got issues,' Ziggy said quietly, shaking her head.

'That he do,' TM agreed.

She gave him a small smile and wandered over to where Marty and Dominika stood, joining them to watch Derrida finish their work. The attendant laid a card down on the counter; Derrida slapped it away with contempt.

'How does this game work?' Ziggy whispered. Dominika shrugged.

'We're not quite sure what any of the rules are,' Marty explained. 'It's fun to watch, though. Bit like volleyball.'

Derrida placed two cards down, one each side of the little stack the attendant had made, then flipped over the top card of the deck. The hapless worker groaned and handed over a fistful of coins, which Derrida pocketed with a wink.

'How did you do that?' Ziggy demanded. They left the confused attendant staring at the cards, Derrida rolling one of their prize coins over their knuckles with glee.

'It's all about knowing how the odds are stacked,' Derrida began to explain, but Marty cut them off.

'Nobody actually cares, Jack,' he said; Derrida stuck their tongue out. 'Jack here,' Marty told Ziggy, 'likes to think they know how to be better than everyone at everything. Exploit the system and whatnot.'

'All systems can be exploited,' Derrida insisted.

'You're so wishy-washy about your philosophy,' Marty said, grinning at him. 'Just because your name is what it is, you can't just assume the legacy of Actual Derrida and roll with it.'

'It's got me this far,' said Derrida carelessly.

'Fair point.'

'Wait,' said TM. 'How far? You've never committed to a job, or a partner, or a favourite flavour of crisp, or... anything, really.'

'Why should I?' Derrida challenged. 'I'm doing fine.'

'You don't decide on stuff, though,' TM said. 'You just think about it until it's too late to make the decision.'

'By which time everything's usually sorted itself out,' Derrida said.

Their meandering took them past an archery range; Dominika perked up, making a beeline straight for it.

'Five arrows,' said the attendant tiredly, handing her a bow and pointing down the range, where five small paper circles were stuck on a wooden wall peppered with arrow holes. Most of the holes were in the wall, the targets conspicuously unscathed. 'Get four out of five in a target, win a prize.'

Ziggy watched with interest as Dominika took the bow, weighed it in her hands, and aimed down the range.

'So this is why she uses a bow in *Hero's Adventure*?' Ziggy asked.

'Oh, yeah.' Marty nodded, watching closely. 'Pretty much anything she can role-play, she can do in real life. She's kind of a badass.'

Ziggy watched with unconcealed admiration as Dominika pulled back the string, touching the cheap plastic fletching of the arrow almost to her cheek, and let it fly. The arrow went spiralling down the range, puncturing a hole right in the centre of one of the paper targets.

'Whaaaaaaaa,' Ziggy exclaimed. 'That's awesome.'

TM and Derrida applauded; Marty gave a whimsical salute. Dominika gave Ziggy a smile, slotting the next arrow onto the string. A khaki-shirted shadow drifted across the range, trailing copper hair and strands of plaited belt, and took the stand next to Dominika. Ziggy stared up in awe; Dominika, oblivious, loosed her next shot, which deftly pierced its target. She looked back at Ziggy with a wide smile of expectation, then tilted her head in confusion and disappointment at the fact that Ziggy's gaze was firmly directed at something that was not her. She turned around to see, and found herself staring at Riegel O'Ryan's chin.

'She's taller up close,' Marty breathed. Ziggy nodded, fixated.

'Hi,' said O'Ryan. Her enormous dog slinked up behind her and presented itself to Derrida, who gave it an awkward pat. 'Don't worry about Keelut,' she said kindly. 'She's harmless, unless she thinks somebody's tryin' to hurt her mama.'

'Keelut?' Derrida said, eyebrows screwed up. 'As in the hairless dog, mythical harbinger of death?'

'Naw,' O'Ryan said, fingers buried in the dog's long hair. 'As in the crater on Callisto. Y'know, Jupiter's second-biggest moon.'

'That's a weird and specific name,' Derrida observed.

'Oh, yeah? What's yours?'

Derrida shut up.

'I just have a little amateur interest in astrological whatsits,' O'Ryan explained. 'Me and Al share that hobby, if nothin' else. Inuit mythology, not so much.'

She took a bow and arrow from the game's attendant, who handed them to her with almost zombie-like reverence. She ran a finger along the curve of the cheap weapon, then in a single sleek movement raised it, drew the arrow back, and released. Dominika looked on, her face dark, as O'Ryan's arrow thudded home within a millimetre of her own.

'Cheers, buddy,' O'Ryan said, holding the bow out to the attendant on one finger. He took it and stood there holding it, staring at her. 'It's good publicity to have a go at all this stuff,' she said, with a wink at the group. She stuck a thumb over her shoulder, where a man holding a camera with an enormous lens immediately tried to pretend that it had been pointing somewhere else and not right at her. 'Gotta say, though, I'm having a lot of fun! Don't get to do this sorta thing an awful lot.'

Ziggy nodded, dumbstruck. O'Ryan looked right at her for a moment, then flashed her a wide smile. 'I'll see you lot for the raffle, yeah?' she said, turning away. 'Keep watching my show!'

The five of them stood for a few moments after she had gone, Keelut padding along behind her. None of them really noticed that nobody else was moving or speaking.

'What just happened?' TM asked eventually.

'That was the most intense moment of my whole entire life,' Ziggy breathed. Marty put a hand on her shoulder, nodding slowly; Dominika gave them all a sharp glare.

'Heeeey,' a voice called; TM turned and spotted Veggie waltzing over to the group. 'Anybody spotted O'Ryan yet?'

'Er,' said TM.

'Yes,' Ziggy answered. The tendons in her neck were a little more visible than usual.

'Aw, heck,' said Veggie, folding his arms with a harrumph. 'I lost her over by the hoop toss.'

'She's... everything,' Ziggy said, a slight strain to her voice.

'Somebody's starstruck,' Veggie commented; Dominika folded her arms heavily. 'Hey, did you guys know her and Al Tyer actually do know each other? Like, other than just both being presenters of stuff? I mean, who would have figured *that*?'

'She said something about sharing a hobby,' TM recalled. 'How do you know, anyway?'

Veggie gestured towards the entrance to the field, stuffing a huge chunk of vanilla fudge into his mouth with the other hand.

'Heard 'em chattering over that-a-way,' he said around chunks of sugary deliciousness. 'It's weird, though, can't tell whether they actually get along with each other or not. She's kind of weird with him, kept calling him by his full name.' He assumed an exaggerated Irish accent. '"As above, so below, Al Tyeeer" – that's how she said it, like, with too much emphasis on the last syllable or something.'

'Probably just the accent,' Marty said dismissively. 'Maybe they're banging.'

'Eh,' Veggie mumbled, swallowing loudly. 'Anyway, she was over here?'

'Yup,' said TM. 'Right next to us.'

'Oh, you lucky buggers,' said Veggie enviously. Dominika huffed and wandered off. 'What's her deal?'

'I think O'Ryan stole her spotlight a little bit,' Derrida said, watching her go. 'I'll go shower her in flattery for a bit, should cheer her up.' They hurried after her, catching up as she turned through some stands and disappeared from sight.

'We have to get back to the stage,' Veggie announced. 'Can't miss the raffle.' His eyes suddenly widened. 'Oh my lord,' he said, breathing faster, 'what if I win? I might get to… to *meet* her, but then – what do I say, what if she thinks I'm *stupid* –'

'Calm down, Veg,' said TM affectionately, taking his partner by the elbow and leading him back towards the stage. Marty put an arm around Ziggy; when she made no effort to move, he took her by both hands and chaperoned her along after them.

'Do you think she has merch?' Veggie chirped as they re-entered the perimeter of the hopeless little stage area. 'I want a keyring, and, like, fifteen T-shirts.'

'Maybe you'll win some,' TM said, as if to a young child who wanted some more juice in their sippy cup.

'Oooooh,' said Veggie.

'Hiiiiii,' trilled O'Ryan, hopping up onto the stage. Keelut padded up behind her, Al Tyer bringing up the rear. His hair was perfectly in place, as was his practised professional smile, but it was clear that he had not been having any fun whatsoever. 'I've been havin' a really bloomin' lovely time hanging out with all of yous and sampling the delights of your fair, so cheers very much!'

There was a general murmur of 'you're welcome'.

'Anyways,' she continued, 'we're up here to announce – well, mostly who's won the raffle – but also where you can see me and Big Al next!'

'HNNNGGG,' Veggie intoned.

'Two weeks from now we'll be at the museum,' O'Ryan announced, 'to launch a brand new exhibit!'

Veggie turned to TM, a pleading look in his eyes. Ziggy's jaw flexed.

'We can go,' TM sighed.

'It is a really rather interesting piece of space rock,' Tyer said, his voice snapping through the crowd like a crisp breeze. 'The cosmos has ever so much to offer these days.'

TM somehow felt that he was scanning the crowd, as if searching for something, as he spoke.

'Yeahhhh, wowie zowie, super cool space rock,' O'Ryan said, reaching her hand into a bowl filled with raffle tickets. She withdrew the lucky winner, holding the tiny slip of paper aloft between index and middle fingers. 'Winner of the first prize of two hundred and fifty quid: Dominika Doležal!'

'How the flip did she know how to pronounce that?' said Veggie.

'Dominika?' O'Ryan called, waving the winning ticket in the air.

'Er,' said TM. 'She's over that way somewhere,' he yelled at the stage. O'Ryan gave him a thumbs-up, pocketing the ticket.

'We'll catch up with her later, I'm sure,' she said, flashing the tooth-exposing smile of a lifelong professional people person. The crowd burbled in appreciation. 'Anyway, number two, walking away today with a bountiful hamper courtesy of local business Barney's Buffets… it's Gary Mackerel!'

'Wooo,' twooted Gary Mackerel.

'Nice,' O'Ryan declared, starting up a round of applause for him. It didn't last long. 'And finally, winner of an officially licensed Surviving O'Ryan keyring –'

'Please let it be me,' Veggie whispered on repeat.

'– Marty Rook!'

'You *cock*,' Veggie said, as Marty waved his arms in the air like a loon.

'Nice one, lad,' said O'Ryan, fishing the prize out of her pocket and lobbing it elegantly in Marty's direction. Veggie leapt on him, tackled him to the ground, and caught the keyring in his fist with a bellow of triumph.

'I was going to give it to you anyway,' Marty groaned from underneath Veggie.

'Ooooookay,' said O'Ryan from onstage. 'Looks like somebody reaaally wanted that keyring. Have another one, man, it's not as if I'm paying for 'em.' She threw another to Veggie, who caught it and screamed like a little girl.

'Yeesh. Big fan, huh?' O'Ryan grinned. Tyer leaned over and whispered something in her ear; she nodded, strands of bright hair floating about her head. 'Thanks a lot for having us, but we gotta scoot, so…'

'Nooooooooooooooooooooooooooo,' Veggie cried.

'Sorry, fella. Places to go, people to entertain. Pop by the museum on Friday, okay? We'll be there.'

'YES I WILL,' Veggie roared at the heavens.

'Right,' said O'Ryan. 'Well. Thanks very much, everyone, and see you again soon!'

The duo waved – Tyer with minimal arm movement, O'Ryan with enthusiastic, sweeping gestures, while Keelut howled in farewell – and left.

'GOODBYE RIEGEL O'RYAN,' Veggie yelled after them.

The small crowd dissipated, happy that their annual dose of celebrity had turned out to be less shit than usual. Gary Mackerel was positively bouncing.

TM eyed the others: Marty was rubbing his chin and grinning, Veggie holding his twin keyrings aloft as if they were the most precious treasure the world had to offer, and Ziggy looked – appropriately, and as was apparently standard whenever Riegel O'Ryan was involved – spaced out.

'You okay?' TM asked, gently touching Ziggy on the upper arm. She snapped out of it, staring at him as if just waking up.

'Oh,' she said. 'Yeah. I think I'm getting used to it.'

TM gave her a firm look. 'What's going on?'

She sighed. 'She's - they're - like, so much *bigger* than me. It's like I'll get crushed or something, so... I can't help but try to make myself as small as possible so they'll just sort of pass over.'

'You're weird,' said Veggie, caressing his keyrings lovingly.

'Hey, Marty,' TM said quickly, 'you wanna come play video games?'

'Heck yeah,' said Marty with relish.

TM glanced at Ziggy. 'Seems as if we could do with it,' he said.

Derrida sidled over, Dominika close behind. 'Somebody say video games?' they asked. Marty rolled his eyes heavenward.

'Darn it, Derrida,' he said. 'You better not Bogart the controller.'

'What does that even mean?'

'I dunno,' Marty said. 'Jack Black says it in School of Rock. "Don't Bogart the mic" or something. It's totally a thing.'

Derrida nudged Dominika, who smiled and gave an evil grin. 'I'm totally doing a *Blackest Spirit* challenge run,' they announced, to which Marty threw his hands up.

'Fine,' he said. 'They are outrageously entertaining. But I get to punch you in the arm every time you die.'

'We're on,' Derrida said, shaking on it.

'Where have you two been, anyway?'

Derrida coughed. 'I managed to get a quick quote out of Al Tyer. I'm writing an article for the paper about... meteorological stuff.'

'Huh.'

'Do us three not get a say in what we're doing?' TM said, slightly miffed at having been missed out of the entire conversation.

'Oh, no, my friend,' said Marty. 'We're doing this at *my place*.'

9. Cheese That Isn't Your Cheese

Marty's house was a marginally more lavish affair than the Veggie Ziggy TM flat-cum-HQ: being in a band that had garnered mild local notoriety might not have been the best earner, but Mr and Mrs Rook – legally Parekh, but Marty had insisted his entire family be referred to by his chosen surname, lest suspension of disbelief be punctured – had made a decent living over the years as a masterful plastic surgeon (moonlighting as an amateur rocket scientist) and her occasionally entrepreneurial househusband.

Marty lived in their attic, a sprawling space - which, with its own mini-kitchen, large bedroom and en suite, and living space larger than TM and Veggie's whole flat, was almost a self-contained property in its own right. It had become a sort of rotating home to all four members of The Inciting Incident (plus Derrida, Dominika, TM, and Veggie, when the mood struck).

'This is where you *live*?!' Ziggy demanded with amazement as her head poked through the trapdoor.

'Heck yeah,' said Marty. He extended a hand to assist Dominika, emerging up the ladder behind Ziggy, but one glare and he withdrew it sheepishly. Dominika catapulted herself up the ladder, leaping into the attic with all the elegance of some unholy leopard-frog hybrid.

Derrida trundled up next and immediately moved towards one of the corners, where an enormous computer tower stood on a desk next to three widescreen monitors.

'Ooooh, ooh ooh,' stuttered Marty, bounding in front of Derrida and reaching to unplug a cable from behind the monitors. 'Ya don't want *these* old things. I got something new to show you.'

'Fancy,' said Veggie, whose head was just popping through the trapdoor.

Derrida watched with interest as Marty carried the cable to a rectangular panel set into the wall. He pressed it firmly; it slid open to reveal a slim projector, into which he plugged the end of the cable.

'You got a projector?!' Derrida practically yelled. TM would have been concerned about the volume disturbing Marty's parents, but serving as a band practice space meant that Marty's room was surrounded by layers of the best soundproofing money could buy. 'I think I've decided I'm coming here more often.'

'Oh, yeah,' said Marty, fiddling with a few settings, 'we'll have *sleepovers* and all kinds of nonsense.'

A loud squeal of feedback turned all their heads suddenly: Ziggy stood under the attic's sloping roof, surrounded by towering speakers and amplifiers. She gave them all an ecstatic grin, eagerly plugging a thick cable into an electric guitar.

'Wurp,' said Marty. 'Be careful with that, okay?'

'Yeah, whatever,' said Ziggy, making devil horns with one hand and spinning the tuning pegs with the other.

'Do you actually know how to play guitar?' Veggie asked, looking on. 'Cos you definitely just tuned it to... like... nothing sharp minor.'

'Best key,' Ziggy declared. 'And yeah, I know how to play. Probably. I mean, why not?' She lifted the neck of the guitar, raised her strumming hand heavenward and brought it down on the strings like the hammer of Thor, producing a huge, invasive block of sound that sounded as if someone had taken the first two bars of every Shostakovich, Stravinsky and Rachmaninov piece ever written and combined all the notes together into one lump of accidentals.

'Ow,' said TM, when the noise faded.

'That was so flipping *radical*,' Ziggy said, breathing heavily and running her hands through her hair. It seemed to have grown longer and more punky somehow, as if the dark purple tint were undergoing some sort of noise-based chemical reaction that was making it significantly more neon. 'I'm gonna be a rock star too, I reckon.'

'I think you killed my goldfish,' Marty lamented, rubbing his ears.

'You have a goldfish?' Ziggy asked happily, returning the guitar to its stand. Veggie wandered over and unplugged it, just in case. 'What's he called?'

'He lost a bet when he got it, so we made him call it Bobfred Livingstone,' TM told her.

'Pfff,' said Ziggy. 'More like *won* the bet. Do all you guys give your pets weird names?'

'Hey,' said Veggie indignantly.

Dominika raised a finger.

'Oh, yeah,' said Derrida, 'she's got a snake called Slithers.'

Ziggy digested that for a moment. 'I prefer the weird names.'

Dominika looked distinctly put out. Derrida punched her in the arm, in what was meant to be a friendly gesture of reassurance; Dominika put them in an armbar.

'Anyway, video games?' Marty suggested as Derrida tapped out, wailing.

'Thought you'd never ask,' Veggie said, settling himself down on a bright blue beanbag. Ziggy plopped a cushion emblazoned with the words 'EFF THE SYSTEM' on the floor next to him, and sat with her knees tucked under her chin.

'Hold on a mo,' Marty muttered, booting up his computer. The entire wall opposite the projector lit up with the image of his desktop; surround sound speakers buzzed to life in the floors and walls all around them.

'Ooooooh,' said Ziggy appreciatively.

Marty clicked an icon, and a box headed with the legend 'Update Wizard' filled the screen.

'You have a wizard in your computer?!' Ziggy exclaimed, hands on the top of her head.

'Oh, yeah,' Veggie told her. 'It's a wizard that everyone fears.'

'Be careful,' Ziggy implored Marty, who waved a hand at her.

'I'll be okay,' he reassured her. 'Just updating, one sec...'

A blue bar crept along until the box was filled; it disappeared, replaced with a full screen of high-definition blackness and a large, flaming logo in the centre.

'What game is this?' Ziggy asked; Veggie pointed at the screen, which read '*Blackest Spirit*' in two-foot-high letters.

'Ah,' said Ziggy.

'Right,' Derrida said loudly, rubbing their arm and picking up a wireless controller. They made to descend into the armchair behind them, but Dominika settled in first, folding her legs up underneath herself with a Cheshire Cat smile. Derrida plonked instead on the arm of the chair. 'What sort of run am I going for?'

'No shield, no dodge, no weapon,' Veggie suggested half-seriously.

'Did that last month,' Derrida said.

'You did *not*.'

'Check the stream highlights, my guy.'

'I absolutely will be doing that.'

'Cheeeeeeese,' TM piped up, perching on the edge of the desk.

'Cheese?' Marty said thoughtfully, spinning around in lazy circles on his boyband-style lead singer stool. 'Oh, heck, yeah. I'll stick the nachos on.'

'Cheese every boss,' TM elaborated.

'Aha,' chirped Derrida, with an excited bounce on the arm of the chair; Dominika, jostled about by the movement, gave them a hard poke in their recently wrenched elbow. Ziggy looked at TM in confusion.

'It's a pretty fun challenge,' Veggie explained. 'This game has, like, a ton of really cool bosses, and they're all super hard and crazy awesome, but there are ways of making pretty much all of them super low-effort. It's not only hilarious, but also makes you feel like the most badass being on the entire planet. It's cheesy. Cheese.'

Ziggy nodded, her expression giving away that she had very little clue what he was on about.

'Just watch,' TM told her. 'It's *awesome*.'

Derrida raised the controller theatrically and hit the start button. A character creation menu zoomed onto the screen; Derrida rattled through the options, naming their character 'Springly Mike' and making her a green-haired thief. An opening cutscene started up, which Ziggy stared at in awe, but Derrida skipped it.

'Awwww,' Ziggy pined.

'It's actually got a really deep story, and stuff,' TM said.

'Lore nerd,' Derrida said accusingly. 'We're just here for the challenge run, bro, forget that not.'

'Don't deride me, Derrida.'

'I've never heard that before,' Derrida said, completely monotone.

'That's so hilarious I think I'm going to die of laughter.'

'It's not even pronounced that way,' Marty piped up.

'*Thank* you,' Derrida said.

Marty nodded wisely, then continued: 'Still funny, though.'

Derrida groaned.

The game started in earnest; Springly Mike awoke to find herself locked in a prison cell. Luckily, some bloke on the roof dropped the key down to her. She let herself out, travelling in erratic bursts of sprints and rolls through the halls, occasionally beating weird pinkish-grey husk zombies to death with her bare hands.

'I don't get it so far,' said Ziggy. At that moment, an enormous fat demon leapt down from the roof (it really did seem to come from the roof, what with the projection of the game occupying an entire wall from floor to ceiling) and she threw herself backwards with a startled yelp.

Derrida glanced over at her for the briefest of moments, and when they looked back Springly Mike was a pile of blood and guts smeared on Fat Demon's ten-foot-long club.

'Shite,' mumbled Derrida, as the words 'YOU WERE OBLITERATED' emblazoned the wall in brightly projected letters. 'Should probably have put some points into vitality.'

'Naawwww,' Marty chided, sliding open another wall panel to reveal a fancy-looking microwave and a cupboard which seemed to exclusively contain boxes of nachos. 'You're meant to be cheesing them, not letting them actually hit you.'

'Point taken,' Derrida conceded. 'I done ballsed up.'

'That you did,' said Marty, slamming the microwave door shut on a plate piled high with nacho chips, cheese and salsa. The microwave hummed obligingly. 'Also, that's one punch in the arm I owe you.'

Derrida restarted their run, getting back to the boss room in record time.

'Okay,' they said, concentrating hard. 'This guy has a pathing glitch, so he'll follow you to the last place where you rolled if you can get the collision detection to think you've rolled into a surface without actually getting interrupted.'

'How do they know this?' Ziggy whispered to Veggie, enthralled.

Veggie snorted. 'They're a hecking *nerd*, is how.'

'That's *so cool*,' Ziggy breathed.

'Soooo,' Derrida continued, ignoring them, 'if I mosey on over to this pillar and roll just alongside –' they did so, and Fat Demon followed him dutifully with thundering footsteps, '– then make this jump over these pots and roll on landing, he'll try to follow, aaaaaand with any luck...'

Fat Demon lumbered over to the pillar, swinging his club aimlessly. Springly Mike hopped over an assortment of ceramic jars, bouncing away from the boss; he tried to change direction too quickly and found himself stuck in the pillar, his animations glitching out and resetting every few frames as he continually flipped left to right.

'And he's stuck,' Derrida finished. 'Cheese complete.'

The microwave pinged; Marty withdrew a steaming plate of nachos. 'Cheese complete,' he echoed, taking the stringiest, melted-est cheesiest, most salsa-est chip he could find and tossing it straight into his mouth. Dominika reached her hands out for the plate and snatched it, resting it on her lap with a satisfied sigh.

Derrida quickly finished off Fat Demon with a few lazy punches to its enormous, jiggling buttocks – 'I don't know why they bothered to animate that,' they said apologetically – and exited the tutorial area through a pair of heavy doors into a bright meadow.

'I think I'm starting to get this whole video game thing,' Ziggy said. Marty took the plate from Dominika's lap, deftly avoiding her grabbing fingers, and passed it around, casting a giant shadow on the wall as he passed through the projector beam.

By the time the nachos were gone, Derrida was three more bosses down. A giant bull with an enormous cleaver had thrown itself off a bridge; a lava-spewing spider with the torso of a woman had somehow managed to stab itself to death; a knight bearing bulky armour and an enormous shield had simply lain down and allowed himself to be repeatedly stabbed in the face. Derrida's cheese was a force to be reckoned with, indeed.

'How are you actually doing this?' Ziggy asked as Springly Mike went rolling through a horde of skeletons to collect her prize: an enormous two-handed sword almost as tall as her.

'Not enough strength to use this one-handed,' Derrida said absently. 'No matter: two handed and we're cooking!'

Marty slotted the last of the nachos into his mouth with a satisfying crunch.

'Video games are super cool, and I'll tell you for why,' Veggie began, but Derrida snapped out of it.

'I'll explain,' they said, pausing the game with a supreme poke of a button. 'The thing about video games is that there are several layers of understanding to them: first, there's the apparent layer, the one you can see and believe yourself to be interacting with. Kind of like what Kant called the *phenomenal*.'

A collective groan arose from the ensemble – except Ziggy, who listened with rapt attention.

'Then there are the underlying mechanics of how it actually works. The physics engine and all that. Understanding what's happening under the surface, what actually causes and affects the stuff you're experiencing on that first level, that's how you learn to be better than the game wants you to be.' They paused for effect. 'When you stop being your character, and start remembering that you're a smart person who's aware that they're playing a video game, that's when you can do things that are impossible.'

Dominika yawned.

'They're actually not as dumb as we'd all like to think,' TM admitted to Ziggy as Derrida turned back to the screen, only to discover that Springly Mike had been beset upon by an angry mob of diseased-looking cannibals. 'Although they do forget that you can't pause *Blackest Spirit*.'

Derrida gave him the finger.

'That's two punches,' Marty mumbled.

Springly Mike continued on with her adventure through the deadly world of *Blackest Spirit*, felling titans and sorcerers and giant magical butterflies with hilarious ease.

'Now then,' Derrida mumbled, guiding Springly Mike through a dark valley. 'We just equip a stat-raising sorcery in the right hand, set out primary weapon to the secondary equip slot, queue the animation then roll and swap equipment mid-action and, ta-da, tumblebuffed,' they explained, helpfully.

Springly Mike swung her ludicrous sword into the hand of an enormous volcanic demon, which did somewhere in the region of sixty-five billion damage and caused it to fall off a cliff.

'I have decided that I am really into video games,' Ziggy announced; TM patted her on the back in encouragement.

'Welcome to the pack,' he said; she beamed with elation.

'Done for now,' Derrida said grudgingly as a nine-headed serpent burst out of a geyser and devoured Springly Mike. 'We'll come back to it.'

Marty switched off the console; TM wandered over to the little hole containing the projector and set to prodding the little machine.

'Whoa there, sailor,' said Marty. 'I only just got that.'

'I'm not gonna take it apart,' TM promised, pulling it out of its niche and peering at it from all angles. 'I just wanna see how it keeps the bulb from overheating.'

'Air vents,' said Derrida. 'Fans. Surely.'

'Yeah, but I need to see how stuff manages not to explode,' TM explained.

Derrida, still balancing on the arm of the cushy chair in which Dominika was lazily lounging, blinked. 'Why?'

'There's a lot -' TM said, carefully prising at bits of casing to get a better look without breaking anything '- of inventions - that I'd like to do - which require management in order to not explode.'

'Why not just make something that *is* supposed to explode?' Ziggy pondered. 'Sounds like that'd be easier.'

TM considered this. 'That's actually kind of a good point.'

'*Veggie Ziggy TM Ziggy Veggie Limited* is not branching out into defence or demolition,' Veggie insisted.

'Yet,' TM muttered; finished with his poking, he set the projector back in its cubbyhole.

'Unless it's to defend ourselves from and/or demolish things belonging to the Swede,' Veggie added, thoughtfully.

'Oh, yeah, so what *is* the Sw-' Ziggy began to ask, but stopped. TM turned his head away from the device set into the wall to look at her; she had gone tight-lipped in response to glances from all three of Derrida, Dominika, and Marty.

Veggie got up and wandered over to the musical corner of the room, picking up a sleek acoustic guitar.

'It's not as if it's still sore to the point that he doesn't want to talk about it,' TM explained quietly to Ziggy, sitting on Veggie's just-vacated beanbag next to her. 'I mean, he keeps bringing it up any chance he gets. Just one of those stories we can't all be bothered to keep going over.'

'You've got one of those too,' Ziggy said, then blushed. 'I mean - sorry.'

TM almost smiled.

Then the sound of the guitar's strings being tuned came from over in the corner: Veggie was leaning over the instrument, listening closely to the shifting pitches as his fingers adjusted the pegs with slow care.

'You can play?' Ziggy asked eagerly, bounding over to him like Keelut proudly strolling along behind O'Ryan. TM suspected her sudden enthusiasm was at least in part to mask the flush still on her cheeks.

'A teensy bit,' said Veggie.

'Pffft,' said TM.

Marty chose that moment to deliver the accrued punches to Derrida's arm; Veggie plucked a low note right as Derrida yelped, somehow harmonising with their voice and setting off a kaleidoscope of overtones echoing throughout the room. Ziggy gasped in astonishment.

Derrida launched themselves after Marty, but he'd already hopped out of the way and launched another game: '*Super Fighter XI*'. He threw a controller to each of Dominika, Derrida, and TM, and took one for himself; as Veggie played a soft series of scales, with Ziggy as his rapt audience, the team of Derrida and TM found themselves repeatedly outclassed by Marty and Dominika.

'That ninja bloke's way overpowered,' Derrida complained after being destroyed by Dominika for the umpteenth time.

'I don't remember you mentioning that in your review,' Marty said, grinning wickedly. 'Seems like the sort of thing a thorough critic like yourself would have picked up on, unless you're just looking for an excuse.'

Derrida threw their controller on the floor.

'Well,' said TM. 'I guess... well, you two win, so... winner takes those two?' He looked over at Veggie and Ziggy.

But Ziggy was asleep at Veggie's feet as he played a gentle classical piece over her head.

Marty glanced at TM, who shrugged. 'Sleepover?' he suggested.

'Absolutely,' said Derrida instantly.

'I was more talking to this lot,' said Marty, 'but I guess you can stay too. It is... like, half four in the morning or something, after all.'

'It is?' TM mumbled, whipping out his phone to check. 'Well, heck.'

Marty stood and stretched, shut down his computer, then opened yet another concealed panel in the wall to reveal a large wardrobe. He withdrew a stack of blankets and pillows, dropping them haphazardly on the floor.

'Sleep as you will,' he instructed; TM got up and strolled over to the pile of soft furnishings, then faceplanted right into it.

'I'll be good right here,' TM said through a mouthful of alpaca wool blanket.

Veggie returned the guitar to its rightful place and opened a door next to the microwave, revealing a smaller room off to the side containing a plush double bed. 'I call shotgun,' he said, hopping inside and reclining smugly.

'You can't call shotgun on my bed,' Marty opined.

'Just did.'

Marty shook his head and stuck his tongue out, lifting TM's head up so he could slide a blanket out from underneath. He carried it over to Ziggy and draped it over her, propping her head up so she wouldn't wake up with a sore neck.

'You better not try to tuck me in,' TM said sleepily.

'I'm being a gentleman over here!'

Derrida slumped down and rested his head on the beanbag that had earlier been occupied by Veggie's buttocks, then TM's. Dominika folded herself into her armchair, bestowing each person in turn with a small smile of goodnight, and pressed her forehead against her knees. Marty leapt into bed next to Veggie, who rolled over onto his face and started snoring.

TM closed his eyes.

10. Rainmaker I (The Spiders From Mars)

'You know what you were saying the other day about how maybe the universe is part of a brain, or something?' TM asked. Aster nodded. She was sprawled out on TM and Veggie's couch, Michel Furcoat lounging on her chest.

'Yeah, vaguely.' She opened one eye to look at him, blowing strands of hair so fair that it was almost silver out of her face.

'I was just thinking about it, I guess.'

'Good for you.'

'How do you think that would work?'

Aster propped herself up on her elbows. Michel Furcoat slinked down the incline of her torso and settled himself in her lap. 'What, like, mechanically?'

'Intellectually, I guess.'

'As in, how would something like the universe be able to generate something like intelligence and consciousness?'

'Yeah, that.'

Aster thought about it. Michel Furcoat looked as if he might be considering the matter too, but was probably just sleepy. TM found himself wishing Maurice Meow-Ponty were around; it was a cold day, they could never afford heating, and the feline occupant of Aster's lap looked like he might serve as a reasonably effective hot water bottle. 'I don't know if there's an answer to that,' she said slowly, 'but I'm not sure it's a question that makes sense to ask, either.'

'How come?'

'I think it might be one of those things you just have to run with,' she said. 'I mean, you're welcome to try to work out how the universe could give rise to a mind, but you haven't really got a starting point because there's no real way of saying how something like a brain can give rise to a mind either.'

'That's kind of debatable, isn't it?'

'Well, yeah, but the debate's never going to be won definitively. We're using our minds to try to learn about our minds. It's self-reflecting. It's never going to get beyond itself. I'm not saying that's a bad thing, necessarily,' she added, seeing TM's look of thoughtful dismay. 'What I'm trying to get to is that we haven't really got a hope of understanding how an assortment of electrical signals and neurons and basically just matter come together to generate something as unique as consciousness. Yeah, we can map parts of the brain to what they do, but that's changing the paradigm and looking only at the constituent parts, forgetting that sentience is totally unlike anything else that exists.'

TM listened quietly.

'So there's no way we can say that a different assortment of bits of matter, arranged in such a way that forces between them acted on each other – electrical signals, or gravity or electromagnetism or nuclear forces or whatever – there's no way we can know whether a mind could arise out of that. So we can't say it definitely couldn't.'

'It wouldn't be the same sort of mind as the one we have, would it? If it was different matter and forces that were... making the framework.'

'Who knows?' Aster shrugged, gently so as not to disturb Michel Furcoat. 'Who even knows that every person has the same sort of mind as every other person?'

'I guess... you can't put minds into sorts anyway, right?' TM said carefully. Aster never made him feel dumb, or judged him for saying something, but she did have a way of coming out with stuff that was so far over his head that he felt self-conscious trying to articulate any sort of idea in case it fell short of the high bar she had set. 'Every mind can only really know one mind, and that's itself.'

'Bingo,' she said, snapping her fingers. 'You can't categorise minds, because nobody has any idea whatsoever what anyone else's mind is actually like.'

'So it's basically meaningless to say that the universe could have the same or different type of consciousness that we do.'

'Or to say that it couldn't.'

TM scratched his head. 'Do you just think about this stuff all the time?'

'Pretty much,' she admitted. 'Don't you?'

'I think I might vaguely wonder about it, but I don't think I often get *very far.'*

'Nothing wrong with being occupied with doing life,' Aster said. 'I don't get things done as quickly as most people, so maybe spending too much time thinking about the world and forgetting to live in it isn't always practical.'

'That reminds me,' TM said suddenly. 'We're out of cat food.'

***

When TM awoke, Veggie was back on his beanbag and staring intensely at the projected screen on the wall. A Post-It note attached to TM's forehead told him: 'Gone to get pick and mix. Back soon. Marty + Derrida + Dom xoxo'. He peeled it off and stretched himself out.

'Whatcha doin'?' he asked Veggie, whose response was simply to nod at the screen. 'Aw,' TM said, noticing what was on, '*yes*.'

Ziggy stirred from under her blanket, rubbing her eyes and pushing her hair back out of her face. It shone with an iridescent shimmer, settling itself into a sleek wave. 'What's going on?'

'We're watching *Wrestle Kingdom 9*,' TM said excitedly, settling himself atop a small heap of cushions. 'Okada vs Tanahashi. We've got super into puro lately, been binging every NJPW show since, like, 2012. No spoilers, 'k?'

'Uh,' said Ziggy. Her face was the picture of non-comprehension, but nevertheless she scooted over with curiosity.

'New Japan Pro Wrestling, bro,' Veggie said, not taking his eyes from the screen.

'Aha,' said Ziggy. 'Cough, fake, cough.'

TM looked at her with something approaching pity. 'You're not supposed to actually say "cough",' he told her. 'Also, don't get Veggie started on –'

Veggie's eyes flitted away from the screen for the first time, staring right at Ziggy. 'It's not fake.'

'I thought,' Ziggy said, then yawned.

Veggie sighed and paused the video, kneeling so that he could look

Ziggy straight in the face. 'Pro wrestling is fake in the same way that porn is fake.'

'What.'

'Don't encourage him, for heaven's sake,' said TM.

'Ah, ba-ba-ba,' Veggie said, holding up a hand. 'Think about it for a second. It's performance art.'

TM plucked one of the cushions out of his pile and buried his face in it, removing himself from the conversation.

'When you watch porn,' Veggie said, to which Ziggy gave an interested 'yuh-huh' – which surprised TM perhaps more than anything else that had happened since meeting her – 'when you watch 'em going at it, you are aware that there is legit bang occurring.'

'Legit bang,' Ziggy repeated, mulling it over. TM let himself go limp, sprawling out over the sides of his cushion bundle in an effort to reiterate that this sort of thing was not to be encouraged. But it was too late: encourage Ziggy had, so Veggie plowed on with renewed voracity.

'The legit-est of bangs,' Veggie agreed. 'There's no getting around it. I mean, they can dress it all up with the fancy lighting and the camera techniques and shot composition and whatever else they wanna use to present it as some sort of fantasy story, but at the end of the day what it boils down to is that you're watching two people who are literally just boning.'

Ziggy nodded thoughtfully.

'Professional wrestling is the same,' Veggie continued.

'It's not exactly the same,' TM felt compelled to interject.

'It *is* the same. You're watching something dressed up to look like a story: a soap opera, an action scene in a thriller movie. Pro wrestling is to fight scenes as porn is to love scenes in… non-porn films. You present it in this way that heightens the drama of it all, but what's really going on underneath is two people beating the shit out of each other.'

'Safely, and using techniques designed to ensure they don't actually injure each other,' TM added.

Ziggy tapped a finger on her bottom lip, thinking it over. 'That makes sense,' she said, after the fifth tap. Veggie fist-pumped ferociously.

'You're probably the first person to say that to him about anything ever,' TM told her. She smiled with pride.

'Right,' said Veggie. '*WK9*, onwards!'

He pressed play; the two men in the projected ring locked up, grabbing each other in a rough tie-up. 'So,' Veggie began to explain, 'the guy in the shorts is Okada and the dude with the weird half-cornrow undercut thing is Tanahashi. He's the champion, Okada wants to be the champion real bad, bish bash bosh, they're fighting about it.'

'There's a bit more to it than that,' TM started to say, but Veggie shushed him.

'There is,' Veggie admitted, 'but the gist of it is that these two have fought each other a whole ton of times, and it's always awesome, and basically they both just want to prove in this match that they're the better person.'

Ziggy looked as if she were doing her best to pretend she understood.

'It's okay,' TM told her, 'you can just enjoy the action.'

'Much like pornography,' Veggie said, and TM groaned loudly, 'in which some people watch the whole thing to get the background and story, and others just skip to the meaty bits.'

'That's gross and weirdly insightful,' Ziggy said.

Early in the match, Okada managed to get Tanahashi strung up outside the ring, draping him over a barricade within inches of the baying crowd. Ziggy stared at the screen, as transfixed as she had been when in the presence of Riegel O'Ryan, as Okada took the champion by the head and fell backwards, driving him face-first into the floor.

'DDT!' Veggie hooted.

'He can do that without hurting him?' Ziggy asked.

'Oh, no,' TM explained, 'it all hurts like heck. They just do their best not to *properly* hurt each other.'

'Ah,' said Ziggy, apparently satisfied, and went back to watching the show.

The match went on, each blow and throw sending Ziggy's eyes and mouth into wider O shapes. The emphatic punctuation of the loud Japanese commentary shook the room. Then Tanahashi pushed Okada down from the top of the ropes surrounding the ring; the challenger fell hard into the squared circle, champion perched above him on the corner of the ropes like a hawk with an unusual haircut.

'High Fly Flow?' Veggie said, biting his nails, and Tanahashi obliged: the champion leapt from the top rope, making a frog-like motion with his arms and legs in midair – 'HIGH FLY FLOW!' squealed Veggie – but Okada rolled aside as he splashed down, and Tanahashi found himself hitting the mat hard.

Okada stood tall over the fallen champion, turning to face the camera and striking a pose. Veggie dutifully stood and mimicked him: legs apart, arms thrust out to either side, palms up, throwing his head back to look skyward. The camera made a dramatic zoom out, and the announcers screamed: 'RAINMAKER POSE!'

'Rainmakaaaaaaaaaaaaaah!' screamed Veggie, and Okada hauled Tanahashi to his feet and stood behind him.

He crossed Tanahashi's arms over his body, holding his wrists from behind, and TM and Veggie drew a collective anticipatory breath. Ziggy looked confused.

'It's his finisher,' TM explained without letting out any breath at all. 'Nobody's ever kicked out.'

Okada let go of one of Tanahashi's hands and pulled hard on the other, sending him spinning away, then yanked on the hand he still held and raised his other arm in a stiff line. Tanahashi found himself pulled rapidly towards Okada, the challenger's arm shooting through the air towards his face.

'OH,' yelled Veggie. Then, 'oh,' said Veggie, as Tanahashi ducked under the swinging arm.

'Nobody's ever kicked out, but a few have dodged,' TM amended.

'What's kicking out?' Ziggy asked; Veggie spluttered indignantly.

'Okay, so to win the match,' TM explained, 'you have to either get the other guy to submit to you – if you see someone tapping their hand, it means they're giving up because they're hurting too bad to carry on – or you pin their shoulders down on the mat for a three-count. When somebody manages to power their shoulders off the mat and break the pin, that's called kicking out.'

'Huh,' said Ziggy. 'Wrestling is kind of weird.'

'It's the best,' Veggie said with an air of dreamy elation.

The match wore on: Tanahashi downed Okada with spinning dragon screw leg whips, rained multiple High Fly Flows from the top rope down upon him, all sorts. Okada fought back as hard as he could, but soon he was limping, worn down by the champion.

'He looks really tired,' Ziggy said with concern.

'He probably is really tired, but he'll also be selling a little bit – putting it on for dramatic effect,' TM told her. 'They've got to make it look as if they're really fighting, which includes acting as if they're really hurt. But he probably is legit super worn out, it's not easy.'

'How do you know?'

'We filmed ourselves having a few matches around the flat a couple of times,' Veggie explained. 'TM's pretty good. Probably 'cos he's so inexplicably good at actual fighting.'

Okada slipped, and found himself with his back to Tanahashi. The champion grabbed him from behind and held him by the wrists.

'Tanahashi's gonna Rainmaker him?' TM wondered.

Tanahashi went for the move; Veggie gasped, but Okada slipped around it, took the champion firmly by the wrists, spun him away and pulled him back into a lariat right to the face.

'RAINMAKER!' yelled Veggie, pointing at the enormous projection as if it were possible to have missed it. 'RAINMAKER!'

Tanahashi went down. Okada dropped on top of him, pinning him to the mat, and the red-shoed referee threw himself across the ring and slapped his hand against the canvas: one, two, thr-

'HOLY HECK,' Veggie yelled, as Tanahashi kicked out.

'OH MY SHIT,' said TM, having accidentally got just as invested as Veggie.

'Okada's lost,' said Veggie dejectedly.

After a few more moves, Okada tried for the Rainmaker again; Tanahashi countered into a bridging dragon suplex – or so Veggie said, although TM had never known the names of all the moves quite that well – that slammed the challenger's neck and shoulders down; Okada went for it again but found himself flying head over heels in Tanahashi's grasp; a final attempt saw Okada land hard on his back, staring up at a High Fly Flow soaring down upon him.

'One! Two! Three!' cried the referee, announcers, and audience in unison.

'That's a shame,' said Veggie.

'That was *amazing*,' Ziggy breathed; Veggie gave a sad smile.

'Yeah, it was.'

There was a knock at the trapdoor; TM pulled it open.

'Can we come in yet?' asked Marty's hair, which was all that was visible of him from TM's vantage point. 'We heard you guys yelling, figured maybe we should stay down here for a bit.'

'Oh, yeah, sorry,' said TM abashedly. 'We were all getting way too into NJPW.'

'New Japan Pro Wrestling!' chirped Ziggy.

'Is that the one where Okada won the title?' Derrida asked, coming into view and examining the screen, which was playing the aftermath of the match. Marty and Dominika hopped up into the attic ahead of them.

'No, it is not,' TM said, as Veggie sniffled.

'Whoops,' said Derrida; Dominika held out a cup of pick and mix to Veggie, which seemed to cheer him up.

'Aww,' he said. 'You got me fudge.'

Dominika nodded, opening her own cup and tipping it up to pour a colourful stream of jelly beans into her mouth. Derrida tossed a cup to TM; Marty handed Ziggy hers. She took it, shook it a couple of times, then hugged him hard. He patted her awkwardly on the back, his own cup in his other hand.

Three more people came up the ladder: a muscular, bright-orange-haired young woman, a long-limbed man with a spectacular mohawk who seemed to be wearing sleeves but no shirt, and a straight-haired girl who looked about twelve. Ziggy retreated, clutching her pick and mix; Marty reached out to her, his empty hand held open and reassuring.

'It's okay,' he said. 'This is the band. That's our guitarist, Obbie Kernel -' the strong woman '- Kurt Eiseldown, bassist -' the mohawked sleeve lad '- and that's our drummer, The Destructionist.' He indicated the young girl, who stuck her tongue out right down to her chin and made devil horns with the index and little fingers of both hands. 'All stage names, obviously.'

'Oh, yeah,' said Veggie, 'band practice. We better bounce, huh?'

'Probably,' said Marty. Ziggy narrowed her eyes at him.

'It's not that he doesn't like us now his other friends are here or something,' TM explained, 'but Marty's priority is rock. Ain't no getting in the way of that.'

'I want to watch,' Ziggy said, still pouting.

'We're doing a show next month,' said Eiseldown in a velvety smooth voice.

'Oooh,' said Veggie. 'You don't even need a bass to play the bass.'

'You say that every time I say anything in your earshot,' Eiseldown said.

'And it only gets truer every time,' Veggie mused.

'Show next month,' muttered Ziggy, as if turning the concept of *next month* over in her head to see what it looked like. 'Yeah. I wanna do that.'

'We'll be there,' said TM. 'Anyway, we probably should be going. Cats to feed, businesses to run.'

'Oh, yeah,' said Marty. 'You've had one jackpot idea, gotta keep that ball rolling.'

Dominika held up the carrier bag in which she had brought the pick and mix, showing off the Veggie Ziggy TM Puncture Repair Kit holding it together.

'Niiiiice,' Ziggy drawled.

'We're on it,' TM said. 'Business meeting scheduled for this afternoon, in fact.'

'There is?' Ziggy asked.

'Yeah, why not.'

Marty grinned. 'Good luck,' he said. 'May your ideas be ever useless, and therefore insanely profitable.'

'I'll try,' Ziggy promised.

Dominika waved as Ziggy slid down the ladder, followed by Veggie and TM; Marty stuck his head out after them, clicking his tongue in farewell, and closed the trapdoor.

'I really like those guys,' Ziggy said, a strawberry lace vanishing into her mouth.

'Yeah, they're pretty cool,' Veggie said. 'Let's head back? I gotta buy cat food on the way home.'

'Let's go home,' Ziggy said happily.

11. The Rent

When they got back to the flat, Michel Furcoat the cat was sitting merrily atop the usual pile of bills and letters imploring them to take adult responsibility for things, soaking the whole lot in liberal streams of piss.

'Thanks, kitty,' Veggie told the cat proudly, nudging the damp mound out of the way with his foot. Michel Furcoat wandered off, a satisfied swish in his tail.

TM's phone beeped.

'Bah-wha?' Ziggy spluttered, spinning around. 'What was that?'

TM took his phone out of his pocket and unlocked it. 'Derrida emailed me,' he noticed; Ziggy's head bobbed back and forth in a perfect double-take.

'Derrida's *in* that thing?!'

'Yes,' Veggie said, deadpan. 'TM keeps Derrida's soul in a beepy thing in his pocket.'

'Waaaa.'

'What they want?'

TM read it out:

Remember how I said I got a quote off Al Tyer for a story I was gonna sell to the paper? Can you give it a quick once-over before I send it off, hook me up with some feedback and that? I mean, you can't reply to this before I send it, so I'll just take that as a yes. Cool, thanks, appreciate it.

'What a dork,' TM said. He wrote a quick reply: *I don't know grammar and that. That's your thing. Overthink it for a bit and then decide it's good enough, OK?*

'So they really were writing a story for the paper,' Veggie mused.

'Well, yeah-huh,' Ziggy said. 'What did you think them and Dominika were doing off on their own where nobody could – oh.'

'Those two?' TM scoffed. 'You think?'

'Stranger things have happened,' Veggie answered, shrugging.

TM shook his head. 'Anyway. *STAR GONE MISSING*, they've called it.'

Veggie kicked the pile of wet post dismissively. 'There's always some celebrity just up and leaving these days,' he said, with something between sadness and total disaffection.

'I don't think it's about that kind of star,' TM said curiously, reading on.

Astronomers the world over are baffled by the complete and unexplained disappearance of one of the stars in the Aquila constellation. Theta Aquilae, a binary star which is – or was – the fourth brightest in its constellation, has entirely vanished. The scientific community is calling this event 'unexpected and super worrying, but also kind of really cool.'

'Derrida's made that quote up,' TM said.

This reporter ingeniously managed to gain a much sought-after audience with local weatherman and resident minor celebrity Al Tyer, who had this to say:

'The effects of a star simply ceasing to be there are unknown. There is no evidence of its death, destruction, or implosion, no supernova or black hole, nothing even to suggest that our view has simply been obscured by some enormous object in space. Assuming that it is truly gone, there must be inevitable concerns about the resultant effects on nearby orbital patterns. What will be the consequence of this shift in gravity? None can say. We must all simply hope that she will come home soon.'

With those wise words, Tyer departed this reporter's company to announce the winner of the local raffle, as this reporter had only really managed to corner him during an unrelated public appearance. This reporter also remains unsure of how qualified a weatherman actually is to comment on astrological matters, but he certainly seemed to know what he was talking about.

'Pah,' said Veggie. 'He's barely even a *minor local* celebrity. They didn't even ask him to turn on the Christmas lights.'

The cosmic science community remains baffled, concerned and more than a little excited, as this latest heavenly event is actually making people interested in studying their field for once. It comes as the latest in a bizarre string of star-related news stories attracting comments such as 'the harbinger of the apocalypse', 'uniquely important in the history, theory and practice of astronomy', and 'nothing major really'. We'll keep you updated, fair city. Turn to page 27 for our horoscopes, in which astrologer Simon Myst will attempt to claim that this all means something that actually applies to your daily life.

'Terrible article,' said Veggie. 'Such an obnoxious writer.'

TM glanced up at Ziggy, then down at his phone, then back up at Ziggy. 'Is this you?'

She nodded, staring determinedly at her own feet.

'You weren't kidding,' TM said, then realised how dumb that sounded. 'I mean. We already knew you weren't kidding, but... it's weird seeing someone else confirm it. You're literally a star, from the sky.'

'I'm literally a star, from the sky,' Ziggy agreed.

'Get with the times, TM,' Veggie said, dragging an enormous bag of the cheapest cat food money could buy in through the door and pouring two streams of nuggets into bowls clearly labelled 'Historian of Idea' and 'Phenomenological Philosopher'. 'They know which one's for which of them,' he told Ziggy proudly. 'Anyway, we're in the twenty-first century. We're all modern and progressive and shit. It doesn't matter what race or religion or sexuality you are, and being a literal star probably falls under one of those somewhere.'

'I'm not saying it matters,' TM said. 'I'm just saying it's slightly non-standard.'

'Brilliant!' Veggie barked, throwing his hands in the air. 'The different-er, the better. If everyone was the same as me, society could never survive. I mean, we'd all constantly be having tons of sex. But also, you know, it takes two to tango, and three to make a carrier bag repair kit, and a few billion to make a society that can come up with stuff like lasagne and Windows Vista without murdering each other.'

'I'm not sure whether that was incredibly insightful or the most meaningless thing you've ever said,' TM said, thinking about it.

'I liked it,' Ziggy said, looking up with a small smile.

Veggie beamed back at her, exposing as many teeth as he could, and Ziggy laughed. Michel Furcoat, the cat, reappeared from nowhere and settled atop her head, pawing ineffectually at her scalp with his purple-sheathed claws; she reached up and took him down into her arms, pressing her nose against his soft head. 'He's adorable,' she said happily, and TM felt able to stop worrying about her.

'Right,' said Veggie eagerly, taking his seat at the table and raising his crayon with glee. 'Ideas!'

Ziggy giggled at him, setting Michel Furcoat down on the sofa. He slipped off, his plastic-covered claws offering no grip whatsoever, and wandered over to the bowls of food. He flopped his tail about for a moment, craning his neck to peer down at the one marked 'Phenomenological Philosopher', then shook his head and tucked into the food in the 'Historian of Ideas' bowl.

'Good cat,' said Veggie. Michel Furcoat farted gently.

Ziggy dropped into the seat next to Veggie, TM settling in on her other side. She rested her head in her palms, elbows firmly planted on the Bedsheet-Tablecloth-Whiteboard. 'You do remember,' she said, 'that the last time we did this, we came up with absolutely nothing whatsoever?'

'Enchi-Ladder,' TM pointed out.

'Absolutely nothing whatsoever,' Ziggy repeated. 'We did better when we just... got out, went for a walk, hung out and let the creativity do its own thing.'

'So that involves... no preparation, no planning, no strategy whatsoever,' said Veggie. 'I love it.'

'Do we need -' TM began to ask, then shut his mouth.

'What?' Veggie chirped.

'I mean,' said TM. 'Do *you* -' he nodded at Ziggy '- need... um.'

'I'm not a tortoise,' said Ziggy. 'I don't need to be kept in a special terrarium or something.'

TM's face flushed with warmth. 'I know, but -'

'You're wondering about how to take care of your new star, though, right?' she said. 'A star is for life, not just for Christmas.'

'I mean...' TM tried to think of a way to express what he was thinking that wouldn't sound completely dumb. 'I'm more thinking, like, do we need to be *careful*?'

'I'm already being careful,' Ziggy said, indignant. 'I'm holding in my light like you wouldn't *believe* over here so I don't get noticed - not that you two bother to keep yours under wraps.'

TM and Veggie looked at each other. Veggie held up his fingers in front of his face, pointed directly into his own eye, and then shook his head. 'Eh?'

'*Oh*,' murmured Ziggy, with an expression that reminded TM of his own the time he'd assumed his dad knew what 'DLC' meant. 'You can't see it.'

'Is this gonna be a problem?' TM pressed. Ziggy shook her head.

'I don't *think* so,' she said, 'not if... hm.' She exhaled loudly through her nose. 'Just don't go lighting anything up too obviously.'

'I will try not to do whatever that involves,' Veggie promised sincerely.

There was a clatter at the door as something emerged through the letterbox, landing with a wet plap on the pile of letters that doubled as Michel Furcoat's toilet. The cat, who had been rolling aimlessly on the floor next to his empty bowl of food (the other bowl, of course, he knew not to touch), got up and trotted over; he nudged the new arrival a couple of times with his nose, then decided he didn't care about it and went for a nap under the sofa.

'Whassat?' Ziggy asked, gazing over at the post.

TM made the extremely short journey across the room to pick it up: it was a folded-up flyer on plain, low-quality paper. He opened it up; one side bore a badly ClipArt-ed proclamation that Riegel O'Ryan and (in much smaller bubble letters) Al Tyer would be unveiling the local museum's new exhibit in a couple of weeks. On the other side was written a message in large felt-tip lettering:

I KNOW SHE'S IN THERE.

TM blinked. He looked at Ziggy, then back down at the message. Then he unfolded the paper the rest of the way and saw the remainder of the message:

Third occupant, higher rent payment starting this month. Your friendly landlord. (Be grateful I can't be arsed to enforce that you're supposed to let me know about changes to your living situation.)

'Ugh,' TM said, throwing the flyer down.

'What?' Veggie asked, one eyebrow halfway up his forehead.

'New museum exhibit -'

'- already knew that, *one hundred percent going*,' Veggie interjected. Ziggy nodded.

'- and somehow the landlord knows about Ziggy and apparently that means we owe him more money for the same amount of space.'

'Ugh,' Veggie agreed. 'We'd better just hang out and do nothing pretty aggressively, then, we're gonna need another good idea.'

'Ooh,' Ziggy piped up, 'I want ice cream. And a movie.'

'Wait a sec,' said TM, realising something. 'You *want* to go to this thing O'Ryan's doing?'

She gave him a thumbs-up.

'I thought being around her was... like, difficult.'

'It's getting less uncomfortable, I think,' she said. 'I think maybe she just makes me nervous because... well, have you *seen* her?'

Veggie nodded knowingly.

'I feel like I want to be where they are, though,' she said, more quietly. 'I need to be. It draws me in.'

She sat there for a second, gazing at something distant, and then Veggie patted her on the head and gave a loud bark of laughter.

'That's called *taste*,' he said. 'I feel exactly the same about... well, a lot of people.' He looked up at the ceiling thoughtfully. 'Marty's hot, isn't he?'

'Ice cream and a movie,' Ziggy said again, more loudly; she danced over to the door and swung it open, gesturing invitingly to the hallway.

'I gotta poop,' TM said.

'Ugh,' said Ziggy. 'Fine. But then ice cream and a movie.'

'Deal,' agreed TM, trotting over to the filing cabinet behind which lay the toilet.

'I think we're, like, triple soulmates,' Veggie said dreamily. 'Three-way besties for ever.'

'That's nice,' said TM, pulling the filing cabinet across.

'Three-way besties,' Veggie said, and TM thought he heard him bump fists with Ziggy. 'We should totally have an actual three-way.'

'No, we shouldn't,' TM said loudly.

'I appreciate the offer,' Ziggy said, 'but I think that if I've learned anything, it's that we're all about a better connection than simple… three-ways.'

Veggie sounded as if he were mulling it over. 'Respect,' he said after a moment.

'I also appreciate this tender moment,' TM chimed in.

'I just realised you're literally pooping right now and I love you and that but this is maybe a bit weird so I'm gonna wait outside okay *byyyeeeeeee*,' Ziggy trilled.

TM finished his business, then followed them outside.

12. No, You Rock

The way Aster walked always reminded TM of a child learning to ice-skate. He remembered the one time he'd been to a rink as a kid – there were never any close by, in the city, so it was a real event if they ever made a trip to one. He'd been nervous, uncertain, always holding onto the wall or his father's hand. Whenever he did let go, it would be for a brief push; he would lean forwards, zooming along so as to reach the next wall as quickly as possible, wobbling the whole way.

Aster, too, was constantly trying to connect herself to the world, whether she realised it or not. Whenever she opened a door or turned a corner, her hand would brush against the wall until her arm was straight and her fingers lost contact. If she passed a fence or hedge, she would raise her hand and let it trail across the surface until she could no longer maintain the touch. She rarely held TM's hand, but always held onto him by the arm. TM wondered whether she was afraid of floating away if she let go for too long.

'Remember what you were saying about needing to see things as a whole and not trying to break 'em down all the time?' TM asked her, one day as they sat on a bench in the park. One of her hands was holding the metal arm of the bench, the other the fleshy arm of TM.

'I was just thinking about that,' she said, looking out at the world. 'I was thinking how beautiful it is just to sit here and watch… everything, you know? The image of the world, just as it is. I'll start looking at individual clouds and hills and stuff in a minute, and I'm sure they'll all be individually great, but I managed to have a moment where I could just appreciate everything in totality.'

'Sounds like the sort of thing everyone could do with a bit more of,' TM said.

'Mm. Sorry, you were going to say something…?'

'Oh, yeah. Veg was telling me the other day about a guy he knew, or read about, or had sex with, I forget. Anyway, the guy had some sort of… brain damage, I think. He had this thing where he kept thinking that everyone he knew was an imposter disguised as the people he loved. He believed that objects in his house were being switched out and replaced with copies that looked exactly the same, but were somehow inferior.'

'Paranoia?'

'Eh, he got pretty paranoid, but it wasn't just that. He wasn't seeing stalkers around corners or anything, just... became unable to recognise the continuity of things.'

'Sounds terrifying.'

'Yeah, it would be,' TM agreed. 'If I thought that you and Veggie were being replaced by identical imposters every time I lost sight of you, I'd probably be pretty messed up.'

'So what happened to him?'

'Oh,' said TM. 'I don't actually know. Veg just sort of told me about the guy.'

'Fair play.'

'Anyway, I was thinking that it's almost as if he lost his ability to see stuff as a whole. Every time he saw somebody, he broke them down into every individual part, and nobody's ever going to look exactly identical every time you see them. Different outfits, hair, expressions even. So the parts never added up to the same whole on two different occasions.'

'He got hung up on the detail and forgot how to look at reality,' Aster mused.

'Something like that, yeah.'

Aster rested her head on TM's shoulder. 'That's a sad story,' she said. 'I'd hate to be unable to see the wood for the trees. Or your face for the features, I guess.'

***

Two weeks later, TM woke up.

It had been something of a continuous welcome party for Ziggy: a large tub of cookie dough ice cream (each), a twelve-hour screening of what claimed to be 'the best indie movie compilation of all time' at the cinema down the road, plenty of pick 'n' mix, and an awful lot of hanging out trying to brainstorm business ideas before getting distracted by video games or spontaneous wrestling matches. Then, finally, the longest nap of TM's life.

When he awoke, feeling better than he could ever remember feeling in his entire life ever, Ziggy was sitting cross-legged on the table, wearing a thick jumper and staring out of the little window.

'Alright?' he asked, rolling his neck around to work out the kinks.

Ziggy glanced around, smiling when she saw him awake. 'Hey,' she said. 'That was a flipping awesome nap.'

'Too right,' said TM. 'Where's – '

Ziggy pointed to a pile of cushions and blankets, topped off with the Bedsheet-Tablecloth-Whiteboard, atop which sat Michel Furcoat. The whole pile seemed to be slowly inflating and deflating; TM slid over and poked it, shifting the mountain of fabric aside and revealing Veggie's sleeping face. Michel Furcoat hopped down at the disturbance, yawning widely to reveal his tiny pink tongue.

'Morning,' said TM loudly; Ziggy slid off the table and scooted over, giving Veggie a poke in the nose.

'Wha,' said Veggie, blinking awake. His stack of hibernation accessories slid off as he moved, like a hatchling turtle emerging from the sand. 'Is over?'

Ziggy nodded down at him.

'Aaaaaaaa,' said Veggie, gurgling languidly. 'That was the best.'

TM nodded, digging out a fresh T-shirt and a chunky sweater from a beaten-up chest of drawers. 'Best ever,' he said with relish.

'Okay,' Ziggy chirruped, checking the time. 'We need to get down to the museum quickety-split, or we won't get a good spot to see Riegel O'Ryan.'

'It's unveily-thingy day?' TM said, having completely forgotten about it.

'It is unveily-thingy day,' Ziggy confirmed. 'And I've been orbiting O'Ryan for a while, and it feels like a good time to...' - she bumped her fists against each other - 'collide, or whatever.'

'You're sure you're gonna be alright?'

'It draws me,' she said simply. 'So we gotta get there soon, else we're gonna be looking at the top of her head over a buncha people.'

'That will not do!' declared Veggie, stripping all his clothes off. Ziggy looked him up and down with mild interest; TM hummed. Veggie pulled on a reasonably clean pair of jeans and a homemade T-shirt emblazoned with the names of their *Hero's Adventure* characters in lurid lettering. 'Let's go harass a celebrity!'

'Woooo!' Ziggy concurred, leaping into the air and punching the sky.

'You were expecting to do, like, a freeze-frame jump-in-the-air pose thing, weren't you?' TM said.

'Maybe,' Ziggy admitted.

'Wait, wait, wait,' Veggie stuttered, waddling over and struggling with the zip on his jeans. 'Let's, let's – ' he positioned TM and Ziggy on either side of himself and bent his knees, poised to spring up, 'three-two-one, YEAH!'

Veggie leapt in to the air, an enormous grin plastered on his face, and pumped his fist with a whoop. Ziggy and TM looked on apathetically as he boinged back down, looking crestfallen. 'You didn't jump,' he said brokenheartedly.

'Sorry,' said TM. 'Again?'

'Don't wanna now,' Veggie said, sticking out his bottom lip and heading for the door.

TM exchanged a look with Ziggy, who gave a wicked grin.

'I'm off,' Veggie announced, and opened the door. TM and Ziggy darted past him as he made to leave, jumping and striking dual midair poses with a happy 'woo'. 'Oh, you guys are the worst,' said Veggie, closing the door behind them.

'Three-way besties forever,' Ziggy chirped, and Veggie laughed despite himself.

'Fine,' he said. 'But next time I want a midair freeze-frame pose moment, y'all better have my back.'

'Promise,' said Ziggy.

***

'It's fopping cold,' Veggie observed as they approached the museum.

'Well, yeah,' said TM. 'It's January.'

'It is?'

'Oh, no, wait, it's February now.'

'Weird how time passes and then you just call it something else,' Ziggy said.

Veggie pondered it all. 'I still think it's kind of weird to have a fair in winter.'

He shivered; Ziggy pulled off her woolly jumper, revealing a layer of knitted cardigan underneath.

'You came prepared,' said Veggie, taking the jumper with a grateful nod and squeezing it on over his T-shirt. He was significantly broader than she was, but it seemed to work.

'Obviously,' Ziggy scoffed. 'Oh, hey, lookie.'

In front of the museum, a tall building that stuck out from the rest – it was almost insistently old-fashioned-looking, as well as having a high roof topped with an angel statue – a thick red rope had been put up. Behind it, up the steps and in front of the doors, stood a pedestal covered by a black cloth. A few people were milling about, but Ziggy barged her way right up to the rope and leaned over curiously. Veggie and TM followed in her wake.

'Space rock,' Ziggy breathed in awe.

'Screw that,' said Veggie, standing on tiptoes to peer up the steps at the object. 'Where's Riegel O'Ryan?'

'And Al Tyer, man!' interjected a bleary-eyed bystander with an impressively patchy beard. 'He's my hero!' He pulled open his anorak to reveal a T-shirt printed with Tyer's face and the legendary words 'Al Is My Guide To The Universe'.

'You're actually here for that guy?' Veggie asked in confusion.

'Heck *yes* I'm here for that guy! He's the most inspiring person in the universe, man. I listen to his audiobook every day! *Every day!*'

'Good for you,' said Veggie, and gently shoved Ziggy and TM towards the other end of the rope.

'I want an audiobook,' said Ziggy absently, trundling away from Al

Tyer's only diehard fan in the cosmos. ('I made this shirt myself!' he called after them. 'I call it Tyer-dye, geddit?')

'As in... you want to listen to one, or you want to make one?' TM asked.

'Yes,' Ziggy clarified.

A buzz of excitement filled the air as they slid along to the furthest reaches of the red rope, spreading from those loitering at the back of the audience towards the front, and as the people around TM started to whoop and applaud, the crowd parted and Riegel O'Ryan came into view. She strode right through the middle of the congregation, Keelut hot on her heels. She raised both fists in the air and the assembly cheered like they were at a rock concert; she ducked under the rope, then held it up to allow her enormous dog to pass.

A slightly less enthusiastic cheer rose up as Al Tyer made his way up to the steps – although his one-man fan club let out an ecstatic bellow as he passed. Tyer raised a hand in acknowledgement, causing the fanboy to swoon from the sheer excitement of it all.

'Hiiiiii,' trilled O'Ryan, voice imbued with a hefty vibrato. The little crowd yelled its approval; she bent backwards sharply, her hair fanning out behind her, then rocketed back up with both hands in the air and her hair flipping over to cover her face.

'She's so rock and roll,' said Veggie dreamily.

TM glanced at Ziggy. Her eyes were fixed on O'Ryan, but her stare was less blank than it had been at their last encounter.

'You okay?' he said to her quietly. They stood still, a rock holding firm in the crashing sea as the crowd around them bounced with raised hands and loud cries. She nodded, her eyes leaving O'Ryan for a moment to give him a reassuring glance.

'Ladies and gentlemen,' began Tyer, thus instantly deflating the entire audience, 'thank you for coming to attend today's unveiling of this, the museum's latest acquisition. Perhaps its most fascinating to date.'

'Yeah!' called the Tyer fan from the ground, apparently regaining consciousness.

'This piece of material from outer space,' Tyer continued, sounding utterly disaffected, 'is, as of this moment, an unknown quantity. What precisely it is? Nobody is quite certain. I, however, am entirely certain that it will prove to be astonishing.'

There was an extremely subdued round of applause.

'Everybody!' O'Ryan said, taking over. A shiver flitted around the audience as its collective attention was recaptured. 'This piece of space rock might hold all sorts of secrets. Maybe it could tell us something we never knew before.'

She looked around for effect, her stare seeming to meet every individual's eye. TM felt Ziggy shivering beside him as O'Ryan's gaze passed over them.

'Or maybe not,' she continued with a shrug. 'But hey, there's potential, and even if it turns out to be absolutely worthless to science, it's still gonna look pretty nice in its brand new exhibit.'

A more enthusiastic round of clapping followed her words.

'Shall we?' said O'Ryan, taking hold of a corner of the cloth.

Tyer nodded, gripping another corner, and the two looked at each other. O'Ryan gave a sharp nod once, twice, a third time, and then they raised their arms and the cloth swooped up between them and fluttered against the sky. Ziggy inhaled as the space rock was revealed: the size of a muscular torso, shaped somewhere between a sphere and a pyramid, it sat in a glass case, glittering as the sunlight ran through the many facets of its surface. It shone, half-transparent, an oil-like shimmer playing over it. O'Ryan balled up the cloth and threw it into the crowd, where a scuffle over who had caught it first immediately started up, then picked up a control box hooked up to a cable running into the museum doors and pressed a button.

'Yeeeeaaaaaaaaaaahhh!' she sang as the hum of powerful bulbs set up around them kicked in, lights powering up.

Appreciative 'ooh'ing and 'aah'ing ensued: thick beams of white light shone through the crystalline space rock, sending rivers of light every colour of the rainbow shimmering out from it. TM looked at Veggie and Ziggy beside him, glimmering spectra lighting up their faces.

'Oh, *hell* yeah,' O'Ryan exclaimed, exhaling in exhilaration as the light danced all around her. 'Okay, guys, this little piece of the cosmos is gonna be out here lookin' pretty for a little bit, and then our pals who actually work here are gonna take it in and set it up, all that shebang. Thanks for coming, watch my show, and I'll see y'all again. Much sooner than you think, some of ya.'

Her gaze passed over the crowd one last time, then she held the door open for Tyer. He entered with barely a further glance at the crowd; she followed him inside with a merry wave. Keelut stalked in behind O'Ryan's heels, the last hairs of her tail barely making it inside before the door closed on her.

The crowd looked around at each other, realised that was it, then dispersed without further ado.

'We have to steal that rock,' Ziggy said.

TM and Veggie gave her the exact same incredulous look as one.

'I'm serious,' she told them. 'We need to steal it.'

'Um,' said TM.

'Yeah, okay,' said Veggie with a nod. 'It'll be good to have a project.'

'I – what?' TM looked at the two of them with astonishment. 'For real?'

Ziggy nodded firmly, eyes fixed on the lump of rock. 'I need it.'

'For what?'

She raised her hand to her mouth and clipped one of her nails with her teeth. 'I don't know. I just feel like… if I have that rock, everything will be alright. Same sort of thing as how I get this compulsion to be around those two –' she gestured at the museum door, behind which O'Ryan and Tyer had vanished '– it just feels like gravity. Attracting forces, in a super literal way. I spent thousands of years in a web of orbits, I know what gravity feels like. I. Need. That Rock.'

'Fine,' said TM. 'If you feel that way, I'm in. Let's just grab it and go.'

He glanced about, making sure there were no stragglers, and made to climb under the rope, but Veggie grabbed him by the upper arm.

'No, man!' he urged.

'What?'

'You can't just waltz up there and grab the space rock in full view of, like, the entire world,' Veggie insisted. 'That's firstly stupid and risky, and secondly not cool enough at all!'

TM considered this. 'I accept your first point. Second, not so much.'

'Aw, c'mon,' said Veggie. 'You can't be satisfied with just yoinking the rock off its pedestal and humping it home. If we're gonna steal this, we've gotta do it the right way!'

'I think I'm getting some idea of what that might be.'

'We need to pull off a heist.'

'You know, somehow I knew that was going to be it.'

Veggie's eyes widened, a dreamy look of pure joy starting in his eyebrows and spreading through his entire body until he couldn't resist fully waving his arms around in the air with exhilaration. 'We're going to pull off the greatest heist of all time!' he wailed, choking up with the utter emotion of how awesome such a thing would be.

TM sighed, turning to Ziggy. 'Are you hearing this?'

She nodded, bouncing with zeal. 'This sounds like the best idea ever,' she chirped.

'I thought you wanted the rock?' TM asked in confusion. 'Surely this'll take time, preparation – you're not going to get the rock for a while, wouldn't you rather just take it now?'

'Heck no,' said Ziggy. 'I want the rock, yeah, but I have to *earn* it.'

TM clicked his tongue. 'And the best way to do that is –'

'A flipping awesome heist,' Ziggy answered, face lit up.

'It's, um.' TM scratched the back of his neck. 'If we do this, we're sort of crossing a line from just being low-level dumb people into actual criminals.'

'It's a victimless crime,' Veggie insisted. 'And you heard what Al and O'Ryan said: that rock could be *anything*. Could *do* anything.' He pointed at Ziggy. 'We've got a human star hanging out with us, why not magic rocks?'

Ziggy scrunched up her eyes as if finding it difficult to look at Veggie as he spoke - as if she were looking at a too-bright light.

'Veg,' said TM. 'There might be consequences.'

'Oh, pfft. You haven't done anything that might have consequences since *she* left, and you're, like, so bored of it that you don't even know what you're doing.'

'Well,' said TM. He sighed. He considered whether he had crossed any lines lately from which there might be no returning, and whether that was something he ought to be doing more of. He looked at Veggie, at Ziggy, at Veggie again, and nodded. 'Alright, then.'

13. Two Steps to Success

When they got back to the flat, Veggie immediately whizzed over to the table, snatched up his crayon and started scribbling all over the Bedsheet-Tablecloth-Whiteboard.

'What are you doing?' TM asked, watching Veggie's hand zipping around. He picked up Michel Furcoat, the cat, who was cleaning his fur on the table, and put him down again out of reach of the zooming crayon lest Veggie draw on him.

'I'm making a plan, obviously,' said Veggie, adding a few stick figures to his diagrams.

'You've just written *HECK YEAH HEIST* and drawn what looks like a flying burglar pointing a dildo at a hippo,' TM pointed out.

'Well, yeah,' said Veggie. 'I'll get to the actual planning stuff in a mo, but there's no point getting started until it's all looking slick.'

Ziggy wandered to the table, looking over Veggie's drawings. 'I like it,' she hummed. 'Very avante-garde.'

'Do you know what that means?' TM asked her.

Ziggy stuck her tongue out. 'Something arty, probably.'

'Do *you* know what it means?' Veggie countered, to which TM could only walk away mumbling.

'Okey-dokey,' said Veggie, putting the finishing touches to his masterpiece. 'Visual excellence achieved, now to start the real work.'

He scrawled the words *SUPER PREPARATIONING* in messy bubble letters and underlined them three times. Then, under that informative heading, he made a list: *1) learn parkour; 2) get good at how to burglar.*

'That is the best and most detailed heist plan I've ever seen,' said TM, which owing to his lack of experience with heist plans was not technically inaccurate.

'I think we need more… steps,' said Ziggy. 'Not that this isn't brilliant, obviously. Just not totally sure it'll be sufficient.'

'Point taken,' said Veggie, rolling his crayon between his teeth. 'Brilliant but insufficient.'

'You'll have heard that one before,' TM said.

Veggie spluttered his objections and threw Michel Furcoat at TM. 'Let's try this,' he said, adding a few points underneath his existing schematics: *2a) enlist the gang as assistants (ideally without telling them); 2b) practice for burgling via Hero's Adventure; 2c) scope out the building.*

'Now *that* is more like it,' said Ziggy happily, giving Veggie a firm pat on the head.

'Too damn right,' said Veggie; TM nodded, having accepted that this was as good as it was likely to get. 'I'll call the gang. We gotta get *on* this.'

***

Less than an hour later, six people were gathered around the table once more. TM passed around the character sheets; Derrida, Marty, and Dominika took their places while Ziggy pored over her stats. Veggie, meanwhile, sat furiously making amendments to his campaign papers.

'Where have you guys been the last few days, anyway?' Marty asked, settling down with a sigh.

'We took a nap for days,' Ziggy explained. Marty nodded in appreciation; Derrida coughed in a way that said 'each to their own', and Dominika gazed wistfully at the pile of cushions under which Veggie had until recently been comatose.

'That sounds like the best thing ever,' Marty said.

'What about you?' TM asked. The trio exchanged amused glances.

'We totally went on a coach trip,' Marty said, grinning irreverently.

'You didn't.'

'Oh, yeah, we went around with a tour guide and looked at historic buildings and whatnot.'

Veggie scoffed. 'Why?'

Derrida pulled out their phone, held the screen out to Veggie and flicked through a series of pictures. 'We took a load of selfies with all these elderly peeps and told them misleading stuff about antiquity and history and whatnot,' they explained proudly.

'Ahh. Nice.'

'Also, I changed jobs again,' Derrida said. 'I write speeches for tour bus guides now.'

'You really need to settle on something,' Marty muttered; Derrida flapped their hands at him irritably.

'You're so settled on punk rock that you Skyped in to band practice from the hotel,' they said. Marty widened his eyes as if to say *well, obviously.*

'So,' said Ziggy, leaning forwards with an eager rub of the palms. 'Where were we?'

Veggie bent over his campaign sheets, running a pencil along the lines until he found the spot at which they had left off. 'Aha.'

Last time, in the epic and astonishing campaign and adventure of the most amazing and efficient heroes of all time ever:

Our protagonists were attacked in the forest by a buncha orcs, whom they summarily and royally mashed up. Iveline got herself a falcon, of all things. L joined the group, and remains both mysterious and enigmatic.

'That's tautological,' said Derrida.

'Shut up, Derrida,' said Marty.

The heroes were heading for the nearest big city in search of grand adventure, and L agreed to lead them there. Our adventure resumes as they wander merrily along in the forest.

Veggie scratched his nose, flipped a sheet over, and grinned slyly.

Oh, and because L failed her perception check at the end of the last session, she trips on a hidden wire and a trapped crossbow launches a bolt directly at her face.

'Whaaaaa?!' Ziggy screeched. 'Way unfair!'

TM thought about it for a moment, then rolled a die. He looked at the result, shrugged, then rolled another one. 'Barry reacts without consciously thinking about it,' he said. 'He jumps in front of L and takes the hit.'

Ziggy gasped. 'You'd do that?'

'Barry's probably got more hit points than L,' TM half-explained. She scrunched up her eyes at him for a second, then gave him a grateful smile.

Veggie leaned over to look at TM's dice, tapping the end of his crayon to his forehead. 'Fair,' he said.

Barry leaps with heroic speed and speedy heroism between L and the crossbow, taking a bolt in the chest for...

Veggie rolled.

Twenty-five points of damage.

'Twenty-five?!' TM exclaimed.

'You got shot in the chest,' Veggie said, shrugging. 'What did you think was gonna happen?'

'I thought I was gonna get shot in the face...'

'Barry's taller than L,' Veggie said, 'and also taking a hit in the face would hurt *even more*, so unless you wanted to specify that Barry was leaning down and got hit harder than you already did...'

'Ugh,' huffed TM. 'Twenty-five. Fine.'

'L thanks him and does some woodland medicine or something,' Ziggy said quickly; Veggie nodded.

'Can we just roll a navigation check and skip the journey?' said TM, scanning the reverse of his character sheet for any items or skills that might prevent further danger and thus save Barry from certain peril. 'I sort of don't want any more low-level encounters until Barry's back on his feet.'

'Also, role-playing just walking through a forest is seriously dull,' Marty added. 'Unless you had something specific to spice things up on the way, obvs.'

'Nah, you're good,' Veggie said, passing sets of dice around to each player. 'Everybody just roll to make sure nothing major happens on the way, and we'll just gloss over the walking part.'

Each player rolled, and Ziggy huffed with dismay.

'I don't think I passed that one,' she said, as the others leaned in to see what score she'd rolled.

'A natural one,' said Veggie, whistling. 'Well, that's not the best.'

'Hold up,' said TM. 'L's meant to know the forest and the route pretty well, she must get some sort of background modifier for that.'

Veggie stuck his pencil between his teeth, thinking. 'True,' he said. 'Gotta have some sort of punishment for rolling a one, though...' He scratched a few lines on his campaign sheet.

Our heroes make their way heroically through the forest, evading traps set by hunters and marauding orcs and whatnot. Iveline's falcon proves itself useful, flying ahead to scout for any impending bandits or such like. All of our courageous wanderers find their way through the trees without incident – except for L, who injures her leg and ribs taking the brunt of a rolling boulder trap accidentally triggered by Barry as he shuffles weakly along.

'Aw, cheers, Z,' said TM.

'Didn't have much of a choice, apparently,' Ziggy said. 'But you're welcome anyway. I think that makes us square.'

L and Barry are in stable conditions, hurt seriously but not critically. The others are able to help them traverse the final stages of the path, and by first light, the group emerges together into the shadow of the great city of Lanriel.

'Woo-hoo,' Marty said, exhaling with relief.

'We need to find some sort of tavern or something,' Derrida mused, tapping their pencil to their skull.

'How comes?' Ziggy asked, to which Derrida gave an incredulous bark of laughter.

'Because that's just what every hero does when they first make it to a new city, Z-ster,' they explained; Ziggy nodded in understanding.

'Gotcha,' she said, winking and pointing finger guns at them. 'Let's tavern it up.'

'Hold up a sec,' Veggie said quickly, tapping Ziggy on the shoulder. She shuffled over and they exchanged huddled whispers for a moment. Then they nodded and split, knowing looks passing between them.

'I know a safe place,' L tells the group. Atgard, who's supporting the weakened rogue by the armpit, nods –

'Hang on a sec,' Derrida interrupted. 'I think I wanna roll for something here.'

'What do you want to roll for?' Veggie asked, looking at them exasperatedly.

'Judgement, perception, knowledge, something-or-other. I need to make sure we can trust this so-called safe place of hers.'

'You're so paranoid,' Marty groaned, to which Derrida rolled his eyes.

'It's saved all of you more than once,' he pointed out. Marty could only fold his arms and grumble.

'Fine,' he said, 'do your roll.'

Derrida threw the dice, sending them bouncing across the table. Veggie erased some text on his sheet and scribbled some more in its place.

Atgard senses that L is telling the truth. Not the whole truth, but she's not lying about anything as such.

'That'll do,' Derrida said indifferently.

'We will follow you to this safe place,' Atgard hisses to L. She nods, grateful.

'And then a new quest,' Marty said.

'How do we get one of those?' Ziggy asked.

'Eh, it's not too hard if he's doing his job right,' said Marty, jerking a thumb in Veggie's direction. 'It's kinda like life, y'know. You wander around until you find something you wanna do. Hopefully he's got some sort of plan to direct us to wherever the important stuff is, or maybe some random guy's just gonna run up to us in the street and hand us a royal decree or something.'

'So unimaginative,' Derrida said.

'Yet effective,' Veggie finished for them.

Veggie guided the heroes to the next phase of their story; L, darting through quiet alleyways and avoiding the gazes of the Lanriel city guard ('Always avoid the guards,' TM advised, 'they're never good news. Plus Barry is wanted in four imperial jurisdictions for crimes he... mostly didn't commit.'), led the party to an unassuming building bearing a wooden sign that read 'Rooms Available'.

Inside, they wandered towards a door guarded by a chap with more weapons than seemed possible for one person to make use of. L exchanged quiet words with him, and they proceeded into a back room.

In the room, sitting at a wooden desk, is a man aged perhaps forty. His hair and beard are starting to grey, but his eyes are gleaming with a young, healthy vitality and grace.

'Your type, is he?' Marty teased.

'He's an attractive guy,' said Veggie. 'Silver fox.'

The man looks up at the party as they enter his room, and gets to his feet when he recognises L at its head.

'It's been a while,' he says, looking half-surprised to see her.

'Perception!' declared Derrida.

'Again?' Marty moaned.

Veggie sighed.

Atgard notices that the man definitely seems to know who L is.

'That's it?!' demanded Derrida.

Veggie threw up his hands. 'What do you want me to say? You wanted a perception check, there's nothing to perceive!'

Derrida folded their arms stubbornly.

Fine: Atgard sees that the man seems to be half-bowing to L, gesturing in deference or respect or perhaps just welcome, but he glances around at the assembly and stops himself.

'I am Rusk of the Leaf,' he says, deftly turning his gesture to L into a bow of introduction encompassing the whole group. 'I sincerely hope that none of you has ever heard of me.'

'Nopely dopely,' says Malachi.

'Oh, come on, Marty,' said TM, 'at least stay in character.'

'Malachi's the sort of guy who says nopely dopely,' Marty said.

'*Nobody* is the kind of guy who says... nopely dopely,' TM pointed out.

'I hath not perheardened of thee, O Rusk of the Leaf, of whom I reiterate that I have not heard,' Malachi intones ceremoniously.

'Not perfect, but better,' TM said.

In smooth tones, Veggie-as-Rusk explained the role of the Leaf: a criminal underbelly responsible for maintaining honour and fairness when the representatives of the law couldn't or wouldn't.

'Keeping the city safe and clean more often than not entails that we do the most unsafe and unclean things,' Rusk concludes.'

'L tells him that we need sanctuary,' Ziggy prompted, pointing at her own leg and TM's face. 'We're hurt.'

'Of course,' Rusk accedes.

'Sooooo,' says Malachi. 'How do you two know each other?' Rusk glances at L, as if checking for her approval.

'I was part of the Leaf for a time,' L says. 'Rusk took me in, and taught me to be who I am.'

'Ooooh,' said Marty. 'Fancy that.'

'And theeeen,' Veggie continued, sliding pages of notes and maps around the table, 'he opens up a door concealed behind a bookshelf -'

'How desperately original,' Derrida sniffed.

'Ancient tradition,' Veggie snapped, 'one of the most extremely effective and most sacred holy laws of thiefdom.'

Derrida snorted.

'Anyway, he takes you down into the basement, which is *not* a weird sex dungeon -'

'I was wondering,' TM admitted.

'- and shows you what you've just been welcomed into: the headquarters of the Leaf.'

'Oooh,' said Marty.

With the help of pictorial aides and sweeping gestures, Veggie described a huge room filled with all an up-and-coming thief could ever need: practice dummies, targets, climbing frames, floors trapped with bells to encourage sneakiness.

'You can train every skill you could need here,' Rusk tells the group.

'Every skill we could need for... what?' asks Malachi.

Rusk stops, sighs, looks at each of their faces in turn. 'This city needs heroes,' he says. 'The Leaf can't do it; we have to stay secret. But you... you ragtag, yet accomplished-looking band of wandering champions, we can train you in our ways and then you can be the saviours that Lanriel needs.'

'Why would we agree to this?' Atgard asks in his trademark hiss.

'You're adventurers!' Veggie spluttered. 'Skills and adventures and stuff are what you *do*! You live to go on quests and heroic journeys, it's your thing.'

'That is a point,' Marty admitted; Dominika nodded in agreement.

'What's the job?' TM asked in Barry's gruff voice.

Rusk sighs, looking down. 'Lanriel used to be a capital of sorts, so it has a high-class... ruling family, for want of a better term. But all the direct descendants of the original rulers are either missing or dead, killed by their corrupted line of cousins who seek to take the power for themselves. The true Lanriel family are all scattered now, supplanted by unrighteous power thieves.' He clenches his fist, staring at his own knuckles as they turn white.

'So you want us to... what, exactly?' says Barry. 'Take out the usurpers? That sounds like more of an assassination than a heroic quest.'

'Hey,' said Veggie, wagging his pencil at TM. 'All heroic quests are... heroic quests.'

'Tautological,' Derrida said again, without looking up. Marty punched him in the arm.

'Just 'cos it's kind of sneaky murder doesn't mean it's not an excellent adventure,' Veggie said.

TM groaned. 'Fine. As long as we're not cutting their throats while they sleep or anything.'

'Oh, no,' said Veggie, blinking down at his sheets. 'They'll make it pretty tough.'

'Well, that's alright, then.'

'And once that's done,' Veggie continued, 'and the evil peeps can no longer drag the prosperity and good name of the city of Lanriel though the mud, the Leaf will... replace them.'

'With whom?' Derrida asked.

'We have a true Lanriel within our walls,' says Rusk with a small smile. 'Possibly the last.'

'So what's in it for us?' Malachi asks. 'If we're going to do all the work and take out this corrupted line, then you Leaf lot are going to put your own ruler in their place... what's the incentive for us to do the job?'

'Gold,' says Rusk. 'Experience points.'

'Don't break the fourth wall, Veg,' TM said reproachingly.

'I mean, gold and the good fame of having restored the rightful regent of Lanriel,' Rusk corrects himself hurriedly. 'Also, the city will return to its former glory, which will mean that its economy flourishes once more. Then all the citizens will need lots of quests doing and have the cash to pay you for it, so you'll be in work pretty much for ever.'

Malachi considers this. 'Good answer,' he says. 'I'm in.'

Iveline nods, and her falcon gives a really awesome caw like it's ready to kick butt; Atgard holds his fist out in a ritual gesture of respect, and nods his weird snakey head. Barry presses his hand to his chest, signalling his approval. L says nothing, but a look passes between her and Rusk.

'Good,' says Rusk. 'Then let me tell you of your objectives.'

Veggie burst into a fit of coughing. 'Sorry,' he said, emerging from under the table a few moments later. 'Doing Rusk's voice is kind of hard on the old vocal cords.' He hawked and spat on the floor; Ziggy shuffled her chair away from the glob of phlegm. 'Right. Two resident… imperial cousins, bad dudes. Two bodyguards. That's four enemies, five of you, easy peasy.'

Marty did a quick head count. 'Can confirm,' he said. 'It's totally not gonna be that easy, though, we're only a low-level party.'

'Luckily,' said Veggie, grinning widely, 'this place has pretty decent facilities, so y'all can just roll each time you train and get a bunch of EXP.'

'Well, that's going to be insanely dull,' said TM.

'Which is why,' Veggie announced, raising a finger, 'I have devised a training plan. The best training plan.'

'Oh, really?'

'Yup.' Veggie stood, sidled over to the sofa and pulled out a games console from underneath. It was still in the box.

'When did we get one of those?' TM demanded.

'When Ziggy made us a buttload of cash,' Veggie said proudly. Ziggy blushed.

'You know we're going to need to come up with something else before too long,' TM pointed out. 'We can't keep living off the profits from the Puncture Repair Kit much longer. Hey, I should probably get started on the Octobike while we still have the funds.'

'Why don't you just get real jobs?' Derrida asked, looking on with total disinterest.

'Because we're disenfranchised Generation Y millennial biznitches who live by the American dream,' Veggie told him. 'Besides, none of you have real jobs.'

'I'm in a band,' Marty said indignantly.

'I write walkthroughs for some well-known sites, you know,' Derrida pointed out.

Dominika reached in her pocket, pulled out a badge and flashed it at them.

'Senior Financial Consultant?' Marty read. 'Huh.'

'We're coming to your house next time,' TM told her, to which she folded her arms and shrugged.

'I wouldn't mind a real job, though,' Veggie said absently, setting up the console. 'I mean, I'd hate the hours, and the work, and everything about it would just suck so many balls that I can't even think about it without wanting to buy a ball pit.'

'But... you wouldn't mind it?' Ziggy asked, eyebrows furrowed.

'Dude, have you ever been to an office where they do... like, low-to-medium-level administration? The sheer number of absolute next-level hot twentysomethings who haven't picked a career path yet, it's...' He gave a wistful sigh, then kissed his fingertips and held his hand up in an OK sign.

'I don't know what that means,' said Ziggy.

'You were saying something about a plan...?' Derrida interrupted, an unmistakeable twang of scepticism cutting through Veggie's fantasies.

'Aha,' said Veggie, finalising the console setup with a knowing flourish. 'Here we go: rotating montage of video gaming-slash-tabletop gaming.'

A blink of mild confusion made the rounds.

'I don't follow,' Marty said.

'I fail to understand,' TM said simultaneously.

'Yeah,' Ziggy added, bringing the backup; TM and Marty fist-bumped her in unison, somehow.

'Three-way fist bump,' Veggie lamented, shooting a betrayed glare at them.

'We'll set one up for you later,' TM said, flapping his hands at his partner to hurry him along. 'Just explain the flipping plan.'

'Right, yes,' Veggie said, with an apologetic scratch of an ear. 'Well, to carry off this most epic of campaigns you'll all need plenty of thief-and-thieving-related skills, such as sneaking. Er, hiding. Burglaring. That sort of thing. So, to really up the immersion, I'm setting up stations.'

He pointed to the table. 'We'll be splitting into pairs, rotating around each activity in turn. Over there, two people will be rolling for stat increases, training to raise their characters' skills until the whole party's good and ready to take on the indubitable greatest quest of all time. Over here –' he made theatrical gestures to present the gaming setup, like a model demonstrating the top prize in an eighties game show '– another team of two will be blasting through some of the classics of the stealth genre to top up their knowledge of the basic tropes of thievery.

'And finally, in the Great Land of Outside, pair number three will be training their awesome parkour skills around the city.'

TM gave him a look.

'What?'

'That's a really dumb idea, but it sounds fun as heck, so I'm game,' said Marty, vaulting the table. 'I call first shot on the stealth games.'

Derrida made to join him at the games console, but the back of Dominika's hand hit them in the chest. There was no sound as her tensed fingers made contact, but they instantly froze and resumed their seat.

'Fine,' Derrida said, leaning away from Dominika. 'You and me –' they nodded at Veggie '– are parkouring it up first, then. 'Kay?'

'Deal,' said Veggie, then turned to TM and Ziggy. 'That makes you two first on super training stat grind duty, then. I'm trusting you not to just add a million points to everything without actually doing the rolls, so don't let me down.'

With that, Veggie and Derrida were gone, Veggie tightening the belt of his jeans as they made to slip down his rear on the way out.

'Are they not going to get changed or anything?' Marty asked without turning around. He flicked the tiny TV on and shuffled himself into supreme comfort on the sofa.

'Nah,' said TM. 'I think they're just gonna go try to be ninjas in Converses and skinny jeans. Or, in Veggie's case, knock-off Converses and jeans that used to be skinny but have stretched a bit.'

'Awesome,' said Marty.

14. Antiquity

By the time Veggie and Derrida made their triumphant return, some two hours later, L and Barry had more than doubled their stats.

'Whoa,' said Veggie, checking their sheets. 'This is legit?'

'Ziggy is... ridiculously fast at rolling dice,' TM explained.

'Fair enough,' Veggie conceded. 'Should have a decent shot at winning this thing now, any rate.' He turned to Marty and Dominika, the latter of whom had taken the controller after the first hour. 'How are you guys doing over there?'

'Pretty good,' said Marty. 'Started with *Steel Cog Sturdy*.'

'A classic of the genre,' Veggie proclaimed.

'I got a couple of stages in,' Marty told him, gesturing to the screen, 'then this crazy woman took over and now we're somehow on the final boss.'

'Huh,' said Veggie, examining their progress. Dominika was scooting about, dodging bullets and diving into a cardboard box for cover (which was proving inexplicably effective). 'There we go,' Veggie declared with vindication, pointing. 'We've learned something valuable today: when in doubt, cardboard box.'

'Yeah, it's all completely worthwhile now,' said Marty, gurning.

TM stood, edging over to Veggie. 'Veg,' he murmured. 'This is what we're doing? As training for pulling off an actual, real-life robbery?'

'Heck, yeah,' said Veggie, affronted. 'It's *perfect*.'

TM stared at his oldest friend for a moment, then went 'pff' and held his hands up. 'If you say so.'

'I do indeed,' Veggie said smugly. 'We are the best friends ever.'

'Don't pretend this is entirely for Ziggy,' TM said. 'You've wanted an excuse to do something stupid but cool for... ever.'

'I'm an extremely selfless person,' Veggie protested, then chuckled. 'Okay, fine, so I'm mostly in it for the sheer audacity of the whole thing, but it makes it more morally virtuous if someone else *also* benefits. Right?'

'Why not.'

Veggie nodded, then waved his arms in the air and yelled 'Station swap!' He and Derrida, who followed dutifully, took their seats at the table as Marty and Dominika left the warmth of the flat for the cold outdoors. TM and Ziggy took over the game station.

'Ooh,' said Ziggy, picking up a box, '*Sliver Nucleus.*'

'You've played it?'

'Naw, I just like the title.' She flipped the box over, perusing the blurb. '*Become the greatest secret agent you've never heard of, because he was so brilliantly sneaky that even history didn't know about him,*' she read. 'Sounds awesome.'

'Haven't played it for a while,' TM said, catching the box as she tossed it into his lap. 'You are Mikkels Stormson, greatest agent of the most secret American espionage agency never to make it into the history books, and it's up to you to prevent the nuclear war to end all wars. Which you do primarily by sneaking around and stuff,' he paraphrased.

'Nice,' Ziggy grinned, adjusting her grip on the controller. 'Sounds more like it.'

'Zig?' said TM.

'Yuh.'

'This space rock isn't some sort of nuclear weapon, is it?'

'Probs not,' she said, reassuringly.

TM sighed, then pressed the start button for her. 'Hey,' he said, as the tutorial commenced.

'Mm?'

TM glanced up at Derrida, who was rolling intently, and lowered his voice. 'You know why we're doing all this, right?'

'Yeah,' she said, pausing the game. 'Practice for the real thing.'

TM nodded. 'You think that if we get this... moon rock... thing, it'll help you somehow?'

She took a break from flicking through menus and gazed up at the ceiling. 'I really hope so,' she said after a few moments. 'I mean, I've been loving staying here with you guys. For real. I literally wasn't even alive before, and to be honest I can't think of a better way to be alive than this.'

'It's been good,' TM agreed.

'The best,' Ziggy said, and suddenly hugged him. 'Thank you,' she said.

'Hey,' called Veggie, who was carefully adjudicating Derrida's rolls. 'Get on with your training, dummies. This is *important*, for reasons.'

Ziggy released TM and hopped over to Veggie, throwing her arms around him too. He patted her on the back, then went back to watching Derrida throw dice. 'Love you too,' he told her.

Ziggy slid back into the sofa, picking up the controller. 'Anyway,' she said quietly to TM. 'This has all been the best. But... I guess that piece of space rock just really feels like something I need to be near, to have. For me. Can't explain why.'

'Maybe it's a bit of you,' TM suggested.

'Don't be dumb, TM,' she admonished. 'I'm a star. We're massive balls of burning gas, not flipping clusters of pebbles.'

'Hm.'

She sighed and ran a hand through her hair. TM thought he could see the colour darkening as her fingers passed along each strand. 'It's just gravity,' she said. 'Just natural forces, pulling celestial bodies together.'

'You're weird,' said TM. Ziggy bared her teeth at him.

'That's the whole reason we get along so well, no?'

TM could not argue with that.

Ziggy started the game back up, controlling the darkly dashing Mikkels Stormson ('That's a pornstar name if ever I heard one,' she said) through the tutorial section; she led him over a quick obstacle course, bounding over nets and walls, sliding under rows of wire. She came to something of a halt when she reached a room trapped with a creaky floor and hundreds of bells dangling in her way, which she had to move through as slowly and sneakily as possible to avoid tripping or making a sound.

'I heard that,' said the agency handler, for the eighth or ninth time. Ziggy puffed her cheeks out in frustration.

'You have to hold this button for stealth,' TM told her.

'Well, that's not intuitive at all,' Ziggy complained. Then she paused the game. 'Hey, speaking of things that aren't intuitive…'

'Are you going to ask how me and Veggie have managed to live together all this time and never… hooked up? 'Cos I get that a lot.'

'I was wondering, but nah.' Ziggy held the controller over her mouth to muffle her speech. 'What's the deal with that guy Veggie really hates?'

'What, the Swede?'

'Yip.'

TM pushed the controller out of Ziggy's face. 'What's made you think of that?'

She shrugged. 'I was just thinking, while we were playing – I can't imagine Veggie ending up hating anybody. Or anybody hating him.'

TM leaned back into the sofa, stretching his shoulders out like a lazy cat. Michel Furcoat sat on his head. 'It was weird,' he said. 'Veg spent a while hooking up with anyone that came near him, but they were always decent. Then the Swede came along, and for some reason Veggie just couldn't see that he was… not decent.'

'So he was just a… bad guy?'

'Basically,' TM said. 'Veggie always saw the best in everyone. He still does, but I think it hurts him pretty hard when people disappoint him.'

'So… when things went bad, he was upset because he thought the Swede was a better person than he was? He'd been fooled?'

'I don't think he thought of it as being fooled. More like wilful ignorance.' TM glanced over at his business partner, who looked up from the table and pointed at the TV.

'Keep playing, losers,' Veggie instructed.

'Anyway,' TM concluded, as they turned back to the game, 'it didn't stop him choosing to believe that everyone was the best they could possibly be. It's almost like he wants to prove the Swede wrong.'

'So that's why he was so happy to take me in so quickly?'

'Might have something to do with it. He might be a bit sore about it, but he figures the best way to get over it is just to… think of everybody as amazing. And here you are, proving him right.'

Ziggy blushed. 'I've never been used for revenge before,' she said, looking pleased at the thought. Then she tried the level again. This time she cleared the room with ease.

'Stormson?' said the handler, as she passed through the door. 'Are you still – good gravy granules in heaven, Stormson, you were quieter than my Catholic grandmother at my gay brother's wedding.'

Ziggy giggled. 'It's got some character,' she said. 'I think I like this game.'

'Just try to follow the plot,' TM warned her. 'It gets complicated reeaaaal quick.'

Ziggy skipped the next bit of plot by accident. 'Whoops,' she said.

'Okay, forget about the plot for now,' TM suggested.

Ziggy complied, moving slowly through a series of walled gardens. She slithered up ladders and over rooftops, making less sound than an enormous stack of stereo speakers with giant bass-enhancing subwoofers and treble reverb that goes up to eleven... all of which are, of course, switched off.

'Okay, Stormson,' said the handler, presumably via an earpiece. 'See that guard on the balcony over there?'

'Not more guards,' Ziggy moaned.

'You'll need to take him out from a distance, without alerting any other guards who might be nearby,' the handler instructed. 'Try your tranquiliser rifle. You could always decide to just shoot him with your pistol, but that sort of noise is going to attract attention. Besides, why kill him when you don't need to?'

'Aww,' said Ziggy. 'I like this guy. He's nice.'

She drew her tranquiliser gun, aimed and fired. The guard went limp and toppled over the edge of the balcony.

'Well,' said the handler in Stormson's ear, 'at least you *tried* not to kill him.'

'That's *such bullshit*,' said Ziggy. 'Next guy I see, I'm leaving him alive, no matter what.'

Stormson slinked through another few streets' worth of slate-tiled rooftops before stopping and staring up at a tall building.

'Alright, this is the destination,' the handler instructed. 'Your target is inside: the codes to the nuclear weapons. They're stored on a computer terminal on the fiftieth floor. You'll need to make your way up there, then hack it.'

'Why are there codes to nuclear weapons in some random office block in some village with hanging baskets in every garden?' Ziggy demanded, scoffing at the screen.

'I dunno,' TM said. 'You skipped the cutscene.'

Ziggy stuck her tongue out at him and waggled it about with almost disturbing levels of dexterity.

'I will hack your building, American,' she said, in a vaguely Eastern European accent, 'for the right coin.'

'That's probably xenophobic,' TM said absently.

'I'm literally from space,' Ziggy said.

TM stared at her for a moment, waiting for an explanation as to how that was a counter-argument. None was forthcoming.

'Anywoo,' Ziggy said, turning back to the game. She took Stormson up into the building via grappling hook, then turned a corner and almost ran into a guard standing with his back to them, silhouetted by moonlight shining through a full-length glass window.

'Thanks for facing out the window,' Ziggy said, creeping up behind him – but, as she approached, he turned and raised his gun. She yelped and shot him in the leg, apparently acting on sheer instinct; he grabbed it in pain and fell to the ground.

'Must have seen your reflection,' TM mused. 'You're lucky this game deals with specific body part injuries, anyway. Some of these things, you shoot a guy in the foot and he goes down holding his head. It's like Premier League football.'

'I tried to kill you,' Ziggy told the guard, who was convulsing in pain in front of Stormson. 'I am sorry about that. But on the other hand, if I hadn't accidentally shot you in the leg I would probably have tranq'd you in the face and made you fall out of the window. So... consider yourself lucky.'

She tapped a button, and Stormson smashed his knee into the hapless guard's face. He collapsed.

'Hey, TM,' Ziggy said, stashing the body away in a dark corner. 'Looks like this guy... *kneeds* a hand.'

'Are you cracking one-liners now?' TM asked, unimpressed. Stormson scampered silently up a lift shaft.

'Heck, yeah.' She pursed her lips in thought for a moment. 'What would you say if, like... you were a suave international agent, and you met your nemesis on a rooftop, and you shot him and he fell off into a vat of baked beans?'

TM blinked.

'You've got to be prepared for this sort of thing,' she said.

He pondered it. 'How about: "be careful when falling... from such a great Heinz"?'

'Not bad, all things considered,' Ziggy said, guiding Stormson up to the very top floor. 'What about: "looks like he's... bean alive"?'

'He's bean alive?'

'Well, he has. He's bean alive, and now he's dead.'

Derrida and Veggie, listening in from the table, burst out laughing. Ziggy looked as pleased as TM had ever seen her. Meanwhile, Stormson clambered out of the lift shaft into a large office room, and found himself staring into the business end of a heavy-looking pistol.

'Stormson,' said the man holding the pistol.

'Ah,' said Stormson. 'Daniel-Dirkham Dangerously, the famed spy known as Triple-D'.

Ziggy stuck out her tongue and made a loud farting noise. 'They ran out of actual names, huh. Also, well-written dialogue. I like how he sounded really angry and super explanatory at the same time, though.'

'Pretty sure the big final boss is called something like Samson B. Nuclear,' TM recalled.

'That's awesome,' Ziggy said, fingers dancing a mad jig as she tapped buttons in time with flashing prompts on the screen: Stormson ducked under the gun and tripped Triple-D with a powerful leg sweep. A decision presented itself as Stormson stood over his fallen opponent: 'PRESS X TO KILL. PRESS A TO SPARE. PRESS B TO KILL (GORY).'

'Spare,' Ziggy decided, causing Stormson to stamp on Triple-D's face. Painful, but technically non-lethal.

'You might regret leaving that loose end,' Stormson's handler warned.

'Fine,' said Stormson, turning away from his fallen opponent. 'I'll enjoy tying it up again if I have to.'

'And *there's* the smart and witty dialogue we all know and love,' Ziggy burbled, snapping her fingers. 'No bother, anyway. We beat him once at the beginning of the game, we'll just beat him again later and it'll all tie up together and it'll be satisfying and great.'

'I need to tell you the storyline for the feud I'm writing just on the off chance I ever get the opportunity to book matches for a wrestling promotion,' Veggie said off-handedly from the table behind them. 'It has all those things, honest.'

Stormson moved over to a computer in the centre of the room – moving sneakily, despite there no longer being anyone to hide from – and hacked it with ease.

'This is all a bit too easy,' Ziggy said.

'It's only the first level,' TM pointed out. 'It gets harder.'

The first level of Mikkels Stormson's grand adventure concluded as he made a note – 'On paper, no less! What a charming, old-fashioned rogue,' Ziggy gushed – of the nuclear launch codes, then fired a full magazine from his pistol into the computer.

'Time,' Veggie called; Ziggy flipped herself around on the sofa, lobbing the controller down onto the floor.

'You guys taking over, then?' she asked, pointing a thumb back over her shoulder at the TV. 'Mikey Stormdude just saved the world, or something.'

'Nice going, Stormson,' said the handler, as if on cue. 'Consider the world saved. For now.'

'Oooooooooh,' Ziggy warbled.

'Yeah, we'll take over,' Derrida said, settling in next to her on the sofa with a sigh and a slump. 'I think I remember a way to noclip through, like, half of this level.'

Ziggy stood and stretched. 'Our turn to ninja the heck out of here, then?' she said to TM, beckoning him towards the door.

'I guess so,' he said, pulling on a light hoodie and digging out the sole pair of trainers he had owned in the past five or six years. As he and Ziggy went to open the door, Marty and Dominika re-entered, red-faced and out of breath.

'How was it?' Veggie asked, taking his place next to Derrida on the sofa.

'Hecking cold,' said Marty.

'Ah.'

'Also, you just told us to go out there and do parkour, which neither of us have ever done before or have any kind of training in.'

'So... good, then?'

'Aw, yeah,' Marty proclaimed, headbanging. 'We were *awesome*.'

Veggie waved them over to the Hero's Adventure table, where Dominika set about rolling with machine-like speed. 'Have fun,' he told TM, who nodded and held the door open for Ziggy. Then they went out into the night.

15. The Dry Run

'So… how do we do this?' Ziggy asked curiously, looking around at the buildings in each street they passed through as they made their way towards the park.

'I have literally no idea,' TM admitted. 'But Veggie is Veggie, and Veggie says we have to parkour if we want to stand a chance of pulling off this museum robbery thingumabob.'

Ziggy nodded, stretching her arms behind her back as they walked. 'Thanks for being up for this whole shenanigan,' she said. 'You and Veggie. I realise this is far from the most organised or professional burglary prep, but… it means a lot anyway.'

'You're our friend,' TM said with a shrug. 'We'd both do the same for Veggie if he decided he wanted to rob… somewhere. Within reason.'

'I mean, Veggie basically *did* decide he wanted to rob somewhere and I just gave him an excuse to actually do it, right?'

TM sighed. 'Something like that.'

They rounded a corner and the park came into view, at which point TM realised that he knew even less about parkour than he'd thought. 'Come to think of it,' he said, 'I'm not sure a flat, open space is actually the best sort of place to practice this stuff.'

'Mm,' Ziggy concurred. 'I was thinking more… like, climbing up buildings, jumping between rooftops. Mikkels Stormson the heck out of this city, y'know?'

TM nodded, thinking. 'We can start there,' he said, pointing to a narrow alleyway leading towards the city centre. Multiple dumpsters stood within, going about their dumpster business. 'Narrow walls, easy to get up to the top, use the bins for a bit of a boost up.'

'I like your thinking,' said Ziggy. 'Then just piss about on the rooftops for a bit, sound good?'

'Heck yeah.'

They took off at a light jog towards the alley; TM drew ahead as they reached the entrance. He hoped to look impressive and not fall on his arse like a dick, but was entirely unconvinced that that would in fact be what ended up happening. He vaulted atop one of the large bins with ease, slapping one palm down hard and hurdling up, then jumped and kicked off against the wall.

'You've done this before,' Ziggy said, folding her arms with a grin as TM hauled himself onto the low roof opposite the bins.

'Believe me,' TM said, 'I'm just as amazed as you that I didn't just miss completely and fall to my ignoble death.'

'My go,' Ziggy proclaimed, hoisting herself up on the lid of one of the bins.

She crouched, holding her arms out for balance and wiggling her toes in her shoes, then leapt for the roof. TM watched as she rose into the air, reaching up and out. He continued to watch as she reached the peak of her jump and started falling back to earth. He started to assemble a consolidating expression on his face, to form some sentence to the effect of 'good try'. He even thought about fumbling his next jump to make her feel better.

She dropped out of view, slammed against the wall with a thud, then came up over the lip and alighted gracefully.

'How the shit,' said TM. He looked her over suspiciously. 'Can you fly?'

'Naw,' she said, sounding half-regretful about it. 'I just… used the wall like a floor. Jumped up. Wheeeee.'

'You're some sort of gravity wizard,' TM accused.

'Possible,' Ziggy admitted. 'Hey, before we go off to be incredibly awesome and all that…'

She stepped back over to the edge of the rooftop and sat herself down, legs dangling off into the alleyway. TM plonked next to her.

'What's up?'

'Eh, I was just thinking about some stuff.'

'Hit me.'

Ziggy's eyes moved around, catching various objects in her roving stare. She seemed to be trying to come up with the right words. Then she sighed through pursed lips, like a smoker blowing the fumes from her lungs. 'Heck, I dunno.'

'Pff.' TM slouched back onto his elbows, crossing his legs. 'I think one of the most human of feelings is that sense of having all sorts of massive thoughts but not being totally sure what they're about.'

Ziggy smiled. 'I guess I must be really human, then.'

'I used to know a girl,' TM said. 'You remind me of her a bit, actually.'

'Ooh, a girl.'

'She was... well, she was a person. Like you. But she also seemed as if she was something other than a person. Not more or less, not higher or lower, just... sideways.'

'Like she had a bit of something else in her?'

'Yeah. A bit like you. You're a person, but you're also something else. I almost said you're not quite a person, but that's not true, you're one hundred percent a person. You just must be more than one hundred percent overall.'

'Hundred percent human, hundred percent giant ball of burning space gas,' Ziggy agreed.

'Anyway, this girl had a lot of thoughts. About a lot of stuff. I felt like I couldn't keep up with her a lot of the time, to be honest.'

Ziggy patted his arm. 'I feel like I can't keep up with you sometimes, Veggie other times, Derrida pretty much all the time, myself constantly.'

'Understanding yourself might be the hardest thing a person has to do,' TM mused.

'I think I understand you more than myself,' Ziggy told him. 'Seems like that's kind of normal, though. Like there's some barrier when people try to know themselves, but it's easier to know other people.'

'Maybe empathy comes more easily than self-reflection,' TM suggested. 'Or maybe it's easier to be honest about who and what someone else really is than what you yourself are.'

'Hmm.'

* * *

'Do you ever think about infinity?' Aster asked TM once, in the middle of the night.

'All the time,' TM replied, much less than half-awake.

'It's kind of misleading that we tend to think of it as just another number, you know?' she continued. TM got the feeling that she would carry on talking whether he woke up and listened or not, but felt that the polite thing to do would be to sit up and attend, so he did. 'But it's kind of like the mind. It's something that's really quite unlike anything else.'

'Makes sense,' TM reasoned. 'Nothing finite can be sensibly said to approach infinity, so...' He trailed off, sleepiness making him forget how the sentence was supposed to end. 'So,' he finished unsatisfactorily.

'So it's sort of in a class of its own,' Aster picked up. 'I don't think we can even really sensibly attempt to comprehend what it actually is. I mean, the universe is infinite, and we're a part of it. I don't think you can even say the universe is made up of us, we're such a tiny constituent. We're like a speck of dust in a cathedral the size of China.'

'Except even that's still way too big.'

'We make up... very, very slightly more than zero percent of everything. The percentage of everything that we take up is a number with a zero, a decimal point, and then infinite zeroes. More zeroes than you could write on a piece of paper that was infinitely large.'

'But if they're both infinite...'

'See, it doesn't make sense to think of it as a number. Writing an infinite number of zeroes won't fit on an infinitely large piece of paper, but the infinitely large piece of paper has to be infinitely larger than the infinite amount of space that the zeroes would take up.'

'Some infinities are bigger than others?' TM hazarded.

'If anything's truly infinite,' said Aster, 'it's got to be infinitely larger than every other infinity. But if those are also true infinities, they also have to be infinitely larger, so I guess every true infinity is both infinitely larger and infinitely smaller than every other.'

TM was beginning to wish he'd just gone back to sleep. 'So nothing can actually be anywhere near infinite, then,' he reasoned. 'Just finitely enormous.'

'I think I could end up thinking about this for an infinite amount of time and not getting any closer to an answer,' Aster said, pulling the duvet up under her chin.

'You wouldn't have any time to do anything else,' TM pointed out. Aster laughed and ran a hand through her hair, which was bright even in the darkness.

'Look at me,' she said. 'I was going on at you about spending less time breaking stuff down, and here's me trying to divide up infinity.'

'Well, we're a part of infinity,' TM said, 'if an infinitely small part.'

Aster bit the inside of her cheek, then sighed and patted him on the chest. 'Did you know,' she said abruptly, 'my name is a part of another word? Or, I guess, the word is made up of the same letters that my name is made up of?'

TM was vaguely aware of at least one word that had 'aster' in it, but let her make her point.

'Disaster means "bad star". "Dis" for "bad", "Aster" for "star".'

'I was thinking mast –' TM trailed off. 'Oh, wait, that's a "u", not an "e".'

Aster ignored that. 'It's because they used to think that comets were evil omens, a bad star announcing hard times to come.'

'I guess they were trying to break down the world into things that affected them,' TM said. 'I mean, if they were right, it would have been useful for survival and stuff. They'd have been able to prepare better for the bad times.'

'If they were right,' Aster repeated. 'Maybe that's why people nowadays forget to appreciate the world. We're all hardwired to be constantly trying to break it down for survival. Only music manages to bypass that, for most people.'

'Music?'

'You can't get that emotional feeling that music gives unless you manage to ignore the drive to be picking it apart. I mean, that's a perfectly valid thing to do, and some people can understand everything about a piece and still get really touched by it. But they'll never again feel the way it made them feel that first time they heard it, before they knew where it was going to go every time.'

'That's kind of depressing.'

'I guess we just need to keep finding stuff to experience for the first time.'

***

'Uh, TM?'

'Hm?'

'Seemed like you kind of zoned out for a bit there. We were just talking, and then…'

'Oh.' TM blinked, realising again that he had feet, and hands, and that there was a cold breeze on his skin. 'Yeah, happens sometimes. Sorry.'

'What were you thinking about, anyway?'

TM sighed. 'That girl I was telling you about.'

'You think about her a lot?'

'I, er…' TM scratched at an itch at the base of his skull. His face and neck felt warmer than the rest of him. 'She pops up every now and then. Not so much since I met you, though, actually.'

'I'm a distraction,' Ziggy said, smiling. 'You said I remind you of her, though?'

'A bit. In some ways.'

She looked away. 'Sorry. Seems like you'd maybe prefer not to be reminded too much.'

'There's no point trying to forget,' TM told her. 'Veggie's not trying to forget about the Swede. He just doesn't let that be part of his life any more.'

'So she's not part of your life any more?'

'Nah, she… left.'

'Oh,' said Ziggy. She seemed to be unable to meet his eyes. 'I'm sorry about that.'

'I'm over it,' TM told her. He was never sure when he woke up each day whether that was true. 'It doesn't do any good to try to forget that it happened, 'cos it did. And it doesn't do any good to think about how it might have been different, 'cos it was her choice and all people deserve to make their own choices and have them respected.' He cleared his throat and fell silent, having said more than he'd expected to.

Ziggy hummed for a moment. 'I think I might be able to tell you the stuff I was thinking now, if you wanted a distraction?'

'Fire away.'

'So when I was being Mikkels Stormson and it was all... like... pew pew...'

'Are you talking about when you shot those dudes?'

'Specifically the one that I didn't want to kill,' Ziggy said, folding her arms. 'That wasn't cool.'

'Oh, yeah, you tranquilised him and he fell off and died,' TM remembered.

'It just made me think about... death,' Ziggy said.

TM sat there for a moment, nodding and thinking. 'Death,' he repeated.

'I don't want to die,' Ziggy said.

TM had not an inkling of what the appropriate response to that might be.

'Me neither,' he said, which seemed insufficient but was the best he could come up with.

'It's weird,' she continued, fingers tapping against each of her arms. 'I don't know that you could say I was alive until a few days ago, but I really don't want to not be alive any more.'

'So what were you before you were alive?' TM asked. 'I mean, you must have been some sort of... thing that existed, if you were able to decide you wanted to run away from the sky and come down here to be with us.'

'I think I was conscious, but not in the same way as I am now,' she said. Her lips opened and closed a few times; her tongue flicked against the roof of her mouth; her teeth bit down on her bottom lip. Then she huffed. 'It's hard to explain.'

'Everything seems to be, these days,' TM said.

'I mean, being conscious is weird,' Ziggy said, as if starting an entirely new conversation. 'It's really, really weird.'

'Totally unlike anything else,' TM concurred, remembering a conversation from long ago.

'And it seems to just kind of pop up as this happy little side effect of the way the brain's put together, which is pretty neat.'

'So who's to say that something similar – totally different, because sentience is so unique, but kind of in the same vein – might not have arisen out of the way other stuff's put together?' TM continued for her. The words felt strange coming out of his mouth. They were his words, but words that had been put there long ago by another star-girl, one long since gone to burn brightly elsewhere in the cosmos. 'Like the universe might have its own mind, in a way.'

Ziggy gave him a funny look. 'Exactly,' she said, sounding uncertain. 'Y'know, I get the sense that you're… I don't know, following a script here. Or repeating something. Like it's not really you saying that.'

'That's the thing about consciousness,' TM said. 'It passes little fragments of itself on to other bits of consciousness, and that way it lives on even when it's gone.'

Ziggy opened her mouth as if to say something, but nothing came out. She closed it again, then laughed quietly.

'What?'

'I just like that idea,' she said. 'Even when we're gone, there'll be bits of our lives, or words we've said, that have reproduced themselves in other minds. Like we're a tree dropping seed pods into other people and sprouting little offspring. Continuing.'

TM shook his head, feeling as if he were tumbling down some rabbit hole into a past life, a memory of a girl that would always live within him but that could never again be real. 'Anyway, maybe when you were a star you were conscious, just in a different sort of way.'

Ziggy nodded, rolling the idea around in her brain. 'Sounds about right.'

'D'you reckon there are more? Like you?'

'Don't see why not,' she said. 'Heck, maybe Veggie's one and you just never noticed.'

TM considered this. 'So… there could be loads of people who are secretly stars, just living as people?'

'I guess. Still fairly convinced I have a twin somewhere. At least, I did up there. Don't know whether she'd have come down too.'

TM clasped his hands behind his head and lay back, looking up at the sky. The stars were starting to twinkle above, albeit behind a thick layer of cloud. 'The world's a weird place, when you get down to it,' he said.

'Course it is,' Ziggy told him, standing and shaking her limbs out. 'It's totally ridiculous that anything even exists in the first place, so you just have to roll with it. Look, I'm starting to freeze out here, so let's tear up these rooftops, yo?'

With that, she set off at a brisk run, kicked off the ground and soared up and over the gap between their rooftop and the next. TM stood, stretched, and thought about how lucky it was that all the buildings in the area happened to have largely flat and traversable rooftops.

'Come on,' she called back to him. 'We've got training to do, or something.'

TM smiled to himself and followed her. He cleared the space between buildings less gracefully than the girl running ahead of him; she began to tumble across the cityscape, spinning and launching herself over the gaps. He was more cautious, hurtling smaller obstacles and stopping to check the distance of larger ones before hopping across. Somehow, he never fell too far behind.

'Oh, hey,' she said suddenly, sliding to a halt atop what TM thought might have been a supermarket. The thought reminded him that they really did need to go food shopping – and soon, and probably buy more vegetables than last time – but Ziggy's insistent pointing put an end to his mental shopping list composition. 'It's the museum,' she said.

'Oh, yeah,' TM realised, following her pointing finger across the street. The museum stood there, as always. It looked less exciting than the last time they'd visited, nothing more or less than a plain building without the crows and the spectacle of the rock on a pedestal behind the coloured rope. Its only distinguishing feature was the high, pointed roof and the generic angel atop it.

'We should scope the place out,' Ziggy muttered, thumb resting on her chin, forefinger tapping her cheek. 'No point practising all this stuff if we get in there and realise we haven't got a clue where we need to go.'

'That would suck,' TM agreed. 'So I guess we just hop down, waltz in through the front door and… actually just visit the museum?'

'Something like that,' said Ziggy, nodding. 'Sort of surprised we didn't already think that might be worth doing.'

'Hm,' said TM. 'First question, though: how do we get down?'

Ziggy shuffled over to the edge of the roof and peered down. 'I don't think we can jump,' she said earnestly. 'So that one's out.'

'Not sure it was ever in,' TM mumbled, scratching his head. 'Any, er… pipes to slide down?'

Ziggy dropped to all fours, craning her neck to examine the wall below. 'There's a few ledges and stuff,' she said. 'Nothing major, but I reckon I got this.'

'What,' TM started to say, but only got as far as 'wh' before Ziggy stood, raised her arms and fell forwards, swan-diving off the rooftop. TM dashed over, staring down to the street, and saw her leaning casually against the wall, both feet safely on the ground.

'How!' he yelled down at her, flailing his arms about so as to communicate both how impressed he was and how utterly distressed and confused he was.

'I just grabbed a few sticky-outy bits on the way down, slowed myself down a bit,' she explained, unsatisfactorily.

'I'm taking this ladder down,' TM said; Ziggy groaned in mock disappointment.

'Let-down,' she accused with a smug grin. 'Fair play for actually spotting that, though. I think I was just excited to jump.'

TM slid down the fire escape, which they had both entirely failed to miss at first glance and which seemed slightly superfluous given that there was nothing whatsoever on the roof.

'What can I say?' he said, spreading his arms in mock apology. 'I'm not a gravity wizard.'

She ruffled his hair affectionately. 'I think I made myself a bit lighter,' she said, looking down at herself. 'Helped with the fall, I guess, but… I don't think I like it.'

TM couldn't tell the difference, if he was honest. On close inspection, she might have been slightly skinnier. He didn't really mind one way or the other.

'This museum is free to get in, right?' she asked him as they crossed the street.

'It was the last time I was here,' he told her, deciding to omit the fact that he hadn't been in over ten years. 'Donations accepted or something, probably.'

They hopped up the steps and entered; the old building was barely any warmer than the crisp outdoors. There were one or two people knocking about: not many, and not enthusiastically.

'It'll be closing soon,' TM said, getting his bearings.

'Ooh, look,' Ziggy twittered, ignoring him, 'they've got a stuffed giraffe.'

'Depressing.' TM shivered, glancing up at the dead animal's face with distaste. 'Let's just look for the rock, yeah?'

'Aw, come on,' Ziggy entreated him, reading a map stuck on the wall behind a thin sheet of what looked like glass but was probably plastic. Or clingfilm. 'We've got, like, a whole hour and a half left before Veggie wants us back, let's have a look around at least.'

TM watched her go for a moment, then followed. She meandered through the corridors, stopping every few steps to read the labels under the rows of jars and plates and ancient masks.

'History is cool,' she said, examining a suit of centurion's armour. 'Can I put this on?'

'Probably not. Hey, look at this: "the constellations according to the ancients".'

'*Boring*,' Ziggy yawned. 'Come on, man, I came down here to get away from all that stuff. How would you like it if you ran away from home and the guys you were staying with kept deciding it would be fun to talk about your parents?'

'I guess that wouldn't be the best,' TM admitted. 'Sorry.'

'No worries.'

She trundled around for a few more minutes, until eventually deciding that it might be time to go and see the thing around which her entire life aspirations had revolved since she first laid eyes upon it.

'I warn you,' she said, half-seriously, 'I may just attempt to take it now.'

'Don't do that,' TM said, trotting after her as she headed for the back of the building. 'Although it might save us a bit of time and effort if you did.'

'I want it,' she said. 'I *want* it. And I don't even know why. Isn't that stupid?'

'I think that might just be normal, actually.'

The largest room, spanning the entire width of the building and boasting a ceiling twice as high as any other room in the place, was reserved for 'special exhibitions'. Generally, this would entail perhaps a guitar once played by some one-time musician who had been entirely the least memorable member of their briefly-notable ensemble; on multiple occasions, when nothing else was forthcoming, it had served as a gallery, walls lined with children's colour-in sheets depicting various historical figures. This space rock, if space rock it in fact were, was quite possibly the most interesting thing ever to occupy the room. In keeping with its lofty status, it had attracted one of the largest crowds ever to attend such an exhibit at this museum: three entire people were in the room examining it when Ziggy entered. TM trundled in behind her, struggling to keep up.

'How does this place stay in business?' Ziggy wondered aloud; TM shrugged.

'By having absolutely no expenditures whatsoever, I guess,' he suggested, noticing the complete and utter lack of staff, security, wallpaper or other budget-draining miscellanea.

'Isn't it beautiful?' said one of the patrons in a familiar voice, lightly accented with the telltale vowels of one who has received extensive training on how to speak 'properly'.

TM glanced up at the rock, sealed within a large glass cube on a high pedestal. Vibrant beams all the colours of the rainbow shone through it from large theatre lights, which seemed to TM not to have been fully thought through on account of the fact that shining white light at the rock scattered whole spectra just as effectively. Then he looked at the man who had spoken, and blinked in surprise.

'Oh, hey,' he said to Al Tyer, who gave a small nod without taking his eyes from the exhibit.

'The cosmos is ever so interesting these days, don't you think?' Tyer asked rhetorically. It might have been the longest sentence TM had ever heard him say, having only ever watched the weather with the sound off.

'I... guess,' TM said; Ziggy nodded wordlessly, her eyes flickering between Tyer and the rock. No other part of her moved a millimetre.

'Stars going missing,' Tyer continued, 'stars dimming. Entire constellations appearing to fall through the sky, if only for a moment.'

'Hadn't heard about that one,' TM said.

'It's all rather concerning, really,' said Tyer matter-of-factly. 'As above, so below.'

'Er, right.'

'You see,' Tyer carried on, and TM became more convinced as time went on that Tyer had no idea that anyone was even there, and was in fact just talking to the rock, 'this place is only the lowest, least fundamental level of an infinite universe. The most… contingent.' He glanced down for a moment, his grey eyes leaving the rock for the first time. He pinched the bridge of his nose as if in discomfort, then resumed his upwards gaze. 'This planet, every planet, is entirely beneath the notice of that which is above.'

'What's above?' Ziggy said; TM thought he detected half a shiver in her voice.

Tyer's head revolved to look at her, the rest of his neat-suited body remaining perfectly still. 'I don't know,' he said. 'That is… above my pay grade, as it were. But whatever it is, it is far more fundamental than anything below it, and it is entirely uncaring.'

'So the universe doesn't care about us,' said TM. 'That's fine.'

'You make your own purpose, then,' Tyer said, not taking his eyes from Ziggy. She stared down at her feet. 'That's admirable, I suppose. Don't you think, though: a meaning you make for yourself, whatever it might be, is by necessity less of a meaning than one ordained by the universe?'

'Nah,' TM said. He stepped back and put a protective arm around Ziggy. Her body felt tense, as if trying hard not to shake. 'You said the universe doesn't care about me, so I don't give too much of a shit about it either.'

'Hm,' said Tyer. His gaze made its way to TM's face. 'We need our stars back.'

TM shook his head and started dragging Ziggy towards the exit as gently and surreptitiously as he could while keeping his eyes fixed on

Tyer.

'Reality is just forces,' Tyer proclaimed. 'Gravity gives no thought to the damage that could be done by a shift of a few degrees in an orbit. The changing of the stars...' He shook his head as if disappointed. 'Gravity may unintentionally be collapsing everything.'

'I thought you were a weatherman, not a conspiracy theorist,' TM said. He narrowed his eyes at Tyer, doing his best to get Ziggy – who shuffled slowly, too slowly as he pulled her along – away from him.

'I am a local celebrity,' said Al Tyer. 'We are many things.'

'Great, good for you,' TM told him, reaching the door at last. He had no idea which door it was, no guess as to which corridor or section of exhibits it might lead to, only that it would take them away from Al Tyer.

He pulled it open.

'Have a nice day,' he said, and stepped through. Tyer's eyes, unblinking, followed them until the door closed. TM had never been so glad to have a few centimetres of wood between himself and another person.

Beside him, Ziggy let out an enormous lungful of air. It sounded as if she were breathing for the first time since they had encountered Tyer.

'I want to go home,' she said, her arms folded around herself. TM could see her upper arms turning white as her fingers dug into them.

'Yeah, I think so,' TM agreed, leading her down the corridor.

Ancient masks, suits of armour, rusted weapons leered and loomed down from the walls on either side; Ziggy shrank away from them, making herself as small as she could. TM, one arm still around her shoulders, thought he could feel her body physically shrinking.

They emerged into the street; the sun was half-visible over the rooftops, setting more quickly than TM would have liked. He looked up, and the few stars that were already visible seemed to shake, then flare brightly. He blinked, and everything was back to its normal luminescence.

'I'm real, but I'm not real,' Ziggy whispered. 'Real, but not real.'

'Whoa,' TM said, holding her hand firmly. 'What's up?'

'He got to me,' she said, her free hand moving across her body from hair to arm to chest and back again. Her fingers clenched and wriggled as if trying to scratch an itch, hold onto something so she didn't drift away, and cover herself for protection and warmth all at the same time.

'I know he's a bit weird,' TM concurred, leading her through the streets back towards the flat, 'but... you don't have to feel anything about it. You're with me, we're going home and we're gonna just be the most generally sweet people in the world, okay?'

'He's not just weird,' she said. 'He's not *from* here.'

TM stuttered and sighed, stuttered again and sighed again, then settled for: 'Are you okay?' It was a dumb question, he knew it, but he needed to say something.

'Him and O'Ryan,' she muttered. 'O'Ryan and him, and... me.'

'They make you feel weird, right?' TM said, grasping for something he could latch on to, something he could identify. If he could identify something, he might be able to fix it. 'You never seem to be able to move around O'Ryan, even just on TV.'

'Imagine standing between two walls pressing in on you,' Ziggy said. Her eyes pointed blankly to the ground, her feet moving along as if she thought she might forget how to walk if she stopped even for a moment. 'Or two black holes. All that gravity, fundamental forces, all of that pulling you and pushing you and imposing a place on you.'

'That's what it's like for you just being around them?'

'It's like how I felt when I had an orbit to stick to. Nothing to do but fall down the path set by the gravity of all the other stars. Like being on a rollercoaster, going around the loop and forgetting which way is up. Every direction just feels like falling, and you couldn't leave the path of the rails if you wanted.'

TM concentrated on walking for a few moments. Then: 'What did you mean, real but not real?'

Ziggy shook her head. TM felt as if she were trying to shake something free, or perhaps to remind herself of where she was, and that she even was in the first place. 'I killed people,' she said. 'In those video games.'

'You didn't really kill people, Zig,' TM told her. 'They weren't really people, just... skeletons of binary bits under source code muscles wearing pixel skins.'

'But I did,' she insisted. 'Just because they weren't the same sort of people as you and me doesn't mean that they didn't exist. How would we be talking about them if they didn't exist?'

'Metaphysics isn't my strong suit,' TM had to admit.

'If we're talking about something, then that something exists. If only as a thing we're referring to and not as an actual physical thing, but it's still real. If something's fictional, it might not be part of the same level of reality as you, but that doesn't mean it doesn't have an existence. Like... you can say you killed someone.

'That means nothing unless you're really talking about something. Or... Okada lost to Tanahashi. That's a sentence you can say, and it's true, even though it's a story and they're characters and he didn't really lose because the result was predetermined.'

'So... existence is just a matter of which level of reality you're on.'

Ziggy stumbled, then righted herself. 'How are we supposed to know which level we're on?' she wondered. 'When I die, maybe I'll only be dead in this little bit of existence but someone on a higher level will be able to just... look back and see me when I was still here. Like starting a new game, bringing all those people back to life that you spent so long murdering.'

TM frowned as he worked out the implications. 'I guess since we've decided they do exist in some meaningful way, that means that they really are alive or dead, or... dying. So... we really do kill them, in a sense.'

'It's all just in a sense,' Ziggy said. TM could feel her leaning, more of her weight depending on his support to keep moving. Her hair was losing its colour. 'Everything's just... in one sense or the other.'

'We're back,' TM told her. She released a breath and nodded.

TM pushed open the door of the flat, still holding her hand tightly, and they swept in to see Veggie, Derrida, Marty and Dominika all taking their seats at the table. All four heads turned in their direction as the door swung open, and Ziggy collapsed into a seat between Marty and Dominika.

16. Boss Battle

'You guys okay?' Marty asked.

'Bit of a weird... encounter,' TM explained.

Veggie flashed a concerned look at TM - who had wandered over to the table and was standing over the group, feeling as if he had forgotten how to sit down - then at Ziggy, who was resting her head on Marty's shoulder and looking as if she might cry. 'Whassup?'

'We, er, ran into Al Tyer.'

Derrida tucked their foot behind the leg of the chair beside TM and pulled it around so that the seat was behind him; TM let his knees go loose and slumped into it.

'It was kind of surreal,' TM said, rubbing the back of his head.

'Al Tyer?' Derrida said, pouting. 'Wouldn't have had him down as the parkour type.'

'He's not, as far as I know. We just popped into the museum, to check it out before -' he became conscious of Derrida, Marty, and Dominika's eyes all on him '- before the space rock exhibition's over. And, well, Tyer was there, and he kinda freaked Z out.'

Dominika reached over and put her arm around Ziggy; Ziggy squeezed it gratefully.

'What did he do to freak you out?' Veggie asked Ziggy; she shook her head.

'Just said some stuff,' she said quietly.

'As above, so below,' TM recalled.

'That's what I heard O'Ryan saying to him,' Veggie said thoughtfully. 'He seemed kind of freaked out by it, but...' He trailed off, exhaling uncertainly. 'I guess weathermen are just a weird sort of bunch.'

'Seemed like more than that,' TM said quietly. 'Like he was... scared, or trying to scare us. Like he knew something we didn't, and he wanted us to know it.'

'Forget about that guy,' Marty said, patting Ziggy on the shoulder. 'He's barely even a minor celebrity, what does he know?'

'Maybe his very low-level fame got to him,' Derrida suggested. 'He's had a teensy tiny taste of the high life and it's driven him crazy. Or something.'

'The way he was talking,' TM said, then paused and thought about it for a second. 'I don't know. It's just, the way he sounded, I don't think I'd be surprised if something's got to him and made him... a bit... not right.'

'Huh,' said Veggie. 'So Al Tyer's had a breakdown. Might see if I can sell that story to the papers or something.'

'I'm writing it first,' Derrida said quickly.

'Ignore the dumb weatherman, Z,' said Marty quietly. 'What would he know about anything anyway?'

Ziggy gave a hesitant nod, fingers digging into her cheek. Then she sat upright, breaths spilling from her body in hesitant waves.

'Need a distraction?' Veggie asked. She nodded: first to him, then to Dominika, who released her tight hug reluctantly but kept a hold on Ziggy's hand. 'Awright,' Veggie said, flourishing his campaign papers with an overly dramatic flick of the wrist. TM caught his eye and gave him a small smile; Veggie's eyebrows twitched reassuringly back at him.

Okay! So!

Since we left off, our most excellent and well-travelled heroes have been training like crazy for many days, down in Rusk's lovely basement. The time spent down in his training camp has made everyone stronger, more dextrous, more agile – even smarter and more charismatic. They're well-rested, fully-healed, levelled-up and just generally better stats'd to high heaven.

One morning, about a week after they first made the acquaintance of the Leaf of Lanriel, Rusk gathers our brave adventurers in his fancy office above Leaf HQ.

'Mornin', fella,' says Malachi.

'Oh, come on,' Derrida said despairingly. 'We're one minute in and you're already out of character?'

'Sorry,' said Marty, his tone entirely unapologetic. 'Gotta get back in the right mindset, or something. Hang on, let's give this a go.'

'Lo and behold, Master Rusk, he who commandeth the Leaves, and the Branches, and the Berries. May all creation and its bountiful tree be the

willing and honourable subject of thou and thee's brilliance.' Malachi does a backflip and a curtsy and a salute all at the same time.

'It's thee and thine,' Derrida corrected. 'Also, you should have had to roll for that.' Marty made a 'pfft' noise and waved his hand to indicate something flying right over his head, to which Derrida could only sigh. 'Fine,' he conceded. 'You talk how you want.'

'Sup,' Malachi says.

'Good morning,' Rusk says, studying the heroes. 'You all seem to be well-developed.'

'Is he saying we have nice boobs?' TM asked; Dominika snorted.

'No, he's –' Veggie rubbed his forehead in exasperation. 'He's talking about your development in the areas of heroic-ness and theivering-itude, you know?'

'You all appear to be well-trained and as if you have become more skilful,' Rusk says, very clearly and unambiguously.

'Why, thank you,' says Barry. 'We appreciate the generosity of the Leaf, allowing us to use these facilities to train and heal.'

'I think loaning you the use of these headquarters is the smallest of prices to pay in return for the liberation of this city.'

'He's very optimistic, isn't he?' Derrida observed.

'Today,' Rusk continues, without breaking step, 'is the first day of the beginning of a new era of the lives of the people of the city of Lanriel.'

'... of the country of the nation of the continent of the world of the universe...' Marty muttered; Dominika grinned, and the corner of Ziggy's mouth perked upwards for the first time since the museum. Veggie looked ready to defend himself, but saw Ziggy smiling and dropped it.

'Today is the day of a big quest,' Rusk clarifies.

'We're ready,' says Barry..

'Good.' *Rusk spreads a set of floor plans and a few pages of notes across his desk.*

Veggie obligingly slid his own, hand-drawn copies of the documents across the table; the group peered in at them.

'These are the plans to the Imperial Citadel of Lanriel,' Rusk explains, pointing helpfully. 'They should help you to navigate. And these are some

notes on the residents.'

'Looks like there are possible hostages in there,' Malachi says thoughtfully, casting his eye over the pages. *'Two imperial cousins of the corrupted line, Lanfal and Linske Lanriel-Lanlanar, are usurping the power and holding the citadel with the help of their trusted bodyguards Tank and Fist. Then there are a few other cousins from one of the more well-liked branches, including Lienna, Lalto and Limlia Lanriel-Lestenal –'*

Marty broke character again for a second. 'You're terrible at coming up with names, Veg. I mean, do all the members of the Lanriel family have names beginning with L?'

'Yup,' said Veggie proudly. 'And aaaaaall the cousins.'

'We're never going to remember them all,' TM said.

'Fine,' said Veggie, looking distinctly put out. 'There's Evil Cousins 1 and 2 and Nice Cousins 1, 2, and 3. And Bodyguards 1 and 2.'

'That's probably easier,' Marty said. Veggie pulled his pages of notes back across the table, crossing out a few lines.

'I did a whole family tree and everything,' he said dejectedly.

'Anyway,' says Malachi, *'we'll basically want to eliminate both Evil Cousins, plus both bodyguards, while also saving the Nice Cousins.'*

'That's about the essence of it,' agrees Rusk.

'Well, sounds easy enough,' Malachi says. Atgard hisses his willingness to go off and do violent stuff.

'We'll prepare you,' says Rusk, *'with tools, equipment... items. That sort of thing.'*

'Oh, good,' said Derrida, 'tools *and* equipment.'

Veggie pulled out a pile of tokens from somewhere and cast them across the table, each a hand-cut circle of cardboard with the name of some useful piece of gear embossed in marker pen. The group scrabbled to collect them; Dominika immediately plucked out 'grappling hook' and 'super jumpy boots', at which everyone else groaned enviously.

'Zig, you're a roguish type,' said Marty, picking up 'hidden blade' and 'awesome parachute'. 'You can probably make best use of these.'

'Aw, thanks,' said Ziggy, taking the tokens gratefully. TM watched her expression as she added the little cutouts to her stack of papers and ability cards: to his relief, the uncertainty, confusion and fear that had been written all over her face a few short minutes ago seemed to have faded away.

'We won't let you down,' says L.

Atgard preps himself with spring-loaded pile bunker gauntlets designed to pierce, punch, pummel and generally precipitate progress.

'He's not much of a climber,' Derrida admitted, 'but he can bash his way through anything you lot can scamper up.'

Malachi sorts himself out with a bulky tome of spells designed for concealing, revealing, sneakily assassinating and such.

Meanwhile, L kits up in the accoutrements of an accomplished rogue, equipped with a folding repeater crossbow, a pouch of curved throwing knives, a hidden extending blade in a bracer at her wrist, a light cloak shimmering with charms of camouflage, a folded parachute in a satchel strapped at her back, a set of daggers of many trick varieties, a pair of goggles imbued with magics of revealing -

'Whoaaaaa now,' said Marty. 'Where are you getting all this?'

'Menemenmnenmn,' said Ziggy, grinning at him.

'Hm,' said Marty suspiciously.

'Look,' said Ziggy, 'the whole thieving, sneaking, roguey thing? Kind of my deal. L's deal.'

'Fair point.'

Anyway. Barry has a brand-new, all-black set of leather armour, flexibly designed to enable him to make the best use of his Shadowguard abilities, and a set of small pouches filled with various powders explosive, smoky, toxic and all sorts. And a map, because that'll probably be useful.

Iveline has a new assortment of compact bows and crossbows concealed in various places on her body, and a quiver of different types of arrows, plus her shiny new grappling hook and a pair of slim-fitting leather boots with extra-springy heels for added jumpage.

'I think I might have given out too many gadgets,' Veggie noted.

'Naaaahhhhhhh,' TM drawled. 'I'm sure they'll all come in handy.'

'I will be extremely satisfied and thoroughly shocked if every one of these things turns out to specifically come in handy,' said Derrida.

'Good luck on your quest,' says Rusk. 'We will all owe you our freedom and gratitude for as long as we live, if you should succeed.'

'When *we* succeed, you mean,' says Barry in a really heroic voice.

'A really heroic voice?' Derrida said. 'I think you should probably have to roll for that.'

'Fine,' said TM, and rolled. Both of his dice landed face up, both displaying the highest possible result. 'HECK, YEAH!' he declared, leaping up out of his chair onto the table and fist-pumping with great ferocity.

'You'll probably wish you'd saved that luck for a more dangerous time, ya know,' Veggie warned.

'Bitch, I don't care,' TM dismissed him, resuming his seat. 'Barry's fuckin' heroic.'

'WE SHALL SURELY NOT FAIL IN THIS DIVINELY-ORDAINED QUEST WHICH YOU HAVE SET, O MASTERFUL RUSK,' bellows Barry in the most amazing heroic voice anyone has ever heard ever.

'Oh, good,' says Rusk, slightly taken aback by Barry's phenomenal lungs. 'Anyway, you should set out today. Spend the day in the city, gather information, and then at sundown make your move.'

'What sort of information do you mean?' asks L.

'Oh, y'know.' says Rusk off-handedly. 'Stuff.'

'You don't actually have anything planned for the day, do you?' TM said.

'Nope,' admitted Veggie. 'Skip to sundown?'

'Skip to sundown,' everyone agreed.

'Farewell!' declares Rusk, and the group embark out into the city.

'Oh, hang on,' said Veggie, 'I need everybody to quickly roll a research check, 'kay?'

'There's no stat for research,' Derrida complained.

'It's the average of your perception, knowledge and charisma,' Veggie told him. 'I made up a new stat.'

'You can't do that,' Derrida exclaimed, taken aback. Then they looked around at each of the group. 'Can he do that?' Everybody made some variation on the same 'ehh' noise and expression of utter apathy. 'Fine, make up your stats, whatever.'

Everybody's dice rolled, as did Derrida's eyes.

'Okey cokey,' said Veggie. 'You, you and you -' he pointed to Ziggy, Dominika and TM in turn '- all gain one useful fact about the building or its residents, which I shall reveal to you when the time comes. You -' a point to Derrida '- alienate all the citizens and nobody tells you a damn thing.' He examined Dominika's dice more closely. 'Oh, and somebody tries to steal your falcon, but it pecks their eyes out. So now the guards'll be looking out for somebody with a falcon.'

'What's its name, anyway?' Marty asked; Dominka slid her character sheet across the table at him. He flipped it over and read aloud, under the 'Pets and Familiars' section: 'One falcon. Sharp talons, good at scouting, fun icebreaker. Named Dogpet.' He handed the sheet back to her, apparently unable to help a grin that revealed his upper teeth in a somewhat creepy manner. 'You named a falcon... Dogpet.'

Dominika nodded firmly.

'I like it,' Marty said. 'High five.'

'I think we got this,' Ziggy said, folding her arms behind her head with all the lazy casualness she could muster. 'We good.'

'That's the spirit,' said Veggie.

The day passes, and each of the heroes spends some time checking out the local inns and taverns and... bars. Pubs. That sort of establishment. At any rate, all except Atgard, who being an enormous snake with giant metal punchy fists is not super conducive to friendly conversation, manage to learn something from the locals of Lanriel. When the sun goes down, our adventurers reunite before the walls of the Imperial Citadel.

'Why is it called the Imperial Citadel anyway?' Ziggy said suddenly. 'I thought the family was, like, just kind of broadly in charge, not running an empire.'

Marty laughed loudly, patting her shoulder. 'You're one of us now for sure,' he said, 'picking apart Veg's skills as Adventure Master.'

'I'd like to see you do better,' Veggie retorted.

'You know none of us could,' said TM reassuringly. 'That's why we keep you around.'

'Thanks, I think,' said Veggie, and continued.

Before the walls of the Imperial Citadel, so named because it was once home to the line of emperors who resided in Lanriel -

'Ahh,' said Ziggy.

- the heroes look up, and take in the sight of this enormous, white castle. It is a symbol of the pure, fair power and justice wielded by the Lanriel family, but that is now corrupted, so dark ivy and purple crawlers line all the perimeter.

'Subtle,' said TM.

Inside are the two cousins who currently hold the wallets paying the guards, and therefore the power of the city itself. Those are the targets of our fair and brave heroes, and before the sun rises again they must both draw their last breath.

Ziggy clapped politely as Veggie finished his speech.

'Everybody roll perception,' Derrida suggested. 'We need to find a way over these walls.'

Iveline spots a section of wall covered in thick branches of climbing plant, underneath which are various holes in the brick which could act as viable footholds. L and Iveline climb up easily with their high agility; Malachi manages to scamper up with the help of a charm of weight loss, which he just happens to have lying around and not because he's self-conscious or anything, and by hooking his sorcerer's staff over the lip; Barry absorbs himself into the many shadows crawling about, and slithers over in the darkness cast by a nearby tree.

Atgard punches the wall really hard to make bigger footholds.

'That better not have made too much noise,' TM said warningly.

'Nah,' Derrida said. 'Atgard might be a seven-foot snake built like a brick with superpowered gauntlet fists, but he's pretty light on his feet.'

'That's true,' said Veggie, looking down at his notes on each character. 'You did put it in, right there under "backstory and miscellaneous attributes": "pretty light on his feet".'

The heroes clear the first outer wall, and alight carefully down on the other side, in an open garden with lots of willow trees and babbling brooks and such.

'Well, this is nice,' *says Malachi.*

'We need to get inside without being detected,' L tells the group.

'Yes, you do, actually,' Veggie said, 'since the thing that L found out on her researchy travels today is that there are a ton of charms and spells and sorceries and magicks, and other such things, placed on the entrances to the building. If you go in through a main entrance, or get spotted by a guard before entering, alarms are gonna be sounded and everyone in the building's gonna be coming down to get you. Plus the important rooms will be sealed off by magical walls and traps.'

'Sounds intense,' said Ziggy.

Iveline swings her grappling hook about pointedly, and sends Dogpet the falcon up to peer in through a window.

'Window,' says Barry thoughtfully. 'Can we all make it up there?'

Atgard pounds his fists together. 'Why not,' he hisses.

'Okay, Iveline,' says Barry, taking charge. 'Get that hook up there -'

Iveline clears her throat, and Barry sees that she's already done it.

'Of course she has,' TM said.

Iveline makes her way quietly up the rope; L easily follows her, and they slide open the window and clamber in. L fans out her cloak, creating a wide shadow in the moonlight down the side of the wall; Barry sinks into it, using his special ability of moving through shadow, and travels up the wall.

'I guess I'll need to roll for this one,' Marty said, as if anticipating impending disaster.

'Naturally,' Veggie said. 'Derrida, you haven't got a chance on this one so I wouldn't even bother, to be perfectly honest.'

'How am I meant to get in, then?' Derrida demanded.

'There are lower windows,' Veggie said, shrugging. 'How'd it go, Malachi?'

'On the edge,' Marty said doubtfully, examining his stats and dice.

'I got this one,' said Ziggy.

L pulls out a folding ladder from one of her many pockets filled with many wonders. It pops out in spectacular fashion and Malachi climbs up.

'Why didn't we all just use that to get over all the things?' Marty wondered.

'I'm assuming Atgard is too heavy for a folding ladder,' Derrida said; Veggie nodded with an air of infinite wisdom.

'Atgard, wait here,' Barry instructs. 'We'll try to disable the security spells so you can just come in through the door.'

Atgard hisses unhappily, but does as instructed, folding his arms and leaning against a sturdy tree trunk.

The four sneaky heroes find themselves at the end of a long corridor, to the sides of which are several doors. Barry takes a peek at his map.

'Do I have to roleplay checking a map?' TM asked. 'I mean, there's a map right there.' He pointed at the map Veggie had painstakingly drawn, which Veggie quickly concealed under a few pages of notes.

'Well, yeah,' Veggie said, 'but Barry doesn't know that. Which is why I kindly gave you *this* very useful map, so you're welcome.'

Barry checks his map carefully and with extreme gratitude.

'I have absolutely no idea which window we came through,' Barry admits.

'I do,' L says.

'You do?' TM said.

'Yeah, I think so,' said Ziggy. 'Right?'

Veggie nodded. 'She's got, er, really high map-reading stats. I also made up a map-reading stat.'

'This is the main gate,' L says, pointing on the map, 'which makes this the wall we came over. Then we headed straight through the garden, crossed the stream at this bend, and this is the window we came through on the second floor.'

'Nice,' says Barry.

'Which means,' L continues, 'that we're now in this corridor.'

Barry and Malachi look down at it closely. Iveline just sort of loiters in the hall, since her Blindsight isn't quite ridiculous enough that she could read a map with it. 'So... the Nice Cousins are in one of these rooms?' asks Malachi.

'Looks that way,' says L.

Iveline, hearing this, starts walking slowly along the corridor, listening to any sounds within the rooms. Dogpet toddles along on the ground beside her so as not to make any distracting flapping noises. She stops beside one of the doors, and points to it meaningfully.

'We should really get Atgard inside before we start completing objectives,' TM said; Derrida nodded.

'Too right,' they said. 'Atgard's getting antsy waiting outside. Plus I don't want you lot getting all the EXP without me.'

'We must proceed, for now,' Barry says. 'We may need Atgard's help.'

Iveline nods in agreement, but gestures towards the door behind which the Nice Cousins reside. L nods, and nudges Malachi meaningfully.

'What?' says Malachi.

'You've got a nice soothing voice,' says L. 'Tell them we'll come back for them. They've heard us here now, so we can't just walk away without letting them know.'

'Fine,' says Malachi, pressing his ear against the door to listen. 'Hello?' he says, and hears a desperate-sounding voice from inside call 'Hello?' back. 'We're brave heroes, here to rescue you and depose your evil cousins,' Malachi says reassuringly.

'Roll for it,' Veggie said. 'See how they respond.'

Marty slapped an ability card down, reading 'Soothing Words'. Then he rolled. 'Add one eight-sider to that thanks to my excellent oratory skills,' he said, tapping Soothing Words, 'and with that I think you'll find that that's a critical pass.'

'Not a natural crit, though,' Veggie said, 'so no super bonus.'

'Aw,' said Marty. 'I was sort of hoping Malachi might tempt one of the Nice Cousins into a bit of nookie.'

'I don't even want to know what sort of check you'd need to roll to actually have intercourse,' Derrida said.

'I do,' Ziggy chirped.

'It's in one of the expansions,' Veggie said absently.

'We're alright,' says a shaken female voice from within. 'My brother is not well, but... we are safe.'

'We have to go and... sort out some stuff,' says Malachi. 'But we'll be back, I promise.'

'I believe you,' says the voice from within, 'but please hurry!'

Malachi nods heroically and the group make their way down the corridor, following Barry's map.

'You know they couldn't see you nod, right?' Ziggy pointed out.

'I'm sure they heard it,' said Marty, flippant.

Turning a corridor, the group suddenly find themselves face to face with an enormous man whose arms are covered in tally marks.

'Hello,' says Barry.

'Intruders?' says the man, who is clearly not particularly smart, and picks up an enormous club. 'Tank smash!'

'Really?' said Marty. 'Tank smash?'

'Hey,' said Veggie, 'it's not easy coming up with this many distinct and interesting characters.'

'Apparently not,' TM said, smirking.

'Hey, what are the things on your arms?' says Malachi, pointing to the tallies.

'Number of Tank victims,' says Tank.

'Pff,' says Malachi. 'Come, Mr Tally Man, tally me banana.'

'Then I wave my dong at him,' finished Marty.

'Somehow that doesn't surprise me,' said Veggie. 'Roll for it.'

Marty paused. 'Ehhhh,' he said uncertainly. 'I'm not sure I wanna risk a critical fail on this one. Daren't think what might happen to the old wang.'

'Fair enough,' said Veggie. 'Roll priority, y'all.'

Tank makes the first move, springing forth with surprising speed, and swings his club down on Iveline. She manages to sidestep most of the blow, but takes damage to the arm.

Dominika tapped insistently at a ticked checkbox on her character sheet, and rolled.

Iveline's Counter Strike ability, which she gained training with the assassins of the Leaf, lets her strike back in retaliation. She puts a deep cut on Tank's arm with her long knife, then cartwheels athletically out of range and sends Dogpet in to peck at his eyes. He falls back, his giant hand clutching at his face as the falcon sets upon him.

'Marty, your shot,' said Veggie.

'Malachi uses…' Marty began.

'Ooh, ooh,' said Derrida excitedly, waving a hand in the air. 'Buff me, buff me!'

'You're not even in this fight,' Marty observed. Derrida sank back with disappointment. 'I'll use Charm of Strength on Barry.'

Malachi calls the power of ancient warriors to his staff, and casts a great magic upon Barry to increase his strength. L then dashes towards Tank, ducking down to slide between his legs, and pops up behind him to slash at the back of his legs. Tank falls to his knees, groaning in pain.

'There's darkness about, right?' said TM, scratching his chin.

'Yeah, why not,' said Veggie.

Barry sprints down the hall, sinking into the long shadows along the walls, and emerges in midair before Tank, where he strikes with his long sword in both hands and takes off the kneeling Tank's head.

'Wait, what?' Marty said, blinking in surprise.

'Hm,' said Veggie. 'I guess you all increased your stats more than I was expecting.'

Tank falls down in front of the group.

'That was easier than anticipated,' Barry says.

'I wouldn't bet on it continuing to be so easy,' Malachi replies. 'Something tells me that some god watching over this and divining our fate will likely see our easy progress and decide that it would be really fun to make everything more difficult.'

'Oh, stay in character for once,' Veggie bemoaned, to which Marty grinned, stuck his tongue out and gave him the finger.

'I need food,' Ziggy said; TM, who had spotted her looking down at her knees, brow furrowed, at Tank's death, decided it might be time for a wrestling break.

17. Tenseless and Inadequate

'Pick and mix run?' Marty suggested as everyone stood up.

'Oh, heck yes.'

'I'm not getting up,' said Veggie, 'you lot get this one.'

Marty and Derrida were out of the door faster than anyone could have said 'greedy buggers'.

'Well, this seems to be going well,' TM observed.

'I'm slightly concerned that it might be going too well,' Veggie mused, making a few alterations to his campaign paperwork. 'Might not have sufficiently planned for this whole… trainingamebob.'

'Time is weird,' Ziggy murmured, as TM ushered her onto the sofa. Dominika, whom TM had sort of forgotten was still there, sidled in next to her.

'Are you feeling alright?' TM asked the celestial body on his sofa. 'I know Tyer weirded you out and stuff, but… you feeling any better?'

'I think so,' she answered. Dominika, ever sensitive to emotions, patted her encouragingly on the arm, then yawned and folded her hands behind her head. 'Just… I don't know. Don't you think it's weird that time is a thing?'

'Extremely,' TM reassured her.

'Time is an illusion,' squawked Veggie, who was busy trying to find a video of Wrestle Kingdom 11 on their crappy little laptop.

'If you believe J.M.E. McTaggart, it's either tensed and contradictory or tenseless and inadequate,' TM said, remembering something Aster had told him.

'Time's kind of like a fourth dimension in addition to the three spatial ones, right?' Ziggy asked. Nobody was qualified to answer.

'I… guess?' TM eventually offered, in the absence of any other response.

'And the universe is expanding in the three spatial dimensions at least, so maybe what we perceive as time moving forward is just the time dimension expanding.'

'So when inertia kicks in and it all starts coming back together...'

'Time might go backwards,' Ziggy theorised. 'Heck, we might already be on the backwards run. We wouldn't know, 'cos our brains can only analyse time as moving one way.'

'Well, that's funky,' Veggie said, hooking the laptop up to the TV. 'Now let's watch Okada versus Omega, 'kay? Okada's champion at this one.'

'Okadaaaaa,' Ziggy trilled, a genuine-looking smile returning to her face.

'Is this the one Meltzer gave six stars out of five?' TM asked.

'That's the one,' Veggie announced, grinning.

'Oooooooooh,' said Ziggy.

Dominika went to the cupboard and returned with a packet of chocolate cereal, which she dropped on the sofa between herself and Ziggy; the two set to demolishing the contents of the box.

When Marty and Derrida returned, the four of them were sitting completely unmoving, absorbed in the match as it neared its end. Dominika's hand was halfway to her mouth, pieces of cereal trickling between her fingers; Ziggy's hand was buried in the cereal box.

'We got pick -' Marty started. He was immediately shushed.

Omega kept hoisting Okada onto his shoulders, preparing to end the match with his finishing move, but Okada was too nimble.

'One-Winged Angel?!' Veggie breathed as Omega made the set-up for what felt like the tenth time, but no: Okada slithered free.

'Rainmaker!' Ziggy squealed in excitement: Okada grabbed Omega from behind, holding his arms across his body. Omega, who had spent the match doing his best to avoid the Rainmaker - though, to TM's disbelief, he had managed to kick out of one - unleashed a barrage of kicks to Okada's face, but the champion held on to his challenger's arm.

'Ooooooh,' went the audience on the sofa in unison. Okada hoisted Omega up, holding him upside down, then dropped to his knees and spiked Omega's head into the ground. Then came the Rainmaker.

'One! Two! Three!'

'Okada wins?' Ziggy demanded, hand still in the cereal box.

'Okada wins,' Veggie confirmed. Ziggy tried to go 'woo' and raise her arms, which sent cereal flying everywhere.

'Can I talk now?' Marty piped up, as TM scrambled to clean up the mess.

'No,' declared Veggie. 'I just remembered I need to tell Ziggy about the feud I'm totally writing.'

'Oh, yeah,' said Ziggy, sounding legitimately intrigued.

'So what it'll be, right,' said Veggie, leaning forwards, 'is there'll be this tag team - two people who team up to fight together - and they'll start sort of expanding and bringing in more people. And then one of the biggest stars in the company will want in, because their new gang is so awesome, and when they join it'll make this *other* guy who's like the number one superstar on the roster super jealous because that dude was supposed to be his rival and now he's all just hanging out with his new mates.'

'Okaaay,' said Ziggy, who was clearly struggling to follow.

'And then,' Veggie continued undaunted, 'the number one guy teams up with another guy who was super under-appreciated or something, and then he makes that guy such a big deal that the two of them can take on the big buncha other dudes.'

'Who's the bad guy in this situation?' Ziggy asked, chomping on cereal.

'Whichever,' Veggie said. 'But then, right, the little guy who just got all built up betrays the big shot, and then... they have a match and it's really cool.'

Ziggy waited. 'Oh,' she said after a moment. 'That's the story.'

'Isn't it cool?!'

'That sounds like a very slight variant on an angle that must have been done, like, a billion times,' TM told his business partner; Veggie stuck his bottom lip out and crossed his arms in a sulk.

'I thought it was cool,' he said.

'This is your Octobike,' TM said, to which Veggie grinned reluctantly.

'Can I talk *now*?' Marty said; Veggie nodded magnanimously.

'We got pick and mix.'

'Yusssss,' Veggie growled, snatching his cup from Derrida's hand. TM passed Ziggy's from Marty to her; she flicked the lid off with a thumb and fished out a piece of fudge.

'Fanku,' she mumbled.

'Welcome,' Marty told her, then kicked the laptop shut. 'Come ooon, bros, we've got adventuring to... adventure.'

Veggie leapt to his feet, as if he'd completely forgotten, and whirled over to the table like a pick and mix-eating tornado. 'This is delicious!' he declared. 'Perfect adventure food!'

The group reassembled themselves at the tabletop; Veggie swallowed loudly, thrust his glasses onto his face, and slammed his cup down on the table.

'RIGHT,' he boomed. 'Where were we?'

'Barry just decapitated a guy,' Marty said merrily.

'Oh, yeah.'

'I'm still outside,' Derrida prompted.

'L knows the way,' Ziggy said with confidence.

L leads the group down numerous twists and turns ('How big is this place, anyway?' asks Malachi, not entirely rhetorically, but nevertheless nobody bothers to answer). As far as Barry, doing his best to keep track of their progress on his map, can tell, she's heading for the dead centre of the place. Eventually they reach a large, open room with large curving staircases at either side leading down towards a man with outstretched arms, standing in front of an enormous rotating ball of energy. On the other side of that are two large doors which look like they lead to the outside

'Well, I guess that's a thing we've gotta deal with, then,' says Malachi.

The man hears him -

'Oh, bugger,' said Marty, 'sorry about that.'

- and turns, arms majestically dropping into a wise sort of pose- you know, like a kind of... beard-stroking, other arm folded... thing.

'Anyway,' Veggie finished lamely, 'he's seen you and he's not too happy about it.'

'You must be one of the bodyguards,' Malachi calls down.

The sorcerer gives a deep, wide bow. 'I am the one they call Fist.'

'Wait,' said Ziggy. 'This one's Fist?'

'I'm getting to it,' Veggie shushed.

'I am called Fist,' says Fist, 'because I do not need to use my fists.'

'That's frickin' dumb,' says Malachi.

'Marty,' said Derrida reproachfully.

'Sorry,' said Marty. 'Just to reiterate, though, and I'm saying this out of character now: that's frickin' dumb.'

'Thou speaketh odd,' Malachi clarifies.

Fist raises a fist, shrouded within his enormously roomy sleeves, and extends his fingers with great force, like Bruce Lee but more wizardy.

'You're really having fun describing this guy, huh?' said TM.

Veggie nodded happily. 'Let's have ourselves a fight, folks.'

Barry does nothing.

'Wait, what?' Veggie whipped his glasses off his nose with astounding speed and force, staring at TM.

TM shrugged. 'I got a Plan.'

Veggie's brows furrowed. 'You didn't seriously make a Plan, capital P Plan,' he said in disbelief.

'Maybe,' TM said proudly.

Dominika rubbed her hands together; Veggie held his hands up and huffed. 'This isn't anime, folks - you can't just capitalise Plan and suddenly have a… thing.'

'Plan,' Ziggy finished for him, helpfully.

'That.'

'Wait and see,' TM said, shuffling smugly.

Veggie pouted, then stuck his glasses back on his face with just as much force as he'd taken them off and slightly less accuracy, poking himself in the eye in the process. 'Whatever,' he said, blinking. 'Fist's next, anyway.'

Fist waves his arms around in a super cool magical way, and in a few moments he's glowing with extreme luminosity. Iveline sends in Dogpet, but Fist, glowing just as bright as the magical sphere behind him, easily dodges.

'Sounds like he's buffed himself,' said Marty, 'so... let's just try to bring Derrida in, maybe.'

'Aw,' said Derrida. 'How nice.'

'I reckon that big ol' ball of glowiness behind him must have something to do with the magical wards on the place,' Marty mused, leafing through spell cards.

Malachi sets about combining a spell from his tome, a charm of unlocking and unsolicited entrance, with a hex of pure and great force.

'Is combining spells allowed?' Derrida said; Marty threw a pencil at them.

'I'm trying to let you in on the action here!'

'Oh, yes,' said Derrida. 'I mean, that's definitely a thing that's allowed.'

Veggie sighed. 'It'll take two turns, but can't see any reason not to allow it.'

'Muchas gracias,' said Marty.

A bolt from L's crossbow rips towards him, but he simply holds up a hand and it disintegrates before it can reach him.

'This seems like a problem,' Ziggy chirped.

'Anyone got any... like, dispel magic... nerf bullets?' Marty suggested. Ziggy raised a hand, then put it down again. She thought about it for a moment, then put it up again.

'I *think* that's what this does,' she said, holding up an ability card, 'but if I'm honest I have no idea.'

'That might work,' Marty said, squinting at it. 'No harm in trying, is there? If we think there's a chance something might work, then the universe will make it work. Maybe. If we roll super well.'

'Top of the round, then,' said Veggie. 'TM?'

Barry does nothing.

'Oh, right. The Plan,' Veggie muttered. 'Iveline?'

Dominika shook her head.

'Iveline holds her action,' Veggie said, one eyebrow raised, 'presumably also to Capital-P-Plan whatever. Malachi spends this round charging his spell-thing, so... L?'

'I use the thing!' Ziggy exclaimed.

L casts a simple spell on one of her daggers and hurls it at Fist. He tries to stop it, but whatever she's done to it sends it straight through his magic and into his upper arm. As Fist staggers backwards, his luminescence seems to flicker; he holds up his hands and a shimmering barrier appears, like a wall between him and the party.

'Plan!' TM exclaimed.

Iveline draws her bow and nocks the heaviest, sharpest, most magically enhanced arrow in her quiver to it, then with a motion of her head directs Dogpet. He launches from her shoulder, swoops about the room, and flies past L, his talons grabbing the parachute out from under her cloak. As the falcon's flight path takes him between Iveline and Fist's enormous glowing self, she releases the arrow. It punctures the folded parachute, which unfurls in the air and billows out behind the flying arrow, casting a fluttering shadow in its wake.

'Aaand...' TM rolled the dice.

Barry leaps forth, descending down into the shadow of the billowing parachute, and rides it speedily behind the arrow. The arrow lodges in Fist's barrier - but the shadow of the parachute, flapping about in the light cast by Fist's glowing body and the giant magical ball behind him, casts itself for a split second on the inside of the magical shield. Barry erupts from the shadow, on the inside of Fist's shield, and sinks both his blades into Fist's face.

'Oh, *shiiiiiieeeeeet*,' Marty hollered, punching the air with glee.

'That was *awesome*,' Ziggy yelled, punching TM on the shoulder with slightly too much force.

'Please say you're gonna allow that,' Derrida implored Veggie, who could only sigh.

'That was a pretty awesome bit of roleplaying-cum-ingenuity,' he conceded. 'Gotta allow it.'

'Woop,' chirped TM.

Fist sinks to his knees, at which point Malachi releases the spell he's been preparing. It zips through the air and blasts Fist in the chest, knocking him backwards; the magic carries on until it hits the big glowy ball thingy, which implodes gloriously.

'That's the security down, then, presumably,' said Derrida, 'so...'

Atgard bursts in -

'Wait,' said Veggie. 'How does he know it's open?'

Derrida tapped their fingers on the table, mouth half-open. 'Instinct,' they said after a moment.

'Ugh,' groaned Veggie. 'Roll for it.'

Atgard's suddenly bizarrely sensitive perception of magical forces kicks in, and he realises the door is no longer alarmed, so he batters it with his awesome gauntlets, kicks it down with his massive snake foot and barges in with a great hiss-roar thing.

'I hate your good luck,' Veggie moaned, shaking his head. 'That's your turn, though, so...'

Fist, down but not out, grabs Barry by the head and squeezes. Barry can feel the wizard's ludicrously strong fingers crushing his skull, sparks of painful magic simultaneously flickering from fingertip to brain.

'Oh, that's not good,' said Ziggy. 'I help!' She rolled the dice, then yelped in distress.

L attempts to shoot her crossbow at Fist, but in her haste fails to load it properly. The string snaps, causing the bolt to flop uselessly onto the floor.

'Bums,' muttered Ziggy.

Iveline shoots an arrow into Fist's chest, but he's still holding on. Barry tries to fight back, but to no avail.

'Balls,' TM huffed.

'Don't worry,' Marty said, 'every good story has one of the good guys die unnecessarily - I mean, in a heroic sacrifice.'

'Does it have to be *me*, though?'

Derrida sighed. 'Don't worry,' they said. 'I got this.'

Atgard activates his recently-acquired ability of Religious Fervour, drawing zeal and energy from his faith that the great Blood Gods will be eagerly watching such a brutal battle, and then he rips off both Fist's arms.

'Flipping heck, Derrida,' Marty exclaimed.

Then he imbibes the blood spurting from Fist to absorb the magical strength it holds, pulls back a mechanical-gauntlet-powered hand, and punches him so hard in the face that his head explodes.

'Christ,' agreed TM.

Derrida yawned contentedly, as if they and not Atgard had personally just feasted on the flesh of their foes.

'I have a healing… thingy,' Ziggy announced, waving a card inches in front of Veggie's face.

'Salve,' he said, eyes crossing.

'I salve the thingy on Barry!' Ziggy implored.

'Okay,' said Veggie. 'Barry's skull is made more better. Moving on -'

'Moving *on*,' Marty interjected, 'what time is it?'

Veggie took his phone out of his pocket and checked. 'Like four in the morning.'

'Ah,' said Marty. 'I was thinking it might be time to call it there and head home, but on second thought maybe it might be time to call it there and head to *your* room, which I bagsy.'

'You can't do that,' Veggie protested, jumping up and running to block the bedroom door. Everyone hopped out of their seats, dashing to claim a good space to make their bed on the sofa, the floor, or - in Dominika's case - simply right there on the table. She curled up atop it like a cat, and was soon appropriately joined by Michel Furcoat, the actual cat. He rubbed his nose affectionately on hers before settling down beside her.

'Night, all,' said Derrida, yawning widely.

'Night, gamebreaker,' Marty called from the bedroom, having barged his way past Veggie.

TM - who was on the floor, since Veggie had immediately taken *his* bed instead - threw a dressing gown over himself, tucking it under his body so that he looked like an enormous fluffy caterpillar. He glanced at Ziggy, who lay with a smile on her face a few feet away.

'You seem happy,' he said quietly.

'I have friends,' she answered. 'Night.'

'Night,' TM said. Then, overcome by a sudden and contented

weariness, he slept.

18. The Others We Carry On

'You know,' said Aster, 'for... like, forever, people have been trying to work out the answer to the ultimate question.'

'Forty-two,' said TM.

'That might not actually be that far off, though,' Aster mused. She was holding a mug of tea TM had made for her, but had been staring into its depths since the moment her hands wrapped around it. TM was beginning to think she might never get around to drinking it. 'I mean, the whole point of the forty-two thing is that nobody knew what the question was.'

'I read something by this guy,' TM piped up, 'who was saying that the idea that the universe just emerged from nothing out of a big bang, or that life just happened to arise out of matter by accident, was trying to answer the ultimate question by pretending it didn't exist.'

Aster took a sip of tea. Finally, TM thought. 'Questions don't exist unless you ask them,' she said after a moment. 'Seems like this phrase – "the ultimate question" – is just shorthand for something to the effect of "a big meaningful thing that must be possible to conceive of, but we don't really know what it actually is". It's sort of lazy.'

'Lazy?'

'Well, referring to this so-called ultimate question kind of negates the problem of having to work out what it might actually be. I mean, not all questions make sense. Maybe the ultimate question is "what's twelve plus fish divided by Nintendo"?'

TM couldn't help but try to work out what the answer to that question might actually be. He didn't come up with much.

'There's no ultimate question,' Aster said. 'Maybe each person has one question that's the most important one in their life, but you're never gonna be able to come up with a single question that represents the most meaningful thing any one person could ever possibly ask.'

TM scratched his head. 'Well, then maybe the ultimate question is "what is your individual ultimate question?" or something like that.'

'That's recursive,' Aster admonished, though not without a slight *smile.*

'You're *recursive,*' TM told her.

***

TM awoke to find the flat empty - except for Michel Furcoat, who appeared to be using the sink as a toilet. He stood and stretched, waddled over to the kitchen and found himself a single slice of dry bread for breakfast, then flicked on the TV.

'So, you see,' said Riegel O'Ryan from the screen, 'it's really all about ingenuity. Thinkin' outside the box.'

TM exhaled and glanced around. Nobody was in - no Veggie to squee over his hero, no Ziggy to… whatever it was Ziggy did in the presence of television personalities.

'All we gotta do,' O'Ryan continued, 'is figure out a way to make what nature's got to offer us do what we need it to do. And, fortunately, I got a gizmo or a thingy-bob to make pretty much whatever I can find into pretty much whatever I need.'

She indicated her broad belt, with its array of variously-sized pockets and pouches, and pulled out a little metal tube. 'This,' she said, 'is a spile, and with it I can turn almost any tree into a source of fresh water.'

Then she put the spile down and took out a utility knife. 'But, hey. I'm me. I have a spile on me all the time. Most people don't. *This* is the only thing I *really* couldn't go without, though,' she said, knowingly tapping her nose with the flat of the blade. 'With this little beauty, I can improvise almost anything.'

She set to carving a piece of wood into a second spile, then stuck her creation into the trunk of a tree and grinned at the camera. 'Nobody's a match for old O'Ryan, not even Mummy Nature.'

TM turned off the TV. He doubted he'd ever need a way to get drinking water from a tree, and if he were to find himself in that situation he'd probably have a bunch more very significant problems that a spile wouldn't be likely to fix. Better to have a gadget for all eventualities, he tended to think; grabbing a pencil and an unopened envelope, he scribbled a couple of quick designs. Working out how to make something to solve a specific problem, that was his forte, but he'd barely taken any time to think about inventing new products - either for the business or just for fun - since the whole Ziggy thing had happened.

Once Ziggy was on his mind again, it was near-impossible to focus on creating, so he dropped the doodles on the floor and sank back into the sofa. Anything where she was concerned was so *huge* that it took over everything. Not that he resented that, or her for it, but it was awfully hard to get used to a status quo that involved sharing his life with an actual star from space. He'd always figured that just knowing Veggie was enough unusualness for one life.

'How do,' said Marty, emerging from the bedroom. TM tilted his head at him.

'Didn't realise anyone was still here.'

'Oh, yeah, the others went to get supplies or something.' Marty plonked himself down on the sofa. 'You alright? You look... thinky.'

'Thoughtful?'

'Thassa one.'

TM rubbed the back of his neck, trying to think about what exactly it was that he was thinking about. 'It's all weird,' he said after a few moments, 'and I'm not sure what the point of most of it is.'

'Yeah,' said Marty. 'Go figure.'

TM blinked.

'That's how it is for everyone all the time,' Marty continued, 'and if anyone says otherwise they're lying or extremely poorly-adjusted. You just gotta do the stuff that makes things feel like they make sense, even if it's just for a few minutes at a time.'

'Finding your own meaning is the only real meaning,' TM said quietly.

'I mean, if you wanna get with the Dao or whatever about it, then sweet.' Marty looked at the ceiling thoughtfully for a moment. 'Just don't say meaningful-sounding stuff like that if Derrida's in earshot, they'll have a field day with it.'

TM bobbed his head up and down.

'Like, I'm just gonna keep being punk rock about everything forever until something feels more right than that,' said Marty. 'Can't think of a better plan, so why not?'

'What if...' TM paused, swallowed, then started again. 'What if I don't even really know what's supposed to be going on right now - what feels like the right thing to do in this moment - but I'm pretty sure there's some big important stuff going on that I should probably be more concerned about?'

Marty ran a hand through his thicket of blue hair. 'I don't think there is a *supposed to be*, really, but I do think you can't go too far wrong just by doing the stuff that feels important when it feels important. We're all only human, can't always know exactly what's best in the bigger picture.'

'We are all only human,' TM agreed, perhaps a little too insistently. Marty raised an eyebrow.

'Well,' he said, 'I mean, I wonder about Veg sometimes, but eh.' He leaned back, hands clasped behind his head. 'You gotta think,' he said, taking his time on each word, 'that if there's no... like, ultimate thing taking care of a big cosmic plan or whatever, then we can't really go wrong 'cos there's nothing to deviate from - and if there is, then it'll happen whether we try to make it happen or not. Which, 'cos it's a big cosmic plan, we probably can't deliberately do anything about.'

'So we may as well just do what... feels right,' TM said. 'Stuff might turn out to have been leading up to some bigger thing or it might not, and it's all good either way.'

Marty made a face as if he'd tasted something sour, tongue moving around in his cheeks. 'I sound like Derrida,' he said. 'Or... well, you know who.'

TM looked down at his knees. 'Slightly,' he said. 'But that's OK. We all take bits of each other, right? Ideas from other people become our own, bits of their thoughts carry on in ours, all that.'

'Now *you* sound like her,' Marty said - then, quickly and quietly, 'no judgement, though.'

'Be weird if I didn't, if we're all constantly absorbing parts of the people we hang around with.'

'That is very true.' Marty blinked a few times, then looked at TM and made a pensive face. 'Am I stoned? This feels like a stoned conversation.'

TM grinned. 'Not as far as I know.'

'Hm.'

The two sat there for a few moments, gazing off at nothing in particular.

'Life is weird,' said TM.

'May as well roll with it, then.'

TM chuckled. 'Heh. Roll. Like -'

'Dice, yeah,' said Marty. 'We gotta stop making that joke every time we play.'

TM opened his mouth to deliver an amused and, he was certain, extremely witty response; before the words left his mouth, though, the flat's door burst open and Veggie, Dominika, Derrida, and Ziggy piled in, arms laden with bags of what looked like absolutely no healthy food whatsoever.

'Oh, good,' said Veggie, 'you're awake. Now come *on*, we've got an adventure to wrap up!' Ziggy nodded her head rapidly behind him.

TM closed his eyes and smiled. Big picture or not, he and this place, and these people, were what existed right then. That was good enough.

19. Plot Twist

After a brief flurry of movement, during which snacks were distributed mostly according to individual preference but somehow also mostly to ensure that Dominika would have easy access to the maximum number of different foodstuffs, Veggie threw himself back into his chair and leaned forwards, elbows on the table, eyes twitching with glee.

'Okay. So. Um...'

'Atgard just ate Fist,' Derrida reminded him.

'That's the one.'

'*Now we're all here, time to go finish the mission,*' Malachi suggests. '*Take out the Evil Cousins.*'

Atgard nods, gore dripping from his mouth and hands. He has grown much stronger from undertaking many days of training in the Leaf's basement and also from consuming a large quantity of extremely sorcerous plasma. The group scurry back up the stairs, to the middle landing, and then further up from there to the highest reaches of the Imperial Citadel.

A series of simple skill checks got the group past a range of mechanical traps, and then they were standing in front of a large pair of wooden doors.

'*In we go, then?*' says Malachi.

'Strength check,' Veggie prompted.

Malachi tries to push open the doors, but they really are rather heavy and he only has little frail wizardy arms. So Atgard punches them into splinters instead.

'*Ah,*' *says one of the two people within, a dark-haired, slender woman with vaguely familiar features.* '*You must be the ones taking out our bodyguards.*'

'*That we are,*' *says Barry.* '*You're going down, Lanriel-Lalamala... evil branch.*'

'*I,*' *says the woman,* '*am Linske Lanriel-Lanlanar. My brother, Lanfal, is also in the room.*'

'Perception check,' Veggie instructed, his voice cracking a little as he dropped from Linske's falsetto to his own baritone.

None of the heroes can see Lanfal.

Dominika raised an eyebrow.

Or hear him.

Ziggy hummed, fidgeting in her seat. 'Are we fighting?'

Veggie spread his hands. 'Up to you,' he said.

'You can leave now,' L says to Linske, who looks at her with surprise. 'We don't have to fight. You can just go, and let the people be free.'

'Free?' says Linske. 'Of what?'

'Of your corruption,' Barry says heroically.

'On the contrary,' Linske says. 'We are the only thing standing between the people and all the corruption that the world would bring upon them.'

'Ugh,' said Ziggy. 'This is useless.'

L dashes towards Linske, striking at her with a dagger in each hand. Linske's arm flicks around in a wide circle, and both of L's blows find themselves deflected.

'Didn't the man who sent you tell you?' says Linske with a smile, turning her hands to reveal long, slim blades, so thin as to be invisible when viewed edge-on, extending from each palm. 'We are more than capable of being our own bodyguards.'

Linske raises her arms to her sides, and something shines in the air in front of her. Iveline, sensing the danger the others can't see, fires off twelve arrows in the space of a second, and twelve blades, so slim that they become completely invisible to the naked eye when pointing towards the heroes, drop to the ground in front of Linske, struck by the arrows.

'Twelve in a second?!' Derrida exclaimed in astonishment.

Dominika winked and pointed to three ability cards stacked before her: Quick Draw (fire four arrows in one attack), Rapid Counter (multiply each arrow by two, to a maximum of eight, when deflecting an enemy's attack), and Skill Shot (add four arrows to a trick shot when shooting multiple targets).

'You can do that?' Ziggy said.

'Technically, yes,' said Veggie, sticking his lower lip out.

Linske smiles, looking as if she wants to present a superior front, but -

'Perception check.'

- but everyone can sense that she's slightly rattled by the display of skill.

'Lanfal,' she calls. 'Get the archer.'

'Dominika, roll,' Veggie ordered.

She did.

'Ooh,' said Veggie. 'Saving throw, if you will.'

'Noooooo,' TM moaned.

An arrow rockets out of nowhere, shooting from an invisible bow, and hits Iveline dead in the chest. She collapses onto her back: alive, but barely.

Dominika stood abruptly and returned a moment later with a tub of ice cream from the freezer; she stuck a spoon into it and nibbled mournfully.

Malachi starts calling the Barrier of Ages and Titans to him, a powerful shield that can protect every person in the party. It'll take a couple of turns to cast, during which time Malachi will be basically defenceless, so he really ought to have positioned himself better.

'Cock,' said Marty.

Atgard lunges forwards towards Linske -

'Roll... attack and evade.'

The dice clattered from Derrida's hand.

Atgard finds himself stopped in his tracks by a barrier of slim blades, floating in the air before Linske. One of the blades punctures his chest, but he stops his attack before it can go too deep, or any more points can find a home in his flesh. He pulls out the offending weapon, thrusting it back towards Linske and scratching her cheek, doing almost no damage.

'Sorry, Derrida,' said Veggie, 'but your weapons skills are absolutely atrocious.'

'Minmaxed it for the unarmed attack, didn't I?' said Derrida regretfully.

The scratch is enough to break Linske's concentration; the blade barrier in the air in front of her vanishes, and Barry flickers behind her, stabbing at her back.

'Decent damage,' Veggie noted, jotting it down. 'I might have raised her HP a teensy bit to make up for how overpowered y'all bitches made yourselves, though.'

'High HP means nothing compared to the power of immersive roleplaying,' Marty proclaimed.

Another arrow flies out of a different dark, concealing corner, striking Malachi in the shoulder.

'Take that in your immersive roleplaying,' said Veggie. Marty grabbed Dominika's spoon, stealing a scoop of ice cream.

L grabs Iveline and uses the ranger's grappling hook to take them both up into an alcove high in a corner, out of immediate harm's way. Iveline -

Veggie tossed a pair of dice across the table.

- barely makes it up thanks to her super jumpy boots of jumpiness. L applies the remainder of her healing salve and some colour returns to Iveline's face; she struggles to a sitting position, saved but not stabilised. With difficulty she nocks an arrow to her string, pulling it back to her cheek.

Dominika dropped a card on the table: 'Strike Undetected.'

'You want to... strike the undetected guy? Doesn't *Strike Undetected* mean you can *be* undetected while you strike?' Veggie asked. She shook her head violently, picked up the card, and slapped it down again. 'Ehhhhh...'

'Wait wait waitwait,' Ziggy spluttered, thrusting her hand into the air. 'I have goggles of revealing!'

'Won't help Iveline,' Derrida said, their chin resting on their index finger.

'Oh, balls,' said Ziggy. 'Can L put them on and... like, point?'

Veggie consulted his notes, then shook his head. 'Fine,' he ruled. 'Apparently I did not specify that that wouldn't be something that would help.'

Iveline looses the arrow, her Blindsight letting her shoot at the undetected archer. It flies true, striking flesh somewhere out of visibility; a dark-haired young man, the mirror image of his sister, falls from the walls and lands in a heap.

'Lanfal!' Linske screams; Atgard takes advantage of the distraction, darting through her temporarily disabled wall of knives, and punches her as hard as he can in the face. She falls, a couple of teeth soaring off in a blood mist and half her face pretty much disappearing under his fist.

Linske's brother - Lanfal - sees his sister collapse, and with a cry of distress dashes to her side. Barry takes the opportunity to stab him in the side.

'We are the most powerful people in this city,' Lanfal says defiantly, grabbing Barry's hand, still gripping the knife buried in Lanfal's flesh. 'You cannot stop us.'

With that, he raises a hand to Barry's face, and with his long fingers gouges his eyes out.

'Aw, heck!' TM exclaimed. 'You serious?'

Veggie thought about it. 'Roll for it,' he said after a moment.

TM rolled; Veggie watched the dice scatter with interest.

Yup, he gouges Barry's eyes out.

'Alas!' Barry cries, flailing back in pain.

'Alas?' Ziggy repeated.

'Roleplaying, man,' said TM. 'Barry's not gonna say *fffff...*'

'Fffff?'

'You know. The F word.'

'Fuck?'

'Oh. Yeah.'

Barry falls to the ground, effectively taken out of this fight for now.

Linske, beaten but still alive, raises a hand slowly. A sphere of tiny blades begins to form around her; Lanfal darts away, back into the shadows.

'After him!' Derrida declared.

Atgard, who with his snake-like senses can detect the smell and heat of the Evil Dude's blood, pursues Lanfal ferociously, grabbing him as he tries to make his way up the wall and pulling him back to terra firma. Around Linske, the blades begin to quake.

'It's gonna blow,' Malachi warns, finally finishing his spell: all of the heroes gain boosted defence.

'I need priority,' Derrida said urgently.

'Dude,' said Ziggy, 'it's not your turn for, like, three.'

'Three.'

'Three... turn.'

Derrida made a noise like a skydiving donkey, and held their hands up exasperatedly. 'Fine, just keep hitting them.'

Iveline fires an explosive arrowhead into the centre of Linske's array of blades, which causes several to scatter across the room. They are instantly replaced by twice as many more.

L throws a knife at Lanfal, taking him in the back; he struggles, but can't escape Atgard's grip.

Barry can't do anything because he's in incredible pain.

'Oh, thanks,' said TM.

'Atgard, do your thing,' Veggie said; Derrida cheered.

Atgard hauls Lanfal off his feet, drags him over to his sister and holds him aloft as the thin blades surrounding her shake more violently. Then, just as the barrier explodes, sending thousands of tiny knives flying outwards, Atgard tosses Lanfal right on top of Linske.

'Niiiiiiice,' said Ziggy and Marty simultaneously.

Lanfal takes most of the impact of the millions -

'I thought it was thousands,' TM interrupted.

'She made more,' Veggie said.

- billions of almost invisible blades, all shooting outwards at the same time. He pretty much disappears in a cloud of shredded flesh. Linske howls from the pain of her destroyed face, the expenditure of the energy to cast the spell, and the gory death of her brother right in her face.

'Yeowch,' said Marty. 'Nice thinking, though: high HP, so we use his sister's high magical attack to take him right out.'

'Ain't I great,' said Derrida, mostly seriously.

L bends down to the blood-covered Linske, looking her straight in the eyes. The imperial cousin's eyes widen in recognition as she fully examines L's face for the first time.

'Lina,' she breathes.

'Let me guess,' said Derrida. 'L's a Lanriel.'

'Possibly,' said Ziggy teasingly.

'Let me be the first to assure you that we absolutely all knew that already,' Marty said.

'Plot twist!' Veggie declared, doing jazz hands.

'I think we all got that,' Derrida reiterated.

'Let me have this moment,' Ziggy protested; Derrida smiled faintly.

'It's me, cousin,' says L.

'No,' Linske says quietly, looking terrified.

L leans down, whispers something in her cousin's ear, then slams her foot down into the ruined half of her face. Linske howls in pain as L loads her crossbow and fires a corrosive bolt point-blank into her remaining eye; the imperial cousin wails and screams, her head dissolving until she finally lies still and silent.

'What the shit,' said Marty.

L stands up, facing the heroes. 'I am Lina Lanriel,' she says, throwing her cloak off regally.

'We had guessed,' Malachi says.

Barry says -

'Oh, yeah, I forgot,' Veggie said, interrupting TM. 'Barry's dead.'

'What?!'

'Well, Lanfal's body couldn't absorb all of those trillions of little blades, now, could it?'

'I guess -'

'Y'all can deal with the grief in a bit, we got plot here.'

'Barry dying *isn't plot*?!'

Veggie thought about it for a moment. 'Nawwwww.'

Iveline comes slowly down from her alcove high up in the walls, her sightless eyes staring at L.

'Now I reclaim my place,' L says quietly.

'Yes, you do,' says Rusk, entering the room.

'How did he get here?!' Derrida demanded.

'He just did, okay?' Veggie explained.

'Now you will support Lina as she takes her place,' says Rusk.

Dominika put her ice cream down with a thud, and made the most intense roll TM had ever seen.

'That's a pass,' Veggie said.

Iveline raises her bow, pointing it at L.

'Whaaaaaaaaat,' TM said helplessly.

'What are you doing, Iveline?' says L. 'I'm your friend, aren't I? It's me, L. We had adventures together, we took over this city together.'

'Took over?' Malachi repeats. Atgard puts himself between Rusk and L, hissing at the head of the Leaf.

'What is this?' says Rusk.

'Everybody roll,' said Veggie seriously. 'Except you, TM. You're dead.'

Everyone, including Veggie, rolled. He took a few moments to look it over, then sighed.

Everyone moves at once. L raises her crossbow and lets fly at Iveline; Malachi releases all his magical might; Iveline looses her arrow, while Dogpet soars down in front of her; Rusk leaps into the air, acrobatically flipping over Atgard; the Serpentine Monk employs the greatest of the Blood Monk's martial arts.

Around the table, each person held their breath.

L falls back with Iveline's arrow buried in her forehead. Dogpet lands hard, skidding across the ground in a pile of feathers with L's crossbow bolt in him. Rusk takes a bolt of magic right to the chest in mid-flip; Atgard grabs him as he falls back to earth, tearing him limb from limb.

'How the heck did that happen?' TM asked, leaning over the table.

Veggie pointed at the dice. TM examined them: three twenties from Marty, Derrida and Dominika, and two ones from Veggie and Ziggy.

'Holy flip.'

Veggie nodded.

'Wait,' said Marty. 'How come Dogpet got hit?'

Veggie shrugged. 'L and Rusk had to do *something* right.'

The heroes, breathing heavily, look at each other with sadness. Malachi closes Barry's eyes, a single tear falling onto his face. Iveline bends down, picks up Dogpet, and hits him hard with something she's been carrying around for a long time: a Stone of Resurrection.

'What?!' TM yelled. 'You got a one-up and you used it on Dogpet?! What about Barry?!'

Dominika looked at him unblinkingly for a moment, then winked and pointed both index fingers at him.

'That is not an answer,' TM said, though he was unable to help a grin.

Dogpet settles on Iveline's shoulder happily, the bolt still sticking out of him. Atgard devours Rusk's remains.

'And then we all take power and rule the citadel with fairness and justice,' Derrida finished.

'The end,' Veggie agreed.

There was a collective release of breath.

'Whew,' said Ziggy after a moment. 'That was a hell of an adventure.'

'That it was,' TM agreed.

'So how come you were evil, anyway?' Derrida asked.

'Oh, right,' Ziggy said. 'Yeah, basically, L was the last daughter of the Lanriel family but she got disillusioned and ran away, and then Rusk found her and took her in, found out she was one of the Lanriel line and decided to raise her up to be his pawn to take over the city.'

'Nice,' said TM.

'Yeah, we were gonna have them monologue it out,' Veggie said, 'but you sort of killed us before we could.'

Dominika finished her ice cream, then applauded politely.

'Speaking of people who got killed before they could do stuff, TM,' Derrida said, eyeing the empty tub for any stray remnants, 'we're all extremely grateful for your heroic sacrifice in the name of emotional denouement... ness.'

'Any time.'

Derrida tapped the table thoughtfully, their rapping finger muffled by the Bedsheet-Tablecloth-Whiteboard. 'So L was secretly a major celebrity, I have no idea how come when we were researching in the taverns nobody pointed any of this stuff out - and I swear we never even got to use any of the facts we apparently found out while we were doing that - and were the Evil Cousins actually... good cousins?'

'Yeah, probably,' said Veggie.

'That's deep,' said Derrida, eyes wide.

'You've been playing too long if you think that's *deep*,' TM said, throwing a cushion at them.

'Darned celebrities,' Derrida said, the cushion bouncing apparently unnoticed off their face. 'Always turn out to be evil.'

'Do they?' Marty asked, looking vaguely concerned. 'Only I kind of want to be a huge rock star and I don't want it to corrupt me or whatever.'

'It absolutely will corrupt you,' Derrida told him.

'Aw,' said Marty. 'So you believe I'm gonna make it!'

'I don't think I said -'

'You said *will*, not *would*!'

Derrida frowned. 'Consider it a compliment, then, I suppose.'

'On that note,' Veggie chimed in, looking at the clock on his phone, 'don't you have a show tomorrow?'

Marty thought about it. 'Yes.'

'Shouldn't you... be setting up, or rehearsing, or something?'

Marty thought about that too. 'Yes.'

There was a brief period of stillness.

'Oh, right,' said Marty after a few moments. 'Byeeeeeee.'

He climbed over the table rather than squeeze past Dominika, then wandered out the door with his usual casual stride.

'And I -' Derrida said, '- should probably go and attempt to do some work.'

'Work?' Ziggy squeaked. 'Weird.'

'Gotta make a living somehow,' Derrida said, shrugging.

'How's the somehow these days?' Veggie asked.

'Started painting miniatures and building model planes and that sort of thing - for people who really like the idea of having a collection of things into which they had to put effort but really don't like the idea of actually putting in any effort.'

'Smart.'

Derrida stood and wandered out; Dominika nodded sagely, which TM took to mean that she was also going to work, and meandered off. Michel Furcoat hopped down from the kitchen counter and watched them go curiously, then decided they weren't all that interesting and went to sleep in the middle of the floor.

'You said you had two cats, didn't you?' Ziggy asked, watching the snoring Michel Furcoat.

'Oh, yeah,' said TM. 'He hasn't actually come out yet while you've been here, but Maurice Meow-Ponty'll be around somewhere. Or not. He's very nice, honest.'

'I'm sure he is.'

'He cares about us really,' Veggie mused. 'Or he's found another home. One of the two.'

Ziggy took a deep breath as if she were about to say something, then just sort of didn't. TM watched her face redden as she sat with a full breath of air, and when she could finally hold it no longer the words all came spilling out of her at once: 'So-I've-been-thinking-I-really-need-to-get-over-this-not-being-able-to-deal-with-celebrities-thing-in-case-Marty-gets-famous-and-then-I-can't-hang-out-with-him-so-can-we-watch-TV-thanks.'

TM blinked at her a couple of times. 'You wanna try… like, exposure therapy?'

'Is that a thing?'

'I think so.'

'Does it mean gradually trying to get used to something so it's not as hard to deal with?'

'… Maybe?'

'Then *yes*.'

Veggie scratched the side of his nose. 'And this is in case Marty gets famous?'

'Well,' said Ziggy. 'I mean. Partly. Sorta. But also 'cos I just generally think it's probably better if I don't have a whole *thing* every time I even see an image of some superstar.'

'Not unreasonable,' Veggie conceded.

They piled onto the sofa; Veggie flicked on the TV, quickly navigating to his recorded shows - which included, of course, entire Riegel O'Ryan boxsets. His thumb went to the button that would start the show, but didn't press it.

'You sure about this?' he asked, looking at Ziggy.

She nodded, holding a cushion under her chin as if ready to cover her eyes at any moment.

He pressed the button.

TM found himself holding his breath as the show started.

Then the power went out.

'Aw, balls,' said Veggie. 'I thought we'd actually paid for electricity for at least, like... more than now.'

'Man,' said Ziggy, dropping the cushion. 'Money doesn't go far, does it?'

'We've taught her all there is to learn about modern life,' Veggie announced, waving his hands around in some combination of pride and frustration. 'Our work is done.'

'Our work is very much *not* done,' TM countered, 'since we apparently need money again and money means work.'

Veggie slumped like a deflating blimp. 'It's not worth it,' he mumbled. 'Money isn't even real and life is endless struggling.'

Ziggy hopped around on the sofa, turning to face Veggie and pulling her knees up underneath her at the same time. 'So let's just do a quick struggle to make some fake money and then enjoy the not-fake stuff we can buy with it.'

'You're suggesting we do another spectacular inventioning session and make a bunch more dollars,' Veggie said slowly.

'Yes,' she said, then turned her head to look quizzically at TM. 'Wasn't that clear?'

'It was very clear,' TM reassured her.

'Then,' said Veggie, his voice starting low and rising to a great shout,

'I, Veggie, accept your challenge to overcome great odds and once more achieve the dizzying heights of just about keeping a business afloat!'

'Sure,' agreed Ziggy, unfazed.

Several hours later, the floor was covered in empty crisp packets and the Bedsheet-Tablecloth-Whiteboard was covered in words, lines, and doodles of all colours - only a few of which, to Veggie's credit, were dicks. The trio stared at it for a few minutes, nodding in silent appreciation, then somehow all managed to fist-bump each other at the exact same moment.

'That,' TM said, 'is badass.'

'Dang right,' Ziggy concurred.

'I'm pretty sure we're already somehow billionaires just from writing that all down,' Veggie said, inaccurately.

Before anyone could say 'confirmation bias', the power came back on.

'Oh, heck,' said TM, for a moment wondering in spite of himself whether they really had somehow acquired money from the future through some sort of awesomeness osmosis. Then his phone buzzed; he glanced at the screen and saw a message from Derrida.

Power's just come back on at mine, hope the cut's over at yours too.

'Um,' TM started to say, but Veggie and Ziggy were chatting excitedly about how their phenomenal powers of inventiveness had transcended space and time. So he just smiled and agreed.

20. Wrestler Intelligentsia

'Morning,' Ziggy said, nudging TM's head with her foot.

'Hi,' TM said, eyes firmly shut. 'Please say it's not actually the morning.'

'Naw,' Ziggy tooted. 'It's, like, three in the afternoon.'

'Oh, thank God,' TM said. 'I thought for a moment that you were actually trying to wake me up before noon.'

'I wouldn't do that to ya, bud.'

'Appreciate it.' TM slowly pushed himself upright until he was reclining on one elbow, rubbing his eyes with his other hand. Slowly, they peeled open. 'Where is everyone?' he asked, peering around the flat. He was on the floor, covered by a blanket; Ziggy stood in the doorway of the bathroom, the filing cabinet pushed aside; other than the two of them, nobody seemed to be in the flat (excepting Michel Furcoat, who appeared to be fully asleep).

'Er...' Ziggy held up three fingers, counting them off. 'You're on the floor. I'm here. And Veggie's at Marty's gig. Or helping prepare or something, I think he said it didn't start until later.'

'Oh, yeah.' TM blinked a few times, realising that he had just assumed that one or more of Marty, Derrida, or Dominika would have been more likely than not to have stayed the night. 'Not a sleepover night. So... why am I on the floor?'

'We did this awesome invention brainstorm thing,' Ziggy said, pointing insistently at the Bedsheet-Tablecloth-Whiteboard, 'and then we were super happy so we ate a bunch more food and watched some old movie about an alien and then all just sort of went to sleep.'

'Oh, yeah.' TM yawned, then sat bolt upright. 'Wait. You said Marty's gig.'

'Yar.'

'You've never been to one of Marty's gigs.'

'Nar.'

TM leapt to his feet, grabbing her by the hand. 'We have to go,' he told her. She maintained eye contact for a moment, then looked down.

'Um,' she said.

'Oh, right,' TM realised, pulling the blanket up over himself again. 'Why was I naked when I went to sleep?'

'I'unno,' she said, shrugging. 'Comfort? Seen both of you now, anyway, so 's only fair.'

'Sorry.'

'Pretty sure I'm fine with it, long as you are.' She looked away for a moment, thoughtful. 'I think bodies are just, like, things that are cool 'cos they work and stuff, anyway. Minds are weirder, and more awesome. Little universes.'

'Still, I'll probably keep wearing clothes for the time being,' TM said, picking up the crumpled outfit he had left on the floor and striding to the bedroom. He tossed yesterday's gear into the corner that passed for a laundry pile and grabbed some fresh clothes, pulling his own Inciting Incident T-shirt over his head and sliding his legs through a pair of jeans with very deliberately ripped knees, then opened the door and meandered out to street level.

He led Ziggy towards the city centre, practically skipping as they got closer; as they passed a supermarket, she slowed and looked in.

'Hungry?' TM asked, realising that he too was pretty much famished. She nodded, looking as if it was an effort to keep from actually licking her lips at the sight of rows of sandwiches and packets of crisps. TM checked his watch, then immediately remembered that he hadn't put it on. 'We've got time,' he decided.

Moments later, they re-emerged, Ziggy noshing on a triple-decker BLT sandwich while TM did his best to stuff an entire baguette packed with southern fried chicken into his mouth.

'Right,' TM said around mouthfuls of chicken and soft bread. 'Gig!'

Ziggy followed earnestly as TM made his speedy way into a side street packed mostly with pubs. He stared up at the signs outside each, stopping at the one declaring tonight to be 'THE NIGHT OF THE INCITING INCIDENT'.

'Whoa,' said Ziggy, gazing up at the sign. 'Marty's band is really successful, huh?'

'They're doing pretty good,' TM agreed, leading her in.

The interior of the pub was darker than the street outside, as the inside of buildings almost invariably tend to be during the day. Veggie stood, leaning against the bar and watching the band tune up; TM hopped up behind him, slapping him on the shoulder.

'Oh, hey, Sleeping Beauty,' said Veggie, eyebrows raising in mild surprise. 'Didn't realise you were coming. Or doing anything today.'

'Dude,' said TM seriously. 'Ziggy's never seen them play.'

Veggie gave an enormous gasp. 'Heck, yeah! Omigosh. You're gonna flipping love this.'

'Are you actually squeeing over the band of a guy we hang out with, like, every day?' TM said.

'I'm a fanboy,' Veggie said. 'It's what we do.'

'Er, hey,' said Marty, tapping his microphone, his other arm draped over the neck of his guitar. Behind him, the rest of the band - Obbie Kernel on guitar, with her orange hair and lean arms; Kurt Eiseldown on bass, clad in traditional Eiseldown garb that covered nothing between shoulder and waist, but for some reason still included sleeves; The Destructionist on drums, looking for all the world like she'd skipped school to be there - looked poised and ready. 'So, uh, I know the sign says we're playing... tonight, but the owners have actually only given us the pre-teatime slot. Thanks, Gary, not Gary Mackerel from the fish shop but Gary the barman whose surname I can't remember.'

'Welcome,' said the barman.

'So we're gonna wait for like two minutes. Then it'll be half an hour after our advertised start time, so that seems like a reasonable time to wait for the usual fashionably late crowd.'

There was a murmur of appreciation as Marty removed his lips from the microphone and turned back to his bandmates.

'Does it get busier than this?' Ziggy asked disappointedly, looking around at the mostly empty space.

'Oh, yeah,' Veggie said, swigging from a glass bottle of fruit juice. 'He wasn't kidding about people turning up late.'

As if on cue, the doors swung open and a flood of people in assorted punk and ironic pop culture T-shirts made their entrance, swarming the seats and bar area.

'Hey, guys,' said Marty, 'glad you could make it.'

An enormous cheer rose up from the assembly, and The Destructionist started to tap on her hi-hat rhythmically. Of course it was rhythmic, TM thought, for some reason: what use would a non-rhythmic drummer be?

'This one,' Marty said, his stance and tone dripping with the mostly-justified cockiness of a rich-ish boy in a mildly well-known local rock band, 'is called *Wrestler Intelligentsia (Get Sexy, Yeah)*. Some of you might know it.'

Ziggy bit her lip, apparently trying not to laugh, and glanced at TM, who mouthed they're hecking awesome at her. She nodded, apparently reassured, and turned back to watch.

'Alright - one two three fo -'

Before 'four' had fully left his mouth, Marty and the Inciting Incident launched into a heavy, juddering, bassy riff. The crowd went, it was fair to say, wild, including Ziggy, who leapt up and down in time and banged her head around so that her hair trailed out behind, floating around her head in waves as if she were underwater.

'OH!' yelled Marty into the mic. His audience duly yelled back.

Oh, he's had a whole bunch of in-ring capers

And contributed to academic papers

IQ of two-two-five, and in the ring he's no berk

Solving the Goldbach conjecture is his life's work, wa-uh-oh

Wrestl-aaaaaah

intelligentsi-aaaaaaah

So woah uh-uh-oh, now get sexy-aaaaaaah

The building shook with the bounding of the masses.

***

Nine songs later, the Inciting Incident slowed the pace a little.

'This one,' said Marty, 'is a new one, that we've never played before ever.'

The crowd went wild.

'Well,' Marty corrected, holding a hand up to quiet them, 'we obviously did, like, in practice and stuff. But not in front of a crowd.'

The wildness intensified.

'This one is called *I Got My Buster Sword* and it is full of tons of references to, like, video games and anime and stuff, and if you get them all you're a nerd.'

A girl near the back of the room screamed and lifted her top up, to which the crowd yelled ecstatically and Marty calmly winked. 'Thanks,' he said politely. 'Appreciate it.'

Who the hell do you think we are?

How do you think I got my lightning scar?

'That's not a video game or anime reference,' Ziggy yelled over the noise to TM, her tone sounding almost cheated.

It's time to tighten the outer walls

Titan, tighten, homophones are cool

'Chorus!' Marty yelled.

I got my Buster Sword

And I got my Keyblade

I got dragon's balls

And they're here to stay

Marty held the microphone out to his bandmates, who yelled in unison:

This goose is here to ruin your day!

Then Marty lifted his head to the sky and screamed, a piercing vibrato that somehow seemed higher than any noise TM had ever heard yet simultaneously reverberated with booming bass, vibrating the entire building.

'Marty is so hecking cool,' Ziggy mouthed at TM, who misunderstood what she was trying to say but nodded anyway.

***

It was the dead of night by the time they left. The barman-cum-owner had finally managed to get the Inciting Incident to stop playing their apparently endless repertoire, almost the entirety of which seemed to have been faithfully memorised by everyone in attendance. Ziggy held her arms skyward, twirling about in the cold night air in breathless ecstasy.

'That was the best thing ever,' she said joyously.

TM watched her for a few moments, unable to stop smiling.

'What?' she said, stopping mid-revolution to look at him.

'I'm glad you're happy,' he said sincerely.

'Whaaaaaaaaaaaaaa,' Veggie yelled, tumbling out onto the street. 'That was pretty tiptop, yeah?'

'Yaaaaaaaaa!' Ziggy agreed, grabbing him by the hands and spinning him around.

'What kept you, anyway?' TM asked.

'Oh,' said Veggie, actually blushing. 'I might have decided that Marty is really, incredibly attractive.'

'Fair play,' said TM and Ziggy at the same time.

'I want food,' Veggie went on, eyes glazed as if staring at a far-away pizza. 'You get this one, I didn't bring money. Or...' He trailed off, in that dangerous *I've got a brilliantly terrible idea* sort of way. 'This might be because I'm slightly drunk off the pure amazingness of that gig, but why don't we do the heist now?'

'Er,' said TM.

'No, I'm serious,' Veggie said, all apparent tipsiness suddenly gone. 'It's the dead of night, we're fully trained up on video games and *Hero's Adventure*... I think we're ready for this.'

'Um,' TM said, in addendum to his previous comment.

'I think you might be right,' Ziggy said, her eyes very wide. 'Let's do this.'

'You guys are serious?' TM said helplessly.

'Heck, yeah!' Veggie exclaimed. 'We're doing this, so why not do it now?'

TM sighed. 'Fine,' he said.

Thus, of all the ways, began the heist.

21. Extreme Hardcore Parkour

They made their way down the street, TM twitching nervously at every unexpected breeze, snapping twig, or drunken chorus of *Like A Virgin* (or, indeed, *Wrestler Intelligentsia*).

'You're jumpy,' Ziggy observed; TM rubbed his hands together, half against the cold and half in the hopes of preventing further embarrassing tics.

'Sorry,' he said. 'I guess maybe I'm starting to get a bit nervous about... you know. Heisting.'

'Don't wimp out on us now, TM,' warned Veggie. 'What is there to be nervous about, anyway?'

'Ehhhhhh,' said TM. 'I dunno. I've just never done an actual robbery before.'

'Heist,' Veggie corrected. 'And yeah, we may never have literally legitimately heisted -'

'Is that a word?'

'It doesn't get underlined by my spell check, weirdly. Point is, we might never have actually heisted an actual building, but now we're trained up, man. We've been working like heck for the last... seventy-two hours, or something like that. Come ooooooooooooon. We got this.'

TM stopped as they drew near the corner of the street upon which the museum sat in wait, and looked at Ziggy. 'You really think... feel like you need to do this,' he said to her, not sure whether it was a question or a statement.

'I do,' she said.

TM took a deep breath. 'Fine,' he said. 'Let's do this.'

Ziggy hugged him; her face pressed into his shoulder, her hair falling onto his skin. It was nice for a second, but then he suddenly found it itchy and uncomfortable and tried to blow the strands away, with little success.

'Thank you,' Ziggy said, holding him tightly. 'For everything.'

'You're welcome,' said Veggie loudly, squeezing them both

obnoxiously. Ziggy gave a quiet laugh; TM felt the breath leave her in his arms. 'Right,' said Veggie eventually. 'Teeeeeeaaaaaaaaaaam - *break*!'

Nobody moved.

'Oh, right, sorry,' Veggie said after a moment. 'I know I said break, and all that, but I sort of got carried away, forgot to let go. So... team break.'

They detached, albeit less basketball-team-esquely than Veggie had probably been aiming for.

'Nice,' said Ziggy.

'Okay,' Veggie said, clapping his hands together, 'ready?'

Ziggy nodded eagerly. TM also nodded, albeit slightly less eagerly.

'We'll make our entrance through a vent in the roof,' Veggie said, pointing upwards.

Ziggy and TM blinked at each other.

'Did you see any vents on the roof?' she said pointedly. TM shook his head.

'Nope,' he said. 'Solid old fashioned stone roof.'

'There must be some sort of opening,' Veggie moaned.

'Don't think so,' Ziggy said. Veggie wailed despairingly.

'A chimney,' he said, 'a skylight, a hole for Santa, for flip's sake.'

'Look,' said TM, leaning around the street corner to peer down at the dark building. 'See that? That is an old style, fancy-ass, impossible-to-get-on-top-of piece of architecture.'

'But... parkour,' Veggie protested.

'We trained for two hours, Veg,' said TM. 'Two hours.'

Veggie nodded, though he looked woefully put out.

'Let's just... try the front door,' Ziggy suggested, to which Veggie gasped with shock and disdain.

'Did you learn nothing from *Hero's Adventure*?' he exclaimed.

'Eh,' said Ziggy.

'We can't just go in the front door,' Veggie opined, aghast. 'There might be magical traps and shit.'

'I doubt it,' Ziggy said, leaving the safety of the corner to make her way openly down the street.

She passed down the centre of the street, weaving gentle loops around the illuminating beams from the street lamps. TM thought her hair was darkening as she proceeded; the purple tint seemed to be fading to pure black, the better to evade detection. When she reached the front of the museum, duly closed to the public for the night, she put her hand on the door and pushed firmly. It swung open with a creak like a dragon with sleep apnoea; TM was vaguely aware of a dog barking somewhere nearby, perhaps startled by the loud noise.

'Creaky,' Ziggy said, 'but open.'

'No alarms?' said Veggie warily, sounding almost disappointed.

'Apparently not,' Ziggy said.

'Not surprised,' TM mused, following her inside. 'It kind of looked like they were pretty light on budget for security when we were last here.'

'Yet they can afford a space rock,' Veggie pointed out, crossing the threshold one finger at a time.

The museum was dead. Which, TM mused, was to be expected: not only was it the middle of the night, but most of the things inside had ceased to be living some centuries ago. They slinked quietly through the corridors, the masks and figures that stared down at them from the walls looking far more sinister than they had in the daylight. Veggie lit the way with the torch on his phone; the beam shuddered slightly every time it passed over any exhibit that had eyes.

Almost immediately, they came to the main room.

'There it is,' breathed Ziggy, staring up at the rock. In the darkness it looked like any other hunk of stone, until Veggie's illuminating beam fell upon it and the room came alight with twinkling reflections and fractured rainbows.

'This is it, I guess,' TM agreed. Ziggy stepped up to the crystalline space rock reverently, then hopped up onto the pedestal with it, her fingers reaching out towards the glass cube encasing it.

Then she kicked the glass.

Hard.

'Er,' said TM, watching on as she slammed her foot hard into the glass case over and over, making an alarming amount of noise. 'Are you sure that's going to break?'

'I'm - not - trying- to - break - it,' Ziggy said between kicks. 'Not - directly - anyway.'

'Not... directly?' TM barely had time to say before the rock, still encased in its transparent cube, toppled slowly off its raised platform.

There was an almighty smash as the glass case hit the floor, followed by a solid, heavy thud as the rock inside came free of its holdings and slammed down. No alarm sounded, though TM couldn't help nervously eyeing the entrance to the room.

Ziggy hopped down, crouching next to the rock. It balanced for a few moments on one of its rounded points, then tipped onto a flatter side and lay still. She reached out a cautious hand, touching the barest millimetre of a fingertip to its crystal-covered surface. Then she sighed.

'You alright?' TM said. She looked up at him, not quite meeting his eyes.

'I... don't know,' she said.

'Go on,' said Veggie, apparently trying to ingest some enthusiasm into the moment. 'This is what we came for.'

Ziggy reached out again, placed her palms firmly on the sides of the rock, and lifted it. TM looked at Veggie, who mouthed at him:

'That thing sounded really, really heavy. Like... *really* heavy.'

TM's eyebrows squirmed back at him in confusion.

'I don't know what I was expecting,' Ziggy said, breaking up the eyebrow conversation. She held the space rock aloft, staring into its surface.

Then she sighed, and dropped it. The rock smashed into the stone floor, leaving a hefty crack. A sliver of the crystalline layer on its surface snapped free and rolled towards Veggie; he picked it up and put it in his pocket.

'Whatever I was looking for,' she said, standing there and watching it vibrate, 'I don't think I found it here.'

'So all this was for nothing?' Veggie said disappointedly. Ziggy's eyes wandered vaguely in his direction.

'Not nothing,' TM said hurriedly. 'We devised, planned, prepared and pulled off a really cool heist, that's something.' There was an extended pause. 'Right?'

'I guess,' said Ziggy. Her eyes traced a path around the room, as if watching something rolling along the floor. 'It feels like all the... all the mass and the gravity, I thought it was here but now it's not. Or... it still is, but there's more of it outside, all just pressing in, so... it doesn't mean anything compared to that. Real but not real. It's all so... *heavy*.'

'Hey,' TM said, taking her by the shoulders. 'I know you thought this would give you... something, but it's okay if it didn't. You've got me, and Veg, and Marty and Dominika and Derrida. And the cats.'

Ziggy met his gaze, though her eyes looked unfocused. 'Could you take me home?' she said, looking as if she might collapse.

TM hoisted her arm over his shoulder, and Veggie rushed in to support her from the other side.

'I'm sorry,' she said, as they half-carried her towards the entrance.

'For what?' TM asked, watching her face with concern.

'I've asked a lot of you,' she said, looking unblinkingly at the floor stretching out before her.

'Yeah,' said Veggie, 'maybe. But we got to pull off a flipping awesome heist, so don't mention it. Fairly sure I speak for both of us when I say we're happy to have been of assistance.'

'It wasn't the *most* amazingly flipping awesome of heists,' TM observed. 'I mean, we didn't actually have to pick a lock or sneak past any guards or climb through any vents or anything.'

'Screw that,' Veggie said. 'Doesn't matter how we did it, we robbed a public building of a rock from space and it was the best. Journey over destination, or something.'

'We didn't actually rob it, technically,' TM pointed out. 'We left the rock in there.'

'Yeah, well. We could have taken it, and isn't that the point?'

'Pff,' said TM.

'Anyway,' Veggie continued, 'I did take a tiny bit with me.' He patted his pocket.

'Nothing really... means anything,' Ziggy said, slumped between them as they turned a corner. 'The universe doesn't care. About anything. I'm just... one dot in the sky, and now I'm just one face in a sea of billions.'

'You're *our* one face out of all those billions,' TM told her firmly.

'I really thought getting that rock would do... something,' she continued. 'I don't know what. Reveal some great truth, maybe, or bestow great cosmic power or something. Maybe it didn't even matter what it did. I just really hoped for... something. Just something that could help all this mean something.'

'How can you say this doesn't mean anything?' Veggie demanded, grabbing her face and forcing her to look at him. 'Zig. We, like, literally fucking love you.'

'I love you too,' she said, her eyes finally focusing.

'So don't you say that this - your life down here, existence, reality in general, whatever - don't say that any of that doesn't mean anything. Cos it does.'

Ziggy laughed quietly, and TM felt her take her own weight on her feet again. He released her gently, letting her stand unsupported.

'You're right,' she said, with a small smile. 'Maybe the universe doesn't care about anything, but... I think I do.'

'That's the spirit,' said Veggie, clapping her on the back.

'I think I might just stay with you guys forever,' Ziggy said decisively. She took her partners' hands, and they left the museum through the still-open front door.

In the middle of the street before them, lit by the yellow beam of a streetlight above, somebody stood with his arms behind his back, staring at the door as they exited.

'Er,' said TM, looking down at Al Tyer.

22. Rainmaker II (Fame)

Tyer said nothing, staring up at them. His suit was as impeccably in place as ever, his hair immaculately combed. His grey eyes focused with unnerving solidity, not moving at all as he gazed up.

'What do we do?' TM heard Veggie whisper. He looked over; Veggie was glancing desperately across to him, a look of absolute uncertainty in his eyes, while Ziggy stood completely frozen.

TM backed up slowly, putting a hand on the door behind him. Inexplicably, but somehow unsurprisingly, it had shut itself and would not budge. The only way out was down the stairs before them, towards Al Tyer.

'We have to go down,' TM said quietly. Ziggy shook her head furiously.

'We can't,' she said, turning to TM. Her eyes were wide, pupils dilated, breathing heavily. 'We can't go that way.'

'What else can we -' TM stopped as he glanced back down at Tyer. He had moved closer.

'Hey,' Veggie called to him, his voice shaking in a way that TM knew was not just from the cold. 'You're out late.'

'As are you,' Tyer said. His voice, as ever, was perfectly steady. 'It is a clear night, with little cloud. Rain is not expected.'

'We're going to... go now,' Veggie said, cautiously taking a step down towards him. 'But thanks for the weather report.'

'I can't let you go,' said Tyer.

'What are you going to do?' Veggie asked uncertainly.

'We need her back,' Tyer said, raising an arm to point, extended completely straight, at Ziggy.

TM felt his stomach freeze. 'No,' he said. 'No, fuck this. We're going home.' He descended the steps, grabbing Ziggy's hand, but found himself stopped halfway down when she failed to move an inch.

'Ziggy,' TM said, looking back up at her. 'We're going home.'

'I think that's where he's come to take me,' Ziggy breathed, completely frozen. TM could not make her move, not so much as wobble, no matter how hard he tugged at her hand.

'What - you mean -' TM looked back down at Tyer, not letting Ziggy's hand go.

'As sad as I'm sure this is, she is correct,' Tyer said, shifting his weight and drawing his hands back behind him, standing in a stiff formal pose. 'A star has disappeared. There are consequences to that, and not ones that any of us particularly want to see come to pass.'

'What sort of consequences?' Veggie asked, narrowing his eyes at Tyer.

The weatherman spread his arms. 'I'm not entirely sure. But, as they say: as above, so below.'

'Nobody says that,' Veggie said defiantly.

'You are below,' Tyer continued, examining his nails. 'The stars are above. Then there is that which is above again. Perhaps there is yet more above that.'

'What are you on about?' Veggie said, stepping down beside TM, shielding Ziggy. 'You're just spouting meaningless bullshit, man.'

'If only,' Tyer said, taking a step towards them. TM and Veggie folded in, putting as much of themselves as they could between Tyer and Ziggy.

'Leave us alone,' TM said, almost pleading. Then he felt Ziggy's hand on his shoulder.

She pushed TM and Veggie to the sides of the steps, slowly stepping down.

'What are you -' TM said quietly, desperately, helplessly watching her descend each step.

'You're...' she said questioningly to Tyer.

He pointed straight upwards, and her head tilted skyward to look. 'I'm gone,' she said. 'And you're dimmed.'

'I am,' he agreed.

'Altair,' she said.

'At your service,' said Al Tyer. He gave her a small bow. 'The eagle has missed you, little sister. Aquila is not the same without you.'

'I know,' Ziggy said quietly.

Tyer stepped the rest of the way across the street, his feet rapping in perfect rhythm against the slabs. He raised his arm, holding his hand out to her, and as TM watched, helpless, feeling like the world was spinning and falling away underneath him, Ziggy took it.

'No,' TM heard himself say, and before he knew what he was doing he found one hand gripping Tyer by the forearm, the other spread protectively between him and Ziggy. 'No. You can't have her.'

Ziggy and Tyer turned to look at TM as one.

'She can't stay,' said Tyer. 'A star is gone from the sky. And without her there, all the forces have become… misaligned. Orbits are changing. Stabilities, bodies held in safe patterns by gravity, have been unbalanced. Before long, all the stars in Aquila will become dispersed, spread across the sky.

'The balance between the heavenly bodies will shift, their masses failing to intertwine, and release them from their places, and as they cross other paths there will be more disturbances, more falling stars. Collisions. As above, so below, and the earth will soon find itself in an unstable position. An imbalance is not sustainable.'

'Surely all that can't really happen from one star going AWOL,' Veggie protested.

'It's about more than that,' Tyer said, 'it's the principle of the thing. You small people have difficulty understanding that the forces in place are there for a reason, and that there are powers higher than what you know which will be angered if they are changed without permission.' He paused for a moment. 'Well. They cannot be angered. That is… overly humanising.'

He looked Veggie dead in the eyes; TM saw his friend look away, apparently unable to meet Tyer's gaze.

'It would be inaccurate,' the weatherman continued, 'to say that they *do* anything, fundamentally, other than exist and react to things. They have no intentions. They just are.'

'Oh, shut up,' said TM, and punched him in the face.

Tyer fell back, clutching at his nose; TM grabbed Ziggy and heaved her up and over his shoulder, then dashed off down the street with Ziggy hoisted in his arms and Veggie hot on their heels.

'Don't let him take me,' Ziggy pleaded, the words coming out broken as TM vainly did his best not to bump her about too much as he ran.

'I'm not going to,' TM told her, breathing fast, darting down narrow streets and sprinting around corners towards home. 'I promise.'

TM slid to a halt as they made it to their street, set Ziggy down on her feet and fumbled about in his pocket for his keys. 'Nice to have you back with us, anyway,' he said, scrabbling about.

'Sorry,' Ziggy said. 'He's... bigger than me. Brighter. It's gravity, like he said. If he pulls me, I can't escape him.'

'It's okay,' TM told her as sincerely as he possibly could, then finally noticed that he didn't actually have keys. 'Veg, keys?'

Veggie dragged them out from the depths of his back pocket and tossed them to TM. He held them up to his face, fiddling about, unable to match key to lock in the darkness.

'I don't want to go back,' Ziggy said. 'I want to stay, and be a person.'

'We won't let them take you,' TM told her, finally slotting the key into the lock. He turned the key, and before he could go to push the door open, an enormous shape bounded out of the darkness at him, knocking him sideways.

'TM!' Ziggy yelled. TM felt himself pressed into the ground by two heavy paws on his shoulders, saw vaguely through the darkness and his fear the face of a golden dog snapping at him.

'Keelut?' Veggie exclaimed in confusion, barrelling into the dog and knocking it off TM. Ziggy grabbed them both by the hand, sprinting away from Keelut, down the street, turning a corner - and then stopped.

'Should have known,' said Veggie, skidding to a stop beside her.

'Hey,' said Riegel O'Ryan, leaning casually on a street corner signpost. Al Tyer emerged around the corner to stand beside her, rubbing his chin. 'Did a bit of a number on Al here, huh? That's actually kind of impressive.' She turned to look at him. 'You'd better not be dawdling down here again.'

He raised an eyebrow a fraction of an inch, every other muscle in his body remaining perfectly still.

'Let her go,' TM said, as firmly as he could.

'Sorry,' said O'Ryan. 'Can't.'

'You could,' Veggie said. 'Couldn't you?'

'We're under orders, of sorts,' O'Ryan said, half-disdainfully. 'Can't leave without her, I'm afraid.'

TM felt Ziggy shiver beside him, standing frozen again like a rabbit in O'Ryan's burningly bright headlights.

'You're my hero, man,' Veggie told her, sounding as if he might start sobbing.

'Well,' said O'Ryan, standing up straight and folding her arms. Keelut padded up beside her, baring her teeth at TM. 'You know what they say: never meet your heroes.'

'Hang on,' TM said, something dawning on him. 'You're... like, a star too?'

O'Ryan pointed upwards. 'I'm a little bit dimmer than usual, but I'm up there.'

TM looked at the sky for a few moments, then back down at her. 'I know literally nothing about stars,' he said.

'You've been living with one, lad,' O'Ryan said incredulously.

'This,' Tyer said, apparently by way of introduction, 'is more than a star. This is Orion, the Hunter.'

O'Ryan stuck a thumb into her belt, waving with the other hand. 'In the flesh,' she said.

TM scoffed, unable to think of anything else to do as he struggled to process it all. 'So, what, you're the... lead star of Ziggy's constellation -' he pointed at Tyer '- and *you're* actually an entire constellation on your own, and she's come to Earth to live some sort of life and you two are pissed off about it so you've... come down too?' He almost laughed. 'Aren't the cosmic forces up above pissed about you two being here?'

'They tolerate it,' said O'Ryan, shrugging with one hand buried firmly in Keelut's long hair. 'The brightest star in her neighbourhood's responsible for bringin' her back, and I'm the Hunter. So they let me come down when somebody needs huntin'.'

'She doesn't want to come back,' TM said, feeling his whole body tense. O'Ryan noticed it.

'What, you're going to fight us?' she said, laughing. 'We're fuckin' stars. I'm the brightest and most beautiful thing in the sky, and I'm about

20 light years bigger than you. So if I were you, I'd probably *back off.*'

'Well, I'm not going to,' TM told her, almost to his own surprise. 'She's my friend. I'd punch the sun for her.'

'I'll tell her that,' O'Ryan said, strolling casually towards them.

Veggie dived at her; Tyer stepped in, effortlessly lifting Veggie above his head and tossing him aside without disturbing a single crease of his suit. TM backed off, raising his fists, putting himself before the motionless Ziggy, and O'Ryan stopped as she reached him.

'Last chance,' she told him. 'Step aside.'

'No,' TM said as loudly as he could manage, which turned out to be a whisper.

O'Ryan looked almost regretful. 'This isn't personal,' she said.

Then she grabbed his arm, lifted him into a fireman's carry across her shoulders, and threw him up in the air. TM started to pray as he went over, his head firmly in her grasp, and then he slammed hard into the ground. He lay there, winded, unable to move, feeling spasms of pain through his neck and back. He could only watch, prone on the concrete, as O'Ryan stood before Ziggy and stared into her eyes.

'Don't,' Ziggy said, so quietly TM wasn't sure he had really heard it. 'Please.'

'Sorry,' said O'Ryan.

She flipped Ziggy around, grabbed her by the wrists from behind, then let go with one hand and pulled hard with the other. Ziggy went spinning away from her, still held fast by one wrist.

'What the fuck,' TM heard Veggie exclaim from the floor a few metres away.

O'Ryan pulled Ziggy back towards her, and slammed her forearm into her face. Ziggy's feet left the ground with the force of it, flipping fully around, then lay still. Rain began to fall.

'Rainmaker?' TM breathed.

Tyer strode over to Ziggy's prone body and lifted her into his arms like a newborn, her arm and head slumping down as he took her up. The rain left tiny dark dots in his suit, but his hair remained impeccably in place. O'Ryan's copper mane stuck to her face, plastered on by the raindrops, as she looked on; Keelut looked about half her usual size with her fur slicked down. O'Ryan put her palm on Ziggy's forehead, looked at Tyer, and nodded.

Then they turned, and walked away into the darkness.

PART TWO
After

23. But Siriusly Though

'She's gone,' said Veggie.

They sat at their old regular café table, mugs of tea cradled in their hands. Rain dripped from Veggie's nose into his mug, splashing droplets onto his hands, but he didn't seem to notice.

Beside him, TM took a sip of his own tea. It was terrible, as usual, but somehow it tasted even more terrible than he had come to expect. Across from them sat Marty, Dominika, and Derrida: despite it being so late that it was now more accurate to say it was early the next morning, all had dropped everything when TM had called. It was astonishing, really, that the café was still open, but TM supposed it was probably just one of those places that defied all reasonable expectations of time and space.

'What do you mean, she's gone?' Marty said after a few moments.

Veggie reached into his pocket, and dug out the two officially licensed Surviving O'Ryan keyrings he had won at the fair. He held them up for a moment, looking at them, grinding his teeth. Then he seemed unable to look at them any more, and dropped them in his mug of tea. TM picked up the mug and put it on another table, lest Veggie decide to break it.

'Ziggy was...' TM began, then paused. 'She was special.'

'She was a star,' Veggie explained, to which the three shared a look of confusion.

'We know,' Derrida said with some hesitation; TM shook his head firmly.

'Nah, not like... how you call people stars, you know?'

'Not... really,' Marty said.

TM sighed. 'You know how there's been those stories on the news lately, about how stars have been disappearing from the sky and stuff?'

Derrida and Marty looked vacant; Dominika nodded, leaning forwards, her eyebrows lowering.

'Well, one of them was her,' TM finished.

'And there were some bad ones, and they're fucking Al Tyer and

Riegel O'Ryan,' Veggie added, slamming his hand down on the table. TM's mug shook in distress; he picked it up and put it beside Veggie's on the other table. 'And they came down, and they took her away.'

'I don't follow,' Marty said helplessly.

Derrida looked about, thinking hard, holding their chin in one hand. 'So... you're saying Ziggy was literally a star, from space, who came down to be in human form. Somehow. And a local weatherman and a survival show host were also stars, and they... what, killed her?'

'I don't know,' said TM, unable to look anyone in the eye. He could feel a burning in his throat and behind his eyes, and in the centre of his brain, and then it was all over his body and he stood up as a prickling hotness stabbed him in every inch of himself and he could not sit still. 'I don't know if she's alive, or dead, or if alive and dead are even words that can be meaningfully applied to someone who's literally an enormous ball of burning gases, but she was my friend. And she's gone.'

Dominika stood, then grabbed TM and pulled him in, resting his head on her shoulder and wrapping her arms around him. TM stood there, finally letting the tears fall onto Dominika's shoulder, shaking in her arms. He was vaguely aware of Veggie standing up suddenly, running his hands through his hair, pacing about, and of Marty putting his hands on Veggie's arms and whispering to him, and then Dominika could no longer hold him and he fell to his knees there in the middle of the café.

'She's really gone?' Derrida said quietly, but TM barely heard them. 'Can't we... report her as missing, or something?'

'She's gone,' Veggie said, shaking free of Marty's grasp. 'She never really existed in the first place, Jack, she was a star. She doesn't have a National Insurance number, or any kind of record, or even a fucking birthday.'

Derrida looked down at the table.

'What would we say?' Veggie said helplessly, holding his hands up. 'Hello, police? It's me, Veggie, and my friend who came from outer space just got kidnapped and probably murdered or rocketed back to space or something by two TV personalities and their dog. Oh, you'll get on that? Thanks.' He gave Derrida a poisoned stare, then shook his head and left the café, slamming the door behind him.

'I'm sorry,' Derrida said quietly as the echoes of the slamming door faded.

'He's just upset,' TM said from his position on his knees, wiping the tears and ugly mucus from his face with his sleeve. 'Sorry I got bodily fluids on your top, Nika.'

Dominika, dabbing at her shoulder with a napkin, gave him a quick thumbs-up.

TM got slowly to his feet, rubbing his eyes with his thumbs, and slumped back into his seat. 'She's gone,' he said finally. 'Whatever they did with her, they wanted to put her back up in the sky where they think she belongs. She's not coming back.'

'Come on, man,' said Marty, pulling uncomfortably at the neck of his T-shirt, as if it were strangling him. 'We've got to... I don't know. Put on some sort of rescue mission.'

'What, you want to build a spaceship and go up after her?' TM said, shaking his head.

'What are you on about?' said Dominika.

TM stared at her.

'You're all like *oh no, I'm so sad, she was my friend*, and yet you've instantly just given up and said *well shit, she's gone so I guess I'd better just immediately accept that she's gone forever and move on.*' She slapped TM in the face. 'Don't be *stupid*.'

'You can talk?' TM said, rubbing his cheek. He looked despairingly at Marty and Derrida; the former looked away awkwardly, the latter simply shrugged.

She took a deep breath. 'This is important, and I'm sure about this.'

'Wait - you don't talk because you're worried that if you're not sure then... you'll look stupid or something? If *you're* not confident in yourself, what the hell chance do any of the rest of us have?'

'Bad experience one time. Look, don't tell Veggie; it's easier having him assume I can't, and I kind of like being all mysterious or whatever. Started 'cos I was scared, kept it up 'cos people seemed to like it.'

That seemed to TM like it might be a problem that Dominika really ought to work through, but all he could say for then was: 'fair play.'

'Point is we've got to at least *try*,' she said imploringly. 'Dunno how, but we've got to.'

TM sighed. 'I don't suppose you can read the stars?'

'Course I can,' she said, hands on hips. TM led her outside, and pointed up.

'Is she up there?' he said, not sure which answer he was hoping for.

She looked up into the night sky, sidestepping to avoid the light pollution of the café's gaudy sign. 'Theta Aquila was the one that went missing, right? And Altair went dim, and so did the whole of Orion.'

'Theta Aquila,' TM said, the name feeling alien on his lips. 'That's her.'

Dominika peered up, revolving slowly. 'She's there,' she said eventually. 'She's back.'

TM pressed his hands to his face, his fingers slowly rubbing down his eyes and cheeks down to his chin. 'They took her back,' he said.

'Looks that way,' she said. 'Altair's back at the head of Aquila, and… Orion's fully lit again, too. They're gone.' She peered curiously around for a moment. 'Oh, and Sirius is back in Canis Major, too.'

'Sirius?'

'Yeah, the Dog Star. It's a pretty big deal, but it only got a few points of visual magnitude darker, so it didn't make the news as much as the other ones that went AWOL.'

'Dog Star,' TM said. 'Of course.'

Dominika dropped her gaze from the heavens to look into TM's face. 'You can't just give up,' she said.

'I know.'

'You're an inventor,' she told him, patting him on the cheek. 'Invent something.'

24. A Slightly More Blank Sheet

One day, Aster left. It didn't matter why, really; what mattered was only that she'd chosen to.

After she was gone, TM spent a lot of time listening to music. He was never quite sure what sort of music to listen to, though. He would put some sad ballad on, or Chopin or something.

It was very easy, TM reflected, to only think of things that could be verbalised as being 'real' or 'valid' or 'true'. After all, so much of everything was done with language. It was a useful thing to have, undeniably, but perhaps everyone was missing something by not just accepting that some things could be true despite not being possible to prove with linguistic reasoning, or even to put into words at all. That was how the music made him feel now.

Other times, he would put on something more upbeat, modern, punky even. It made him smile for a short time, if he was lucky. Ultimately, it didn't seem to matter whether the music was happy or sad. He would feel what the music made him feel for as long as it lasted, and perhaps a little longer, and then he would go back to feeling what he had been feeling before. Happy music didn't take away the sadness, and sad music didn't seem to be providing any sort of effective catharsis.

All in all, TM thought, it was a bit of a shitter of a situation.

***

'Hey,' TM said, closing the door to the flat slowly.

'What?' said Veggie, from somewhere.

TM scouted about for a moment. Michel Furcoat came over to wind himself around TM's ankles, purring quietly; TM patted him gently, then picked him up and carried him over to the table at which they had all played *Hero's Adventure*. Veggie was sitting under it, legs crossed, forehead pressed against the wall.

'No,' Veggie said, reaching behind him to pull the Bedsheet-

Tablecloth-Whiteboard down like a protective canopy. It bore only a few of the words and pictures that the three of them had spent only the previous evening plastering it with - the rest seemed to have been obliterated in angry swipes.

'Veg,' said TM quietly, tugging the sheet off him. 'Don't do this to yourself.'

'Why not?' Veggie said, turning his head very slightly. 'We had a new friend, man, a new partner. She was going to bring us profit and business and fucking happiness and then Riegel O'Ryan came down from space and teamed up with a gigantic dog and a god - fucking - damned -' he smashed his head against the wall with each word '- weatherman and she hits the fucking Rainmaker on Ziggy and takes her away, and -' he slumped against the wall, tears streaking down the wallpaper '- and she didn't want to go, Tom, she wanted to stay here. With us.'

'You've only called me that twice before,' TM said, slotting himself in beside Veggie under the table and putting an arm around him. 'You remember?'

'Yeah,' said Veggie, looking as if he were trying to smile. 'The day we first met, and the day I caught the Swede cheating and you were trying to persuade me not to kill him.'

'You were so pissed off,' TM said, laughing.

'Yeah, well,' said Veggie. 'I guess my sophisticated taste in partners was... less developed at that point.'

'Pff,' TM agreed.

'She's, like, properly gone,' Veggie said after a moment.

'Yeah,' TM said, reluctantly.

'And there's nothing we can do about it.'

'Don't say that so soon,' TM admonished him. 'I said that too, but Dominika and I had a bit of a chat and -'

'You had a what?'

'Through sign language, and stuff,' TM corrected hastily. 'Anyway, she made me see that we have to at least try to get Ziggy back.'

'What are you suggesting?' Veggie asked.

'We're inventors,' TM said. 'Let's build a flipping spaceship.'

'You know that's an absolutely ridiculous plan.'

'I do. Let's do it.'

Veggie thought about it for a moment, then held up his fist. TM bumped it.

'We need funds to make a spaceship, though,' Veggie said thoughtfully. TM opened his mouth hopefully, but Veggie cut him off: 'We're not doing the Octobike.'

The sounds of scratching came from above their heads, and then Michel Furcoat lunged down off the table and came to rub his body against them. Disturbed by the cat's movements, a piece of paper drifted off the table in his wake.

'What's that?' Veggie said; TM reached over and picked it up.

'It's Ziggy's character sheet,' he said. He glanced away, unable to look at it.

'Hang on,' said Veggie, taking the sheet eagerly. 'Look what she's written here.'

TM stared at it. There were three words neatly pencilled under the tables of stats.

'Hot dang,' said Veggie. 'I think Ziggy's just made us a ton of money again.'

25. We Got A Real Job, Kinda

Ziggy's idea turned out to be the single most successful thing ever to pass through the brains of *ZVTMII* (as the company formerly trading under *Ziggy Veggie TM, Inventors Incorporated* soon became known, acronyms apparently being more fashionable these days). At the first pitch, based on the name alone, Veggie - to TM's enduring astonishment, although nothing could quite shock him where Ziggy was concerned - somehow managed to secure enough of an investment to kickstart Ziggy's venture:

Muscles and Mussels.

She'd even scrawled some ideas for the layout on the corner of the Bedsheet-Tablecloth-Whiteboard that had escaped Veggie's furious erasing. They bought an old gym, refurbished it, stuck in a seafood bar, moved into the flat above (much larger than their old one) and Bob was their uncle - which was to say that for once, the oft-tested pairing of TM and Veggie was actually making a steady income.

Life seemed to have improved, although TM never thought either of them was quite the same as they had been before Ziggy had abruptly entered, and just as abruptly exited, their lives.

'I think we're nearly ready to go, y'know,' Veggie said one day, two-and-a-bit years after M&M's grand opening. They were sitting at the bar, taking turns slurping the cheapest seafood they had in stock (it wouldn't do for the owners to eat the stuff that paid the bills; that needed to be saved for people who would actually pay for it). From their vantage point, they could see their gym. It wasn't exactly crowded, but it was doing well enough for them.

TM peered up from the notebook he'd been scribbling in; the whole gym-seafood thing might have been their main business these days, but if anything it had only given him the opportunity to spend more time dreaming up inventions that nobody in their right mind would ever actually need.

'Go?' he asked, wondering whether Veggie was asking permission to use the toilet.

'The spaceship,' Veggie clarified. 'Y'know. Go. To space.'

'Oh,' said TM. 'That.'

'What?'

'I just… sort of thought it would never actually happen, you know?' TM scratched his chin, sighing.

They'd diverted as much of their funds as they could justify into hiring a warehouse just outside the city, in which something vaguely resembling a rocket was in the process of being assembled. Marty had borrowed some of his mother's books on the subject of rocket science, which none of them could understand; between the three of them, plus Dominika's god-tier DIY skills and Derrida's unhelpful interjections about how they were doing it wrong, they stuck a load of components together into something that at least looked a bit like a spaceship.

As far as Veggie was concerned, the fact that it looked like what it was supposed to be meant that it was definitely going to work. TM was less convinced, but had never been able to shake the feeling that Ziggy's very existence meant that maybe physics and all that other science stuff wasn't quite as rigid as it had seemed.

Maybe there was some unknown law of the universe that said that being pretty cool was actually sufficient to make a thing function well. It wouldn't be the strangest thing.

'I think I know what you mean,' Veggie mused. 'We sort of started doing it because we felt like we had to, but we didn't really think about finishing.'

TM nodded. 'We just wanted to be doing *something* to get Ziggy back. I don't think we thought about how it would actually work. Just that… the effort would pay off eventually, some day we wouldn't have to think about yet.'

'Well, now I feel like we've let her down,' Veggie said. His hand went to his chest, where TM knew he kept the little fragment of space rock on a chain.

'It's just… funny how things seem like such good ideas until you have to *do* them,' TM said.

'We managed to do Muscles and Mussels, no? That was hard work.' Veggie gestured at the building around them: concrete proof that they had, in fact, achieved something.

TM had to agree, but something continued to bother him. 'Do you feel like we've… forgotten her?'

'Not a chance.'

'I mean, I know we both remember her, but… I don't know. I don't think we've remembered her in as active of a way as we should probably have done.'

Veggie gave TM a searching look, undermined only slightly by the shrimp sticking half out of his mouth. He sucked it in, chewed and swallowed, coughed a few times, then resumed the deep stare. 'This is about Aster,' he said.

TM blinked. 'What?'

'Remember Aster?'

'Are you really asking me that?'

'Just… this is about her for you. I think.'

'Well, thank you for that insight.'

'Welcome.'

Veggie's phone vibrated on the counter; he swiped it up and held it to his ear. '*Moshi moshi*, Veggie *desu*.'

TM had another prawn.

'We'll be over,' Veggie said, and hung up. 'That was Marty,' he told TM. 'He says the rocket isn't *finished* as such, but he's done everything he knows how to do in order to make it as rocket-like as possible, so we may as well give it a go.'

'Baller.'

26. Hunky Dory

They took a taxi to their warehouse, a medium-sized unit among hundreds of other identical grey cuboids. Marty was waiting outside, wearing tight dark jeans and a peacoat.

'I had a great idea for a new dish for M&M,' he said as they pulled up. TM got out and wandered over, patting him on the shoulder; Veggie made a faff out of fishing change out of his pocket to pay the taxi driver. 'It'd be soup, but the most stylish and decorated soup of all time.'

'What's in it?' TM asked.

'Doesn't matter,' Marty said. 'It's superficial soup.'

'Superficial Soup Official,' TM hummed. 'I'll run it past the chef.'

'Derrida and Nika are heading over now, by the way,' Marty told them. Veggie, having paid the driver, hopped over and planted a kiss on Marty's cheek.

Veggie and Marty had supported each other after Ziggy had gone, which perhaps inevitably led to a relationship blossoming, and within the year it was fully official and they were engaged (Marty had proposed by yelling out 'Will you marry me?' in the middle of a performance, which had led to record-breaking sales of CDs and merch).

The pair spent roughly equal amounts of time at Marty's undeniably swanky pad in his parents' house and the new, less-swanky-but-still-better-than-the-old-one flat above Muscles & Mussels.

'So... look, I haven't got a clue about the first thing to do with space travel and that, but I've made this thing as cool as possible and that's the best I can do,' Marty said, beckoning them inside. 'Derrida says it's stupid, but Nika likes it and she's usually pretty good at knowing... stuff.'

Inside the unit stood a cylindrical contraption clearly designed to look as much like a stereotypical spaceship as possible. It had things that resembled wings, things that looked a bit like thrusters, a thing that might well have been the rough shape of a cockpit.

All of these things were, TM was assured, held together in one way or another.

'That looks...' Veggie began, taking in the sight. The rocket was around four metres high - not as big as a 'proper' rocket, perhaps, but as large as they could fit in their little warehouse - and bright orange (chosen for being the cheapest colour of paint, according to Derrida). Stacked in the corner were a group of old-fashioned consoles with green screens and a small speaker so that everyone on the ground would be able to hear the pilot. TM tried to gauge his partner's reaction; Veggie examined the machine closely, then took a deep breath.

'... A-flippin'-mazing,' he finished.

'I know, right?' Marty agreed, grinning.

'And we're - we're just going to do it?! Right now?!' Veggie demanded, bouncing around like a small dog. 'This is the *best*!'

'Far be it from me to curb your enthusiasm,' Derrida interrupted, entering the warehouse with Dominika in tow, 'but actually attempting to fly that thing is a terrible idea. I mean, a really legitimately terrible idea.'

Dominika's dark hair was now grown out almost to waist-length and dyed so that various blues and pinks flashed from under the dark red when she moved; Derrida had had the same hair for years. They wore a waistcoat over a shirt with the sleeves rolled halfway up their forearms, holding a jacket over their shoulder by one finger; their usual smartness looked incongruous against the dirty warehouse.

'You helped make it,' Veggie countered, pouting.

'I thought it was some sort of catharsis thing,' Derrida said. 'I didn't think anyone was planning to actually get in it and *launch*, for heaven's sake.'

'It *is* some sort of catharsis thing,' TM said, 'but may as well try to get the most possible emotional whatnots out of it.'

'So basically,' Derrida said, 'you're just doing this because why not.'

'That's pretty much it, yeah.'

Derrida sighed. Dominika nudged them. 'As good a reason as any, I suppose,' they conceded. 'Let's do this.'

They all exchanged glances for a few moments, then realised that they had failed to plan for this part.

'So, er...' Marty scratched his head. 'Who's flying it?'

'TM,' Veggie said immediately, to TM's surprise.

'Really?' TM asked, wondering whether this was Veggie's way of teaching him something beautiful about the universe, or perhaps letting him know that he believed in him.

'Yeah, you're pretty skinny, you'll fit.'

'Oh, right.'

'We probably need to move it outside,' Marty pondered, looking up at the roof. 'I mean, we could just blow a hole in the unit, but I think you might have to pay for that.'

'Did we build it on wheels?' TM asked.

'Er...' Marty leaned down and peered under the structure. 'Narp.'

Dominika sighed, then shrugged and toddled over to the rocket, stuck her hands underneath and heaved. The ship tilted; she glared pointedly at the rest of the group. Derrida and Marty took up positions around the machine; between the three of them, they crab-walked the entire spaceship out of the warehouse (with some difficulty getting out of the door, like a scaled-up version of trying to move a sofa out) and plonked it down on the concrete outside.

'I don't know if it should be light enough to just pick up like that,' TM said. 'Not trying to sound negative, but I'm about to get in that thing and go to space.'

'It's *fiiiiiiiine*,' Veggie reassured him, which was entirely unreassuring.

'Much as I hate to relinquish my usual stance of total cynicism about everything,' Derrida said, brushing their hands off, 'I think the only way to make sense of the way the universe works, in the light of what we know about Ziggy and stars becoming humans and all that, is to accept that things are broadly just a bit weird and perhaps usual scientific standards aren't in fact the best way of measuring whether something's likely to work or not.'

'This one gets it,' said Veggie.

'What you're saying,' TM said uncertainly, 'is that maybe this will work not because it's built in a smart way that makes sense by normal standards, but because... our standards of what makes sense are different, and if we think this makes sense to us then it'll just work in real life?'

'Something like that.'

TM sighed. 'Fine,' he said. 'Strap me in.'

***

I got Green Dragon, I ride Red Hare

I'll beat the heck out of Monobear

I'm a ghoul, I'm a Death God, I'm an Anti-Spiral

It's past time for a Grim Fandango revival

I got my Buster Sword

I got my Keyblade

Got dragon's balls

Shove them in your face, yeah

I wear my Mega Ring

I go Bankai

I bust out my Scissor Blade

And show you why, yeah!

TM ejected the cassette. 'I'm flattered that you gave me a recording of *I Got My Buster Sword* -'

'Latest version, trying out a couple new verses,' Marty chirped through TM's headset. 'What ya think?'

'I think the fact that you fitted the rocket with a *cassette player* is immensely reassuring,' TM said, checking out the rest of the cockpit.

He was strapped into what seemed to be a repurposed rollercoaster seat, surrounded by buttons that, for the most part, seemed to be there for stylistic purposes and were not in fact hooked up to anything. A small window pointed skyward, a rectangle filled with blue.

'Anyway, I'm flattered by the gift, but don't you want the tape back before we go? It might not come back.'

'Naw, you gotta keep that,' Marty said. 'That tape's gonna be the first of many Inciting Incident demos sent into space and enjoyed by all the many inhabitants of the cosmos.'

'Righty-ho. Can I speak to Veg?'

There was a crackling over the headset as Marty handed his mic over.

'We should probably have got more than one of these things,' Veggie said when the sounds of movement faded.

'Hm.'

There were a few moments of silence. 'What's up?' Veggie asked eventually.

'Just... I thought that after Ziggy was gone, things would get less surreal and more normal-reality-like, and now I'm literally about to try to shoot myself into space in a can built by people who know nothing about space travel.'

'I read a book,' Marty yelled from a distance, his voice tinny through the headset.

'I know what you mean,' Veggie said. 'About the Ziggy thing. She made everything... weirder.'

'That she did.'

'I think she's just changed us for all time, y'know. I don't think things are ever going back to normal.'

TM nodded slowly. 'Wouldn't have it any other way.'

The muted, static-laden sound of discussion burst through the headset, then Derrida took the mic.

'We're ready for launch,' they told TM. 'I'll be your co-pilot on the ground.'

'So, er... how does this actually work and what do I do?' TM asked, thinking that these might have been questions he should have asked earlier.

'We put engines on, so we're pretty sure that'll do something. I'll talk you through your end of it; Dominika's drawn you a map so you've got some idea where we're going.'

TM cast around the cockpit and spotted it: a piece of lined A4 blu-tacked onto the wall. She'd drawn, in purple felt tip, a circle labelled 'Earth' and a dot labelled 'star-Z'. An arrow pointed from the Earth to the star, the words 'go this way' written next to it. That was all.

'Thanks for the map, Nika.'

He thought he heard her give a thumbs-up.

'Right,' said Derrida. 'Let's switch some shit on.'

'Technical,' Marty retorted; his voice came through clearly, as if they were squished together at the console.

Something started to vibrate. TM's whole body shook with the force of the entire pod, the cocoon to which he had entrusted his body, building up force around him. Then it all stopped.

'Er.' TM could hear Derrida tapping at something on their end.

'Was that supposed to happen?' TM asked.

'Not as such,' Derrida admitted. 'It looks like we just didn't give the thing enough power.'

TM closed his eyes and sat there. It was stupid, he thought, to have really believed that they would be able to shoot him into space and bring Ziggy back, and yet he had believed. It seemed so much easier to believe in things that made no rational sense now that he knew that something like Ziggy could exist in the universe, but this... might have been a step too far.

'I mean...' Marty began. TM could hear his voice wobbling slightly, as if he were tapping his feet, unable to stay still. 'At least we didn't run out of power halfway to space? That would have sucked.'

'Better not to have to fall back down, I guess,' Derrida agreed. 'Sorry.'

Veggie's voice came over the headset next. 'Dom, what are you -' There were sounds of a struggle, then a loud burst of static as the microphone got knocked over. TM winced. 'TM, she's stealing my space rock necklace!'

TM sighed. There was a knock on the window, and he looked up to see Dominika crouching on top of the rocket, clutching the sliver of space rock. 'What are you -'

She thrust the rock meaningfully in his direction.

'That... meant something to Ziggy,' TM realised. 'She didn't know what, but she felt something in it.'

Dominika nodded furiously.

'She was linked to it somehow.'

More nodding.

'You think it can get me to her?'

A casual shrug.

'I'll take those odds.'

Dominika saluted and hopped down. TM heard scratching and banging around the sides of the rocket.

'She just put my space rock in the engine!' Veggie wailed.

Everything started to shake again.

'Er, ground control to TM?' Veggie's voice came over the headset, almost drowned out by the noise of the rocket coming to life. 'I think it's working.' The shaking and booming intensified until TM was aware of nothing else. He tried to yell down the headset:

'I think it might be -'

Everything was silent.

27. Oddity

'- launching,' TM finished.

The window showed nothing but black.

'Um.'

Hissing, distorted voices whispered down the earpiece into TM's brain:

'TM!' That one sounded like Veggie.

'It - launched, just - gone!' Marty, TM thought that one was.

'Can - hear us?' Derrida, probably.

'...' That'd be Dominika.

'Wait, did you come all this way for *me*?'

TM tried to sit bolt upright, but the straps holding him tightly in wouldn't let him move. 'Ziggy?!'

'It's me, I think, but I don't... where are you? What are you doing here?'

'We made a rocket and put the space rock in it, and now I'm in space, I think, and - what do I do?!'

The gravity of TM's situation suddenly hit him: he was floating in a cobbled-together hunk of metal somewhere in space, having spontaneously travelled from there to here, no idea how or where or when or what could return him safely to the place he'd started - nor, indeed, how he was (at least for now) failing to die in the hostile reaches of space, since he had no suit and the ship couldn't be enough to keep him safe...

'TM?'

'Oh, yeah, sorry, I'm here, but... I don't really know where *here* is, or how I got here.'

The ship broke apart around him then, the loosely-joined sheets of metal separating and going their separate ways off into the universe. TM caught the Inciting Incident cassette as it floated past his face.

'Sounds familiar,' Ziggy's voice said. 'Well, you're here now. May as well appreciate the view.'

The pieces of TM's tin can capsule dissipated into the far reaches of space; he pulled himself free of the straps holding him into the chair and let it fall away. He hung there, trying not to think too hard about how he was breathing and not imploding in the atmosphereless vacuum. Then he must have rotated, or perhaps just opened his eyes, because the blackness all around lit up with tiny fireflies dancing around each other.

'I might have wanted to get away from the whole being-a-star thing, but I've got to admit… things could be worse.' It sounded as if Ziggy were sighing wistfully.

'All the lights in the sky,' TM said slowly, trying to touch the whirling fabric of pinprick flames.

'Not sure exactly where you are, but you might be able to see me,' she told him. 'Hang on, I'll…' One of the lights in the tapestry dimmed, flickered, then let loose a radiant burst. 'See me?'

'That's you?' TM breathed, staring at the little star with wonder.

'That's me.'

'You're… beautiful.'

'Aw, thanks.' TM could hear Ziggy smiling. 'You might be able to see Earth from here, if you know where to look. It's all blue.'

Dominika would know where to look, TM thought. Then he shook his head, trying to clear the fuzz that had come over it. Thoughts of the people back home returned; thoughts of the reason he had come. 'How do I get you back?' he asked.

'Yeah, that's… not really… y'know.' The little light that was Ziggy pulsed as if thinking about something very important. 'I wish I could come back.'

'You can't?'

'I want to. I do. But… I went down. I did that. I was human with you. Now that's over, and I'm back where the universe says I need to be.'

'Fuck the universe,' TM said.

'I want to come back and live more of a life with you and Veg and everyone else,' Ziggy told him. 'I really do, but I can't spend that life being chased forever. Orion, Altair… they wouldn't ever let me go. You'd get hurt, and I can't do that to you.'

'I don't care,' TM declared. Tiny, white-hot droplets of water forced their way out of his tear ducts and drifted off into nothingness.

'I really am sorry,' Ziggy said. 'Believe me, if I could choose my life I'd choose the one I had with you. It's not like I'm just giving up, though. I'm not done. I'm in the same place you all came from and the same one you'll all make it back to eventually. You're just on a longer road, but… mine was a one-way shortcut. I'll be waiting, don't worry.'

'You really can't come back,' TM whispered.

'I really can't,' she agreed. 'But you never know. You might see me again, somehow. Wouldn't be the weirdest thing. I thought me turning into a person was the strangest thing that could happen in the universe, but I think you and Veggie and everyone made a million even weirder things happen every day just by… being people.'

'Can I stay here?'

'I think you've probably got to go back, same way as I had to.'

TM took several deep breaths of oxygenless space air. 'What about - you had a twin or something? Or… are there other stars like you? Ones we can help?'

'There are always stars popping down to visit,' Ziggy said vaguely. 'I can't tell from up here, to be honest. You and Veggie shine just as bright as any star.'

'I don't want to leave you.'

'I don't want that either, but -' Ziggy's voice cut out in a hiss of interference.

'Ziggy?' No answer. TM flapped his limbs, willing his body to move towards the distant star that was his friend. 'Ziggy?'

The weave of stars was swept away like a cobweb, or maybe TM was sent spinning. Out in the endlessness he saw, flashing before him, the intricate dance of the galaxies, held together by the forces that had put them there.

He beheld an enormous spiral, composed of billions upon billions of tiny stars, making its inextricable way towards its closest neighbour, and knew that the two would one day collide and start a new, two-person dance.

'Tell everyone I love them,' Ziggy's voice said, faint in TM's ear.

28. Re-Entry

'Can you hear me, TM?'

Something hit TM in the face.

'Earth to TM!'

Somebody was moving around him, people chattering somewhere off to the side.

'What *happened*?'

'His circuit died, something went wrong, I don't -'

'*Something* went *wrong*?! That's a pretty huge fucking understatement, don't you think?'

'I'm sorry! We couldn't have known -'

'Guys?' This was the voice closest to TM, a familiar voice. Veggie? 'I think he's waking up.'

'The stars look different from up there,' TM said, opening his eyes.

'Oh, fucking hell, TM.' Veggie collapsed next to him, wringing his hands through his hair. 'I thought you were dead.'

'I'm not totally sure I wasn't,' TM said, sitting up.

'Where were you?!' Derrida asked. They sprinted over, closely followed by Marty and Dominika. TM glanced around and noticed, to what might once have been surprise, that he was sitting on the floor of the warehouse. 'You just went and then you just came back!'

'I disappeared?'

'The whole ship did,' Marty said. His face was white; all of them, in fact, looked thoroughly shaken. TM supposed he could understand it. 'Just blasted into... nowhere.'

'That space rock worked too well,' Derrida muttered.

'The... space rock.' TM felt around in his pocket and withdrew Veggie's space rock necklace, still on its chain. 'Must have floated in there at some point.'

'So what happened?' Veggie asked, taking the rock from TM gently.

'Oh, this is...' TM took Marty's cassette out of his other pocket and tossed back to him. Marty caught it, realised what it was and gave something halfway between a roar of laughter and a sob. 'I was here and then I was somewhere else. Floating. The... the ship broke. Sorry,' he said, looking around at everyone. 'I know how much you put into making it.'

'Screw the ship, we thought you were broken,' Derrida said.

'You were floating?' Veggie coaxed. 'In space? With no ship?'

'All of that, yeah.'

'And you didn't die?'

'Seems that way,' TM reasoned.

'Well, thank heck for that,' Veggie said, hugging his partner. Then he withdrew, looking as if he knew the next question he was going to ask but didn't want to ask it. 'And... Ziggy..?'

TM breathed, remembering. 'I met her, sort of.'

Veggie broke into a wide smile, then bit his lip. 'She hasn't come back, though?'

TM shook his head. 'I spoke to her, but... she couldn't come back. She wanted to, but she couldn't.'

Veggie nodded, exhaling loudly through his nose. 'I don't know whether I really thought we'd actually get her back.'

'Me neither,' TM admitted. 'I hoped. But... I dunno. I think we carry her on, somehow.' He sighed and scratched his chin. 'You still think this is about Aster for me?'

'Not sure,' Veggie said slowly. 'Maybe... partly?'

'I think I get what you meant, though,' TM told him. 'When Aster left... it was because she wanted to. She just decided that it was time to move on, so I had to respect that and... I wanted to chase her, to bring her back, but I couldn't. I couldn't even be angry with her, because it was just the right thing for her to do.

'But Ziggy, she didn't want to go, so I could finally try to get somebody back. I could be angry about her being taken away.'

Veggie watched him. 'And now?' he asked quietly.

'I'm still angry,' TM said, 'but she wouldn't want me to be. So... I guess I'll remember her, and live for her.'

'Sounds like a plan.'

'She told me to tell you all that she loves you, by the way,' TM said, louder. Marty looked down at the tape in his hands; Derrida coughed awkwardly, looking as if they weren't sure whether to smile or cry; Dominika blew a kiss skyward.

'So... what do we do now?' Marty asked, after a few moments of reflective silence.

Veggie checked the time on his phone. 'We've got to get back to work,' he realised.

'Oh, that's so *dumb*.'

PART TWO-AND-A-HALF
A Bit More Afterer

29. An Inauspicious Communication

The next few months passed relatively without incident. TM found himself feeling something like closure, even if things hadn't resolved the way he would have liked. Life went on, as it were.

Then, three years to the day since Ziggy was carried away, Veggie got an email.

'Oh, you are hecking kidding me,' he said. TM, legs folded underneath him in a fancy leather office chair, pushed off his desk and wheeled over, peering at the screen of Veggie's laptop (moderately high-spec, bought on sale).

'Oh, heck,' TM agreed. 'It's the flipping Swede.'

Dear Jonathan (began the email)

I realise we have not spoken for some time, nor did we part on the best of terms. It is, I fear, not with the most auspicious of tidings that I now address this electronic communication to yourself.

'God, he's pompous,' said TM. Veggie scrolled down, grinding his teeth together so hard that the veins on his neck stuck out and his cheeks turned whiter than the background upon which the black text of the email sat. Michel Furcoat, the cat, who had been sat on the desk, saw the expressions on his owners' faces and buggered off, purple-covered claws tapping lightly against the floor as he scarpered.

You see (the email continued), *it has come to my attention that your little business venture is now running a certain establishment of sorts: a gymnasium, the selling point of which (or 'U.S.P.' as I believe is the fashionable, current and correct business terminology, my attention to which you will doubtless appreciate, I am entirely sure) -*

'Twat,' said Veggie.

- is that it is conjoined with a seafood restaurant, such as the term may herewith apply. 'Muscles & Mussels', I am informed: how quaintly alliterative. Thus commences the source of my quibble.

'What ridiculous phrasing,' TM observed.

'He hasn't changed,' said Veggie sourly.

Unfortunately, I believe, and my lawyer tends to agree, that you may, in running such an establishment, be, knowingly or unknowingly, infringing, maliciously or not maliciously, upon my, intellectual and trademarked, property.

'Too many commas,' said TM, leaning over and deleting a few words in an effort to make it all make more sense.

Unfortunately (TM's revision read), *I believe that you may be infringing upon my intellectual property.*

'Still not perfect,' said Veggie, making an alteration of his own.

Unfortunately, I am a colossal asshat.

'Amusing, but not entirely useful,' TM said, hitting ctrl-Z.

I, you see (the Swede's email went on), *have been operating a very similar marine-delicacy-cum-physical-improvement-themed franchise (the equally, if not more so, pleasingly named 'Fish and Fitness') for some years. I hope the issue maketh itself clear to you now: your enterprise is concerningly alike in its particular oeuvre to my own businessitudes.*

'Is 'businessitudes' a word?' Veggie said.

'Doubt it,' TM said; Veggie looked satisfied.

As such, I find myself concerned. If you are making money from what I assert to be ultimately my idea, then be assured I shall want a share. I attach for your reference a copy of my documents regarding this matter.

Veggie clicked the attachment.

'It's flipping password-protected,' he said.

'Email him back for the password?' TM offered; Veggie raised a hand in absolute denial, so quickly the air vibrated.

'I'm not emailing him back,' he said. 'Ever.'

'Hang on,' TM said, 'there's an address.'

I look forward to hearing from you with the money to which I am rightfully entitled (concluded the email).

Yours

J.K.

Below that, an address gave the Swede's current residence as '5-12 The Mansions', which Veggie scoffed at.

'I've got an idea,' said TM.

'Is it 'kill the Swede'?'

'Not exactly.'

'Then I'm only mildly interested.'

TM raised an eyebrow. 'I propose,' he said, 'a heist.'

Veggie folded the laptop shut, staring at TM in apparent disbelief. 'You must be fucking joking,' he said.

'Why?' TM demanded. 'We trained so hard for the last one -'

'We spent six hours playing games and shit,' Veggie interrupted. 'Plus, that *last one* ended in our three-way soulmate being abducted into space.'

'Well... yeah,' TM admitted, suddenly feeling a weight descend on his shoulders. He hunched over in his seat; the feeling physically pushed him down, compressing him, dizzying him as he tried not to think about the image of Ziggy being carried away, then the flashes of the light in space that was her and the crashing together of the galaxies.

His experience in space might not have killed him, against all odds, but he would not forget it in a hurry.

'But he says he's got some proof or other that he came up with this idea,' he continued, trying to sit up again, 'so I say we should go and steal it.'

Veggie looked unconvinced.

'And maybe destroy his house a bit while we're there,' TM added.

'Fine,' said Veggie. 'I'm in.'

TM's phone vibrated.

'Er,' TM said, looking at the screen: unknown number calling. It wasn't all that uncommon for them to receive unknown calls since starting up the gymnastaurant (the unofficial term for the type of establishment M&M was), but something in TM's stomach told him the timing was too convenient.

'TM,' he said, picking up the call.

'Hello, Thomas,' said a Swedish voice, overly articulating every letter in an attempt to conceal the accent.

'Johan,' TM said coldly, rolling his eyes at Veggie, who mimed shooting himself in the face (including loading his imaginary gun in alarmingly acute detail).

'I am telephoning yourself,' said the Swede, 'because I suspect you will be more favourable of reaction than dear Jonathan. Which is to say, less absurdly apoplectic.'

'You're probably not wrong,' TM admitted; Veggie mouthed *'don't tell him he's not wrong'* despairingly.

'I assume he's read my email,' the Swede said silkily.

TM nodded.

'Hello?' said the Swede down the phone.

'Oh, right, sorry,' said TM. 'Yup.' Veggie facepalmed.

'And the response?' demanded the Swede.

'Nah,' said TM, and hung up. Then he turned his phone off. 'Ready to heist?' he asked Veggie, who nodded in a way that suggested he was just sort of agreeing, his mind apparently still on thoughts of murdering the Swede.

TM leaned across, flipped Veggie's laptop open again and jotted down the Swede's address. 'He's conveniently nearby,' he noted.

'Hang on,' Veggie said, standing. 'I think Marty's downstairs.'

'You want to bring him along?'

Veggie thought about it for a moment. 'Nah,' he said. 'Best not involve him in the illegal stuff.'

'Fair play,' TM agreed.

'Dominika, though,' said Veggie thoughtfully.

'Ahhh,' TM mused. 'She probably would come in handy.'

'No question,' said Veggie.

'If she's downstairs,' TM suggested, 'we bring her.'

Veggie nodded, and moved to his bedroom (they had separate ones now). TM made to stand up, but a ping from the laptop brought him back down.

By the way (read the new email) *don't fuck with me.*

Also, I heard your partner no. 3 got herself, as it were, disappeared. I imagine you're useless without her. As I hear it, she was... shall we say, extremely persuasive to investors. Almost incredibly so. I wonder what sort of trouble I might be able to get you in if I were to report that she... traded herself for your fortunes? It need not even be true, although I imagine most would believe it.

Kind regards

Give me my fucking money.

'Oh, you are so fucking dead,' TM told the screen.

***

Downstairs, which was to say in the gym, Veggie found Marty doing his best to keep up with a treadmill.

'Didn't have you down as a... jogging person,' TM said, coming up behind.

'Yeah, well,' Marty said with some difficulty. 'Gotta keep the rockstar physique, you know?' He rammed the speed setting, slowing the treadmill belt right down, and looked them over. 'What's up with you two?' he said, sweating and panting profusely. 'You look like someone promised they'd get you a three-course meal and came back with a Flump.'

'Emails,' said Veggie, the word forcing its way out through his lips as if it were some sort of throat-dwelling alien parasite.

'Say no more,' Marty said, leaning down to kiss Veggie on the cheek.

'Ew,' Veggie said, wiping Marty's sweat from his face. 'Have you seen Dominika?'

'Slacking, natch,' Marty told them, pointing with a glistening thumb towards the bar area of the gymnastaurant. 'See you later?'

Veggie gave him a quick peck goodbye. 'Later,' he said. 'Don't spend too long here - don't you have a Battle of the Bands to prep for?'

'Heck, yeah,' Marty said in realisation as they walked away.

Dominika was, indeed, slacking. Soon after the opening of Muscles & Mussels, she had applied to work for TM and Veggie, much to their surprise. Veggie had conducted the interview, which apparently she had 'absolutely aced, don't ask me how because I have no idea but she basically just nodded and we have to hire her' and that was that: she left whatever other mysterious employment she might have had and came to work as general manager of the business, leaving TM and Veggie with more spare time to pursue their more eccentric, less profitable and ultimately much more fun ideas. This was all when they weren't all working on the spaceship (now sadly obliterated), of course.

At that moment, she was leaning on the seafood bar, chugging oysters and cider in her black Muscles & Mussels T-shirt.

'Dom, you can't be doing that in uniform,' Veggie said; she froze, an oyster halfway to her mouth, then quickly slurped it up and dropped the empty shell down on the bar guiltily.

'It's fine,' TM said, almost laughing. 'We're not gonna be big corporate a-hole bosses, no worries.'

Dominika leaned over the bar, pulled out a cold bottle of fruit cider and took a hefty swig, looking relieved.

'We might need your help,' TM told her.

Dominika raised an eyebrow in a way that said 'tell me more'.

Veggie shifted about, then took a breath and explained, spitting the words out in one clump of noise: 'theSwedeemailedme.' Dominika nodded in understanding.

'He kind of wants to sue us or shut us down or something,' TM added. 'So we've decided the only reasonable solution is to break into his house.' Dominika's shoulders rose and fell in a way that said 'fair enough'. 'Also, he kind of said some stuff about Ziggy…'

'He did?!' demanded Veggie, his fists clenching so hard TM thought his knuckles might pop out; TM nodded reluctantly. 'He's so dead,' Veggie said, the words vibrating behind his teeth as if he wanted nothing more than to scream them out. Dominika raised her bottle in agreement.

'So, anyway,' TM continued, as cheerily as possible, 'we're going to break in, steal-slash-destroy whatever evidence the Swede might think he has, possibly kill him - we're not totally sure about that yet - possibly blow up his house - same situation - then come back and have a takeaway or something.' He breathed deeply, having forgotten to do so for the entirety of his speech.

'And then go watch a Battle of the Bands and forget the entire damned thing,' Veggie finished.

Dominika slammed her bottle down on the counter enthusiastically, sending splashes of dark purple cider up the neck and out onto the polished surface. She mopped it up sheepishly.

'I'll take that as a yes,' TM said. She nodded firmly.

'Alright,' Veggie said. 'Get someone to cover you, Dom, we're going heisting.'

30. Wait, We're Actually Getting To Do It This Time?

By mid-evening, the trio stood before the gates of the Swede's mansion, which much to Veggie's irritation was easily within walking distance. They were fairly sure they had the right place, because the legend 'RESIDENCE OF JOHAN KARLSSON' was wrought into the gates in foot-high, solid iron lettering.

'Ready?' Veggie asked, pulling a balaclava over his face.

'Ready,' TM affirmed, suiting up.

'Let's go fuck up a Swede,' Veggie declared.

'Oh, hang on,' TM said quickly, opening his securely-strapped shoulder satchel and passing out a few choice things. 'I... may have been working on some inventions that might help.'

'That's suspicious,' Veggie hummed, taking the proffered gadgets.

'Eh,' TM said, 'I thought maybe we might need to pull off a slightly better heist some day, and I've sort of ramped up on making weird things since, y'know, we've actually had the money and time to invent stuff. Also, this gizmology is *cooool*. If, legally speaking, technically unmarketable.'

'Fair play,' Veggie shrugged. 'I feel kind of satisfied that our one day several years ago of *Hero's Adventure* and stealth games and parkour was not wasted, then. Not that it would have been a waste anyway doing that stuff for the fun of it, but you know. It's just quite nice to be doing an *actual* heist at last.'

Dominika gave TM a questioning look.

'We might have robbed the museum,' he admitted under her gaze. 'Amazed it didn't end up on the news, actually.'

Dominika gave a low, heavily accented chuckle. Veggie almost jumped in surprise; TM tilted his head at her conspiratorially.

'Aaaaanyway,' said Veggie after a moment, staring at Dominika. 'Let's go be homewreckers.'

TM leapt up the Swede's front wall, fingers gripping the top, and levered himself slowly up to peer over. The side of the house he could see was ludicrously extravagant, a monolith of grandeur like something out of a *Real Housewives* show.

'He's got a guard and everything,' he told his fellow would-be burglars happily.

'When did you get so… ninja?' Veggie demanded. 'Also, you didn't actually need to do that cos there's an iron bar gate we can see through literally right here.'

TM dropped back to earth silently. 'We've owned a gym for, like, three years,' he explained. 'It was almost inevitable that I'd get vaguely in shape at some point.'

Veggie wagged a finger at him. 'I think you've just been preparing in the hope that we would eventually get to pull off another heist, sir.'

TM shrugged. Dominika scouted around a corner and beckoned them over; they scuttled along the wall, leaning out to peer around.

'Clear,' Veggie whispered; they left their cover and followed the wall around. 'We need to find some sort of way in that isn't the front door this time.'

'Yeah, it won't be that easy,' TM said with a grin.

Dominika lifted herself up, staring over the wall into the garden. A tilt of the head told TM to check it out for himself, which he did, revealing a long row of white rose arches spanning from the wall across to the building itself. There was one person in view: a gardener, a young woman in thick gloves shearing rogue branches off a bushy hedge.

Dominika hummed, staring intently at the gardener.

'What's going on?' Veggie hissed, bouncing up and down; the top of his head sailed a few inches below the top of the wall at the zenith of his boing.

'Think this might be our way in,' TM whispered down at him. Veggie rubbed his fingers together with excitement.

TM waited, looking down; Veggie blinked back at him, then coughed.

'I'll need a leg up,' he said sheepishly.

TM hopped down, crouching to offer his back to Veggie. His partner stepped up on top of him and levered himself over with some difficulty; TM followed him over, dropping down on the other side as Dominika alighted lithely.

'We're in,' Veggie said excitedly in a quiet (albeit abnormally deep and spy-like) voice.

The trio quickly shuffled under the row of arches, Veggie crouching the whole time, moving with what TM could only think was intended to be a cool, casual sneak. As they came under the tunnel of roses, Veggie's languorously sneak-stepping foot caught on a thorny tendril, breaking it off with a loud snap.

'Cock,' Veggie said as the gardener turned towards them in alarm. 'Um. Dominika, you get this one?'

Dominika dashed out of cover towards the gardener, who bared her teeth and brandished her shears threateningly. Dominika swatted them aside, flipped up and wrapped her legs around the gardener's neck, swinging around and forcing her hapless opponent to tumble over onto the grass. The breath exploded from the gardener's lungs, then the general manager of Muscles & Mussels fell on top of her and applied a sleeper hold, wrenching it in until the gardener went limp.

'Er,' Veggie said.

Dominika stood, brushed herself down, then picked up the gardener's arms. She tugged off the unconscious woman's gloves, held her by the wrist and stood for a moment. Then she gave a happy thumbs up.

'I really hope that means she *didn't* kill her,' Veggie said with mild concern.

'Hang on a sec,' TM said as Dominika rejoined them. 'We're both wearing masks and plain clothes, but you -' he gestured to Dominika '- are not only barefaced but wearing a hecking Muscles & Mussels T-shirt.'

She raised her chin half an inch in a way that very clearly communicated 'I'm just that good, bitches.'

'At least turn the logo inside out or something,' TM said exasperatedly.

She sighed and complied, stripping the T-shirt off to flip the logo to the inside; Veggie, TM noticed, averted his eyes for the brief time she was standing in just her sports bra, which TM thought was rather sweet. Marty had been good for Veggie, he thought.

'Happy now?' said Dominika's unimpressed tongue-in-roof-of-mouth expression when she was done.

They proceeded down the white rose hallway towards the mansion, climbing on the walls of which were yet more roses.

'This butthole got really into roses,' Veggie mused disdainfully, spitting on the nearest flower.

Dominika pulled on the gardener's thick gloves, leaving a few bare inches of bicep between her sleeve and the almost elbow-length leather, and took hold of one of the thick stems covering the wall. She pulled herself up cautiously; the tendril bent slightly under her weight, but did not break.

'I don't think either of us is light enough to do that,' Veggie said quietly to TM, watching Dominika make her way up towards a window. In her thick gloves, black T-shirt, and skinny jeans, topped off with fashionable but enormously impractical sneakers, she looked like some sort of hipster ninja.

'This is really cool,' TM had to admit. Dominika scampered up to the window and gave it a shove; it opened easily. She stared at the opening for a moment, then pulled it closed again.

'What are you doing?' Veggie hissed up at her; she dug about in a pocket (with some difficulty, owing to the gloves), pulled out one of TM's devices - a tiny half-sphere, the flat side of which bore a plastic rubber sucker like the ones on Christmas window decorations - and affixed it firmly.

There was a quiet hum as the gadget did its work, and then with barely a cracking sound the glass pane split into two, broken straight down the middle. Dominika caught the *TM Window Splitter* deftly as the two halves of the pane fell down, their landing muffled by the grass, and popped it into her pocket; then she hauled herself gracefully through the window.

'That,' said Veggie, looking up after her, 'is really cool.'

'Told ya,' said TM.

'So... what do we do now?' Veggie asked after a second.

'I guess... we wait for Dom to take out the magical security systems, if it's anything like *Hero's Adventure*,' TM suggested.

'I'm not so sure it is,' Veggie mused. 'More like... wait around and maybe eventually hopefully pull off some parkour or video game style nonsense.'

'Hopefully,' said TM. There was a pause. 'Hey, Veg.'

'Mm.'

'Do you ever think maybe we have a slightly... exaggerated idea of how reality works?'

Veggie thought about it for a second. 'Nah,' he said reassuringly. Then he yelped as Dominika poked him on the shoulder from behind.

'Oh, hey,' said TM. 'What's up?'

Dominika beckoned them around and led them through a back door, unlocked from the inside. It led them to a small, albeit almost unnecessarily well-stocked, wine cellar; Veggie pulled out one of the bottles, smashed the neck on the corner of a shelf and poured a stream of dark red liquid into his mouth. Then he gagged in disgust, spat and hurled the bottle over his shoulder, where it shattered against the wall.

'I feel *awesome*,' he said.

'Yeah, good times,' TM said, hurrying him along. 'We need to find this evidence, whatever it might be.'

They moved quietly over to the corner of the room, where a sterile white light shone down from up the stairs, and headed up cautiously. Dominika led the way, her stolen gloves sticking out of her back pocket. In the first corridor lay a uniformed guard; Dominika kicked him in the head, almost affectionately.

'Uniformed guards?' Veggie spluttered. 'Who does this mothertrucker think he is?!'

'Nice job, though,' TM said, scurrying past. 'Don't suppose anyone has a floor plan or anything?'

'Unfortunately not,' Veggie muttered, stepping over (which was to say, *on*) the guard's prone body. 'We didn't have a secretly evil head of the local thieves' guild helping out on this one.'

'Why did he give us legitimately useful help with stuff, anyway?' TM asked, stopping in the middle of the hall. 'If he was evil?'

Veggie's mouth opened and closed for a few moments, then he shrugged uselessly. 'Needed the plot to move forward,' he said eventually.

They took a few more steps, then TM stopped again. 'Shit!' he said suddenly, smacking himself in the forehead with his palm.

'What, what what?' Veggie hissed, casting wild stares around the corridor.

'We never even saved the nice cousins,' TM lamented.

'Ah, screw them, they were probably secretly also evil anyway.'

They slipped down the next hall, stopping at the corner. Dominika pointed up with a finger, picking out a security camera set into the corner between ceiling and wall. It hummed gently as it swivelled from side to side, casting its black lens eye around the length of the corridor.

'Didn't know there were cameras that actually did that,' Veggie mused.

'Think *Sliver Nucleus*,' TM suggested. 'You are Mikkels Stormson, man.'

Veggie looked prouder than TM had ever seen him, nodding firmly; then he darted out as the camera faced away from them, scooting in under its blind spot. He practically leapt into the air with excitement, then put a finger to his chin.

'What do I do now?' he mouthed at them. TM shrugged; Dominika rolled her eyes, then cartwheeled along the wall to join Veggie, which TM thought was extraordinarily acrobatic but not entirely necessary. She slipped one of the gloves over a hand, then reached up and pulled out the cables, sending sparks flying.

'Won't that... let them know we're here?' Veggie said with vague concern.

Dominika shrugged.

'Eh,' said TM. 'We got this. Besides, I didn't think you would mind if the Swede started realising his precious mansion was under attack.'

'You make a good point,' Veggie said, eyes lighting up.

They made their way towards what they hoped was the centre of the building, hiding in doorways to avoid guards. The Swede's mansion was superlatively, superfluously large. When they came to a wide, open room, stairs at either side and a guard positioned at the top, facing away from them, TM couldn't resist: he leapt onto the banister of the stairs, flew up and around, jumped up to grab the railing behind the guard and pulled himself over, retrieving a home-fashioned Taser of sorts from a pocket in midair and jamming it into the man's neck before he even landed.

'Wooooo,' Veggie chirped from below, applauding as the guard dropped. 'Seriously, TM, I'm impressed.'

Dominika, as if not to be outdone, clambered up the wall and scampered cat-like over the railing, culminating in a handspring flip with a twist and an almost obnoxiously well-stuck landing.

'Yeah, well,' TM said, flashing his tongue at her as she strutted past, 'you've always been a ridiculous ninja. I *learned* it.'

She gave him a slow clap. Veggie jogged up the stairs the old-fashioned way, scooting up to them merrily. 'We must be near the hub,' he said, rubbing his hands together with excitement. 'There'll probably be *traps* and shit.'

'Fun,' TM said, gently pushing open the door to the next corridor.

The two guards inside turned towards them in surprise.

'Ah,' TM said.

Dominika sprinted down the corridor between the two guards; one turned to follow her, the other sticking with TM and Veggie. He fumbled at his hip for a second, then they were on him. Veggie tackled him to the ground, knocking the wind out of him, and rolled away, leaving the guard sitting dazed on his arse. TM took the opportunity to run at him and kick him as hard as he possibly could in the chest.

'Niiiiiiiice,' Veggie burbled. The guard sat up slowly, groaning in pain; TM and Veggie looked at each other, then at the guard, then back at each other.

'Can we?' Veggie pleaded.

'Oh, we can.'

The guard attempted to wobble upright, just about making it to his knees; Veggie and TM grabbed an arm each and grinned at each other, raising their free hands to point at the ceiling before each driving a knee into one of the man's shoulders. He crumpled back, groaning, and wisely decided not to get up again.

'He'll live,' was Veggie's reaction.

Meanwhile, Dominika had the other guard prone on the floor; seeing

TM and Veggie delivering their tag team finisher, and not to be outdone, she took a run-up of a couple of steps before throwing herself into the air, legs flying over her head as she flipped backwards and landed stomach-first on her target.

Then she stood up and kicked him in the head, partly for good measure and partly because just landing on someone doesn't actually do all that much in a real fight unless you happen to be a fair sight bulkier than Dominika.

She brushed herself off, looking satisfied.

'That was so impractically cool that I think I'm going to try it,' Veggie declared.

'Do *not* try to do a shooting star press,' TM said, 'you'll break your neck.'

Veggie huffed. 'Well, I obviously can't now you've made me doubt it, but I totally could have done it if I hadn't realised how dumb it would be.'

'That... actually sounds kind of like how the world works lately,' TM had to admit.

Around the final corner was the Swede's office. The door actually had his name on it, which seemed odd given that they were in his house in the first place, and opened onto an enormous library, complete with sliding ladder. In the centre of it all sat an unnecessarily large desk, topped with no fewer than six unnecessarily large monitors.

'It's got to be on here,' Veggie said, plonking himself down in the unnecessarily large office chair and firing up the computer.

'Can you hack a computer?' TM asked curiously.

'Nah,' said Veggie, 'but he has written his password on a Post-It, so I think I got this.'

'Aww,' said TM disappointedly. 'I had a thing for this that let you see infrared traces of thermal contact on the keyboard to work out what keys were pressed most often, thought that might come in handy.'

'Sounds awesome,' Veggie said, tapping in the password. 'Don't ever use that on my laptop.'

He opened a few files, clicking aimlessly; Dominika wound her way around the walls, checking out the Swede's vast library of antique-looking books. TM followed her, leaving Veggie to it. She pulled out one of the thickest, heaviest, oldest-looking books on the shelves, and opened it. Then she snorted and passed it to TM. He checked the hard, faded cover: some Russian-sounding classic he'd never heard of, except possibly vaguely in passing. Then he flipped to a page somewhere in the middle, took a look, and laughed.

'Pretentious bastard,' he said in Veggie's direction. 'He's just put a fancy cover on a flipping telly magazine.'

'Least it's not porn,' Veggie said, clicking through the Swede's folders.

'I dunno,' said TM, looking around the room, 'there's a lot of books in here.'

'Can't believe I ever,' Veggie mumbled. 'Worst decision ever, and if everyone lives on in the minds of everyone they affected then that dickhead's still in my brain somewhere and that's just…' He trailed off, then: 'aha!' he declared, pointing triumphantly at one of the screens before him.

TM scurried over to look, leaving Dominika to peruse the shelves. At the end of Veggie's pointing finger was a single file, titled 'EVIDENCE AGAINST JV + TM (SEAFOOD GYM)'. Veggie clicked it.

A notepad file filled the screen. It was blank.

'That arse,' Veggie said, jaw tensing and grinding. 'He doesn't have anything. And if he did it would be a flipping dot-TXT file.'

'Oh, but I do,' said a smooth voice.

'Aw, for heck's sake,' Veggie moaned.

The Swede stood above them, leaning over a rail mounted in the top of one of the many high shelves for no apparent good reason. He was a tall man in a cream suit, blonde-haired and blue-eyed, and was in all outward appearances almost ridiculously Swedish-looking.

'You see,' proclaimed the Swede in grandiose tone, 'I may not have any real evidence with which to assault your legal and financial sensibilities, but what I now have as a result of causing you to believe that such evidence was in my possession is…' He paused, took a deep breath and smiled widely. 'You.'

'You're saying it was a trap?' TM asked, just to make sure he'd fully understood the Swede's typically lengthy proclamation; the Swede nodded regally. 'Pff.'

'You find this amusing?' demanded the Swede. TM pulled something out of his pocket. 'What is that?' said the Swede, craning over the rail to look.

'I call it the *TM Super Bomb*,' said TM, tossing the object up and down in his hand.

'Super... Bomb?' the Swede repeated.

'Oh, yeah,' said TM, moving the *TM Fingerprint Detector* around as much as possible lest the Swede get a good look at it. 'See, I figured this might be a trap, so I thought if we're going to walk into it I may as well come prepared to blow the whole damn thing up, you know?'

As he spoke, Dominika, who had been against the wall under the Swede's railing and thus gone undetected, cautiously and quietly began climbing up the shelves of books. The Swede looked down at them, apparent shock on his freckled face, then cast about wildly.

'I wouldn't make any sudden moves,' TM said. The Swede stood still.

'By the way,' said Veggie, 'your computer sucks.' Then he stood up, knocked the chair over, swept the monitors off the desk and set to punching them to pieces.

'Oh, I wish you wouldn't do that,' said the Swede haplessly.

'You really didn't think this through, did you?' TM asked. The Swede could only shrug. Then Dominika reached the top of the shelving, grabbed him by the shirt and hauled him over the railing. He hit the ground hard, wheezing as he sat up.

'Why do you even bother?' TM asked, pocketing the TM Fingerprint Detector. 'Do you really hate Veg that much?'

'Not at all,' the Swede said, spitting out a tooth. 'Someone wanted you here. Someone very persuasive.'

'You serious?'

'What?'

'Someone else told you to do it? That's just an absolutely terrible justification for being such an enormous anus.' The Swede chuckled, then wheezed. 'What, you cheated on Veggie because the other guy just told you to?'

'No, I did that because I was bored,' the Swede told him, climbing to his knees. Veggie growled and picked up one of the more intact monitors, striding towards him, but TM got there first.

'Oh, fuck off, Johan,' he said, and kneed the Swede in the face. He collapsed on his front, arms splayed out. Veggie let the monitor drop, looking impressed.

'That'll do,' he said with satisfaction.

'Pafffff,' the Swede choked, rolling onto his back. 'I still win in this situation, I hope you realise.'

'How do you figure that?' TM asked contemptuously.

'Because I still have more money and greater success than you,' the Swede said, grinning, 'and I haven't lost the most successful part of my business.'

Veggie picked up the monitor again.

'I'm sure the two of you can find ways to make up for what she brought to your little partnership, though,' said the Swede. 'I imagine you can be just as persuasive as she, when you put your minds to it. It doesn't exactly take a special person to suck -'

Veggie whacked him in the face with the monitor, which smashed everywhere. The Swede collapsed.

'She was special,' Veggie said angrily. 'Is.' He turned away, then quickly back. 'Also, she didn't do that anyway, and furthermore *fuck you*.'

'Er,' said TM. Dominika scooted in and pressed two fingers against the Swede's neck, then slapped him in the face; he coughed weakly. 'See ya, Johan,' TM said to their fallen foe. The Swede moaned in response.

'He'll be fine, probably,' Veggie said. 'He's had what he deserves.'

Dominika nodded.

'You don't think that was a bit... much?' TM asked half-heartedly. 'Feels like we've switched gears from light-hearted roguishness to... I dunno, assault.' Had the Swede done a triple backflip, TM reflected, the whole thing would have felt more tonally appropriate, but simply beating up a man who hadn't fought back felt like a less satisfying resolution than he might have hoped.

'It's merited,' Veggie growled.

TM couldn't disagree.

Dominika nudged his shoulder, gazing curiously up at the railing behind which the Swede had stood. There was, TM noticed now, a door set into the wall behind.

'Well, we've come this far,' TM mused. 'May as well find out what he had in his most hubby of hubs. And if there really was someone who told him to trap us for no reason.'

Dominika flashed her teeth, then set to climbing back up the shelves; Veggie elected to slide the ladder over, which TM scooted up behind him.

'I don't get it,' Veggie said as he climbed. 'I know he's an arse who'd do anything just for the sake of sticking it to us, but... really, what was the point?'

He hoisted himself over the railing and collapsed in a heap on the other side; Dominika held out a hand to him, which he accepted with mild embarrassment.

'He's not *stupid*,' Veggie continued as Dominika waved at the door, inviting him to be the one to open it. 'I don't see how it makes sense to lure us here with some *evidence* that doesn't even exist just to... just to have us here? I mean, what was gonna happen after that?'

He shook his head, took the handle, and slowly turned it. The door creaked open, and Veggie led the trio inside.

Behind the door was a medium-sized, verging on small, room: a simple lounge containing a TV, a square table upon which sat a chess board, pieces left in the middle of a developing game, and a single armchair, upon which sat Al Tyer.

31. Precipitation

'What the actual shit,' said Veggie.

'*Ah*,' said Al Tyer weakly. His hair, always so perfectly in place down to the follicle, was messy and ruffled; his suit, usually creased exactly as it should be, hung loosely on him. Sweat patches had soaked through, and every inch of material seemed to have been either damaged or dirtied. He looked gaunt, smaller. He looked ill.

'You look terrible,' TM told him.

Tyer laughed, which immediately turned into a wheeze. 'I do rather, don't I?'

Veggie punched him in the face. Tyer's head snapped to the side, and when he turned back to look up at them his cheek bore a visible dent. It was as if his skin were stretched over modelling clay rather than muscle and bone.

'You took Ziggy,' Veggie told him. 'You took her.'

Tyer looked off at a spot on the wall, like an old man struggling to remember some detail of decades past. 'I did,' he said uncertainly. Even his voice was worn, hoarse, a far cry from his old perfect professional cadence.

'What happened to you?' TM asked. He had never felt so clueless as to how to feel: furious, curious, heartbroken, pitying, wrathful, even a little sad.

'I empathise more with your friend than perhaps you realise,' Tyer said slowly, still staring at the wall. 'One gets to enjoy the magnitude of being a star in the sky, and… tired of the backdrop.'

'You came down without permission,' TM realised. 'Not just this time?'

'Not just this time.'

TM extended an arm, putting a barrier between Tyer and Veggie, who looked more than ready to hit him again. Dominika, meanwhile, leaned against the door impassively with folded arms. 'Orion,' TM said. 'She must know - she must be…'

Fear swelled up inside him, and he turned towards the door, but Tyer held up a hand. It looked as if it took all his strength simply to raise his elbow from his knee.

'She's not coming, not for me,' he said. 'She knows. She always knows. But she tolerates me, because... I always find my way back on my own.'

'Or she just doesn't think you're worth wasting her time on,' Veggie spat.

'She has a lower opinion of me than might be hoped,' Tyer conceded, then an exhalation turned into a hacking cough. He wiped his mouth, breathing heavily. 'I cannot say it is entirely inaccurate, however.'

'Oh, shut it with the self-pitying nonsense,' TM said, tired of hearing the old star's croaky rhetoric. 'You made decisions. Apparently, you got away with them. She didn't. So fuck you.'

'Not unreasonable,' said Tyer quietly.

'You're not even a *good* celebrity,' Veggie told him. Tyer gave something between a choke and a chuckle.

'Not as much a star on earth as in heaven,' Tyer admitted. 'Your friend came in her entirety; unless I am invited, I leave some of myself behind so as not to... overstep *her* patience.'

'And, what, because you haven't shot to stardom this time you're out of juice?'

'I am... out of juice. It demands a goal. For your friend, simply existing did the trick. For me, failure even to read the weather successfully has depleted my strength somewhat.' Tyer cast a bleary grey eye over the three of them; faded and dull though it was, TM could feel the force of it. 'You ought to be careful letting so much of your own show.'

The trio exchanged confused glances, looking for whatever Tyer was talking about.

'We're not stars, though,' Veggie said slowly.

'We all have a bit of special sauce,' TM remembered. He became aware that Dominika was fidgeting behind him, and sighed. 'We're done.'

'Wait,' said Veggie, his mouth hardly moving. 'What about Ziggy?'

'She is where she belongs,' Tyer said; Veggie hit him again, TM too slow to stop him. 'It's the truth, I'm afraid,' he said, half his face crumpled like a car bonnet in a collision.

'How do we get her *back*?' Veggie demanded.

'We've been through this,' TM protested, suddenly drained of all willingness to stay in the room with Al Tyer any longer, but Veggie shook his head.

'I know she said we couldn't,' he said. 'But this one - this one does it. So… so couldn't she do it too?'

'I do not think she would be so selfish as to put you in danger again,' Tyer said. 'Not that she can feel anything now, of course. She exists, and that is really all we can be said to do up there.'

'It's not,' TM told him. Tyer looked at him questioningly. 'She wanted to come down, so she did. You - you miss being who you were down here, so you do it too. I went and *spoke* to her!' Tyer blinked at that. 'You can't tell me you don't feel anything when you're up there!'

Tyer thought about it, head swaying side to side as if he were watching a very slow fish in a distant aquarium. 'Perhaps not,' he said eventually. 'Still, the things above us… they do not feel. If feeling causes them to act, then we would be better off not feeling.'

TM pressed his palm against his forehead, inhaling deeply. 'I don't see what else there is to do here,' he said to Dominika, who nodded; Veggie punched Al Tyer again.

'There is one thing,' Tyer said through his half-broken mouth. 'Why do you think I asked Johan to bring you here?'

TM shrugged. 'Doesn't matter. So you could both work out how to hurt us best, probably.'

'I have… a warning,' Al Tyer said, very slowly. 'She knows.'

TM and Veggie looked at each other. 'Knows what?' TM asked.

'Another.' The breath sounded as if it were having to swim through treacle to escape the old man's mouth. 'You have another.'

'Another… Ziggy?' TM almost burst out laughing, or crying, or screaming. 'No, we don't! There was only one of her, and you saw to it that she couldn't stay with us.'

'I think I see it,' Tyer rumbled, looking very closely at Veggie. 'Still. She won't stop.'

'What do you mean?' Veggie asked, raising his fist again. 'And why the hell would you warn *us*?'

Tyer considered this. 'I don't believe I can help it,' he said finally. 'My sister, your friend, would understand what I mean by that, I think.'

Veggie growled. 'You didn't answer the first question. What do you mean, another?'

'I shall return to my place now, I suppose,' said Tyer.

'What do you *mean*?!' Veggie bellowed, hitting him in the face again.

'Veg,' said TM quietly. Veggie punched Tyer twice more, the ex-weatherman's head caving under his fists like wet bread dough. 'Veg,' TM said louder, warningly. Veggie raised his fist again. '*Jon!*' TM yelled.

Veggie paused. 'This isn't even a person, TM,' he said.

'Ziggy was,' TM told him. 'He's the same as her.'

'She was a person,' Veggie repeated. Then he stared down at Tyer, who looked back at him with sunken eyes, his face fractured and misshapen. 'She was.' He sighed, turned, and left.

'I will be going now, I think,' Tyer said, the words hissing out like gas escaping from a ruptured pipe. 'Yes, I will be going now.'

'You're scared to go back,' TM told him, half-questioningly.

'Hmmmm,' Tyer murmured. 'I know very little of the things above me. Fear of the unknown might be the most human of feelings.'

'It's your place,' TM said; Dominika nodded, TM thought almost with sympathy.

'Yes,' said Tyer, and then he was gone, a fine golden mist evaporating up into the air.

TM watched him go, then turned and followed Veggie out of the small room, leaving the empty suit that had been Altair's crumpled on the armchair.

'Hey,' said Dominika quietly.

He turned back to her. 'Yeah?'

'Veg,' she said. 'He's angry.'

'You don't say.'

'Hey,' she said, taking him by the shoulders. 'Don't let it get the better of him. Or you. That's how shit goes bad.'

TM thought about it for a moment, then nodded. 'You're right,' he said; she patted him on the arm.

'Of course I am,' she told him. 'Look, I gotta go home, but… I'll see you guys at Marty's thing next week, yeah?'

'Veg'll be there. I've got stuff.'

She nodded. 'Take care of him,' she said, then wandered away.

32. Station to Station

Veggie collapsed into the sofa, releasing a stream of air from his bulging cheeks. Michel Furcoat popped out from underneath the cushions as Veggie descended; the cat glanced up as if telling his owner off for the inconvenience, then wandered away to find food.

'That was... interesting,' Veggie said after a moment.

'Yeah,' TM agreed, not sure what else to say.

'Al fucking Tyer,' Veggie murmured.

'It's... kind of sad, what happened to him,' TM said, descending onto the sofa next to his partner.

'My heart bleeds,' Veggie said. 'Fuck him, TM, he took Ziggy.'

'I know,' TM reassured him.

There were a few moments of silence.

'Oh, stick the TV on or something,' Veggie moaned.

TM picked up the remote and hit the power button with a loud click.

'I'm back,' said Riegel O'Ryan.

'You,' Veggie half-groaned, half-screamed, 'have *got* to be kidding me.'

'It's been three looooong years,' O'Ryan drawled in her soft Irish tones. 'I've been all over, place to place, station to station, and now I'm back to take on my greatest challenge yet. So tune in to my new show next week, and you'll see survival in the most -'

TM turned the TV off. He sat there for a moment, his skin feeling burning, prickling hot all over.

'She's back,' Veggie said quietly. 'He wasn't kidding, she's really come back.'

TM nodded silently, holding himself by the arms and trying to make himself as small as possible so there would be less of him to feel the burning.

'So... there must be another runaway star,' Veggie said, looking down at his feet.

TM nodded again.

'Oh, balls to this,' Veggie said, covering his face with his hands. 'Look, she's on TV in, like, Bhutan or something, she's already taken Ziggy, what more does she have to do to us?'

'Probably enough,' TM said quietly. 'Tyer seemed to think she'd be after us again. As if he thought we had a second Ziggy.'

Veggie sank further back into the cushions. 'Look, whatever Weather Bastard said, he was old and grey and broken and we *haven't* got another star so… just let's forget that Irish-Greek-cosmonaut-whatever-she-is friend-killer and move on, yeah?' he said, looking and sounding more tired than TM thought he had ever seen him.

'We already had to move on once,' TM said, trying not to think about it.

'Then let's not give her the satisfaction of having to do it again,' Veggie argued. 'Let's just… forget about it.'

TM collapsed as far into the soft fabric of the sofa as he could. 'Fine,' he agreed.

'I'm not happy about this either,' Veggie told him.

'I know, I can tell.'

'But… Marty's got his Battle of the Bands next week, so I just want to try to forget it, be there for him, that sort of stuff. You know?'

'I know.'

'Good,' said Veggie, and went to bed.

TM stayed on the sofa for a while, wondering how it had gone from Dominika telling him to take care of Veggie to his partner trying to tell him to keep calm. He stared at the TV screen. He could still see O'Ryan's face staring out at him, her charismatic presenter's smile firmly in place. Then he looked at the ceiling for a bit, then at his feet. Then he went to bed too.

***

'You know, Junior,' TM's father was saying, a week later, 'it's nice to see you and Jonathan doing well and having success with your Muscly

Shellfish thing - and I think it's wonderful that he and young Benjamin are together, I listened to some of Benjamin's band's music and I think it's quite spectacular - but you do seem ever so down since that nice young lady dumped you.'

'She didn't dump me,' TM said, for what must have been the fiftieth time. 'We weren't *together* like that.'

He re-read the menu in front of him; he'd decided what he was having a good few minutes ago, but didn't feel like looking up yet. They had come to an Indian restaurant; TM had suggested they go to Muscles & Mussels, but apparently his parents hated seafood.

'Oh, that's right,' said Senior, though he clearly didn't believe it.

'Junior doesn't want to talk about that, Tommy,' Lily chided her husband.

'It's okay,' TM said, trying to smile. 'I don't think Mum wants to hear about it on her birthday, though, Dad...'

'You really ought to come and see us more often than just on birthdays,' Lily told her son.

'Yeah, I know,' TM said, scratching his nose. 'Things are kind of...'

'Busy?'

'I was going to say weird, but I guess that too.'

'It's good to keep busy,' Lily said.

'Hm.'

TM kept re-reading the menu. Senior cleared his throat and leaned over. 'You know, you can talk to us. About things. We'd very much like to be there for you, and... whatnot.'

'Yeah, I - oh, hang on.' TM pulled his phone, which was vibrating away cheerfully, out of his pocket. 'Derrida's trying to video chat, for some reason...'

'Go on - we won't be going anywhere,' Lily said with a faint smile.

'Cheers.' TM stood and trotted out of the restaurant onto the night-time street. 'Derrida?'

Derrida's face, poorly lit and stuttering around in the low-quality video, filled his phone screen. 'TM!' they yelled, barely audible over the sound of a roaring crowd. 'This is amazing!'

'What's going on?' TM asked; Derrida pointed to their ears and shook their head.

'Can't hear you,' Derrida bellowed, 'but you've got to see this!'

They held their phone up to show TM where they were; the camera flashed past the flushed, beaming faces of Veggie and Dominika before capturing an enormous room, every inch of floor space lined with a bouncing mass of people.

To each side, cutting the audience into an H shape, stood a large stage. On one stood the Inciting Incident, facing across the room and breathing heavily. On the other, four women wearing white-constellation-patterned black jackets; the picture wasn't great, but TM thought they looked strikingly similar, with high cheekbones, stern, bright eyes, and almond-shaped ears sticking out from under their long black hair. 'That's Lauren and the Ire!' Derrida exclaimed. 'They're sisters or something!'

'How's it going?' TM said, putting his mouth as close as possible to the microphone. Derrida whipped the camera back onto their own face.

'They've done, like, two songs each, and they're both *awesome*,' they trumpeted. 'Ooh, ooh, they're switching their lineup!'

TM caught a glimpse of narrow turquoise beams fanning out above Derrida's head, and heard Marty's amplified voice declare proudly: 'That's our laser harp. It's new.'

'Ooooh,' went Derrida, along with the rest of the crowd.

'Fancy,' said the lead singer of Lauren and the Ire - Lauren, presumably. Her voice was soft, like a chamois cloth.

'I like your cello,' Marty said. Derrida's head flipped side-to-side as each of them spoke, watching as if the exchange of words were a tennis match across a sea of baying fans.

'It's a double bass,' Lauren shot back.

'Fitting,' Marty said, 'because you're about to get double *bossed*.'

'OHHHHHHHH,' roared the crowd.

'Dang, son,' TM heard Veggie exclaim.

'What do you say, you ridiculously amazing audience?!' Marty yelled. The crowd screamed. 'What do you say, something.jpg?!' Marty bellowed. More cheers.

'Something.jpg?' TM tried to ask Derrida.

'Their mascot!' Derrida shouted, possibly because they had heard TM or, more likely, because they had predicted the question. 'They got an iguana mascot! Called something.jpg!'

'Look, Derrida,' TM tried to say, but Derrida was bouncing around enraptured. 'Thanks for showing me and all, but I need to...'

'I'll let you get back to it,' Derrida bellowed, as the Inciting Incident launched into *I Got My Buster Sword*. 'Can't hear you at all, but this is great! Wish you were here!'

'Love you,' TM quipped, and hung up.

'Well, that looked like fun,' Senior boomed. TM whipped around.

'How long have you been there?'

Senior hiccupped and patted his son on the shoulder. 'Since the laser harp,' he said. 'What an invention! Did you invent that?'

'No, Dad, I didn't invent the laser harp.'

'You have invented some rather good things, though,' Senior said. 'Like, erm... well, I seem to remember just after my birthday a few years ago there was a good one.'

'Oh, yeah, that was the day Ziggy invented the Puncture Repair Kit.'

'That's one of yours?!' Senior bellowed, slapping his thigh. 'I use those all the time!'

TM smiled. 'Glad to be of assistance.'

Senior guffawed, then sighed heavily and plonked himself down on the kerb. 'You know, Junior, I don't get to see you as much as I'd like -'

'That's my fault, I know that.'

'- but I know when you're not alright. You were ever so down after that Zebra girl left, and then I thought you were getting over it, but today you seem as if you've just lost her again.' Senior stared out into the lights of the city; TM was, as he had been before, surprised by his father's perceptiveness. 'You've hardly been this sad since you were a teenager with terrible skin,' Senior continued, shattering the illusion somewhat.

'That was years ago, Dad, you can stop bringing it up now.'

'But it's my acne-dote,' Senior said, crestfallen.

'Pff.'

'Look,' said Senior, shuffling up closer to his son, 'I think I might be able to understand how you feel, a little. It's not sad, not as such. More like you just don't have all of yourself any more, at least not in the place you thought it all was.'

'Something like that,' TM conceded. 'How do you..?'

'I thought I lost your mother once,' Senior said. 'When you were born, she was...' He sighed. 'It could have ended very badly.'

'I didn't know.'

'Not the sort of thing you tend to bring up.'

'But she was okay,' TM said. 'You got her back.'

Senior nodded. 'I did, but... if I hadn't, I would have carried on. I wouldn't have been alright, but I wouldn't have given up. I would have had you to take care of.'

'So you're saying... I just have to tough it out?'

Senior hummed a few low, ponderous notes. 'You have to find the things you can carry on for,' he said after a moment.

TM thought about it. 'That might be one of the wisest things you've ever said.'

'I do alright, from time to time.' Senior stood, stretched out, then threw his enormous arm around TM's shoulder. 'Do me and your mother a favour and come back in now, would you? I'm absolutely bloody starving.'

TM shook his head, smiling as he and his father walked back into the restaurant together. 'Know what you're having?'

'Bit of everything, I reckon,' Senior said.

33. Because 'Gary's Mackerel' Would Have Been Too Obvious

TM wandered down the streets towards home, belly full of korma. As promised, Senior had eaten one of almost everything, with Lily quite happy to fill up on whatever he left. TM was glad to have gone to the meal; he really ought to see them more, he thought.

His phone rang again. Veggie this time.

'Veg?'

'Hey,' Veggie said. 'How was the thing?'

'It was good, actually,' TM said. 'Yours?'

'Ohmigosh best thing ever,' Veggie burbled. 'The other group won, but I don't even care.'

'They must have been pretty good.'

'Yeaaaaaaah... I mean, obviously the Inciting Incident were totally better, but the show was just awesome so it's good all round.'

'Taking part that counts, right?'

'So lame. But yeah. Oh, and apparently your dad knows Marty's bandmates? They were all, like, hyped to call him and tell him about it.'

'He said he was a fan,' TM remembered. 'Sounds weird that they're apparently best mates now, but somehow not surprised. You heading home?'

'Nah.'

TM waited for an explanation.

'Oh, yeah, that's what I was calling about!' Veggie remembered, sounding as if he'd surprised himself. 'Can you come over to the arena?'

'What for?'

'Well, Lauren and the Ire - that's the other band -'

'I know, Derrida video-called me.'

'- anyway, those guys, they asked if me and you and Marty could meet them in their dressing room in half an hour.'

'Er.'

As if sensing TM's thoughts, Veggie made a stuttering noise and clarified: 'Yeah, I know, four girls, three guys, dressing room - don't worry, they just want to talk to us about some collaboration or other. Pro bono, no boning.'

'Why do they need me and you there? Surely if they're collaborating with anyone it'd just be Marty and the band?'

'They've got this idea for a concept album where they do the music with Double-I - that's what we're shortening "Inciting Incident" to now - and we invent a product for each song. It's totally, like, multimedia postmodernism.'

TM swapped his phone to the other ear and tried to work out where exactly he was. He'd been walking in the general direction of Muscles & Mussels on autopilot, but now he was trying to think about how to get to the Battle of the Bands location, he was at a bit of a loss. 'I'll be there in... a bit,' he said. 'Gotta hang up and satnav it, though, okay?'

'See you in a bit,' Veggie said. 'Don't take too long, or we might all just end up banging after all.' He hung up.

TM hoped it wouldn't come to that; with Marty and Veggie spending regular nights in the same flat as him, he'd already seen more than he needed to of... that. He pulled up a maps app and stuck in the address of the arena, which was a shorter way across town than he'd thought. Small world.

'Spare some change?' somebody asked as TM turned a corner. He rummaged about in his pocket and found a spare pound, which he held out. 'Thank you kindly, sir,' said the person sitting on the corner. TM looked down at him.

'Gary Mackerel?'

'Oh. Hey, TM.'

'I haven't seen you since... when you won that hamper at the fair three years ago.'

'Things have gone a bit downhill since then,' Gary Mackerel said mournfully.

'What happened to Gary's Fish?'

'Oh, the fish and chip shop. It just... sort of stopped making money.'

'Man, that sucks.'

'I should have called it something about mackerel,' Gary Mackerel muttered, as if scolding himself. 'I didn't want to go for the obvious pun, but apparently *Gary's Fish* isn't marketable enough...'

'You know,' TM said, 'we've got a place that does... fish... stuff.'

Gary Mackerel brightened. 'You do?'

TM nodded. 'Know anyone who might be up for helping us out? We're growing, we could use some new hands to help us with seafood supply and that sort of thing.'

Gary Mackerel burst into tears. 'Are you... really?! TM!' He leapt up and wrapped TM in a smelly, damp embrace.

'Just, er... go let yourself in,' TM said, extricating himself. 'Door code's 080147; you can use the showers and we'll be back a bit later.'

'I can't believe this,' sobbed Gary Mackerel.

'You know where it is?'

Gary Mackerel nodded between blubbers. 'I can't believe you would - thank you!'

'Everything'll be alright,' TM told him, and found himself starting to believe it too.

'I won't let you down!' Gary Mackerel blurted. He gave TM one more hug and dashed off in the direction of Muscles & Mussels.

'See you later, Gary Mackerel,' TM called after his new employee, and carried on down the road.

***

TM wandered up to the entrance of the arena, a large building that had no business being where it was in among the residential streets. Marty and Veggie were waiting outside, still sweaty and flushed from - TM hoped - the Battle of the Bands.

'Hey, loser,' Marty said as he approached.

'I heard you were the loser,' TM retorted. Marty winced.

'Set myself up for that one,' he admitted.

'Oh, Veg,' TM said, before he forgot, 'I think I just hired Gary Mackerel to come work for us, just so you know.'

Veggie nodded, not seeming to think that this was an odd turn of events in any way. 'Fair play. As long as he doesn't try to change the name to "Muscles & Mussels & Mackerel" or something.'

'I think he'd probably just go for "Muscles & Mussels & Gary", but point taken.'

Marty shivered. He was wearing a thick jacket, but TM could see his usual stage attire of a thin T-shirt underneath.

'Shall we go in?' he suggested. Marty nodded and hopped through the doors. Veggie made to go bounding after him, but TM put a hand on his business partner's arm and walked him in. 'So... this band just asked you if we would help them out?'

'Yeah!' Veggie declared. 'Isn't it awesome?'

TM thought about it. 'Don't you think it's a bit weird that they just knew that we were inventors? Like, what are the odds they just met Marty today, heard about us and came up with this plan?'

'They probably just Googled Marty and found out about *ZVTMII*,' Veggie said dismissively. 'We're all kind of famous now.'

'I guess,' TM said.

'We've always just rolled with stuff up until now,' Veggie pointed out.

'I think maybe... not that just going with it wasn't great, but I feel like I don't ever choose to do anything,' TM said, thinking out loud. 'Weird stuff just happens around me and I react to it.'

'Best way to live,' Veggie said. 'C'mon, their dressing room's just around here.'

Veggie dragged TM down the corridors of the arena, following Marty through backstage areas filled with instruments and various unused scenery and prop items; they turned a corner into a hall labelled 'Talent Zone'.

'This was our dressing room,' Marty said proudly, pointing to one of several doors around the walls of the Talent Zone. 'And this one...' He moved a couple of doors along. 'Pretty sure this one was theirs.' He knocked, then, when there was no response, slowly pushed the door open.

'Helloooooo?' he called. 'I'm coming in. Don't be naked.'

'Or do,' Veggie piped up.

Marty swung the door all the way open and wandered in. 'Nobody's in here,' he said, looking around. TM thought he could hear movement nearby, a low growl like a breeze whipping through a narrow crack. Then Marty yelped and disappeared under the dark mass of an enormous dog.

'Marty!' Veggie yelled, sliding in and kicking at the beast; it hopped back, then leapt and pounced on him, pinning him down. 'What the - Keelut?!'

'Oh, shit,' said TM, frozen in the doorway as Riegel O'Ryan's dog snarled and drooled in his partner's face. Marty stared from the hound to TM, frantically mouthing 'What do we do?!'

'Keelut,' said a soft Irish voice from behind TM. 'Don't eat his face, there's a good girl.'

'Motherfucker,' Veggie wheezed.

TM didn't even bother turning around. 'What are you doing here, Orion?'

She swished past him, strands of her hair brushing across his arm. She was even taller than he remembered. 'Come on, girl,' she said to the enormous mass of muscle and fur that was Keelut, and the dog relinquished Veggie and padded over, wagging its tail. 'Good dog.'

'What did you do with Lauren and the Ire?' Marty demanded, sliding over to put himself between Veggie and the Huntress.

'Oh, that lot,' Orion said, fingers buried in the fur around her canine companion's ears. 'Don't worry yourself about them, they're fine. Promise.'

'What the hell are you doing here?' Veggie bellowed at her. 'You took Ziggy away from us, isn't that enough?!'

'I mean, you know what I do,' Orion said, shrugging. 'You can't figure it out?'

'If you're anything like Altair, you just fancied another day in the limelight,' TM spat at her.

'Oh, no. Poor Al. He was ever so fond of being all famous-like, even though more people loved him in the sky than they ever did on their TVs.' Orion sighed and leaned against the wall. 'No, I'm here 'cos we've lost another one, if you catch my drift. Kind of a big deal, this one. Real rock star.'

'So somebody had to come down and bring them back, huh?' TM said, a kind of sour resignation making its way through his body.

'Naturally,' Orion said, bowing. 'Not to strum me own harp, but yours truly does it best, or so I'm told.'

Veggie scoffed. 'So you thought you'd come beat us up again. What makes you think your runaway's with us this time?'

'Not all that much, to be totally honest,' Orion said, shrugging. 'Thing is, you're sort of a weak lead, but probably the best one I've got right now. You're the last known harbourers of one of our little... refugees, and I've been picking up some luminosity in your area, so I figured we'd start with you lucky chaps.'

'That's it?!' TM exploded. 'After what you did to us - to Ziggy - you really want to show up here because you figure maybe, just maybe, because we happened to meet her, we might just possibly have some vague inkling of where this other runaway star might be?'

He strode towards Orion, pushing his face up towards hers, standing on tiptoe to look straight into her eyes with as much wrath as he could muster. 'Are you celestial idiots so *fucking incompetent* at keeping tabs on your own people that you came down here, burst in on the most tangentially maybe possibly relevant people you could think of, and you thought that would solve all your problems?!'

Orion returned his gaze, though TM thought he might have caught her lip give the briefest of twitches. 'Well, when you say it like that...'

'We don't know where your damn starfriend is,' TM told her venomously. 'You took the only one we knew, okay? So go back to your bosses, tell them to leave us the hell alone, and leave us in peace. And while you're at it, ask them to give us Ziggy back.'

'I don't think I can do that,' Orion said quietly. She broke TM's gaze for a second, glancing down at Keelut as if asking for guidance. The dog looked up at her, tongue lolling out. 'Orders are orders, and order is order,' she said softly, almost as if to herself. Then she sighed and gazed at Veggie; Marty held his arms out protectively. 'As above, so below.'

'Altair liked saying that,' TM told her.

'Ah, yeah, he did at that.' Her gaze moved back to him. 'I heard about your run-in with him, y'know. Did quite a number on him, from how they're telling it.'

'He was afraid, and so are you,' TM said. 'You're all scared shitless of whatever's up there, above even you.'

'Mice fear cats,' she said. 'Elephants fear poachers. I know my place in the food chain.'

'It's not at the top, is it?' TM asked her, staring so intensely that his eyes began to hurt.

She exhaled, then shrugged. 'Doesn't matter. I'm here to bring back a target, and that's what I intend to do.' She reached into a pocket and withdrew a business card with two fingers, slipping it deftly into TM's back pocket. 'Give us a shout if you do happen to hear anything.'

Then she was gone, Keelut bounding out after her.

'That utter bitch,' Veggie hissed.

'So she really is... evil?' Marty asked, looking helpless.

'I don't know,' TM said. 'Altair – Al Tyer – he said something about things on this level not being good or evil, just sort of existing according to the laws of physics and stuff.'

'She's evil as shit,' Veggie said. 'She was my hero and she's literally the most evil-est person in the world.'

'What do we do now?' Marty said. 'Do we just... carry on like normal? Like nothing happened?'

'We go home,' TM said.

'And when we get there,' Veggie continued, 'we call Dominika, and we discuss how we're going to murder Riegel O'Ryan.'

'I don't know if –'

Veggie stood and strode over to TM, grasping his shoulders. 'Tom,' he said. 'She killed Ziggy. Maybe not in the normal fully-dead sense of the word, but to all practical intents and purposes, that's what she did. I thought I could ignore her if she wasn't *here*, but she is, she's in front of our faces and I am *fucking furious* with her.'

'I know, and I get it, I do, but I don't see how –'

'It doesn't matter how!' Veggie snapped. 'If we have to hold O'Ryan hostage to get Ziggy back, then great. Whatever. But she's here, she's back in our city, and she won't just let us go, not a chance. Someone's gotta stop her, and it sure as hell isn't gonna be anyone else.'

TM sighed and looked past Veggie's red face to Marty. 'What do you think?' he asked.

Marty took a few deep breaths. 'I don't know,' he said eventually. 'If she's here, then somebody else is going to lose someone like Ziggy, like we did. It... feels like we've got to do something.'

'Can we just go home and think about it there?' TM groaned.

'Fine,' Veggie said. 'I'm calling Dominika.'

34. Ultimate Showdown of Ultimate Destiny

When TM, Marty, and Veggie entered Muscles & Mussels, Gary Mackerel was sound asleep on one of the gym's benches.

'Oh, he's adorable,' Marty cooed. 'Nice hire, TM.'

'I thought so.' The three of them headed to the stairs in the back, making their way up to the flat above the gymnastaurant and leaving Gary Mackerel to snooze.

'I think Dominika's on her way,' Veggie said, closing the door behind them. Michel Furcoat, the cat, looked up at the noise, then went back to sleep on TM's desk. 'Hard to tell over the phone, but sounded like she nodded. What's on that card Survival Bitch gave you?'

TM pulled Orion's card out of his pocket; the only thing on it was a local address, which he read aloud.

'Wait a sec,' Marty said, pulling out his phone and tapping the address in. 'That's one of the warehouse-y container-y things, like the one where we built the rocket.'

'You're shitting me,' said Veggie.

'Nuh-uh.' Marty showed him the screen. 'Looks like it's almost right next to the one we hired.'

'Did we ever... like, stop paying rent on that?' TM asked. 'I mean, we're not using it any more.'

'Problems for another time,' Veggie insisted. 'What are we going to do about the Riegel O'Ryan situation?'

TM scratched the back of his head. 'Is it really a situation?'

'Are you serious?!'

'Well... she's here, but we genuinely don't know where the poor sod she's after is, so... she hasn't got any reason to mess with us, right? She'll just wait for us to call, leave us alone if we don't?'

'We've been through this!' Veggie exclaimed. 'She's already messed with us just by showing up - and besides, she's here to take somebody away from a life on Earth. We can't let that happen to someone else, not when we know how shit it was going through it.'

'Look,' said TM, trying to collect his thoughts, 'I hate her as much as you, I just... don't know what to do about it.'

Veggie let out a growl, pacing about. 'Me neither,' he admitted grudgingly.

There was a knock at the door; TM opened it to let Dominika in.

'Dom!' Veggie burbled. 'Thank Christ. You always know what to do about... everything, right?'

She eyed him warily.

'We have to take out Riegel O'Ryan,' Veggie implored. 'So... how do we do it?'

Dominika shook her head and gave him a questioning look.

'She showed up,' Veggie explained, 'at the arena. She's probably killed Lauren and the Ire, and her stupid dog nearly killed me and Marty.'

She shook her head sadly, as if expressing how much that sucked.

'And there's another star down here somewhere that she's trying to track down and... we have to help them! We can't let her do it again.'

Slowly, Dominika nodded. Then she pointed right at Veggie's chest.

'I don't...' Veggie said. Then he pulled out the piece of space rock that still hung around his neck.

'Space rock,' TM murmured.

'Space rock!' Veggie squealed. 'Dom, you're a genius!'

'I think I'm missing something,' Marty said; TM shrugged at him.

'Remember we stuck this in the rocket and you got teleported into space or something?' Veggie babbled. 'There's something to this little bit of meteor whatsamebob, something powerful!'

'Maybe,' TM said, 'but we've got no idea how it works or what it does, or even whether it's got any juice left after blasting me into the far reaches of the cosmos.'

Veggie gave a groan of exasperation and thrust the rock right in TM's face. 'We had no idea how that rocket was going to work,' he said. 'We just knew that it would, because it had to. Same thing.'

'Our luck's going to run out,' TM warned him.

'I don't think it's luck,' Veggie said. 'I reckon all people have a bit of Star Power, and people like us have it in spades – not as much as the actual star people, but I reckon we're pretty dosed up on stardust, probably 'cos of hanging out with Ziggy – and I reckon that this Star Power is an actual force in the universe that we can use to do cool shit that shouldn't make any sense.'

'Ziggy did say the two of us burned brightly,' TM remembered, 'when I spoke to her... and Tyer, he said some stuff about seeing why Orion would think we had a star, and how he couldn't help but help us. I mean... it seems really unlikely, but maybe that's what they meant?'

'Of course it is,' Veggie proclaimed. 'The more audacious a thing, the easier it is to get the universe to accept it via Star Power. And that's why this will definitely work.'

TM nodded, overcome by the hype. Then he raised a finger. 'Er... what exactly is it that's going to work?'

'We're going to use the space rock to blast that starfucker back where she belongs,' Veggie announced, holding up the little bit of rock on the chain around his neck. 'Cos we *definitely* have superpowers.'

TM sighed. It made as much sense as anything else that happened these days. 'I guess that's what we're doing.'

'You're in!' Veggie yelled joyfully. 'Dom? Marty?'

Marty's expression made the rounds from confused to decisive to uncertain back to resolved, and he nodded firmly.

'This is stupid,' Dominika said.

'She can talk now?!' Veggie exclaimed. TM could tell that the cocktail of emotions bubbling away inside him had reduced the shock from utter astonishment to something like an exasperated 'of course she can'.

'Only when it's important,' she said, 'and it's important that we're all in agreement that this is absolutely one of the dumbest things we've ever come up with.'

'I know,' Veggie admitted. 'I am in fact fully aware that this is a really, really bad idea. It's not even an idea.' He gave Dominika a hard stare; for perhaps the first time TM had seen, she found herself unable to meet it. 'But we're doing it. For Ziggy, for Lauren and the Ire, for this other poor ba-star-d who decided to go AWOL and now has that fucker chasing his or her celestial arse. Nobody deserves that shit.'

'Well said,' TM had to acknowledge.

'Eh,' Dominika offered, looking unimpressed. 'It's still dumb, but it's less dumb doing it with me here than if you'd just run in on your own.'

'I appreciate that most back-handed of... sort-of compliments,' Veggie said. 'So you're in?'

Dominika stuck her tongue out. 'Yeah, why not. You've got me to agree to weirder than this.'

TM desperately wanted to ask, but knew it wasn't the time.

'By the way,' she said, pointing accusingly at Veggie, 'I really don't like Dom. Nika's fine, if you have to shorten it, but Dom? I dated a Dom. He *sucked*.'

'Fair point,' Veggie conceded. Then Dominika stopped talking again, and the four of them headed out.

***

The address on Orion's card, as Marty had said, led to what looked like a disused unit among the warehouses that had once housed the *ZVTMII* official spacecraft. They took a taxi there, piling into every seat. Dominika took the front.

'Are you... okay?' TM asked Veggie uncertainly on the way. His partner was shaking next to him, opening and clenching his fists.

'Probably not,' Veggie said. 'I'll be better when Orion's gone, for good. But not okay.'

'So what's the plan of attack?'

'Haven't thought about it so much.'

'You want to just march in and... punch a constellation and her dog in the face?'

'Hey, we live in a world with more than six Star Wars movies, more than three of which are decent. Anything can happen.'

'Anything...' TM pondered. 'Hey, who ended up winning? Out of Okada and Tanahashi, I mean.'

'Oh,' said Veggie, thinking, 'I don't even know. Kenny Omega, probably. There was all that Rainmakering and High Fly Flowing, and then Omega came along and kneed a bunch of people in the face.'

'Huh.'

'Never can tell how things'll end or what the point'll be. Maybe that's the point.'

The silence that lasted the rest of the journey wasn't comfortable, but TM didn't have anything else to say. He dropped Derrida a quick text to pop in and feed the cats, and then they were there.

'Sixteen quid,' the driver said, staring at them slightly menacingly in the rear view mirror.

'That's outrageous,' Veggie said disdainfully, but he picked a twenty out of his wallet and handed it over.

They exited the vehicle, Veggie pocketing the four pound coins he was handed in change (the driver huffed when none was offered as a tip, and drove away a little too quickly).

The door was open; or, at least, there were a few clear inches of space between the sliding iron sheet and the concrete below. TM slid underneath on his belly, shuffling like a soldier; Veggie and Marty rolled under, while Dominika opted for the classic baseball slide. Inside, the space was larger than it appeared from the outside - and certainly bigger than the one the rocket had been built in, which was understandable since it had been the one with the absolute lowest rent - a high square room surrounded by walkways and filled with big black boxes. Veggie flipped the latch on one, which swung open to reveal a tower of amps. Dominika inspected a couple more, which contained various instruments and cables.

'Somebody's supplying a rock band in here,' TM mused.

'Yeah, something like that,' agreed a voice from up on the high walkway.

TM looked up, and was only half-surprised to see a girl with long dark hair, elfin features, and a black jacket emblazoned with white stars leaning on the rail, legs crossed, watching over them curiously.

'Lauren!' Marty gasped.

'Should have known,' Veggie growled. 'You lot all stars too?'

The rest of The Ire emerged on the walkways, one peering down from each of the four walls.

'Yeah-huh,' Lauren said, gesturing around at herself and her bandmates. 'I'm Beta Lyrae. That one over there, also Beta Lyrae, and those two are a coupla Epsilons. Not totally sure exactly which, but who really cares?'

'Lyra,' TM said. 'So are you the one who's lost somebody?'

'Yeah, our lead singer went missing,' Lauren said, biting a nail absently. She pronounced things carefully, as if hiding an accent, but the occasional ethereal vowel slipped through. 'Vega.'

TM looked at Veggie.

'So we're down here to come get our brightest star back, with Orion's help,' Lauren explained. 'Seems to be how it works, no?'

'Wait, you're not even the lead singer?' Veggie asked, sounding almost smug about it.

'Not generally,' Lauren said, 'but I think you'll agree that I do pretty well at it.'

'You made such good music,' Marty mourned. 'You're not supposed to be evil. We could have made such a sweet collaboration!'

Veggie stared up at her for a moment, then shook his head. 'We're not here for you,' he told her. 'We're here to kill your boss.'

'What, Orion?' Lauren looked around at her bandmates, who grinned back. 'She's not our boss. No, no. Vega's our boss, we're just… not sure where he is. Or she. Never can tell. Orion's kind of our assistant while we're down here.'

'Where is she?' Veggie demanded. 'She in here?'

'Uh, nuh-uh.' Lauren shook her head. 'She left us to look after the place.'

'While she does what?'

Lauren smiled, and tapped a button mounted on the rail. TM heard the door descend the last few inches and close fully behind them, sealing them inside the warehouse room. 'She went to your place.'

'What?!' TM exclaimed. 'Why?'

'Are you actually going to make me monologue this out for you?' Lauren glanced at their faces, then sighed. 'Fine. We reckon you've got Vega. So we arranged a meeting between us and -' she pointed at TM, Marty, and Veggie in turn '- you and him and his BFF - sorry, fiancé, and congratulations, by the way - and then Orion showed up and gatecrashed and then gave you this address, knowing you'd come after her. Now you're out of the way, and she's gone to search your place for Vega.'

'Why not just kill us?' TM asked. 'Why not just *wait until we were out*?'

Lauren thought about it for a moment. Then she shrugged. 'Not actually sure,' she said thoughtfully. 'Would have made sense. I think Big O's actually a little bit... scared of you guys. Anyway, I don't know if you noticed, but she's not the most stable of peeps. Tends to come up with these plans that hurt people most, even if they're not the most effective.' She leaned over, whispering exaggeratedly: 'Between you and me, she's a bit unhinged.'

TM sidled over to Veggie, as did Dominika, the three of them doing their best to huddle together without attracting too much undue attention. Meanwhile, Marty yelled something up at Lauren about selling out and not respecting her artistry any more.

'Derrida's at our flat,' TM whispered. Veggie groaned quietly. 'She'll murder them.'

'I know,' Veggie hissed.

'So's Gary Mackerel... shit. We've got to get back.'

'What are y'all whispering about down there?' Lauren asked, leaning over curiously.

They broke the huddle; Veggie looked up at her and sighed. 'Well, we're in a bit of a fix, Laurelino.' She raised an eyebrow at that. 'See, we need to get out of here to go back to our place, beat up Survival Bitch - and her little dog too - and then go back to living our nice peaceful, happy life that we had before all you arses showed up.'

'Yeah, I can sort of see why you'd be wanting to do that,' Lauren said, 'but unfortunately that's what we're here specifically to stop you doing.'

Veggie reached into his pocket, pulled out one of the pound coins from the taxi and threw it at Lauren as hard as he could. She flicked it away easily, but Dominika took advantage of the distraction to make a dash for the door. She kicked it once, hard, and it dented under the blow; she pulled back for another, but two of Lauren's bandmates were suddenly upon her, one holding her by the arms from behind as the other hit her hard in the stomach. TM dashed towards them, but Lauren herself dropped down in front of him.

'Sorry, man,' she said. 'Wouldn't have had to do this if you'd just stayed here like we wanted.' Then she kicked him in the head.

TM collapsed, dropping, his flesh and bones feeling loosely connected, like a sock filled with marbles. He lay there for a few moments, face pressed against the floor, his eyes just about able to look around at the scene. He saw Dominika brought to her knees, smashed over the head with an electric guitar that exploded into neon splinters like a tiny firework; the same member of the Ire turned and kicked Marty in the chest, sending him flying into a wall; Lauren and one of the others - the double bass player, TM suspected - set upon Veggie. The bassist picked him up with ease, holding him over her head, then dropped him across her knee and onto the concrete as Lauren whipped a foot into his back on the way down. Veggie lay there, contorted in pain, and Lauren and the Ire resumed their places around the perimeter of the room, now leaning against the warehouse walls on the lower level.

'Sorry,' Lauren said, sounding genuinely apologetic. 'It's really not that we want to be doing this, honest. There's just... stuff more fundamental and important to the universe than you guys, so if we have to kick a few heads in to restore balance then that's what we're gonna do.'

'You think Orion only does this cos she has to?' TM asked, slurring. He could just about move himself, though the very definitely square room kept bouncing around in his vision until it looked almost spherical.

Lauren chewed the inside of her cheek for a few moments. 'Partly,' she said.

TM chuckled, and the vibrations that went through his body with the movement were enough to force his head back to the floor. 'We don't have your star friend,' he told her firmly from the ground. 'We don't know anything.'

'You're probably telling the truth, that's the annoying thing,' Lauren said. 'But we've gotta do what we've gotta do, and all we can really do on that front for now is chase up our last known perps. Which, unfortunately, happens to be you lot.'

'It's not us this time,' TM said. Veggie gave a spluttering wheeze. 'But if it was, we'd defend your star until you finally got around to killing us.'

'I believe you, which might not be a good thing for you,' Lauren said, sighing.

'You lot can understand it anyway, right?' TM said, sitting up again. The world wasn't shaking quite so much any more. 'Altair got around to knowing the feeling, too. He ended up liking being down here so much that he let himself waste away on earth before he finally went back up to heaven.'

Lauren and The Ire exchanged glances. TM didn't know whether they were glances of disdain, uncertainty, agreement or something else entirely, but he pressed on.

'You love being stars, right? - not, like, literal stars - rock stars! You had that entire audience cheering for you!'

'There's something about being adored,' Lauren admitted, almost absent-mindedly. 'I mean, it's all well and good having people watch you from a distance, love you through a telescope, but... man, it was awesome looking out and actually being able to see people filling a room with love for us.'

The four of them looked wistful, TM thought. No wonder they had to keep a hunter like Orion on hand, if coming down to be incarnated as humans was so intoxicating.

'You're all going to end up back down here too before too long,' TM said. 'You won't be able to resist, and then they'll send her after you.'

'Eh, maybe,' said Lauren. 'You really don't know how lucky you have it, being able to have your own life for... well, your whole life.'

'I think I'm coming to appreciate it.' TM saw Dominika stirring out of the corner of his eye, her fingers twitching amidst the fragments of guitar, and brought himself to his feet unsteadily. 'Now, we really need to get going.'

'Oh, man,' Lauren said, pushing off the wall and slowly walking towards him. 'You know we're not gonna let you do that.'

TM wobbled towards the door, which still bore the dent from Dominika's kick; suddenly the entire four-piece was standing between him and the exit. 'Don't make us hurt you,' Lauren pleaded, and TM believed that she meant it.

'I don't know what else to do,' TM told her.

'Then...' She shook her head, and strode towards him. 'Have it your way.'

The door of the warehouse exploded inwards, flying off its hinges and smashing straight into two of Lauren's bandmates. She turned, shocked; a huge man barrelled into her, knocking her away from TM.

'Sorry we took so long!' called an orange-haired woman, storming in and busying herself with fending off Lauren and the Ire's bassist.

'Had to wait for TM's dad to give us a lift,' yelled the man with the mohawk and no shirt who was diving onto the broken door, trying to keep the two women under it from breaking free. A preteen girl with long, straight hair dashed up and started jumping on the sheet of metal.

'Wait, what?' TM breathed.

'Hey, guys,' Marty greeted the newcomers weakly, propping himself up against a wall. 'Thanks for coming.'

'Any time,' said Obbie Kernel, guitarist for the Inciting Incident, as she delivered a devastating haymaker.

TM looked over at Marty. 'Did you -?'

'Texted soon as Lauren started monologuing,' he said, coughing. 'Figured we might need some accompaniment.'

'And I wasn't going to let them come alone!' declared TM's father, drawing himself to his full height. Lauren lay sprawled before him. 'She's just sleeping,' he said apologetically, half to TM and half to Lauren. 'She'll be alright.'

'Dad - I don't - what are you doing here?'

'My new friends over there got the message while we were having a video chat - did you invent video chat?'

'No.'

'Well, it's quite something,' Senior confided. 'Anyway, I thought you might be in trouble, and I'd just got home safely with your mother and sat down so I didn't need to be anywhere, and you know I said I wanted to help you and -'

TM ran to his father and wrapped his arms around him.

'This is exceptionally nice,' said Senior, squeezing TM like a boa constrictor with enormous biceps, 'but I think I ought to help our musical friends.'

'Oh, yeah,' said TM. He let go; Senior thundered over to where Obbie was dodging punches, put his considerable mass between the two women, and stood there absorbing the blows while Obbie took the opportunity to catch her breath.

TM dashed over to Veggie and helped him clamber to his feet with some difficulty; Marty slung Dominika's arm around his shoulder and carried her towards the blown-open door of the warehouse. 'We have to go,' Veggie wheezed, clutching his side. 'Jack.'

'Go,' said Thomas Major, Sr. 'We can handle this.'

'I -' TM began, but the steel sheet that had been the warehouse door went flying into the air with an almighty crash, Eiseldown and The Destructionist still atop it, as the two flattened members of Lauren and the Ire burst free.

'I think this fight is ours, don't you?' Senior muttered. 'You have bigger fish to fry. And a mackerel to save, if I heard right.'

TM couldn't argue with that. Still supporting most of Veggie's weight, he followed Marty and Dominika out of the warehouse, leaving his father and the Inciting Incident to face off against the astral four-piece.

'Everyone okay?' TM asked when they were around a few corners, realising that it might have been a dumb question. Dominika gave a half-shrug-half-nod. 'Marty?'

'Bit winded, nothing too bad.'

'We got lucky,' TM said.

'What about Veggie?' Marty said; TM glanced at Veggie's face, which wore a distant expression.

'Took a bit of a hit,' he murmured. 'Be alright. Had worse knocks from *Guitar Hero* championship afterparties.'

Even with Dominika still leaning on him, Marty ignored TM's protests and took Veggie's weight, propping his partner up with a kiss on the forehead. 'How are we getting home?' he asked TM quietly.

'I... might have a warehouse of my own around here,' TM said, looking around, trying to remember.

'You what?'

'I might have been a bit busy with serious business-y-type stuff over the last few years, but there was one thing I had to finish doing,' TM explained, spotting the right number among the homogeneous rows of buildings. 'Knew it would pay off, eventually.'

Veggie looked up at him, wincing as the muscles in his neck took the weight of his head. 'You didn't.'

TM pulled a key out of his pocket, stuck it in the lock, turned and lifted. The door slid upwards, and the four of them dragged themselves inside. TM hit the light switch.

'Holy shit,' said Veggie. 'It's the fucking Octobike.'

35. Meow, Bitches

The Octobike streaked out of the warehouse, leaving a motion blur trail of red and purple (TM had been thinking about changing the paint job, but never got around to it).

Dominika and Veggie sat in the sidecar, held in by a rollercoaster-style safety bar and a dome of what the vendor claimed was bulletproof glass; TM manned the cockpit, surrounded by wheels and ridiculous machinery, with Marty stuffed in behind him. Veggie had raised mild concern at the idea that TM should be driving with what was probably at the very least a slight concussion, since Lauren's kick had given him a definite head injury, but none of the others was in any better state. Besides, TM was the only one who knew how to pilot the thing.

He had been working on the Octobike for almost the entirety of the last three years, as something to keep himself occupied in his spare time and as a project of his own, something to give him his own building space outside the collaborative rocket project and the joint business that had become most of his life. It was still very much a prototype, and in its current form most resembled a Meccano Cthulhu with wheels, but it was his. It was also categorically not road-legal and almost entirely untested.

TM steered the vehicle down narrow streets, glancing periodically over at Dominika and Veggie. His partner looked pained every time their momentum shifted; TM did his best to take the corners gradually, making the most of the Octobike's top-notch manoeuvrability and cranking it up well over the speed limit in the straights. He could hear Veggie wheezing with exhilarated laughter as the Octobike zoomed through the city, back towards Muscles & Mussels and their flat.

They scorched past the park where they had first encountered Riegel O'Ryan and Al Tyer; the Octobike slingshotted itself around the corner on which Ziggy had first been standing, the day she had told them about the inventor of cable ties and subsequently entered their life to an unexpectedly deep degree; they whizzed through the last few streets, the museum spinning past them in a blur, the bar where the Inciting Incident had once played a gig with Ziggy in the audience flashing alongside.

Then they were back, and TM vaulted from the Octobike as it skidded to a halt in front of their building. Dominika hopped down beside him; Veggie fell out of the sidecar. TM thought about making him stay there, but knew there was no point. Veggie would follow them no matter what, and was probably no safer outside besides.

TM pushed the door open. As expected, it was unlocked. The gymnastaurant was empty, quieter than most graves, with the small exception of Gary Mackerel snoring peacefully where they had left him.

'Marty,' TM whispered, 'you're in the best shape. Get Gary Mackerel out of here, okay?'

'Be careful,' Marty shot back, then hauled the groggy Gary Mackerel to his feet and guided him out of the door.

Dominika grabbed a bottle of cider from the bar and took a lengthy swig before they headed up the stairs to the flat above the gymnastaurant, which felt longer than they ever had. TM stopped just short of the door as he reached the top, Dominika half-dragging Veggie up the stairs behind him.

'Oh, heck,' Veggie wheezed.

'What?' TM asked urgently, whipping around.

'Nika...'

Dominika leant in to hear Veggie's words.

'Totally forgot to tell you, but you won two hundred and fifty quid in that raffle.'

'Not the time,' TM said, and peered around the door.

'Maybe they really don't,' an Irish voice said from within. 'I mean, I know it was a long shot anyway, but... damn. Seems a bit of a waste if we go back with nothing.'

There was a low growl in response, which sounded to TM like agreement.

'Maybe I was a little bit overzealous,' Orion admitted, coming into view; she turned over furniture and ripped open cushions, but whatever she was looking for, she evidently hadn't found it. 'I think I wanted it to be these lads, you know? I think they just plain rub me up the wrong way, to be honest, so maybe I was sort of hoping I'd get to... devastate them again.'

'You're a real bitch,' Derrida said, obscured from view. TM saw the shadow of Keelut stalking towards the kitchen, then heard Derrida yelp. Next to TM, Veggie took a long breath and held it, trembling.

'And you're a fuckwit,' Orion said in his direction. Then TM saw her bend down, looking at something on the table. 'What's this?' she said with interest, holding up an envelope.

Veggie coughed.

'Shit,' breathed TM.

Orion opened the door, as if inviting them in.

'Oh, hi,' she said, looking them over. 'It's funny, actually. I was just about to come looking for you lot.'

'Let Derrida go,' TM said firmly.

'Oh, this one? I guess I don't need to keep 'em, now you're all here, but damned if it isn't just more *fun*.' She picked up TM with one hand and slung him over her shoulder, though he struggled; Dominika threw a punch, but the Huntress easily snatched her up under one arm and grabbed Veggie with the other. She threw them all in a disgruntled heap in the corner of the kitchen, Veggie spluttering as he hit the floor.

'What are you doing?' Derrida hissed. They were in one piece, though sporting a black eye. 'Why did you come back?'

'Heard you were in shit,' TM told them.

'Well, now we all are,' Derrida pointed out.

Orion waved the envelope in her hand at them smugly, looking down at the pile of people from above. 'So,' she said, with an air of satisfaction. 'Looks like I've got a gas bill here, and who should it be addressed to, I wonder?'

TM blinked at her cluelessly. 'Me?' he ventured.

'Actually,' said Orion, holding the envelope up to her eyes exaggeratedly, 'it's for the attention of one Mister Jonathan Vega.' She actually giggled, putting her hand to her mouth. 'I mean, I know Orion, O'Ryan, not the most inventive, but come on. You *actually* used Vega as your surname?' She prodded Veggie's ribs with her toe; he hacked up a wad of phlegm onto her boot. 'Ew.'

'Veggie's not the one you're looking for,' TM told her. 'He's been my friend for... years. Like, for ever.'

'You'll forgive me if I don't fully believe you,' Orion said, voice dripping with sarcasm. 'You harboured one of ours before, so you're in a bit of a cried-wolf situation here, know what I'm saying?'

TM sighed, closing his eyes for a second, thinking. 'Please,' he said after a moment, unable to come up with anything better to say. 'Please don't take Veggie too.'

'Sorry, little fella,' said Orion; she wandered casually towards the group, but Dominika and Derrida clambered to their feet and put themselves between her and Veggie. 'Ugh. Really?'

'Don't,' said Veggie.

'I'm gonna,' Orion sneered, cracking her knuckles.

'No,' Veggie wheezed. 'Nika. Derrida. Don't.'

They turned to him, confused and afraid; Veggie hauled himself upright, using the kitchen counters for support, and wobbled towards Orion. Keelut, pacing behind her master, stopped and cocked her ears curiously.

'What are you doing?' Derrida hissed.

'Making a choice,' Veggie said.

'You can't,' TM breathed.

Veggie turned to his business partner. 'You know how this goes,' he said. 'She'll go through everyone to get to me.'

'But... you're not the one she's looking for.'

Veggie looked at the floor, the muscles in his jaw tense. 'I don't think so,' he said, 'but I don't think she agrees.'

'You can't!'

'Tom,' said Veggie. 'She gets me one way or another. Or she rolls through us all and then she gets someone else, she puts more people like us through more...' He drew in a sharp breath through his teeth. 'Through more.'

He turned to Orion, pushed Dominika and Derrida aside gently, and strode right up to the erstwhile survival host. 'Come on, then, bitch,' he said.

She raised an eyebrow, her expression flitting between satisfaction and bemusement. 'Selfless choice,' she said. 'I can commend that, at least.'

Then she hit him, just once, caught him in her arms as he fell, and turned to the door.

'Don't let them leave,' she instructed Keelut. Then she reached out the hand that was not holding Veggie's limp body, closed the door behind her, and was gone.

'No,' TM breathed. Derrida looked frozen, staring helplessly at the door; Dominika was trying to hide it, but TM could see her shaking as she kept her eyes on Keelut.

'We have to go after him,' he said. 'We have to.'

'He... decided,' Derrida said, sounding as if they'd never been less certain of what to do in their life.

'I don't care,' said TM. 'We're going after him.'

Keelut stalked over, growling threateningly; Derrida and Dominika rushed to TM's side protectively.

'Whatever opportunity you get,' TM whispered, though he was certain the dog would hear, 'you gotta take it.'

Then he grabbed an orange from a bowl on the counter behind him and lobbed it over the dog's head; Keelut turned to watch as it sailed past her, and TM launched himself past the enormous canine towards the door. His hand was almost on the handle when he felt a powerful set of jaws clamping down upon him, and Keelut lifted his whole weight from the floor, suplexing him back into the corner by the ankle.

'Bad dog,' Derrida said exhaustedly as TM slumped down against the kitchen cupboards.

Keelut's shoulders lowered, teeth flashing, saliva dripping from her jaws as she turned to face them.

'Wait,' said TM, holding his hand up to her. 'Your master said don't let us leave, she didn't say kill us.'

Keelut growled; TM could smell her breath as the warm air hit him.

'Please don't,' he said helplessly.

Keelut tensed, ready to spring. TM closed his eyes.

Then there was a loud wailing, an exclamation that sounded like an exploding wind section, and a tiny furball threw itself out of the darkness and put itself firmly between the dog and its helpless prey. Michel Furcoat, the cat, stood as a sentinel protecting TM, Dominika, and Derrida; Keelut gave a confused whine. Michel Furcoat leapt at the dog, hissing and squealing, and struck her in the face.

Keelut stood, disinterested, as the cat's purple-plastic-covered claws bounced harmlessly off her furry skull.

'Shit,' said TM.

With one golden paw the size of a stack of bricks, the dog knocked the cat aside, eliciting an ear-vibrating squeal. Michel Furcoat hit the wall and slumped down.

'We're doomed,' TM said quietly, almost accepting it.

Keelut advanced, skulking towards them and exposing her teeth.

'Don't you have another cat?' Derrida asked uncertainly, and then the bare, unsheathed claws of Maurice Meow-Ponty sliced through the air. Keelut yelped, recoiling as cuts opened on her face, drops of blood pattering down like heavy raindrops. TM took the opportunity to slither past, dragging Dominika and Derrida behind him, and made for the door, grabbing a few bits on the way out and stuffing them into a carrier bag held together by several *Ziggy Veggie TM* Puncture Repair Kits.

Dominika and Derrida dashed through the exit - Dominika hurled a butter knife at Keelut, which bounced off ineffectually, but it was the thought that counted - and TM glanced back to see his cats, each no bigger than his forearm, fending off a dog the size of a small shed. The door closed behind him, leaving the sound of pained yapping from within.

'Where do you think she's taking him?' Derrida said breathlessly as the three of them dashed down the stairs, through Muscles & Mussels and out onto the streets.

'I have no idea,' TM admitted, bursting out of the door and sprinting over to where the Octobike sat patiently in parked majesty. 'But I'm not gonna let her just take Veggie too. I can't.'

Dominika tugged on his sleeve.

'What?'

She pointed.

On the horizon, hanging just above the skyline, was a star, shining brighter than any TM had ever seen except the sun. He blinked at it for a moment, then lowered his gaze a few degrees.

Directly underneath from TM's perspective, the distinctive angel of the museum seemed to be pointing up at the star, and the star seemed to be pointing down in response. TM, lacking as his knowledge of astronomy was, thought he knew that star.

'The museum,' TM said, and hopped in the Octobike.

'What the heck is this?!' Derrida exclaimed; Dominika hauled them into the sidecar by the collar.

TM revved the machine, sending vibrations through the entire contraption. 'It's the Octobike,' he said.

'The flipping *what*?'

Then TM put his foot down, and the Octobike burned the rubber of its many tyres as it launched into the night.

36. See, It All Came In Handy

TM practically vaulted off the Octobike as it screeched to a halt outside the museum, dashing straight in through the open front door.

Above the building, the bright star gazed down; inside, the halls were empty and dark, just as they had been the night Ziggy was taken. Dominika and Derrida followed, dashing down the corridors after him; TM skidded around corners and down rows of artifacts, heading for the main exhibition room where, he knew, the space rock (minus the sliver Veggie had taken for a necklace) still sat.

'We can't just burst in,' Derrida hissed as they drew closer; TM came to a stop.

'There are balconies around the side,' TM said, 'about halfway up the walls. Pretty sure that vent there goes through to them.' He pulled something out of his carrier bag.

'What is that?' Derrida said uncertainly.

'It's called the Enchi-Ladder,' TM told him, unfolding a tiny rod of metal out into an H-shaped contraption. 'I came up with it ages ago as a side thing, to help reach Mexican food on high shelves, ended up making the prototype one day when I had nothing better to do...' He shook it about a bit. Nothing happened. 'Wait. Bugger.'

Dominika sighed, and pulled a burrito out of a pocket.

'Why do you have a burrito?!' Derrida exclaimed in disbelief.

'Thought it might come in handy,' Dominika said, shrugging, and tossed it up into the vent. The Enchi-Ladder sprung to life, telescoping out into a ladder that reached up into the rafters.

'Well, it works,' TM said in response to Derrida's open-mouthed outrage.

They scampered up the ladder, which folded back into a single metal rod in TM's hand, and scrambled into the vent. Dominika picked up the burrito and stuffed it back into her pocket.

'That's really gross,' Derrida said.

TM edged through the vent on his hands and knees, trying to make as little noise as possible. When they reached the metal grate covering the exit, he reached back into the bag and pulled out a tiny tub that had once held hair gel but was now marked 'Super Grease'; he rubbed a little of the substance around the edges, and the grate slid cleanly off without a sound.

'Okay, that is genuinely impressive,' Derrida admitted from behind.

'We were going for lubricant, but we ended up with incredibly corrosive... something,' TM explained in a whisper, sliding himself into the vent.

'Real sneaky stuff feels more terrifying and less epic than *Hero's Adventure*,' Derrida said.

'If Veggie was right about this whole Star Power thing, we only stand a chance if we do things in the most epic way possible,' TM mused, shuffling on his hands and knees through the small space until he could slide out and onto the walkway.

He could see Orion below, standing over Veggie's prone body before the space rock, which was in a new glass cube on its pedestal. The earthbound incarnations of Lyra were there too, the four members of Lauren and the Ire leaning against the wall with practiced casualness.

'Why are we here again?' Lauren asked; TM sneaked around the upper walkway to the enormous theatre-style lights, tucking himself away behind one in an effort to conceal himself from view.

Behind him, Derrida gave a muffled gasp. 'They got out?!' they whispered; TM tried not to think about it.

'Because,' Orion said impatiently, 'I can hear them here.'

'You can... hear them?' Lauren said, looking doubtful.

'Hmm. I'm not sure what it is, but... this rock. There's something about it.'

Ziggy had thought so too, TM thought. Though the sliver of rock, which he hoped beyond hope was still around Veggie's neck, had somehow had - or at least catalysed - power of some sort, Ziggy had never been able to explain what it was that had attracted her to the thing. Perhaps it was some sort of... star catnip.

'No, there's not,' Lauren said flatly.

'Doesn't matter, in the end,' Orion said, sounding weary. 'There's really nothing about anything except what a mind makes of it, and a few strong minds tried to make something of this one.'

'So... what are they saying?' Lauren enquired.

Orion closed her eyes for a moment, then looked down at Veggie. 'He'll do.'

'He'll *do*?' demanded Lauren, walking up behind Orion. 'So it's not him?'

'It doesn't matter if this is the original Vega,' Orion told her. 'All that matters is that he will burn brightly enough, and that he will.'

Lauren scoffed. 'Nothing matters with you, does it?'

Orion grabbed her by the shoulders, staring down into the smaller star's eyes with a dark intensity that TM could feel even from his high vantage point. 'It's not *supposed* to,' she hissed. 'Remember that. As above, so below - nothing matters to what's above us, so nothing can matter to us either. If it starts to feel like it does, that's when things go *tremendously fucking wrong*. That's when Altair's little idiot and *your* stupid lead singer start thinking it'd be fun to come down here - that's when orbits fall into chaos and galaxies start colliding.'

Lauren looked away. 'Even you're not immune, though,' she said. 'Even you call the things above *them*, like they were people. Even you *feel* things.'

Orion slapped her. 'It. Doesn't. Matter,' she reiterated, voice low and dangerous. 'Disagree, and it'll be you I'm after as soon as I've killed this one.' She gave Veggie a stiff kick.

Derrida made a choked noise of distress; TM clapped a hand over their mouth, but all five of the heavenly bodies below were already staring up at them.

'I'm actually impressed,' Orion said, although she sounded more frustrated than TM suspected she would have liked to admit. 'You got past the dog?'

'Might have done,' TM said, trying to sound brave as he stepped out from behind the light.

'Ugh,' said Orion.

'You don't even care about what happened to your *dog*?!' Derrida yelled at her. 'You're a monster!'

'I don't -' Orion closed her eyes, rubbing her temples with a finger and thumb. 'You just *do not* get it.'

She picked up Veggie and carried him towards the door. 'I'm taking him up,' she said as she passed Lauren. 'Deal with this.'

'You're not taking him!' TM yelled after her, but she was gone. He fumbled about desperately in his carrier bag, and pulled out the last two items. 'Grab,' he said urgently to Dominika and Derrida, who each took hold of a corner of the Bedsheet Tablecloth Whiteboard; then he leapt over the railing and the three of them descended to the ground floor, hanging under the billowing sheet like a parachute.

Lauren and the Ire came to meet them, but TM soared over their heads and the band found themselves entangled in the enormous sheet, struggling to free themselves.

'Hope my dad hit you hard,' TM said, kicking the flailing mass with all his strength. Dominika and Derrida set to attacking the struggling foursome too, Dominika with undeniably more success.

'It's too late!' Lauren yelled, throwing the sheet off, and she leapt on TM. 'You can't stop her. You shouldn't even *want* to stop her! We're trying to balance the scales here!'

'Not with my friend,' TM said defiantly, and punched her as hard as he could in the face. She fell backwards, a hand pressed to her cheek, and TM held a small sphere aloft. The Ire-women stared at it curiously; Derrida and Dominika took the opportunity to get behind TM.

'What's that?' Lauren asked, rubbing her bruised face.

'This is the TM Super Bomb,' TM told her, grinning evilly.

'Oh, that,' Lauren said, looking fantastically unconcerned. 'I heard about that. Just a fake, right?'

'Oh, no,' TM said, shuffling towards the room's exit. 'I brought the real one this time. And if you don't want me to blast you right back up to high heaven, you're gonna tell me what you did with my dad and the Inciting Incident and then you're gonna let us go.'

Lauren looked at his unwavering eyes, then up at the tiny device, then back at him. 'You're bluffing,' she said.

'You sure?'

Lauren narrowed her eyebrows, then sighed and rolled her eyes.

'They're fine,' she said. 'We put them in a big box with a bunch of speakers and stuff.'

'You didn't kill them?'

Lauren swallowed. 'Look,' she said. 'I know what we have to do, and I gotta go along with it 'cos we really do have to do it. But I'm not gonna go offing people if I can help it.'

'Thank you,' TM said.

She exhaled heavily, nodding at the floor. Then she started to tense, and TM knew she was about to risk it. So he turned, pushed Dominika and Derrida out of the door into a corridor, and leapt after them, throwing the Super Bomb back over his shoulder.

The room exploded behind them, the walls collapsing as a spurt of flame and force brought it down. Dominika rolled halfway down the corridor nimbly; TM scrambled out of range less impressively, but Derrida, still suffering from their experience with Orion in TM's kitchen, stumbled and tripped before they were all the way out.

TM scrambled to turn back for them, but Dominika made it first, leaping back and throwing Derrida clear just as an entire wall's worth of bricks and wood came down.

'Ow,' TM heard, and then the rubble stopped falling. A cloud of dust billowed down the corridor, but the structural damage didn't seem to extend beyond the room; the sounds of destruction halted, the dust settled, and Derrida scrambled over to Dominika, who was lying just beyond the point where the devastation had stopped.

'Are you OK?!' Derrida yelped; Dominika thought about it.

'Actually, yeah,' she said. 'I mean...' She nodded towards her left arm, which was under a pile of stone chunks. 'That might be a problem.'

'Oh, *shit*,' Derrida breathed. 'You... sacrificed your arm for me.'

'Well, no,' Dominika said, 'I saved you and then didn't get my arm out of the way in time. Also, it actually feels fine, so either I've somehow got it stuck but not crushed or I've stopped being able to feel things.'

'You're safe here, at least,' TM told her, pacing back and forth between his fallen friend and the building's exit.

'We've got this,' Dominika said; TM couldn't tell whether she was resolved or resigned.

'You've gotta get *her*,' Derrida snarled, sitting down beside Dominika. 'I'll take care of Dominika -'

'I genuinely don't need it.'

'- because Dominika obviously needs someone looking after her and also I am *not* going out there.'

TM allowed himself to smile, just a little bit. 'It's OK,' he said. 'I think I've gotta go do this one on my own anyway.'

Then he turned and walked out of the museum.

37. Rainmaker III (Ch-Ch-Ch-Ch-)

Orion was there, looking back at the building and the cloud of dust rising from it. She dropped Veggie on the pavement as TM emerged, staring up at him with shock and hatred in her eyes.

'Are you serious?!' she exclaimed, holding her hands up in disbelief. 'What does it take to get rid of you?!'

'More than what you've got, apparently,' TM said. His hands trembled, but he squeezed them together behind his back and out of sight.

Orion scoffed. 'You're nothing,' she said. 'You're not even anything special, and I can't even believe I'm having to take care of you myself.'

'That's us humans,' TM told her, standing on the steps defiantly. 'Nothing special.'

She strode towards him, shaking her head; though TM braced himself, the first punch lifted him from his feet and slammed him into the arch of the doorway. He felt something break, and all the air whooshed forcefully from his lungs, burning his throat on the way out. She hoisted him up with one hand, then tossed him down the stairs and bounded down after him.

'You stupid little man,' Orion said, kicking him in the ribs. TM went flying, landing next to Veggie. 'Why did you even get involved in the first place? Why care about some dumb fake person you'd only just met? Why not just let me do what I came here to do and mind your own fucking business?'

'I'm nothing,' TM told her, the words leaving him in painful shudders. 'You're right about that. But it's about more than just me.'

His hand snuck its way to Veggie's neck, finding the chain with the fragment of space rock and pulling it free. Veggie coughed.

'First sensible thing you've said in your life,' Orion said disdainfully, striding over and driving her knee into his throat as he tried to sit up. TM fell back, gasping for breath. 'It's about more than just you, or him, or any person. It's about the universe.'

'The universe doesn't care,' TM tried to say. The words came out as a series of sharp hisses and coughs, but Orion seemed to understand.

'No, it doesn't, but you live in it and unless you let me fix it it'll quite happily destroy your entire planet,' she said.

TM gazed up at the sky from his place in the road, lying face up on the tarmac. The star hanging above the museum seemed brighter than ever, like an enormous white fireball growing ever larger and closer.

'I didn't want to hurt you,' Orion told him, hauling him to his feet and staring into his eyes. 'At first. But now I think I do.' She headbutted him, keeping hold of him by the shirt, then punched him in the stomach. TM felt something start to slip away inside him. She let him fall once more, and TM felt something like peace as he landed on his back again.

'You're done,' the Huntress snarled.

'Fuck you,' said Veggie.

TM lifted his head with a great effort, staring at his best friend. Veggie, prone on the ground, eyes wide open, had reached up with one hand and grabbed Orion by the ankle as she stood over TM. The starlight from above grew ever brighter, bathing the scene in pure white while dark shadows played underneath.

'Oh, *wow*!' Orion let out a hysterical cackle, shaking free from Veggie's grip with ease. 'You're not dead? Holy shit.'

'Like he said,' Veggie grunted, somehow hauling himself to his feet, 'we're nothing special, each of us. Not on our own. But he is to me, I am to him, and that means something.'

'This is *so lame*,' Orion muttered, rolling her eyes. 'There's no power of friendship moment to be had here, y'know.'

'I'm not using the power of friendship,' Veggie told her. 'I've got Star Power.'

He threw himself at Orion, and TM thought for one strange moment that a blazing shroud of light had appeared around Veggie's body, but Orion simply slapped him to the ground.

'Bullshit,' she said, gazing down at him. 'Sure, you're brighter than most humans, but what did you think was gonna happen? I'm a damn *constellation*.' She folded her arms, then stuck her tongue in her cheek and sighed. 'Okay. Look. In recognition of your absolutely idiotic but undeniably unusual courage, I'll give you a chance here.'

Veggie hacked up a wad of red phlegm in the direction of Orion's boots.

'You wanna quit while you're ahead, I'll let you go,' said the Huntress. 'I'll go after Vega, the real one. You help me find it, and then you can go back to whatever meaningless shit you fill your days with. Sounds more than fair, no?'

TM's eyes widened.

Veggie pushed himself to his knees, then wobbled back to his feet. 'Hell. The. Fuck. No.'

Orion raised her hands in front of her, mouth open as if exasperated at a child who wouldn't stop asking 'why?'. 'Really? Fuckin' *really?*'

'I'm done anyway,' Veggie said, directing his words at the space between Orion and TM. 'Better me than you start again, go after Vega, put more people through more shit. And you wouldn't - leave us alone, I mean. Any time you thought there was another one of your runaways around here, you'd be after us. You'd hurt Derrida, or Dominika, or Marty.' He took a deep breath, which sounded as if most of it didn't make it to his lungs. 'I can't let you do that.'

Orion blinked a few times, the muscles in her face tightening in various quick movements. 'Well,' she said. 'Alright, then.'

'No,' TM wheezed.

'I got this one,' Veggie said quietly, and then Orion hit him one last time.

For a moment, the Huntress stood still, just looking down in thought. Then she turned to TM.

'Well,' she said, as if nothing had happened, 'that was intense. Nothin' else to do but end you too, looks like.'

TM didn't have the strength to say anything, to shake his head, to breathe. Every bit of energy in his body was dedicated to pushing tears out of his eyes as he lay there, helpless. The little bit of space rock still in his hand felt sharp, painful.

The star above really was beautiful, he thought, watching it shine through the sheen of tears like the moon reflected in a rippling lake. Maybe Veggie, lying still in the road a few metres away, could go and be as beautiful as that, too. Maybe he would get to be something like that himself, once he was gone from this earth. It was so big, so bright. So close. He almost thought he could feel its warmth as it grew larger, drew nearer. It was so clear that he thought he could see something in the centre; a small, dark shape, surrounded by burning brightness.

Wait.

There was something. Someone he knew.

Orion picked him up for what he knew would be the final time, and held him with his back to her, gripping him tightly by the wrists.

'Goodbye,' she whispered in his ear. 'I'll be making some changes up there when you're gone. Maybe reconfigure some stuff, see if I can't make life tougher for your friend. Ziggy, you called her, right? I think I'm going to push her into a black hole, and I'll watch. You know how that works? Far as she knows, she'll fall in and be gone - but for me, on the outside? She'll just stop. I'll watch her frozen on the event horizon for all eternity, and I'll hope you can feel the pain of it too, wherever you end up.'

'Changes?' TM whispered hoarsely.

Orion whipped him around, releasing her grip on one of his arms. TM spun away from her, and then her forearm was rocketing towards his head. The first drop of rain touched his forehead as she pulled him in for the Rainmaker. TM looked up.

'Turn and face the strange, bitch,' he said, and ducked under her arm. Then he jumped up and smashed his knee into her head.

Orion stumbled back, holding a hand to the side of her head, staring at him in pain and confusion. TM leapt forwards and, believing with all his might that it would work, thrust the piece of space rock in his clenched fist into her face; she went soaring backwards like an arrow fired from a bow, landing ragdoll-like in the middle of the road.

'What -?' she wheezed, staggering back to her feet.

TM pointed upwards, then collapsed. The brightness in the sky descended, burning as intensely as the sun, and the shape of the girl within it bent and extended her legs like a frog as she fell to earth.

Then Ziggy landed on Orion with a High Fly Flow powered by all the weight of the fall from space.

Orion disappeared into the concrete, battered down by the falling star that had hit her from above.

TM watched as the burning of the star faded and a faintly glowing shape picked herself up from the earth and walked slowly towards him.

'Hey,' Ziggy said. She looked exactly as TM remembered her, albeit perhaps slightly more luminescent.

TM could only laugh, a pained and breathy sound.

'What's funny?' Ziggy asked, folding her arms and looking down at him.

'I thought the universe didn't care,' TM said, staring up at her.

'The universe doesn't care,' Ziggy said. 'But I do.'

TM nodded, a few tears falling from his face. It might have been the pain, or something else. He wasn't sure.

'Did you hear what I -'

'Turn and face the strange, yeah,' Ziggy said, grinning. 'I liked that. Would have said it myself, but you sort of beat me to the punch.'

'Is she gone?'

'She'll go back up now, I think,' Ziggy said, glancing at the presenter-shaped hole in the road. 'Doubt she'll be back down for a while, though.'

'What about...' TM trailed off, staring at Veggie, who still lay unmoving.

'He's gone,' Ziggy said. 'I'm sorry. I tried to get here faster, but... well.' She looked down at her feet. 'I don't think he would have wanted me to ruin his heroic sacrifice, anyway. Would have sort of defeated the point.'

'How are you even here at all? I thought you couldn't...'

'Not sure,' she admitted. 'Doing a sort of Lazarus thing, I guess. You guys have a lot of my brightness in you, and you were *really* burning up - even brighter than *her*, I think, between us - so... it was sort of as if I was already here anyway.'

TM closed his eyes, feeling a familiar burning in his chest, more fundamental than the sharp cuts of the broken bones. 'What now? He'll... go up?'

She nodded. 'I'll take him, show him what's up. Put him at the head of Lyra. Then everything will be back in place, and... hopefully you can just go on with your life, or something.' She bit her bottom lip, looking at him gently.

'Yeah, that'll be easy,' TM said, unable to look anywhere without seeing something that made him want to disappear.

'I'm sorry,' she said. 'I wish I could stay.'

'What are you... how are you... are you okay?' TM asked her, not sure how to phrase it.

'Oh, yeah, it's not so bad,' she said reassuringly. 'I mean, I miss you guys. But I can watch, some of the time. And I got to see you, when you came up to visit. That was *ridiculous*!'

TM nodded. 'Compared to some of the stuff we've been through, that seems kind of normal at this point.'

'I'm sorry,' she said again. 'For everything you've been through because of me.'

TM smiled, fully this time. 'Whatever else happened, I wouldn't change that you were part of it,' he told her. 'Not for all the stars in the sky.'

Then she returned to the stars, the iridescent stardust that was all that remained of Orion and Veggie following in her trail. TM watched them go. Then he passed out.

38. Lady Stardust

TM sat on a bench in the park in the middle of the night, looking out at the field that once played host to the fair, remembering.

The last month or so had been... well, it had been.

Dominika had, somehow, escaped injury entirely; the collapsed bits of the museum had managed to surround her arm, trapping her, without doing any damage whatsoever. Marty had taken Gary Mackerel to his parents' house, then sprinted back to help. He was just about close enough to hear the explosion from the museum when it happened, and found TM lying in the road and Derrida inside trying to reassure Dominika (who had continued to insist that she did not in fact need reassurance and would have preferred that Derrida go and get help).

There was no evidence that anybody else had ever been there, except the hole in the road that looked oddly like a tall woman.

For TM's part, the doctors had told him he was lucky to be alive, lucky not to have broken more than two ribs, lucky not to have been arrested. Dominika had somehow managed to talk the police out of arresting them, since they had been the only people at the scene of the enormous explosion that had destroyed half of an 'architecturally significant' building; TM would never know how she had done it, but he wasn't about to complain.

After being released from the hospital, TM had gone back to Muscles & Mussels in an attempt to... carry on with things. Gary Mackerel was, as it turned out, a spectacularly competent employee, so he and Dominika were perfectly capable of keeping things running. Marty, meanwhile, had taken some time away from everything before eventually returning to band practice with the Inciting Incident (who, along with TM's father, had been found unharmed in a large case in the warehouse, as Lauren had promised). TM had spoken to him, once or twice, but there hadn't been much to say that neither of them had already been over too many times.

It would take time, and it would hurt, but they were carrying on.

When he wasn't at the gymnastaurant, he had spent the days...

sitting, mostly, since he had been advised not to do much more than that. Thinking. He was never sure what about, but it was all he seemed able to do.

A young woman sat down beside him. TM glanced over at her; she seemed to be watching her knees as they bent into a sitting position. She was small, pale, with unusually bright eyes, the hood of a thin blue jacket pulled over her hair.

'Hi,' she said, after a moment.

TM said nothing.

'I'm really sorry about what happened to... you. Your friends. All that.' She had a strange accent, TM thought vaguely: somewhere between Welsh and Finnish.

'How would you know about that?' TM said. It was hard for him to talk, with his ribs in the state they were, but her words were not ones to be left unresponded to.

'It's... kind of my fault,' she said.

TM turned his head to look at her properly. 'You're Vega,' he said after a moment. 'The real Vega.'

'In the flesh,' she said, smiling sadly.

'My friend got turned into a ball of gas because of you,' he told her.

'I know,' she said. 'I heard about that whole... incident.'

'Incident?' TM said. 'I think it qualifies as more than that.'

'Yeah,' Vega admitted. 'I'm sorry.'

TM breathed several deep breaths, feeling the rage and denial and fury and numbness work its way through him again. Then he sighed. 'I forgive you,' he said. Vega looked at him, her already wide eyes widening further.

'I came here to ask for that,' she said, 'but I wasn't really expecting to get it.'

'I can't blame you,' TM told her honestly. 'I had a friend, a really good one, and what she wanted most in the world was to live on earth as a person. I know what was at stake for her. So I can't really expect you to... not want that.'

'I heard there are still others like me, down here. One of the binary sisters from Theta Aquila's supposed to be around somewhere, just trying to live a life, you know.'

TM frowned.

'Or... so I heard,' she said, and sighed. 'We're just trying to have the lives you get given from the start, but... that doesn't mean we think we're any more entitled to exist than you. I wouldn't have let your friend go in my place, if I'd known in time.' TM believed her. 'But... since he is up there, instead of me, I'll do my best to make it worth it.'

'You do that,' TM told her.

'You need anything?' she asked, looking at him with what seemed to be concern.

TM thought about it. 'Nah,' he said. 'Just... don't waste what you've been given here. I think that's about all any of us can do.'

She nodded, gave him a quick, gentle hug, and vanished into the night. TM watched her go until he could no longer turn his head to follow her, then turned back and gazed up into the sky. Ziggy and Veggie were burning up there among those stars, he knew. So were Orion, Altair and the Lyra foursome alongside Veggie.

He had no idea which ones any of them were. He'd have to ask Dominika.

Leaning back on his bench, TM sighed, and wondered if there had really been any point to any of it. When after a few minutes he was unable to come up with one, he decided that perhaps all he could do was to take his own advice to Vega, and not waste the existence he had been gifted. So many people were part of his little universe - some still in his orbit, some sailed off elsewhere, and some gone entirely, but all still carried on in some way by the sheer fact that he was still there. It didn't always mean being OK with the fact that people were gone, but the least he could do was keep going so that they would too.

He stood, stretched, and made his way unsteadily over to the Octobike, which sat parked in the field behind a few trees. Vega, to his half-surprise, was still there, examining it.

'Oh,' she said. 'Sorry, I -'

'It's okay,' TM said. 'Just wasn't expecting you to stick around.'

'I wasn't really planning to,' Vega said, 'but then I realised I didn't know what I actually was planning on doing.'

'Sounds familiar.'

They watched each other for a few moments, then both opened their mouths at the same time.

'So what's this -' Vega began.

'So what are you -' TM started.

'Er,' said Vega.

'You go first,' TM told her.

'I was just going to ask what this is,' she said, gesturing to the Octobike. 'I mean, it looks like some sort of vehicle, but not any I've ever heard of.'

'It's called the Octobike,' TM said. 'I invented it.'

'Oh, yeah,' Vega recalled, smiling as she looked the machine over. 'I heard you were an inventor-y type.'

TM watched as she marvelled over the contraption, feeling something he couldn't identify.

'Sorry,' she said after a moment. 'You were gonna say something?'

'Oh,' said TM. 'Yeah. I just...' He sighed. 'This might be stupid, but I was just thinking... I knew someone. Life and love and just hanging out meant a lot to her, and I... thought maybe it would mean a lot to you too.'

Vega paused her inspection and gazed at him with her bright eyes. 'You want me to... come with you? You don't even know me.'

'Last time I let someone I didn't know come be a massive part of my life... well, it ended badly, but I wouldn't have changed it for the world.'

Vega considered it for a few moments, then smiled and extended a hand. TM shook it.

'Do you know anything about how to manage a gym-slash-seafood-restaurant?' he asked her.

'Nothing whatsoever.'

'Do you... like pick and mix?'

'You serious?'

TM gave a quiet laugh. 'We'll pick some up on the way back,' he said.

'Oh – I don't have, like, any... money, or anything...'

'I'll get this one,' TM promised, and helped her onto the Octobike.

The universe might not care about him, but somehow that didn't seem to matter too much.

EACH LITTLE UNIVERSE

Acknowledgements, and Just Sort of a Note

Dear Reader

This book is for you.

Actually, that's not quite right. First and foremost, this book is for *me*.

The story you've just read has been floating around in my brain and on various sheets of paper and bits of data for over five years now, and it's come to mean an awful lot to me. In some ways, this story is me - at least, I identify what I think of the story very closely with what I think of myself as a human being. Not the most healthy or helpful attitude, and I don't recommend it, but there it is.

Honestly, I don't think I'm ever likely to get to a point where I feel that Each Little Universe is really finished, or that it's good enough. Still, it's been bubbling around for so long that the time finally came when I couldn't keep it any longer; happy or not, I simply had to put it out into the world. And... looks like I've done that now. Sweet.

I have to thank my other half, Hannah, without whom would exist none of the several versions of this story which have been started and half-finished and occasionally got to a stage resembling something like completion. She is the only reason I've actually followed my own dream in creating this.

I also owe thanks to... a lot of people, actually. I couldn't afford a proper editor (it shows, I'm sure), but *Each Little Universe* has improved quite a lot, I think, since its first full draft back in November of 2015. (The first pieces of the story were knocking about a year and a half before that, with a couple of conversations between TM and Veggie in this published version still almost exactly as they were in the contextless snippets I first dreamed up in a creative writing module back at university, so depressingly many years ago.) I'm grateful to everyone who's read any part or version of this story; a lot of different minds have contributed to shaping it into what it is now. Too many to list here, even (not least because I'd almost certainly forget a couple of really important people and then feel bad), so I hope it'll suffice to say thank you to a few groups of people and hope that that covers most of it: pretty much everyone who taught me or studied with me at uni, the Gremus, a bunch of video game bloggers (particularly Alex Sigsworth, whose laser-sharp eye for spotting typos has been invaluable), Project Revival, Hannah again, the Mages, and David Bowie.

A brief moment of specificity is required, however, to single out Moses Norton and Blythe Norton, the former for providing a lot of helpful motivation and advice when I was trying to work out how to turn a story into a manuscript into a novel into a published thing and the latter for helping me to bring it to life by creating the wonderful cover art which you hold in your hands (or, probably more likely, which you can view by returning to the books menu of your tablet or e-reader).

This is my first published novel, which I think means I'm a novelist now. I don't really expect anyone to read it, to be honest, but I have now done what I've been meaning to do for twenty-something years and actually published something. That's good enough for me for now.

I may well end up publishing more in the future, and I hope you'll read that too. There are more stories I have to write, and perhaps they'll make their way out into the world before too long.

To keep up with what I'm making, you can find me on Twitter, where I'm @overthinkery1. I'm also on Facebook and (though I can't claim to understand it) Instagram, on both of which I'm 'chrisdurstondoeswords'.

I even made an actual website - chrisdurston.com - mostly because I thought that an Actual Author needed one, so check that out too. If you're reading the e-version of this book within a fortnight or so of its release (in which case I am humbled and grateful), my giveaway of a few signed paperback copies might still be open, so go to chrisdurston.com/blog to find out how to enter.

Thank you so much for sharing this part of myself with me, even if you hated it. I mean, I'm planning to put this page at the end, so I'd be kind of weirded out if you hated it but still read it all the way through and then went on to the acknowledgements. Either way, thank you. I appreciate it more than you know. (and hey if you didn't hate it maybe leave a review to help feed the algorithms thx)

Yours in gratitude

Chris Durston

ABOUT THE AUTHOR

Chris Durston started writing *Each Little Universe* at university in Cardiff in 2015 or thereabouts, and just sort of didn't do much with it for the next five years.

He lives in Devon, where he is, finally, a novelist, and is also the host of Philosophiraga, a podcast about video games and philosophy.

His second novel is, at this point, a mystery even to him, but he hopes it's inevitable.

Learn more at chrisdurston.com.

Printed in Great Britain
by Amazon